INTO THE UNKNOWN

A LEAP OF FAITH

GLENDA C. BROWNE

COPYRIGHT

Copyright © 2018 Glenda C. Browne

DEDICATION

For my dad.

INTRODUCTION

Brought up in a tight-knit Jewish community, then watching his parents brutally murdered, Ishmael flees his hometown with his friend Avraham and together they set out on a spectacular journey. After turning his back on his faith and forced into another reality, will Ishmael realise the true value of the people in his life and what is important?

Will this lead him to be who he was always meant to be?

Or will things turn out to be just a little too much for him to handle?

Find out as you read this tale of love, life and loss.

CONTENTS

About the Author

ACKNOWLEDGEMENTS

To Ian Marchant and Ann Sansom:
Thank you for your time, inspiration and belief when they were needed the most.

To Becca Little:
Through light and dark you have never turned away; you have always been there to listen and advise, help and encourage me. Thank you for your belief in me and all the support you have given. You are an inspiration and I am blessed to have you as my friend because you are a true one.

For my amazing Angels:
Your guidance, strength, love and reassurance has got me through many difficulties in life, and also got me where I am today; this I must acknowledge, always.

For Simon:
To others you are just a homeless man, but to me, you are what human is. You give me your time, you listen to me and you are a real inspiration. You ask for nothing but give your all to someone who talks to you. Thank you, Simon, regardless of your situation, you are a great human being, I am privileged to know you and I am grateful you gave me that chance.

For Ged and Kirsty:
I can't put into words all you have done for me, thank you for always being there when I have needed you, for supporting me through the good times and the bad.

For my Hub family:
To all the staff, volunteers and clients at the Hub, thank you from the bottom of my heart for all the support and encouragement this last year. The opportunities given, plus the space to grow personally which I have had, has completely changed my life. You have supported me massively, not just as a volunteer, but as an author, with something that means the world to me: my writing.

For Darren:
Thank you for always being there through the dark and light. All you did, is why I am where I am now, you never gave up on me which motivated me to not give up on myself. You have never left my side and I am forever blessed and grateful for it.

INTO THE UNKNOWN

A LEAP OF FAITH

GLENDA C. BROWNE

1 A LIFE CHANGING DAY

My village was only small, yet beautiful. Everyone I knew was Jewish, going about their daily business, buying or selling goods, or farming with their big carts.

The carts were pulled by some of the most beautiful horses I had ever seen. I would often watch them walking down the main path which went straight through the village, from one end to the other. Then they would pass by the yellow cornfields that could be seen shimmering in the distance on a warm sunny day, brightening the surrounding areas on days when rain fell, before the farmers would become just a black speck in the distance.

I would often write by the fields, or play by the river which ran through the village with my friends Avraham and Benyamin. These were times when I wasn't helping my father, or during the days that he was taking things to market.

Mama was a devoted housewife, her fondness for the family showing in all she did. I would sit chatting to her on rainy days; she would give me freshly baked food just out of the oven, which I would eat while she continued working.

Humming happily, she would smile at me as she went about her tasks. I would sit at home to write at times, too. Mama took a great interest in this, hovering occasionally over my shoulder, giving me encouragement.

She was very pretty, with chestnut brown hair which was tied neatly in a braid, not a strand of it out of place. She wore an apron over her clothes which were always immaculate. I often wondered how she managed to keep her clothes so clean, especially when her jobs consisted of tasks such as clearing the fireplace, then filling it with coal for the evening fires. She was medium height with a slender physique; her eyes were green and looked like emeralds twinkling in the sun. Mama was kind-hearted, her voice was warming with a soft tone; she was also a superb cook. It was easy to see why my father adored her, we both did.

Papa was quite the opposite, he was a lot taller but carried some weight, although you could tell he was a man of strength; I often admired his muscles.

He wore a white shirt which was always covered in dirt by the time he came home, along with brown pants which, to me, always looked like they were too short. He said they let him move around efficiently, but he did look funny, especially with his big, brown working-boots, well, at least to me. He never left home without his cap, which sat gracefully on his short black hair.

To many people, he looked fearsome, he could easily give others the wrong impression at first glance, yet my father was a gentle man with good humor. He had a beard which I watched him trim at times, he took great pride in that. His eyes always gleamed when he arrived home, his face would light up when he saw us. His excited voice was loud and could easily be heard, even at the back of our house. He would tell Mama how beautiful she had become from when he had left in the morning, then would turn to ask me, jokingly, if I'd grown since, it always made me chuckle.

He did the same thing every day.

Some people may have thought they were an odd couple, but together they were perfect. They had been together since teenagers, yet their love blossomed more as the years went by: this was obvious to anybody.

1947 is a year I will never forget: it changed everything for me. One morning my father left for his usual errands, only to return much earlier than expected-panic stricken. He called my mother repeatedly, his voice quivering. Alarmed, she rushed outside, I followed her, somewhat confused with an unsettling feeling in my stomach. They looked at each other for only a minute, but to me it seemed much longer. I watched them, lost in the moment, before Mama turned to me desperately, grabbing my arms at the same time.

"Hide, Ishmael, hide: they are coming."

"But Mama, who? Why?"

I stood there wondering what was happening. I could see the fear in her eyes, but I could give no comfort. I wasn't sure what would happen, I only knew whatever it was, it wouldn't be good.

"Ishmael, please, go into the barn: you must hide well, be safe. Always know you're very loved by us both."

"But?"

"Ishmael, go now; GO."

Mama never raised her voice, this frightened me because it was something much more serious; I felt completely panicked by this now. Instinct came, forcing me to throw my arms round her; I hugged her tight not wanting to move. I glanced over at my father who seemed frozen on the spot, there was no emotion visible, nothing. The permanent sparkle he always had was now evaporating, leaving only fear in its place. Mama pushed me away from her.

"Ishmael? Whatever happens, you must stay in there. Hurry; go now, we love you."

I was too tongue-tied to reply, I only listened to her words then darted to the barn; I regretted not running to my father, too.

I opened the big doors then stepped inside, closing them behind me as quickly as I could. It was a big creepy building, one I always felt uncomfortable in every time I entered. It was a dark place, too, somewhere I never liked being in for long, either. I always had a feeling of being watched, almost like there was something lingering in the shadows.

I looked around to see light coming in through a large crack, which time had eventually worn away. Under it, there were haystacks scattered around, I pulled some over before stacking them to make a seat. Sitting down I looked through the crack to where I could see the house. All was quiet now, I just sat waiting anxiously wishing my mother or father would call me out; I never got the call.

A short while later I saw soldiers pull up outside, then step out of an army truck. They moved up to my house, banging on the door impatiently; I now became very uncomfortable. Papa opened it, he was immediately dragged out, followed by my mother, whose cries I could hear. I saw them struggle as they were pushed to the ground. A few words were spoken, but I could not make out exactly what was said.

I could tell my father was trying to reason with them, while my mother begged for mercy, but it was to no avail.

Covering my ears, I tried to drown out the noise, but I was unable to take my eyes away. I was fixated without choice. A soldier took out his gun then stared at them coldly, without thought, with no hesitation he shot them both three times, point blank. There was no remorse or guilt, nothing; I thought the soldier, to me, seemed inhuman.

My parents were just left, treated like garbage. I waited silently, watching them whilst trying to hold back my anger; tears now falling for every second that passed. They were my parents, I loved them, now they had gone without any answers as to why. I wondered: what had they done, that was so wrong, to deserve that? They were always good to me, as well as others. I wanted to scream but I was terrified the soldiers would hear me then come back; I never wanted to be found.

As soon as the soldiers were out of sight, I wiped my eyes

then ran out towards my parents . I was shaking with anger now, fear cradling my whole being; every step towards them was painful. I did not want to see them like that, but I could not pull myself away. I had to go to them no matter how difficult, but it petrified me.

I slowly approached them while anxiously looking all around me. Each step feeling like forever to take; I had never felt fear so intense as I did in those moments as I headed towards them.

The gunshots had pierced right through me; I could still hear the shots echoing, on constant replay, in my head.

I was horrified to see my Mama and Papa like that, covered in blood, lifeless. I just stared down at them without moving. Instinct was trying to pull me away, but my mind wouldn't allow it. I was completely helpless, the numbness I felt was building, but inside there were other emotions surfacing now.

Tears started falling again, I was in shock but found myself bending down in between my parent's bodies. The look of terror on their faces was something I would never fail to recall again. I closed their eyes, smearing their blood as I did so, then wiped the tears from mine.

I did not know how much time had passed until my friend Avraham came to look for me, the moments didn't seem real. Holding a bag in hand, he saw where I was kneeling, then started sprinting towards me, shouting my name.

"ISHMAEL, Ishmael, we must leave."

His voice bought me back to the moment, but now I lost every bit of control I had during those silent minutes alone. I got up clenching my fists, my body turning one way, then the other; the frustration I felt was overwhelming. I put my hands to my head, grabbing my hair, then I just screamed; I could no longer control the explosion of emotions battling inside me that were desperate to come out.

"AAAH WHY? THEY DID NOT DESERVE THIS. Why did they do this? WHY AVRAHAM?"

Avraham hurried over, holding me firmly by the arms.

"Come Ishmael, please? We cannot stay."

"I will never forgive or forget, one day they will pay. Avraham, I can't leave them, I just can't, not here."

I just sobbed now, then more shouting came, I was so angry, devastated, just traumatised. All I knew was that my parents were dead, but I had no idea why that happened or what would happen next. Avraham only listened, trying to offer some comfort. He put his hand on my shoulder softly.

"Ishmael, listen to me, we must; we have no choice. Our home is no longer safe. All that we know is being destroyed; there is nothing left here. Come, gather some things, we must hurry."

"I... I can't leave them here, Avraham?"

"My friend, you're not thinking straight; we cannot move them. Please, the soldiers may be back anytime; we must go. I know how you feel but it's just us now, we can't do anything for them. I'm so sorry Ishmael, I really am."

"What's happening, Avraham? Why do I have the blood of my parents on my hands? I just don't understand any of this?"

"Ishmael, for now, you don't need to. We must look after each other, find somewhere safe."

I still didn't know what to do. A few hours earlier, all was fine, but now my world had been turned upside down without any warning.

Avraham was two years older, he always knew what to do even behind his own grief; I trusted him.

I stood over them, tears falling once again.

"They will pay for this Mama, Papa; they will pay."

Avraham eventually dragged me away. I quickly picked up what I could with his help. We ran out towards the hills, both stopping to take one last look before running into the darkness, which was now creeping in, then into the unknown.

We managed to escape to an unfamiliar area, walking across fields, crossing many rivers cautiously; constantly looking over our shoulders. The terror never left us, but Avraham hid it well: he never showed any fear or other emotion, only his vocals would give that away at times.

At first we came across a few others on our escape, all scared, all cradling every precious possession they had brought with them, but as the days passed, they went their separate ways. I felt somewhat safe with them; I was only seventeen at the time, but I had never left our village before. We were forced to flee which was just as frightening as staying in our village had become. The fear of the soldiers coming for us if we had remained there was a reality that was more than possible, having others close brought comfort.

I was glad of just one thing once they had all departed: that Avraham was with me.

His family had also met the same end, before mine; now he decided there was nothing left there to stay for, and he was right. It was a risk, but we had to take it now, we had no choice. The chance to maybe find something better was far more appealing to our young minds, just as much as the necessity of it was. We had no idea if we would find it or not, we just fled.

We walked for weeks, rationing what food we had between us. Neither of us had any idea where we were going, or where we would end up. Turning back wasn't an option: only continuing on, in hope we would reach safety soon, kept us moving. Avraham was a little taller than me, slim build with hazel eyes, just like his father. He had started growing a beard which was becoming more noticeable by the day. Long ringlets from the side of his head where falling in front of his ears. He always looked well presented, ready for any introduction.

We were both so tired, any rest we had was not doing

anything now other than exhausting us more. While still trying to keep our Jewish tradition going, we would pray we would make it. All we had was our faith now, as well as each other.

Avraham always looked out for me, he would insist that I have more food, more sleep than him. Always the first one to keep watch of a night, until he, too, fell asleep. He would not show emotion or complain, he was just there, guiding the way. Maybe he saw I was more vulnerable in many ways, or it was just the fact that I was younger than him, but he knew how I was feeling. Perhaps he knew that keeping his feelings hidden was only going to help me, he never said, he just got on with it; I admired him for that.

One evening as the darkness was drawing in, I turned to him: one question had been niggling away.

"Avraham, why did you stay after your parents died?"

He just looked at me, somewhat surprised by the question then turned away before speaking.

"You are my friend, Ishmael, I knew if they could do that to my parents they could do it to yours. I could not leave; that's what kept me there. Get some rest, I will keep watch."

"Did you know, that they would come?"

"No, Ishmael, your parents are the first since mine, but I also don't know why; I just knew it was possible. Leaving wasn't right, not for me. Sleep, Ishmael, please; you need your rest."

"So do you, Avraham, so do you."

He looked at me again then stared off into the distance; he looked so detached now, in a world of his own. I could only guess what he was thinking or feeling, with him it was difficult to tell. Seeing him now I knew he was deep in thought, I was unsure whether he would even reply. However, a minute later he blinked then turned to me again.

"That will come, Ishmael, for now it is not about me, you are needing it much more. We may come close to help soon, so you need all the strength to get there. Rest now, we are up early."

A few days later, Avraham's prediction came true: we saw a town at the bottom of the valley. I was frightened at what was down there, but at the same time we needed somewhere to get more food, as much as some wanted rest. It was the first settlement we had seen since we fled, I stood looking over at it. I should've been relieved, but I felt nothing other than fear, which was rising by the second.

The town was surrounded by hills, which leaned against the mountains that towered over it all. Avraham came to stand next to me, yet I did not notice at first: I was lost in wonder at what lay down there. Would it be the making or the breaking of us? Would what we came to hope for be shattered, or could the tension which was building be laid to rest? I was so muddled, uncertain of anything. As I was biting my nail, Avraham put his hand on my shoulder reassuringly, I turned sharply. He then showed a rare smile.

"Ishmael, come; it will be alright."

"Avraham, how do you know? You can't be sure?"

"No, but I believe we have been led here."

"Led here? By who? I don't understand."

"You don't need to, Ishmael; you trust me, don't you?"

"Yes, I trust you, I am just afraid: we have come too far, Avraham."

"Have some faith, Ishmael, we have come far, this far, haven't we?"

I looked at him in disbelief. I was alarmed at his confidence, I didn't understand this either, he should have been the same as me: doubtful as well as scared, but again, he did not show it. My head was racing now: I could not trust this idea was right, I could only trust him. But as much as I did, I knew if we ran into soldiers, then it would have all been for nothing.

I followed him, unconvinced, as we made our way towards the town. All I could think was: 'please let this work out, don't let us be caught, let this decision be the right one'. The same words going over in my head constantly.

I didn't know what I was walking into; I so badly wanted to get there to find out, but the other half was pulling me back, dragging my feet. My heart was thumping erratically, I felt dizzy now. I wanted to catch Avraham up, yet was not able to go any further at the same time. I needed to stop, to sit down for a moment, panic evidently clear again. I was shaking but could not stop it, which only added to the fear already there. Avraham, at first, did not notice; however, I was always under his watchful eyes, which was why he turned a few seconds later. Seeing me sitting down, he came running over, now showing real concern.

"Ishmael, what's wrong? You're shaking?"

"I can't do this Avraham, I just…"

"Okay, just breathe, Ishmael. I know how scared you are; I know your fears, I have them too. But we must at least try, we can't run forever. We owe it to our parents to do this, I will not leave your side, not ever."

After calming a little, Avraham took me by my wrist pulling me up; I tried to put a brave face on.

"Okay, Avraham, you're right: I must try, I am ready. I just need a minute; please?"

"Ishmael, no: that gives room for fear to overtake, we must do this now, come."

We started making our way down the hill towards the town; Avraham as promised, never left my side. We eventually made it there. Vigilantly we moved along the side of a shop, both of us popping our heads around to check for danger, who or what was around there. It was a small, busy place, with various shops, people going about their day. Avraham was quick to step out, but I was still so uncertain; I pulled him back aggressively.

"Avraham, stop; what are you doing?"

"It's fine, Ishmael, come on; we need to find someone

who can help?"

"No, what if they take us away, what if it's a trap, what if...?"

"Ishmael, stop it, calm yourself; you are going to make yourself ill. Trust me, I have a good feeling about this; we can't stay back here forever, can we?"

That moment, while listening to his words trying to think of a plan, I caught a glimpse of a man in the distance. I stared at him then felt a strange calmness blanket me. The urge to go to him was so strong, almost like some invisible force was pushing me; I just had to do it now. I turned to Avraham.

"Avraham, that man, there; we must go to him?"

Now it was his turn to look surprised as he looked in the direction I was pointing.

"Ishmael?"

"That man, over there, QUICK?"

The man just stood looking at me, so I sped out towards him; Avraham came running after me shouting my name. People were stopping to look at two unfamiliar boys running across the town, unsure as to why. The man saw me coming towards him; he just stood waiting, watching. This unnerved me, so I slowed right down to check him out while looking around nervously. Waiting for Avraham to catch up with me seemed to take forever.

However, Avraham soon caught up; now breathless, he was not impressed by my random act in the slightest. We started squabbling for a minute, not realising the man had now come over to us. We were about to run when he touched Avraham on the arm, gently. We knew he was of some real importance, clearly Jewish: he had a big hat with matching black robes, not the usual everyday wear. Like Avraham, he, too, had a fuller black beard, with black hair that was showing at the sides.

"Boys, are you lost? I am the rabbi of this town, what are your names?"

Avraham looked at me, then turned to the rabbi who

was softly spoken, friendly with a calming aura, he had a twinkle in his eyes then showed a faint smile. I knew he was a good man; I liked him straight away.

"Rabbi, my name is Avraham, this is Ishmael. No, we are not lost; at least not in how you think."

The rabbi seemed puzzled by that comment, but he did not force anything. Only kept asking questions, trying to make conversation without scaring us off.

"I have not seen either of you here before; I know nearly everybody, where are you from, Avraham?"

"We are not from here, we are from a little village behind the mountains. I doubt you have heard of it: Rakira? We have come a long way Rabbi; we are tired."

"Yes, I have heard of it, that is a long way. Have you both come here alone? What about your families? Where are they, may I ask?"

I stepped in now, abruptly: I was becoming frustrated with the questions.

"Rabbi, our families were murdered by soldiers. We had to leave that place; we could not stay. We only have each other now. Please, we have travelled for weeks, they won't find us here, will they? I will kill them, I…"

I suddenly felt dizzy again, I put my hand to my head then began swaying; Avraham started to panic as he saw me sitting on the floor.

"Ishmael? Please, Rabbi, help him? I beg you; he is not well."

"I will be alright, Avraham."

"No, Ishmael, look at you? Please, stay there, Rabbi?"

"Ishmael, no, you will be safe here with me; I will help you both, wait here while I get some water. Oh, Ishmael? Apart from being no match, you are in no state to do anything. Stay here, I won't be long."

Avraham now bent down to me looking somewhat confused.

"Ishmael, that was careless, he seems nice, but it could have ended differently; why did you do that?"

"I'm not sure, I just knew it was right: I can't explain it, I'm sorry, Avraham."

"I can't say I'm surprised at that Ishmael, but for now it's not that important. You need to rest, here comes Rabbi."

Rabbi went to the nearest shop then came out with a cup of water. I felt no better, I needed to sleep more than anything now. I had barely had any sleep since my parents were shot. I had been having nightmares, constant flashbacks, which had taken their toll. I was exhausted, I just didn't realise how much.

"Ishmael, can you stand? I will take you to get some rest."

"Thank you, Rabbi, I think I can."

"Slowly, Ishmael; here, let me help you up."

Avraham once again grabbed my arm to help me up, Rabbi only stood there, smiling, before he spoke again, curiosity in his voice.

"Are you brothers, Avraham?"

"No, Rabbi, we are friends, I have known Ishmael for as long as I can remember."

"Come, Ishmael needs rest, you both do."

He led us to his house; it was a friendly place which had bookshelves scattered about in the lounge, filled with a wide variety of books. Many religious symbols were placed around the room; there were big brass candlesticks with used candles, unlit, placed around different parts of the room, too. The open fire was welcoming, the walls were bright with light coloured curtains that were draped from the high windows.

"Avraham, sit Ishmael here, I will have a bed made for him."

He walked out leaving me alone with Avraham, I was weak but turned to him, relief now in my voice.

"We made it, Avraham, I think it will be alright."

"Yes, Ishmael, I do too, but it is not over yet; we must

still be cautious. Rabbi is friendly, but we still don't know if we can trust him."

"No, Avraham, I do, we were brought to him for a reason; I think I now understand your reasons for leading us here."

Avraham stood in thought for a minute when Rabbi came back in with a tray.

"Ishmael, your bed will be ready soon, in the meantime you must have something to eat; drink as much as you can, that will help immensely."

I sat up, then we both started to tuck into various plates of Jewish food, much of it reminding me of home. Avraham filled Rabbi in about what had happened, while my thoughts wandered. I found I couldn't continue eating, even though hunger was gripping me. For me the ordeal was still too raw, the nausea became much stronger now. Picturing their lifeless bodies covered in blood was all I could see, along with the gunshots going off in my head. Avraham noticed I had suddenly stopped eating.

"Ishmael, eat, you need your strength!"

"AAH, AVRAHAM, I KNOW, I know, but I can't: all I can see is them, I'm sorry. Rabbi, please, I am so tired."

"I will check if your bed is ready, Ishmael."

Avraham came over to sit next to me, still tucking into a bit of bread.

"Ishmael, I know how angry you are, I see you lashing out in your sleep, I hear your cries, but…"

"Why did it have to be like this? I wasn't prepared Avraham, I didn't know a person could feel so much anger."

"I know you are grieving, all you feel I felt too, but Ishmael listen to me: you must push through it, otherwise it will consume you. You can't let that happen."

"I am trying, Avraham, that's all I can do; please, just leave it."

He moved away as Rabbi came back, not saying another word. I was then taken to a small room, Avraham followed me in. It was friendly looking; I felt safer than I had done since leaving our village.

There was a bed with fresh yellow blankets covering the crisp white sheets under them. Outside the big windows, there was a stunning view overlooking the hills that we once had roamed. I was looking out when Avraham touched me on the shoulder.

"Ishmael, you are a million miles away, you must rest."

"I was so afraid up there, looking down here. Now I am here, I am still afraid, yet I shouldn't be; nothing is making any sense Avraham?"

"Ishmael, I know, but for now you are safe, you can't make sense of anything because you are exhausted. I know you fear sleeping, I know you fear being awake. However, both are needed, Ishmael, for you sleep is priority now; please, my friend? I will be here for you always."

I got into bed; the softness of it was comforting. It had a familiar fragrant smell which lingered in the bedding. Feeling emotional now, I lay down; Avraham stood over the bed staring at me.

"Try resting easy, Ishmael."

"Avraham, you must rest, too?"

He looked at me while leaning down, slightly touching my arm.

"Don't worry, I will when I can, Ishmael."

He walked out of the room leaving the door ajar, now I just sobbed into the pillow; I don't remember falling asleep.

I was woken later by Avraham shaking me, calling my name. I was having nightmares which made me hysterical, shouting at my parents, cursing the soldiers. My anger had reached a whole new level; I could not suppress it now.

Avraham sat as I yelled out, but he said nothing again. For the first time, I really wanted to hurt someone; I don't know what came over me. I didn't know whether it was because I had had some much-needed rest, which had given me the strength to unleash all that was bottled-up inside, or it was just the nightmare itself which had tipped me over the edge, forcing me to react this way.

I couldn't pretend I wasn't hurting, or that nothing had happened, I was scared of the extent of my anger, but Avraham stepped in as soon as I went to throw something.

"ISHMAEL, easy my friend; this is not the way, you must fight through it. Be angry, you have every right, but don't let it have that control, ask God for help."

This comment unbeknown to Avraham only stirred things more, I hated the world now; I placed blame on everything.

That moment I stopped in thought: I felt maybe it was me, that perhaps I deserved all this? I had no answers, I only had blame to give; I blamed my faith, God.

I started questioning it all which made me distance myself from it, I could not trust it now. I turned to Avraham, hoping that he could explain, maybe make me understand it.

"Why does God hate me, Avraham? What have I done that is so wrong?"

"Ishmael, it is not God that has done this: bad things happen, but I cannot yet tell you why. Don't lose faith, it will get you through this."

"Don't lose faith? Tell me, where has faith got me?"

"Ishmael, look around you, you're questioning faith, yet you were drawn to the rabbi who has helped us? God led us here."

"Why would he do that after doing what he did to our families? You are not speaking sense, Avraham, yes, we got here, but now what? You look around: we have no home or family, nothing. Do you really think God would give us all that?"

"I believe things are meant to be, I know you find it hard; naturally you are looking to place blame, but we have a lot to be thankful for Ishmael."

"Thankful for? I will never be thankful for any of this. Tell me, Avraham: you have lost just as much, why are you not angry?"

"You will one day, we still have each other so regardless of what I have lost, I know things will work out; we will be provided for. Over time I have had much healing, Ishmael, but in time you will, too."

I was so exasperated now, I flung myself round towards him angrily.

"AVRAHAM, THAT DOESN'T HELP, I WANT ANSWERS: SOMETHING, ANYTHING TO EXPLAIN ALL THIS, I... I... AAAAH."

"ISHMAEL, please, I have no answers for you. However, time is a great healer, things are difficult I know, but you are strong, I see that."

"Strong? If I was strong I would have stopped those men; I didn't, that is not strong, Avraham, I failed them."

"Ishmael, no, you can't think like that. You were no match, like Rabbi said, they would have only shot you, too, your parents knew this; I think deep down you do, too. This is not your fault."

"I will never know that: I sat there, watched it happen, yet did nothing Avraham, nothing. I can't forgive myself for that, not ever."

"Anything can happen, Ishmael. In time you will have answers. Blaming yourself is not going to help you; you will realise that, too."

I only looked at him then, he was always so calm, so composed, which infuriated me, even more so now. But it was also my lifeline: I would come to know just how important his way of being was.

After being at Rabbi's a while, Avraham got some work at a farm; I barely saw him. Rabbi kept me distracted as much as he could, but still, I was becoming more bitter, much more out of control as the days passed. I wished I had never witnessed what I did, that my parents were still here. I wished more than anything that the nightmares, all the flashbacks I had, would stop; even for a while.

Attending the synagogue where I met people only helped temporarily, it distracted me from my thoughts for a while, but I still felt alien there. I knew Rabbi would have told people my situation, but I hated that; it made me feel inadequate. It was hard to see families together, too. Rabbi thought he was doing right, and in some ways, he was. But knowing what he did about me, I didn't see the reason as to why he would let me be surrounded by that. I started becoming more isolated, withdrawn, wanting to hide away permanently.

Rabbi spoke of me often to Avraham, but I no longer cared. I worried constantly now that Avraham was making friends; maybe one day he would marry. I started pushing him away: devastated at the thought of losing him, too.

It appeared logical for me to do that, but it seemed I was still always his priority. I knew things had changed, but he never did. He still cared, always tried to be there for me, was always just Avraham. I was very thankful for that, he was like a father figure, young, but wise beyond his years; he spoke sense even if I didn't see it at the time.

Weeks then months swiftly passed by, but I still suffered with the flashbacks, the nightmares along with the emotions; that did not change. We had been there at Rabbi's for over a year now when Avraham came back from work one night. He came into the lounge looking tired one evening, then sat down on the sofa before turning to me.

"Ishmael, would you sit down?"

"Avraham? Yes, what is the matter?"

"Ishmael, I have some news: with Rabbi's help I have secured you a property, it is a flat. You can move in when you're ready."

I couldn't believe my ears; I was speechless, he stood up just about to leave.

"Avraham, wait? I don't know what to say other than thank you; but…"

"But what, Ishmael?"

"How am I going to keep a flat alone?"

"Trust me, it's all been taken care of. Ishmael, I know it's daunting, but you do need your own independence; that will help you in time. We can go there tomorrow, let you see it?"

"Yes, okay, Avraham, we will go tomorrow."

The next day I was up early, part of me was scared to be alone, but the other part of me wanted my own space. I appreciated Avraham watching over me, but at times I just wanted to be by myself, away from people; I knew having my own place would give me that. In some ways I was looking forward to it; but that didn't last long.

We set off, soon arriving at the flat. Looking around its surroundings, it was certainly no beauty, set in a rough looking area crammed with houses. Far different to what I was used to back home, almost another world.

Although the area was no picnic, I still thought it was perfect. We walked in, my curiosity taking over. Somewhere inside I began to believe what Avraham had said about us being provided for; I never expected to have my own place so soon, but it would be mine and would give me some freedom.

Whether that become a good thing, or not, I had yet to find out. For now, behind my concerns, I was still grateful. I went to check out the rooms, Avraham, who was waiting for a reaction from me while I looked around, soon called me, also with curiosity in his voice.

"Ishmael, what do you think? Do you like it?"

"Avraham, it's great, I don't understand why you have

done this; I don't deserve it?"

"Only God can decide that, Ishmael, but you are my friend; you can build a life now, you can try to find some happiness. I know you're infuriated with me at times, but even though you have your own place, I am always going to be there: I know you still need that. I have a spare key just for emergencies; so, you have nothing to worry about."

I couldn't fully agree with that because I knew how I was, and once I was alone, I wasn't sure if I would be able to handle it. I felt that because he had gone to so much effort, I owed it to him to give the same back. I wasn't sure I could keep a flat; I had watched my mother doing housework, but I was no expert. I picked up some cooking tips from Rabbi which was enough to get by, but I still had a lot to learn. It was overwhelming; until I moved in there was no way to know how I would cope. I'd never been alone, but I was reassured that Avraham would be close by.

A few days later I moved into the flat. People had given me bits of furniture to make it a bit more welcoming; for now, it was enough. Rabbi would come around often to make sure all was well or to see if I needed anything. He would give me money for essentials, too. I was appreciative of the help, but I could not just keep taking, yet neither could I work. I had no skills other than writing which I struggled to do at the time, too, so I began to lose control a lot more; I felt useless.

Sitting there one night I found myself becoming very emotional. I was glad to have the space, but too much of it was not something I was used to either. It gave me time to think, I couldn't handle the flashbacks or the nightmares either, especially alone; I was battling with demons until I eventually gave in.

Consumed by emotions I couldn't control, I got up, grabbed my coat, then went to the shop where I bought a bottle of vodka, as well as a bottle of whisky. I had never drunk before but I needed something to take away all that I was feeling; I wanted to feel normal again. This was the start of a downwards spiral; at that point, I didn't care whether I came out or not.

I walked home annoyed at myself for doing it, but seeing it as a way out brought relief more than anything. Once home I completely isolated myself, I needed nothing or nobody except the bottles that sat before me. I poured myself a drink then sat staring at it. I knew it was wrong, but the first sip of whisky I eventually consumed, gave me a warm feeling inside, almost hugging me; it made me feel good.

I was addicted to that sensation straight away. I felt completely alone now, the whole world was outside, but I felt no connection; I felt so empty on the inside, like part of me was dying. I felt nothing other than the warmth which was clinging to my throat, travelling down towards my stomach. I was too wrapped up in my own thoughts, trying to make sense of things, but not even in my drunken state could I do it; yet, it never stopped me from trying.

Avraham became aware that I had begun drinking, inevitably he tried to avert me from it; I was a state. He saw I wasn't coping but could not be there all the time, neither could Rabbi. He insisted on getting me a puppy: he said it might help keep me on the straight and narrow, but I was too drunk to really know what was going on or to even care.

This went on for a while until Avraham gave me no choice in the matter: I was getting worse. He walked in one day shaking me awake from another heavy night of drinking.

"Ishmael? ISHMAEL, wake up, look!"

"No, Avraham, leave me be, please?"

"Ishmael, no, sit up, you must!"

I sat up to look straight at him. I noticed the puppy as the blur from my eyes lessened. Rubbing my face, trying to wake myself up from a hangover, I fell in love. He was a husky, grey with white fur; carefully I took him from Avraham. I was tempted to ignore him, but I couldn't: I was drawn to him instantly. I put my head on his.

"Avraham, he's beautiful; Jonah, I want to name him Jonah. Thank you, I've behaved badly but I will try harder, I just can't make promises: it's too soon."

"Ishmael, to try is enough, Jonah needs you now, don't let him down, you are better than this; it is why I am so hard on you. Please, think about what you are doing?"

"I know, Avraham, but I can't get rid of the flashbacks, the nightmares; it's all too much."

"Yes, I know this, but it will destroy you if you let it. I can't tell you anymore, Ishmael; now it's up to you."

He looked at me sternly then walked out leaving me with Jonah, quietly closing the door behind him. I decided to try to pick myself up. Whilst looking in Jonah's eyes, I felt he would help me, I might have been imagining it but he was there; that was at least a start.

He never left my side, even when I was drunk; he was fearless, comforting at times. Having him there made me feel remorseful for everything that had happened: he reminded me what I had become when I was drunk. His big eyes staring up at me made me feel guilt-ridden every time, yet I could not stop. I thought it strange Avraham giving him to me: I couldn't look after myself let alone an animal. It confused me but, nevertheless, I was glad of the company.

A few months passed and I thought I was doing better. I got up to walk Jonah who had grown quickly. I stopped drinking as much, but it had become a habit now; one I was dependent on. I felt normal having it, I could forget for a while. The comfort was welcomed, but although Jonah was, too, I couldn't just stop drinking, or even wanted to. Still, Jonah always stayed close to me, he knew when I was having a bad day; I never knew an animal could be so loyal or trusting of me.

We had grown a special bond, I was annoyed to allow myself to get this way now, I felt like a failure, so unless I got my act together I wouldn't get very far. Jonah meant everything to me now; I also knew he deserved better than what I was giving him.

Avraham meant well in all he did but, somehow, I always saw the bad side of his actions, but the blame could only be aimed at myself.

One night, just before the anniversary of the death of my parents, I got more drunk than I'd ever been. For me, getting through it this way was far better than being sober. In my drunken state, I eventually decided to take Jonah for a walk, but he would not go. Rocking constantly, and with blurred vision, I could just make him out, lying down by the door. I kept calling him to come until eventually he got up, whining, as well as fighting with me once I managed to put his lead on. He was trying to pull away, but I didn't know why; it was the first time he had reacted that way. I stumbled out of the door as Jonah hesitantly followed. I had no clue where I was going or why, I just needed to get out. It was raining heavily but I didn't care now. Jonah kept falling behind, stopping as often as he could.

Each time he stopped I turned to look at him, he wouldn't move any part of himself other than his eyes, which were fixated on me as rain soaked his coat. I had to keep pulling on his lead, whether he was just checking on me or he sensed something more, or whether he was trying to tell me something, I don't know. I remember I eventually fell, feeling wetness on my face, only hearing echoes of Jonah barking. Lying there I soon heard the faintest voices, but I could not move. Jonah tried pushing me with his head, repeatedly, whining much louder, he knew there was something very wrong happening now but he was as helpless as I was, in my current state; he couldn't do anything other than bark. I mumbled at him. Only silence could be heard, only water could be felt covering my mouth then touching my nose, that's when everything went black; I was out cold.

2 A REAL CONNECTION

The rain was falling heavily that morning, but I knew I had to walk my Jonah. He was pacing, anxiously waiting for me to lead the way. I looked at him, I loved that dog with every fiber of my being. He was fiercely loyal, brave, my best friend; he was grey as a dull day with patches as white as snowflakes. I called him; with one look, pricking up his ears, he came running over to me straight away.

"Good boy Jonah; do you want to go out?"

His face was excited, with a persuasive look about him; I smiled. I had had him since he was a couple of weeks old. We were devoted to each other; he was there when I needed him, gave comfort through my darkest moments, too. He was non-judgmental, which had helped me before now.

I grabbed my bowler hat along with my cloak then put them on.

Putting his lead on him, I moved towards the door, opening it.

"Come on boy, let's go."

I loved to watch the rain, especially being inside with the fire burning, hearing it thrashing against the window. It was one of those days; rain falling heavily now.

However, I could not find the joy in it except for the glimmering, shimmering puddles on the ground where light was reflecting off them. The raindrops were dripping from the leaves of my fir tree fast. The noise was thunderous, drowning out any thoughts of not wanting to go out there.

But I had no choice: my Jonah needed me to, his priorities were greater than mine now, it was the only option.

I stepped out, the first few hits of rain caught my face, causing a chill through my body, signalling the coldness in the air which was becoming very apparent now. Jonah looked around, startled just as much by the cold: realising he couldn't escape it, either. But he wasn't to be phased by it; he just shook his coat, tail still wagging, then looked up at me while blinking to rid the continual drops from his eyes. I chuckled at him, I knew we would be completely drenched, but he was happy regardless; to me, he was worth every second.

"Come on, Jonah, we will just go around the block then come back."

We walked out of the gate where I turned to close it behind me. After walking for a couple of minutes, I saw a glimpse of something in the near distance getting closer. The colours were so bright against the dullness of the day, greyness dispersed from around it. I became increasingly curious by this, hastening my steps to feed my curiosity. The rain eased slightly, allowing me to see more clearly. If I would have been alone, I would have almost been running now, but Jonah would stop at every lamp post to do his business or have a sniff, oblivious to the moment.

I got closer, then stopped dead in my tracks: it was a girl. I hadn't seen such beauty but there she was, like an angel appearing before me. Jonah started panting with excitement, pulling on the lead eagerly towards her, bringing me out from my trance like state. I started feeling myself becoming more nervous, there was something more about her I couldn't put my finger on, drawing me in. I knew I had to speak to her somehow.

Every step she took, she lit the dull streets up, her brown curly hair blowing gently in the breeze underneath her umbrella. She suddenly halted, then, as she started fumbling around in her purse, something fell onto the floor. I rushed over; the opportunity to speak had come so I took it, now forgetting the shyness that had overwhelmed me from a minute before.

I bent down to pick up the item that had fallen, as I stood up my eyes met hers; my heart was thumping, yet I wasn't nervous now. She gazed into my eyes for a second, then smiled at me.

"Thank you, what a beautiful dog."

I stared at her now, the softness of her voice brought calmness to me, I wanted to speak about him, but I didn't expect her to make conversation. The nerves became ever so clear again causing me to blurt out in an alarming way.

"Jonah, his name is Jonah."

She looked at me for a second: trying to figure me out. I almost expected her to storm off in disgust, but surprisingly, she moved in to stroke Jonah with a smile on her face. She was not at all worried by how wet his coat was or that he could become hostile; she, too, was fearless. I was becoming more intrigued by her every second that went by.

"Ishmael, my name is Ishmael."

I held out my hand, she pulled off a glove then took it, gently shaking it.

"I'm Betty, nice to meet you, I have not long moved into my place for work."

"What is it you do?"

"I'm a nurse, I have not long graduated."

"Aah, that's a great job, so, you have a special touch?"

Looking to the side, smiling, she then moved a step closer subtly before gazing in my eyes, then speaking.

"Maybe, Ishmael."

I grinned before she bent down to fuss Jonah; I just watched her, now fascinated. Jonah was friendly, but he wasn't used to attention from strangers, it unnerved me in case he snapped, but he didn't; with her he was content. I relaxed easier seeing this, now I just wanted to know more about her.

Rain was pouring again but I barely noticed: it felt like I was stuck in a bubble, a time warp that I could have stayed in forever. But it wasn't to be, she stood up fixing her coat before putting her glove back on.

"Well, I better go now Ishmael, I have work soon."

My heart sank, whether the disappointment to her comment showed on my face I do not know. I lifted my hand to shake hers again while looking her in the eyes.

"It's been nice to meet you, Betty."

"Yes, you too, Ishmael; perhaps I'll see you around sometime?"

"That'll be nice, too, goodbye, Betty."

She walked off turning back with a grin.

"Goodbye? Hmm, we will see, Ishmael."

I smiled as her presence became hidden once again behind the umbrella. Like a stranger whom I may never have met, if not for the clumsiness of the moment, or for Jonah being a dog.

Jonah was becoming impatient now, much more restless. He had been very patient waiting; our planned walk had been interrupted so he was keen to go now. We were both soaked; but now it didn't matter. I waited; watching Betty get further away until I saw that first glimpse of colour I had seen previously. Only now there was a name, a voice, something which was so hypnotic about her. The curiosity never left my mind; it was in overload now. I bent down to Jonah, he was fed up but still flicking his tail to acknowledge he wasn't completely annoyed.

"Thank you, Jonah; come on, you deserve a special treat."

He stood up with eagerness, constantly looking up at me. I didn't know whether he was checking to make sure he would get his reward, or it was to check I would not change my mind. Maybe he was just thanking me in his own way, or he knew I would keep my word. Or he just didn't know at all, but he trusted me, just like I trusted him.

As I walked, I asked myself "did that just happen?" It seemed almost surreal now: the moments felt like time had stood still, I had never felt that before. I was plagued with questions, but something told me it wouldn't be the last I saw of her.

Maybe I was dreaming, or I had a foresight I was unaware of till now; I didn't know. We spoke few words, but it felt like I'd known her my whole life; I couldn't make sense of it.

All I knew was she had turned up in my life which had me gripped. I felt ridiculous for the sudden outburst, but like Jonah with the rain, she didn't seem put off by it; if she was, she hid it well. I had no clue if her friendliness was just her being polite or, like me, she sensed the same as I did, her last comment made me think this. I was so spellbound by her, she was beautiful, with such a warming aura.

The more I thought about it the more I was desperate to find out more about her; I was obsessed but couldn't help it. I was repeatedly asking myself if we would really meet again, thinking as though my mind would give me the answer. I then wondered if we ever did would my nerves get the better of me again?

The suspense of not knowing was casting a cloud I couldn't flee from. Part of me liked it: it took focus away from the reality which was due to unfold. For a while, even though I had no answers to my never-ending questions, I was content to stay in the thoughts.

Sabbath was not far away which I always dreaded: it was a difficult time since my family had passed. I had lost faith in a lot of things. too, because of it, so never stuck to the traditional Jewish ways now. My last trip to the synagogue was a brief one: I was no longer comfortable, or had the faith to be there now which others didn't take lightly to. I pulled myself away from it gradually until I didn't go back anymore, I also grew distant from Rabbi.

I was bitter as to how I once had everything, and now had nothing, without any explanation or reason as to why this came to be. I had lost my way, but I was happier some ways now, I had stopped drinking at least. Every occasion I would have spent with family made me become more isolated, thinking, questioning all over again.

However, my parents were good people; I always wanted to pay my respects to them. Still, I could only bring myself to light a candle in the comfort of my home, alone. Prayer was a short one where I would then slump into my armchair, reflecting on my life, while staring hard into the flicker of the flames.

The only other person in my life now was my best friend Avraham; he would always come by to check on me during these times especially. He would try convincing me to get out more or go back to the synagogue. As much as that frustrated me, he was kindhearted with much wisdom; he still always had my best interests at heart. He had been there with me through everything, and, apart from his pesky ways, he was still my best friend who meant the world to me.

A few weeks passed, I saw no sign of Betty again. I wondered about her often; I questioned all I had thought, as well as felt, at the time, hoping I would see her again; yet becoming more unconvinced I would as time went by.

The day before Sabbath, Avraham was due to come around. I had a swift tidy up, then took Jonah out, but still had a few hours to kill until he was expected. I was going to read but, oddly, found myself reaching for my prayer book instead. As I went to pick it up the phone rang, confused as I was not expecting anyone, I quickly moved to answer it. I lifted the receiver.

"Hello?"

"Hello, is this Ishmael?"

"Yes, who is this, please?"

"It's about your friend, Avraham, he's been rushed into hospital; he has been asking for you, could you…?"

I flung down the phone without even saying thank you or asking what had happened. Panic engulfed me, shaking my whole being, literally. All I kept saying repeatedly was: "please, not Avraham, not him, don't take him". I had no clue to his condition, so, I assumed the worst.

I eventually composed myself enough to call a taxi, then waited anxiously for it to arrive. Jonah, sensing something was not right, came over, trying to give me comfort; his eyes looking sad. I stroked him, trying to give reassurance, yet it was unconvincing as I didn't know what would happen. A few minutes passed until I heard a beep from outside: it was the taxi. I got up then told Jonah I'd be back soon, before rushing out to get into the car, leaving him to the pleasure of his bone.

Darkness was beginning to overshadow the streets as it was late in the afternoon. Street lights were dim; waiting to reach their full potential. The sky was changing, creating a beautiful sunset over the horizon; I had never noticed it before. I felt a peacefulness, the beauty, just like Betty, had gripped me again. For a second all was forgotten, not even the bumps on the roads distracted me.

Driving through the streets I thought of everything Avraham had done for me; I was blessed having a friend like him. I had been somewhat neglectful to him in many ways, yet he never swayed. I vowed to never take him for granted again if he was to live. He made me see I needed to change, I could not wallow any longer or hide behind my bitterness. Even in his hour of dire need, he still showed me the way; he was still being the best friend from his hospital bed.

I prayed for him, a real prayer now, pleading I would get the chance to thank him. Hoping I could tell him how much I appreciated him, to be there for him now, just like he had been for me. I felt tears forming but quickly came to my senses; no, it wasn't about me, Avraham needed me to be strong. He was my only focus; I just hoped I wouldn't be too late.

The driver soon drew up at the entrance, I was pulled from thought with the jolt of the car stopping. I paid the driver before rushing out towards the entrance, then straight to the reception desk.

"Please, my friend Avraham has been bought in; is he alright, what's happened?"

The lady looked at me then just smiled.

"Okay, sir, if you want to take a seat; someone will be out shortly."

"But…? I…?"

"Please, sir, take a seat?"

She was stern now, leaving me no option other than to turn away, which made me feel even more concerned. Why not just say if he was stable or not, it only worried me even more; I just needed to know how he was.

Taking a seat wasn't an option for me, either. I was very fidgety now; I found myself pacing the waiting area, hoping time would pass quicker as well as calm me; I was naive to think it would do that. It felt like hours until I had a tap on the shoulder.

"Ishmael, is that you?"

I recognised that surprised voice immediately; I spun around quickly, now in disbelief, to see who was standing there.

"Betty? Betty please, where is he? Is he going to be alright? I have been told nothing."

She grabbed my arm pulling me towards a seat; my first thought was he had gone. I closed my eyes as I followed her, muttering under my breath, 'please be alright, Avraham, please be alright.'

Sitting me down, she then gave me that smile again; instantly I felt more at ease.

"It's alright, Ishmael, he has had a suspected heart attack; he is stable, but we are keeping him in to run tests and monitor him for a while."

I was filled with empathy for my friend, and so glad he was still with me. I now felt a surge of guilt: I should have seen the signs, I should have known he was not well. Everything he had done for me, I only gave him selfish behaviour in return. I was disgusted with myself, but now I had a second chance to change that, which I intended on doing.

I just stared at her, she had beautiful eyes, ones I could have gazed at forever.

"May I see him? It's important."

"Of course, but not for too long he needs rest, Ishmael."

She took me to his room, I was still worried for him, unsure about what to say, she saw the look on my face then laughed.

"Ishmael? Hey, he will make it; don't look so worried."

I just snapped now: really agitated at the remark.

"He's my best friend, I can't not worry; you don't understand."

She looked taken aback by this, her smile fading ever so quickly into a regretful expression.

I didn't mean to snap or be so abrupt, but I felt so many emotions coming at me from all angles; a comment like that had activated an unintentional bad reaction.

I walked into the room slowly, he was just lying there with many machines attached to him. He looked so tired, the colour had left his once red cheeks. I barely recognized his ghostly appearance.

I felt a lump in my throat now; he turned to look towards me, surprised to see me standing there.

"Ishmael, my friend, you came?"

"Yes, Avraham, of course, never will I take you for granted again. I'm so sorry, I thought you had, I..."

"Ishmael, stop, sit down; everything will be fine. You worry far too much."

I glared at him, did I? Was I so wrong to worry? I suddenly felt confused again. Whatever did he mean by this?

I sat on the chair besides him.

"Avraham, you are like my brother, when I got the phone call I panicked: I was so scared you wouldn't make it. I can't not worry, you're the only person in my life; yet, I've taken you for granted. I have been selfish, I prayed tonight; I prayed so hard hoping you would be alright."

"My friend, I admire you: you've been through so much, yet you're a wonderful person underneath. You have got lost but I only want to help you. I must ask that you stop pushing me away, live your life. Don't hide behind four walls: you have so much to give, please, don't be so hard on yourself, Ishmael."

I sat there thinking, suddenly the alarms started to go off. I looked at him, now startled: he was lying there still, almost like he had said his final words.

"Avraham? AVRAHAM, NO."

I ran to the corridor frantically; screaming to anyone that would hear me. A nurse came out of a room nearby.

"NURSE, NURSE, please, somebody help? It's my friend."

The nurse came quickly, then more nurses came rushing in behind her. They stopped me from going back in the room as I approached it; a doctor followed a minute later. I stood watching through the glass till one of the nurses pulled the curtains, staring at me the whole time. Now I had to wait again. As I waited, I heard her voice again.

"Ishmael? What is it?"

I lifted my head then curved myself around to look at Betty. There was no smile now, only a look of concern. I felt awful snapping at her earlier, yet she still had time for me even now.

"I am so sorry I snapped, Betty, you see, he is all I have: he's like a brother, a father, everything. I… I can't lose him, not now."

I felt myself welling up, it was getting harder with every second that went by to fight them back. She walked over towards me then gently put her arms around me; I was shocked by her doing this. It was welcoming, but I couldn't control my emotions any longer now; I broke down.

She stood there just holding me, rubbing my shoulder slowly. It had been so long since I had that, a first for me from a girl. Still, all I could think about was Avraham: he was all that mattered now. I was overcome with feelings which completely consumed me.

So many thoughts were battling through my mind: I was faced with my demons, every emotion flowing through me one by one. I just wanted to scream, but the comfort I received from Betty helped me to keep control.

We stood there for a couple of minutes while my tears fell onto her shoulder. The urge to find out what was happening was growing stronger now, but the consolation was a reality I could have easily stayed in, but only with her.

I lifted my head off her shoulder, a cold blast hitting the warmth of my cheek, as though it was blowing my tears away. She stepped back, with a look that appeared to anticipate what I was going to say next.

"Betty, I need to know what's happening with my friend; please, could you find anything out?"

She showed her smile once again, then squeezed my arm reassuringly.

"Sure, I'll see what I can do."

As she started to walk off, a doctor came towards me, I was terrified: he looked so serious, now I had convinced myself of the worst outcome.

"Is it Ishmael?"

"Yes doctor, please? Is my friend going to make it? What is happening? Please tell me he is alright?"

"Yes, your friend is alive but very sick, we have taken him to theatre for heart surgery; we are doing all we can for him, the next few hours are critical."

The sense of relief I felt in that moment was so satisfying. I knew it was early days, but something told me he would get better. I thought, maybe if I continued to pray enough, believe, then perhaps it would be so.

Betty hadn't moved, she just listened quietly, the look on

her face made me think that she, too, believed the same. I thanked the doctor then walked over to take her hand.

"Thank you, Betty: for all you have done today, I won't forget what you did."

"Not at all, Ishmael, I'm glad I could help."

She reached into her pocket, pulling out a small pad and pen she scribbled something on it.

"Here, please take this, if you ever need to talk then give me a call?"

I looked longingly into her eyes then smiled.

"I will Betty, I will call you."

"Good, I will be waiting for it, Ishmael."

She winked, then smiled at me, giving my shoulder a gentle rub, before returning to work. I sat down, so much had happened today, I had almost lost my friend, I was brought together with Betty when I needed it. It was all too much, yet I felt more harmony now which was down to Betty; I knew that.

I turned my thoughts to Jonah: he would have been wondering where I was, but I could not leave till I knew Avraham was out of theatre or on the road to recovery. Hours had passed now, I had dosed off unintentionally, tired from earlier events. The same doctor came over gently waking me; I bolted upright.

"What is it? Avraham?"

"He will be fine, Ishmael, he's very weak but we are positive he will make a full recovery."

I leapt up, just hugging him ecstatically now. Hearing those words was the best feeling I had never thought I would have the pleasure of experiencing. That moment I felt incredibly lucky, that one day had changed my life in so many ways; I was happy to share it with anyone.

"Thank you so much, Doctor, thank you; may I see him yet?"

He laughed as he straightened himself out. Looking at

me, holding my arm, he nodded in agreement.

"He is sleeping but you can have a minute. I think you should go home, too, to get some rest: looks like you need it? He is in good hands Ishmael."

This was a comment I couldn't deny, they had not just saved my friend, but given me a second chance; how could I ever repay that?

"I won't be long, doctor, I promise."

"Very well, Ishmael, follow me."

The doctor led the way, I went in quietly, smiling now: this was my friend, he had colour back, he was no longer the ghost that lay before me earlier. I went over to him, lifting his hand.

"Thank you for everything, I will be back first thing to see you, Avraham, rest now my friend."

I don't know if he heard me; I could only hope. I kissed him on the forehead then left the room. Glancing back, I thought to myself what an amazing man.

As I strolled along the corridor, I saw Betty, now with a coat on, holding a bag. She saw me then came rushing over.

"He is going to be fine, Betty, he will make a full recovery."

She hugged me again tightly: appearing to be thrilled with the news.

"Oh Ishmael, that's wonderful to hear."

"You have no idea, Betty."

I winked at her now, she stared back at me curiously before putting her head down, with a chuckle. She waited a moment then looked up at me.

"Well I'm heading your way if you fancy stopping for a coffee?"

I was obviously keen, but I had to take Jonah out now; he always came first. Thinking for a moment, I turned to her.

"Betty, I would love to, only Jonah will need to go out; he will wonder where I am."

"Is there room for one more?"

I stared at her for a moment then grinned.

"Yes, I think we would both like that."

"Come on, Ish, let's go get him?"

"Ish?"

"Yes, I think it suits you; do you not like it? I won't call you it if it's a problem?"

"Betty, you can call me what you like. Hang on for a minute?"

"Hmm, a minute? I think I can do better than a minute, Ish?"

I walked up close to her now, with my smile growing; she gazed in my eyes.

"Hmm, I think I could to, I'll be right back, Betty."

I pulled myself away towards the reception desk, now chuckling quietly; Betty didn't take her eyes off me the whole time. I asked the receptionist to ring me about any change, then told them I would be back in the morning. We soon made our way to pick up Jonah. Betty showed great interest in me, as well as Avraham; she was as curious as I was. While we slowly strolled, she grabbed my arm.

"Ish, he must be a very special guy for someone to react like that? I have comforted many in my job, but I've never felt such intense emotion as I did with you. I'm sorry: I shouldn't have said anything, it just got me curious?"

"I've known him my whole life, he has been there through everything with me. I lost my family, my faith, my friends; I have been selfish, showed no gratitude. I turned to drink but he has not left my side; I owe him everything Betty."

I looked over to see what her reaction was, I was slightly unnerved by what I had told her.

"Ish, you have been grieving, I can see you have had a lot to deal with, but life must go on. You don't have to deny yourself happiness; being a nurse, I know life is a gift; so we need to make the most of it. We all have regrets, we all feel guilt; that's to be expected. Just don't let it control you: your family would not want that."

I listened to her wise words, I knew she was right. I had been stuck this way for so long that seeing a way out scared me.

"I saw things so much more clearly today; I was given a second chance, one I will not ignore, thank you, Betty."

"Don't torture yourself, I see a lovely guy; I know there's more to you, don't be afraid to show it."

She linked my arm as we got nearer to my house, I had sensed there was something special about her which was proven to be right. I knew I needed her: she would be the one to help me move on, however, I did not know how. Soon that would become clear.

We soon arrived at my house. Upon opening the door, Jonah came charging over: it was clear he had missed me. He seemed pleased to see I was fine, but he was still unsettled, not wanting to leave me alone. Betty followed me in then went wandering round the room.

"Jonah, hello boy, shall we go out?"

I knelt, stroking him fondly before I stood up to grab his lead. Betty slowly moved around the lounge, picking up the pictures or ornaments that I had with great interest.

"Ish, is this your family?"

"Yes, it's an old photo, shall we go?"

"Yes, we have been waiting long enough."

She grinned as she put the picture down neatly into place, with every moment passing, I liked her so much more.

We walked for a short while, soon we came to the place where I had first seen her.

"This is the spot we first met, do you remember? You were like an angel appearing before me."

She gave me a strange look then burst out laughing.
"What?"

"I'm sorry, you are very funny, Ish, so sweet too."
"I'm serious?"

"I know you are, you just sounded so poetic; I didn't mean to laugh."

"I am a poet; a very good one, too, if you don't mind?"

This just tickled her more, she almost cried with laughing: I'm guessing maybe my facial expressions along with my folded arms were much funnier than the actual words were; it was hard to tell at that moment.

"Oh, Ish stop it, please?"

Poor Jonah wondered what was going on; puzzled as to why we had stopped for such madness. I would've been offended if it was anyone else; I couldn't help but grin with her laughing so hard.

"Tell her, Jonah."

He wagged his tail, panting, he then looked straight at me with a look as if to say, "Don't be ridiculous, you know I can't speak", tilting his head one way, then the other, repeatedly. He humoured me all the time; he never failed to do it again now. I really loved that dog. Betty had also taken to him.

"Oh, Ish, he's adorable."

"He's certainly special, I know that much."

"Yes, that is clear to see; he's gorgeous."

"Yes, but I'm thinking he is not the only one."

She immediately looked at me then started laughing again; I just looked at her with a grin.

"You just had to get that one in, didn't you?"

"Yes, I couldn't resist. What? I'm only speaking the truth Betty."

"If you say so, Ish, if you say so."

"Yes, Betty; I say so."

3 A PERFECT EVENING

Her whole being warmed me: she had a calming aura about her. She was lovely from the inside out, watching her took the worries of the day away which relaxed me immensely. This was someone I could be with, but if not, I had found a female version of Avraham: another best friend. I had her in my life, at least for now; I could only hope she would stay.

Betty composed herself as we continued walking, the sky was clear, stars were appearing quickly; it was beautiful, that moment I felt I could take on the world.

We decided to go to the park which was opposite a row of shops. I let Jonah off before looking up at the moon in awe. Betty stood next to me also looking up.

"The night is beautiful, Ish, hope is in the air."

I looked ahead taking it all in before turning to her.

"I know, I have you here; don't I?"

I smiled at her, then with such confidence, she came up close to me, looking me straight in the eyes.

"Okay, Ish? I don't know why, but I've wanted to kiss you since we left the hospital, that's only increased since. There I couldn't, but now there is nothing to stop me, or is there?"

My heart raced so fast, I took her hand moving as close to her as I possibly could while gazing back.

"I don't think I could stop you even if I wanted to."

"I can't explain this, Ish, but you were familiar from the minute I spoke to you; I knew we would meet again."

"Time seemed to stand still when I met you, I also sensed we would meet again, but then time passed making me think otherwise; now here we are,"

She scanned my face with her eyes, then, with a smile, she put her hand behind my head and moved in to kiss me; it would be a kiss I would never forget.

I knew the chemistry was strong but now I was certain it was real; Betty had felt it, too, just as much. After the day I had had, I now felt happy. Betty pulled away, now smiling back at me.

"Wow, Ish, I have no words, but I knew it would be… different."

"I knew it couldn't be anything else, Betty."

We both smiled at each other, she knew exactly what I meant, she then turned to look at Jonah.

"Oh, Ish, look? Jonah."

I turned around to see him sitting there, he was looking slightly confused again, feeling slightly left out. I called him to me.

"Come here, Jonah, it's alright boy."

We both fussed him for a minute or two, Betty then stood up.

"Shall we get a coffee, Ish? I'm parched."

"That's not how I would describe you: I think there are more fitting words."

"Even so I want coffee, come on, now."

I stood up grinning; Betty went to walk off, but I grabbed her unexpectedly, pulling her towards me again.

"What? I couldn't help myself."

"Clearly, Ish, clearly."

"You can stop me, Betty"

"We both know that's not true, Ish."

I kissed her again, not wanting to stop now. The passion I felt the first time was addictive; she didn't hold back anyway, so I didn't either. I found it hard to contain myself as the seconds ticked by, but I had to. Hesitantly I pulled away.

"I'm thinking now is a good idea to get coffee?"

"Say no more, Ish, I felt it too."

We arrived at the café. I tied up Jonah outside where I could keep him in view, finally stepping inside to order drinks. It was a pleasant, quaint little place with an array of colour, which had plenty of life to it.

Old fashioned tables were dotted around, all with identical chairs that looked cozy, I liked it instantly, as did Betty.

"What a place, Ish, bet the coffee is just as lovely."

"Yes, I like it, Betty, although I doubt it'd be as warming as those moments were."

"Well you will soon feed your curiosity, won't you?"

"Yes, I intend to."

I smirked as she looked at me questionably; the waitress came over with our order a moment later. I started feeling the coffee cups, Betty, as well as the waitress, just stared at me.

"Ish, what are you doing?"

"I'm feeding my curiosity, Betty."

I winked at her, Betty started laughing while putting her hand to her face. The waitress looked at me as though I had gone mad, but at the same time couldn't help but smile either; she then left us. Betty turned to me.

"So, what's the outcome, Ish?"

"No competition, obviously."

"You know, I could have just told you that"

"Well you didn't need to, not really."

I gazed at her as she picked up her coffee before continuing on, quickly changing the subject.

"So, do you write, Ish?"

"I did once; its faded with time along with a lot of things."

"It might be something to try again? It will be there somewhere."

"Maybe. What about you, Betty? Why did you become a nurse?"

With a serious look, she picked up her coffee again, taking a sip followed by a deep breath.

"I, too, lost my parents a couple of years ago. Seeing them go through illness; knowing I couldn't help them was very difficult. When they passed I knew I wanted to be a nurse; so, after many struggles, I studied nursing."

Now I understood her compassion and her desire to be there for me: she, too, had been through it. I had great admiration for her: she appeared to have handled it much better than I did. She had moved on with her life, done something positive for herself.

"You have done amazingly well, Betty, you are beautiful on the inside as well as out. I know how hard it is; your parents would be proud of you."

"That's sweet, you're sweet, it was hard; sometimes it still is. But everyone copes differently so don't be disheartened; bad times don't last forever. You will get through this, Ish, I will help you."

"I am so glad you came into my life, I've learned today not to take anything for granted. I've been wrong, so now I want to make it right."

"Admitting that is a start; I know you mean every word. Go easy on yourself: you have had it tough too, but everything will work out."

"It's been good chatting. I have never spoken before about it – not even to Avraham."

"Well maybe you should? Ish, he's your best friend; he will be there."

"I know, he always has been. It just never felt right either, I feel I can talk to you about anything."

"That's because you can; I feel the same, too."

She took my hand squeezing it soothingly.

"Let's get Jonah, Ish: it's getting colder now."

She never failed to warm my heart: she was so lovely with me, with Jonah too. We came as one which she accepted, she also accepted me, my demons. Saw something in me that I could not. She made me want to find out, she was inspiring, brightened up my life so much being in it; I couldn't fail her or myself.

Betty got up to go the restroom before we left. I scribbled some momentary thoughts on a bit of paper. She soon came back so I hurriedly put it into my pocket. She glanced at me suspiciously with a grin, but said nothing about it.

"We'd better go, are you ready, Ish?"

"For you? Any day."

"Oh, Ish, come on, we will be here all night with you, don't?"

I laughed then looked at her.

"Don't what?"

"I know what you're going to say."

"Hmm, why am I not surprised, Betty?"

"Think we both know the answer to that one."

"Well, you can't blame me, sounds like heaven to me"

"Hmm, I can think of better places more fitting for that word, Ish"

She grinned cheekily before I finished the last of my coffee, I then stood up. Walking out we thanked the waitress then headed to the door were Jonah was lying down. He looked very much fed up after being left for a while now. Moving his eyes to look, he got up quickly when he realised it was us.

"Good boy, Jonah, I love you, yes, I do; come on let's go home."

Betty gave him some attention while I untied the lead; he enjoyed every second. Rain had started to drizzle as we stepped outside; the sky had quickly become overcast, coldness in the air hitting us like the sting of a bee, yet, all I could do was smile. Betty huddled into me for warmth while speaking of her family, her work; I listened contentedly. It felt as though we were walking for hours but I was not fatigued or bored. With her everything was perfect.

I walked her back to her house: it was late now. It would ease my mind knowing that she was home safe, besides the fact I wanted to spend every second that I could with her. We soon arrived at her home.

"Well this is mine, I've had a lovely evening, thank you, Ish."

"Tonight has been perfect. Here, take this but open it when I am gone."

I handed her the scrunched piece of paper I had scribbled on, fixing it first to make it look presentable.

"I knew it. It'll be the last thing I look at before I fall asleep."

She walked up to me again, grinning, then kissed me softly again.

"You will be my last thought before I close my eyes Betty: that way I know my dreams will be the best ones."

"You certainly have a way with words, Ish, goodnight; keep smiling."

"That shouldn't be too difficult with you around; goodnight beautiful."

She ran up to her door; I watched as she closed it behind her, then she was gone. Rain became heavier, but that moment felt as though we were immune to it: just like we were encased in a bubble, maybe not even in this world. It was a magical feeling, but like all good things it had to end, at least for now.

I headed back to mine. I made a drink then fixed Jonah some food before filling his water bowl; then I sat down. Today had been very eventful; I needed a moment to reflect on it all. This morning my heart was almost broken, but now? I had a warmth in it that not even ice could freeze.

As I sat in front of my open fire, listening to the crackles of the cinders burning, I wondered what Betty was doing – whether she had read my note – and what might happen next. I realised how lost I had been, how much time I had wasted, now I had to move on.

I also thought about Avraham. It was him who had bought me together with Betty, unknowingly. He had made me see the error of my ways, put things into perspective; he never left my side the whole time. I lit a candle then prayed: I just had the urge to. I gave my thanks for the day, the good as well as the bad, praying Avraham would get better quickly. I could not wait to see him, prove to him that I was on the road to change.

Betty was also thinking while she got ready for bed, for she, too, had not experienced a connection like this before, all Ishmael had felt, she had too. For her, the urge to kiss him so soon was too strong to ignore. She pulled out the piece of paper he had given her then sat on the bed; carefully she opened it.

Like the sun, you came from nowhere
Igniting my world
One kiss you warmed my life
One gaze, I was addicted
A connection which no time
Can ever change
An invisible thread no one can break...
You're so beautiful, and me?
I'm just the luckiest guy around
x

She thought for a moment before she mumbled quietly.

"Two hearts that beat as one; oh, wow, Ish."

The note made her emotional: she was so touched by the words. Taking another look at them, she cradled the paper against her chest. She got into bed still holding it; there she lay on her back thinking about him. She smiled before whispering a goodnight, as though he was there with her. She soon fell asleep, for her it was the perfect ending to a magical night.

Sitting there, I went over everything both Betty and

Avraham had said, the day was a long one. Fatigue was quickly creeping in now, so, I soon headed to bed. I was shattered but felt peaceful, getting into bed I smiled.

"You were my last thought, beautiful, goodnight."

It didn't take long until I fell into a deep asleep, but soon I was awoken by the chimes of my grandfather clock striking the morning hour. A beloved piece of history that had been passed down the family, looking after it was a great pride of mine. My instant thoughts were Avraham, then Betty; smiling, I darted out of bed, throwing some clothes on. I was soon on my way to the hospital. I had picked up my prayer book before I left as Avraham was still very much a part of the Jewish community; I knew the book would be something he would want when he was well enough.

It was strange walking back to the same area where things could have turned out differently. The place where Betty had comforted me. Waiting what felt like a lifetime to hear of Avraham's condition, only to be told he was going to make it, then the events thereafter. I looked around, it looked the same but felt different, so much had happened in that area the day before, now I just wanted to see Avraham. I approached the receptionist who looked up as I got to the desk.

"Good morning, I'm here to see Avraham."

"Aah, yes, of course; he is in the same room if you want to head there?"

"Thank you, yes, how is he?"

"Much better today, he's sitting up, although try not to tire him too much: he needs rest."

I became excited, he really was getting better; my feet couldn't take me there quick enough. I just wanted to hug him, tell him all that had happened.

"Here you are, sir, remember what I said?"

"Of course, thank you."

He did look much better, seeing him like that I was thrilled. I beamed at him as I walked in, he looked as surprised as the first time.

"Ishmael? What are you doing here?"

"Avraham, it's so good to see you, how are you feeling?"

"Good, my friend, good, feeling much better. I can see you have a twinkle in your eyes I've not seen for a long time? Ishmael?"

"Yes, Avraham, things look so much better now; I can't thank you enough."

He looked baffled by this, so I told him all that had happened from that first phone call from the hospital, to now.

"I never meant to frighten you, Ishmael, for that I am sorry. However, it's God's will I am here, so it would have been his if I wasn't; you still have much to learn my friend. Now, tell me about Betty?"

"Avraham, I have never met anyone like her, she is beautiful, smart with much wisdom, compassionate; she has a fun side too. She was there for me yesterday; I could be myself around her, I've never felt a connection like that. We have much in common, I know she is special: she, too, made me want to change my ways."

"Yes, she sounds wonderful."

"I am feeling happy for now, that's all I want, even for a while."

"I'm happy for you, but Ishmael? I'm concerned the community will not approve of her if she is not Jewish?"

"I have not been part of it for a long time, her religion doesn't matter to me; they can't have a say now, surely?"

"Ishmael, if you are to ever marry then you will need their blessing; you will not get that if they are against it. I also do not want there to come to a point where I must choose between my faith or my friend, but I may have to. You are my oldest friend, you are important to me, but you need to think this through carefully. Please, don't be angry, I am only telling you this as your friend."

"I'm not angry, I know all this; I'm not as wise as you but I know she is special. Avraham, I would marry her if it's ever meant to be, but I do not want to lose my friend over it. What do I do? Do I pursue this or let her go?"

"Only you can decide that, Ishmael, you must do what's right for you: whatever you feel in your heart. Don't let others make that decision for you, I will always be there. Just, don't let love cloud your judgement, be sure it's right."

"I will, Avraham, you have my word. Here, I bought you my prayer book, can I get you anything else?"

"No, I am good; bless you, Ishmael. I am a little tired now, but maybe tomorrow we can say a prayer together?"

I hesitated for a moment: acting like it would be so easy was not something I could do unless I was alone. Seeing his face, I knew it would mean a lot to him if I did: so, I agreed.

"Yes Avraham, I will, for you. Rest now, I will come back tonight."

"Ishmael, do not trouble yourself: go now you have much to think about, I'll be here when you need me."

"I will go, but I will still be back tonight. You said for me to not push you away; well don't push me away either, I want to help. I will not abandon you, Avraham."

He laughed at this.

"Okay my friend, okay; I will see you tonight."

"You will, goodbye, Avraham."

He lay back, closing his eyes peacefully. Those moments had given me a reality check regarding Betty: I felt torn now. Things moved so fast with her, I gave no thought to what the future would bring. The thought of Avraham also being torn weighed heavily on me: he meant the world to me, but I was thrown by fate with Betty.

I wondered now if I misjudged it all: just got caught in the moment? Would I risk too much for something that may not work out? I had a lot to think about; I also had to speak with Betty about it at some point. I didn't want to frighten her off or raise any doubts by bringing marriage or my Jewish traditions into it just yet; timing had to be right. I wanted to enjoy every moment until I knew what would happen next, one way or the other.

I left the hospital, but I wasn't ready to go home. I

walked into the town, I'd not been there for a long time just to avoid bumping into people I once knew. It looked so different now; I stopped to look around. The place felt so unfamiliar, yet it was still busy, people rushing round as they always did. I suddenly felt as though I'd walked into another world, so much time had gone by, but I had nothing to show for it. Everything had changed with time; the feeling was a peculiar one.

I sighed, then took a breath when a cafe over the road got my attention; hastening my steps, I moved towards it. The sun was shining brightly, giving out warm rays which fell easy on my face. There were tables standing neatly with chairs on a veranda, which had steps up to it, looking very inviting. Now I was here, I decided to get some lunch. I walked to a table before dragging out a chair to sit down. I picked up a skillfully stacked menu to scan the dishes when a waitress came over promptly.

"Good afternoon, may I take your order, please, sir?"

"Yes, I'll have the sandwich with a white coffee if I may?"

"Yes, that's no problem; someone will bring it over."

I smiled at the girl as she walked away into the café. I sat staring out at the town for a couple of minutes, watching the world go by. I suddenly heard a voice I recognised a couple of minutes later, bringing me back to the present moment.

"Ishmael? Ishmael, is that you?"

I slowly turned around to see Rabbi standing there. I was shocked: he looked so much older now. His once black hair had grayed considerably just as much as his beard, which had lengthened, too; he also had a frail look to him. I knew the voice, but no longer the man that stood there before me.

"Rabbi?"

"Yes, it is I, Ishmael, I can't believe it is you: it has been too long. How are you?"

What did I say? All was well? I was fine? I felt troubled, but I was unsure of telling him why: things felt awkward considering the reason. However, he knew there was something on my mind, Rabbi always did.

"What is it? You seem disturbed about something. Ishmael? Perhaps I can help?"

"I worry for Avraham; torn as to what comes next or what to do."

He sat down on the chair next to me.

"What comes next? Ishmael, you have lost me. How do you mean?"

"Forgive me, see I've met this wonderful girl, Rabbi, I'm led to believe she may not be accepted by our community. If so, I will not be able to one day marry, I am convinced she is the one, but I am doubtful now: not of her, but of how this could go, I just…"

"Ishmael, why do you let this trouble you so? Enjoy it for now, see how you get on. When you know what's right then things will fall into place. Yes, some will not agree but if this is important to you…?"

"It is, Rabbi, but I don't want it to affect my friendship with Avraham, I do not want to make him have to choose: he has enough to deal with. But not just that: he's my best friend, Rabbi."

"Son, I know, but if this is meant to be then it will be so. You, always overthinking or doubting, it will send you mad, not to mention make you miserable. We cannot change destiny; we just need to accept whatever comes."

He placed his arm on my shoulder. I noticed how much I had missed him; he was fair, always had a certain way of making me feel better. A few years had passed but he was so different in appearance; his heart, however, was still a good one.

"I just want to do the right thing, Rabbi, for everyone."

"Ishmael, I can see, but don't forget yourself either, it's clear she isn't Jewish, but…"

"We have a connection, Rabbi, things have happened fast. Why does it have to matter? I have lost my faith; I don't follow the Jewish way now. Pretending to do so, just to be able to marry, is something I will not do."

"Ishmael, I have known you since you were a boy; I have seen you go through so much peril. When you talk of her you have a spark about you. If she makes you happy then I am happy for you. Avraham however, is a wise one; listen to him, but, more importantly, listen to yourself. You won't need to pretend, things will turn out if you are doing what is right by you. I am here if you need to discuss this more."

"Thank you, Rabbi, it is early days but yes, I will, it has been good to see you."

I kissed his hand before he got up. Although his words fell easy on my mind, I was still conflicted: as now I could risk backlash for him, too.

"You too, goodbye, Ishmael."

"Goodbye, Rabbi, thank you."

He wandered off, until the distance had drawn him in, then out of sight. Now I was alone with just my thoughts for company. I had to do something: I could not let my mind take me to a place I could not free myself from. I sat for a moment then got up, barely touching my lunch. I began to stroll round the shops; I started to feel more uncomfortable as I walked: people staring at me, whispering.

I once knew this place well; but now it was an alien world. I went to pass a bookshop, but then stopped abruptly: there was a sign in the window.

POETRY COMPETITION
Do you write? Why not enter to win great prizes?
Ask inside for details.

I went to walk off, but I was almost pulled back. Staring at the sign, I found myself opening the door then entering the bookshop. The shopkeeper was carefully placing books on the neatly stacked shelves. Hearing the bell, he turned as I wandered inside.

"Afternoon, sir, what can I do for you?"

"I am Ishmael, I am inquiring about the competition?"

"Aah, so you write? Come."

I walked over feeling slightly awkward about what he was going to say or do next. He was a bubbly chap, fairly short, with a brown moustache, beady eyes. He had brown hair, some which was sticking up on top of his head. He had a white shirt with a red dickie bowtie, smart looking, but not overly; he seemed an interesting man. As much as I wanted to run out of there now, I found myself moving towards the counter cautiously.

"Ishmael, come, come over. The competition is for poetry only, very popular. If you want to enter then send your work to this address; don't forget to put your details on it, too."

"I have not written for so long; but I was drawn here."

"I, too, wrote once, but since my sister and her husband passed, I have had my niece to look after. She has her own life now, but I'm still so busy."

I just stared at him, was he Betty's uncle? For some reason, I believed this to be an accurate assumption. I was about to leave; but turning towards the door I looked back: curiosity now taking over.

"Is your niece a nurse?"

He looked up at me, surprised.

"Why yes, she is, do you know her? Betty, she's called Betty."

This was scarily coincidental, I was unsure as to what to tell him or say, so I kept it brief.

"Yes, I know her, she's a wonderful girl."

He seemed pleased with the compliment but his look quickly turned to a saddened gaze.

"Yes, she is, I'm very proud of her; yet she is troubled."

I wondered what he meant by this, nevertheless, it wasn't appropriate to pry. It was an awkward comment, but it was obviously one which weighed heavily on his mind: for that I could sympathize. I had learned something because he didn't know about the relationship that was growing between Betty and me. I was stuck as to what words would be right.

I thought just leaving for now was the best thing, staying curious was also right. The need to leave became strong now, so I turned to him, hoping I could at least reassure him some way.

"I'm sure things will work out, thank you for your time. I must go, your help is appreciated; have a good day, sir."

"Anytime, Ishmael, anytime; good afternoon to you."

I hurried out of there thinking what on earth had just happened?

Being led to one thing then coming away, somewhat concerned by the words said which regarded something else. I had to see Betty now before I went back to the hospital; I just hope she had not yet left for work. Jumping into a cab to her house, I stopped at the florist on the way. It didn't take long to arrive. Paying the driver I got out and dashing up the steps, I heard voices arguing from inside; this startled me, instinct forcing me to now bang on the door.

"Betty? BETTY?"

I knocked desperately, then heard silence, a minute later there were heavy footsteps coming towards me; the door flung open almost knocking me over. It wasn't Betty who stood there, but a big burly, aggressive looking man; he did not look happy whatsoever.

"Who the hell are you? What do you want?"

"To see Betty, is she there?"

"She's busy, now leave before you become a part of the pavement."

"I want to see she is alright; only then will I go."

"Look I will not tell you again, go now: I'm warning you."

I turned to go, flowers still in hand. He slammed the door hard behind him, annoyed at my interference. I just thought to myself: what have you got involved in, is this what the bookseller was referring to? My fear for her was scaring me now. I felt cowardly for not doing more, but I was no match. He would have seriously hurt me, but especially Betty more; I had to think of her first.

I did not know what was happening, only that I had to stay out of it, at least for now. I went home to prepare my visit to Avraham. I was not looking forward to seeing him now: he would know something was wrong instantly then forbid me to get involved, but I already was.

Nobody could understand my feelings, or why I had to be there for her. She had helped me, so, as troubled as she seemed to be, I had to help her. I hoped my turning up had not caused Betty even more trouble. I was reeking of guilt, my fear for her was increasing. My stomach was in knots now; I wanted to go back taking Jonah with me, but something told me not to. Betty knew I was here; I just prayed she was alright.

I had a couple hours to spare, I made a cup of coffee then sat down. I remembered the details from the poetry competition. I took them out to study the paper then reached for a notepad; but I just felt nothing, neither could I concentrate. Betty took priority in my mind, worry for her was increasing more as time went by. I placed the notepad down on the table, I was foolish to believe I could just pick up from where I left off, especially now. But I felt the need to write for the first time in a long time. I had so many other thoughts spinning round.

My focus was missing which exasperated me, I leaned back in my chair, thinking. It wasn't long before I heard a tap on the door; I shot up to open it. Betty was standing there, terrified, with her body shaking. Tears were falling on her slightly swollen face, I could tell he had hit her; I was completely horrified.

"Oh no, Betty? Let me help you; why has he done this? I'll kill him."

"I'm so sorry, Ish, I didn't know where else to go."

"Hey, don't worry: you are safe for now, here sit down."

I led her in, fixed the couch for her before I got a cloth

with some cold water to bathe her face. She was really hurting; my heart felt as though it was breaking seeing her like that. I felt so angry now at myself, but especially at him; how could he do this? Why did I not do more?

"Betty, you are not obliged to tell me anything I und..."

"No, Ish, I disagree: I want you to know, no secrets. I wanted to tell you but..."

"Hey, it's alright Betty, you don't have to explain; not now. Let's get you more comfortable."

I put the cold cloth against her face making her wince with pain. She looked like a shell of herself; completely different to when I saw her last. It was like the part of her which was full of life, was gone: now she was sitting there scared, feeling many things as well as being in a lot of pain. I saw straight into her soul; it was still beautiful. I was not going to let anyone touch her again: that moment I knew I would kill, or die, for her without thought.

Jonah came up to her, quietly yelping, he sensed her pain too, so was now wanting to give her comfort, but not knowing his own strength or the fact that he could unintentionally hurt her more. I didn't want him causing her any more pain.

"Jonah, here boy, come here."

"It's okay, Ish, let him be: he's trying to help."

He lay by her and never moved a muscle. He, too, had become very fond of her; by his reaction I could tell he was willing to protect her, too. He, like myself, just seemed to know.

"Betty, you need to report this: he cannot get away with it. I'm not going to pressure you but after what he's done?"

"I know, but you don't know him: he will always find me. I moved to escape, but he found me again. I am scared, Ish, that's not an option for me."

"Who is he? Can I ask? What does he want?"

"His name is Jerry, after my parents died I went down a rocky road. I met him at a bar; he allowed me to stay with him, but wanted money for keep after a while. I got involved with drugs then…"

She sighed heavily putting her head down in shame; I could see this was traumatising for her. I placed my arm gently round her as she took a moment.

"You don't have to tell me now; I understand it's hard."

She carried on, completely ignoring my comment.

"I got involved with drugs then he changed, he wanted me to work for him, but I couldn't do it. It was only by pretending to that I managed to escape to a church. I was eventually picked up by my uncle; he looked after me. I changed after that; I wanted more for my life, so I went to college to become a nurse, like I said, then I met you. Oh, it's such a mess, I don't blame you if you walk the other way."

She put her hands up to her face, now sobbing: it was clear how haunted by her past she still was. All the mistakes made, she had dealt with them; now this man was abusing her still, it had to stop.

"Betty, I won't turn away: all those things I said to you, I still mean them. You were there for me when I needed someone, now I am going to be here for you."

I kissed her aching head softly, a smile appearing now. I thought her amazing that she could still manage that. I was falling for her hard with every passing minute. Wanting to make her happy, to make her smile permanent was my main aim now; nobody deserved to be treated like that, especially her.

"Betty, how much will it cost to get him gone? I could kill him for doing that to you."

"He wants a thousand; too much for me to afford. If I don't pay, I will keep getting this to repay it; that's how it goes. Now he has found me there isn't any escape, I don't want to move again, I can't afford that either."

I was shocked at her words: I couldn't understand how somebody could even be so cruel? How somebody could turn someone so beautiful into a shell that sat in front of me? I was going to get it somehow, repay what's owed to him. If he ever came back, then he would see my dark side, too. But Betty had seen enough, I hoped it wouldn't come to that.

"I will find the money, Betty, some way. He will not touch you again, because if he does… I will kill him."

Her eyes lit up, I knew she believed every word. I just didn't know how I would manage getting so much money, but it was my concern now; I would find a way. I started clearing up when she grabbed my hand.

"Ish, when this is over, I want to make you happy: I've never felt so safe as when I am with you, I…"

She paused, appearing to be unable to find the courage to say what she was about to; I sat back down by her, now curious.

"What? Betty, what is it?"

"It doesn't matter."

"Betty?"

"No, it's fine, Ish."

"Get some rest now, everything will be alright."

"Wait, it's just… I love you, Ish, I'm sorry."

She put her hands to her face again, I pulled them away then lifted her chin, I grinned at her.

"Betty, hey, it's alright, remember my note?"

"Ish, of course, two hearts that beat as one."

I chuckled at this: she had given the missing piece to the riddle of words I had written. Part of me was amazed, and the other…? Somehow, I just knew she would.

"We are the same, I love you, too, Betty; I couldn't love anyone but you, I knew you were the one."

"Oh, Ish, I have so many feelings when I am not with you, but they're confirmed when I am. It is so strange, saying that is so quick, too, I know that, it's why I hesitated. But yes, I knew you were the one, too, maybe that is why I couldn't hold back? I never thought it possible I could smile today, you always manage to make that possible."

"I, too, have felt it all, Betty, it is not wrong to feel how we do, time will not change it. I've done nothing but smile with you; you're beautiful do you know that?"

"No, but you certainly make me feel like that, Ish."

"Well, that's how it should be."

We just stared at each other then. That moment, through all our doubts, all the insecurities, it seemed nothing could pull us apart. We both had our issues, but we knew we were there for each other through anything life threw at us. We both knew that she could always confide in me if needed, just as I could with her, she was vulnerable in some ways, the same as I was.

I was uncertain about a lot of things still, but we had each other there to help; that was a good feeling. I felt anguish now as Avraham was expecting me, but I did not want to leave her alone; I couldn't.

I glanced at the clock as Betty lay down by me; she noticed straight away. She sat up now, looking unsettled.

"What is it, Ish?"

"Don't worry, it can wait."

"What can?"

"Avraham, he will be expecting me but…"

"Go, Ish, you must, I will be fine with Jonah."

"No Betty, I can't: I will only worry about you. I'm thinking that you could come with me? Get yourself looked at, too? I'd love you to meet him?"

"I'll be fine, Ish, I'm a nurse after all. As for going, I don't know: look at me, I'm a mess."

"You're beautiful, it would be one way I would know you're safe."

"Ish…"

She moved in, kissing me passionately. I felt every inch of it; she held onto me like she never wanted me to go. I knew life would be good with her in it, I felt so lucky to have found her, I also knew she was worth crossing any ocean for, in a heartbeat I would do it.

We got lost in the moment until Betty pulled away.

"Every kiss, always as good as the first, Ish."

"Everyone better than the last."

She laughed softly before moving her finger down my face, just looking at me.

"Whatever way you want to look at it, Ish."

"Aah, I'm happy with either."

I winked at her as I went to get up, she caught my hand, her face solemn again.

"Ish, you're a special guy; I always knew that."

"I'm so lucky; I know that. Come on, Avraham will be wondering where I am, are you ready?"

"Yes, Ish, nervous, but I'm ready."

"Don't be: he can be overprotective, but you will like him, I think he will like you, too."

"We will see, Ish."

"No, you will know before long, it's Avraham after all."

She only giggled at this as we headed outside. We made our way to the hospital, I watched her hair blowing in the wind. You wouldn't think she was so troubled: her fighter spirit with oodles of optimism was shining just as brightly as she was now. I just wondered why on earth she even picked me?

4 A BOLD MOVE

We arrived at the hospital where we made our way to Avraham's room. I opened the door, beckoning Betty in: she just stood there with a sense of uncertainty, wondering what would happen next and if she was doing the right thing. I reassured her enough to get her to walk in; Avraham was out of bed, fixing some books.

"Avraham, you're up already?"

"Ishmael, my friend, yes, I am doing better than expected. It is so good to see you. Aah, who's this? Is it…?"

"Yes, Avraham, this is Betty."

He walked over slowly to her, shaking her hand. He noticed her face, a slightly alarmed look fell upon his. For the moment though he said nothing, just greeted her in a welcoming manner.

"I've heard much about you Betty, come, pull a chair; please sit down."

Betty sat quietly on the chair; I sat on the bed, keen to make conversation from the silence that had fallen around us.

"Avraham, you look very well."

"Yes, I may be able to come home tomorrow, I am feeling much better."

"I am so pleased, I hope me bringing Betty was the right thing?"

She gripped my arm while he looked towards her for a minute, thinking. With a vague smile he then replied.

"Yes, I am very pleased to meet you. Ishmael, I would love a cup of tea, would you?"

"Of course. Betty I won't be long, it's okay."

She looked at me almost begging me not to go; I felt bad, but it was obvious Avraham wanted a minute alone with her.

"So, I hear you are very fond of Ishmael? No, fond of each other?"

"Yes, he is wonderful, Avraham. I've not met anyone like him before, I want to make him happy as he does me."

"You are aware he is Jewish, yes?"

"Sir, I am, I don't know what will happen, but my life is better now he is in it. I am extremely fond of him, but I don't want to cause problems for anybody."

"No, I can see that. Ishmael said the same. Pardon me, Betty, I am happy for you both. He is my good friend, someone I have always looked out for, too; I will continue to do so, but I will interfere no more."

"He is your friend, you have every right to be concerned for him; but I love him, he's an amazing guy."

"Yes, he really is. Betty, forgive me for this but I will say what is on my mind: I am alarmed by your bruising, may I ask what happened? Are you alright?"

"I am fine, thank you for asking, but I…"

Avraham could see it was difficult for her; Betty had been caught off guard by the question, not really knowing what to say. It was awkward, but Avraham would never have meant it intentionally. He touched her arm gently.

"Betty, I shouldn't have asked: you don't need to answer to me. If you are both alright, then I am good with that."

I walked back in a few minutes later, I knew words had been said but I didn't know what about. They both seemed a little disturbed, but nothing major. I didn't want to aggravate anything by asking, so I said nothing.

"Thank you, Ishmael."

"Avraham, Betty…"

"Relax Ishmael, I am happy for you both. I will not

interfere any more as I said to Betty; just take care of each other, that is my only ask."

"I saw Rabbi today."

"Really? Where?"

"I walked to town after seeing you. I told him what you said, he gave his blessing, too, but said I should listen to you. I love Betty, but you are my best friend, I don't want to lose either of you, Avraham."

"Rabbi is a fair man, very wise. I am your friend, Ishmael. We only want what's best for you, I can see Betty is a good influence; don't let what people say spoil what you have."

"Avraham, thank you; I appreciate that, he said the same about you. I want you to stay with me until you're well enough?"

"No Ishmael, I will be taken good care of. I won't burden you, I shall be fine; I know you are there if I need you."

"Yes, anytime, you only need to ask, but Avraham? You are never a burden."

Betty, who had barely said a word, was watching us both, her forthcoming humour came out of nowhere.

"You are both like an old married couple; should I be worried?"

We both looked at her before erupting into laughter; I could see her point. Poor Avraham holding his chest, laughed the hardest. So much so that a nurse popped her head in, grinning, somewhat intrigued as to what was so funny. It had been some time since I had seen him laugh like that, that was also a rarity.

I felt like the bond had been cemented between us. Now I was confident in believing that, under his defenses, he really liked her; that was a great weight off my mind.

"You have much humour, Betty, it will serve you well. Now I should get some rest."

"Ish, he is right, drink up so we can let him sleep."

Avraham nodded towards Betty in an appreciative

manner, we drank our drinks then got up; he called her closer.

"Look after him for me, he is a good man."

She smiled at him, eager to reassure him she placed her hand on his.

"I know he is, do not fret, Avraham; I will look after him, always."

I looked at them both warmly. I had my best friend as well as the girl of my dreams here, it was a great moment, one I was so grateful for.

I wanted to speak to Avraham in more depth about her situation: get his advice. But, seeing they had taken to each other, I didn't want to mention it now. I felt I was allowing them to meet under false pretenses, but I wanted him to see her without any clouded judgment. In this way, I knew that if, for any reason, I still needed to go to him, then he would have a much fairer view. I also knew it was for me to fix now, but I still didn't know how. All my worries from before seemed petty compared to hers: Betty was in real danger, time was running out. I had to start making plans to get the money as quickly as possible; I just hoped I could get it in time.

"Goodbye, Avraham, I will come tomorrow."

"No, Ishmael, I will be home."

"Yes, but I want to make sure someone will be there, just in case."

"Fine, Ishmael I won't argue. It was nice to meet you Betty, I hope to see you soon?"

"Likewise, Avraham; take care, goodbye."

"Bye, my friend, see you tomorrow."

We both walked out then Betty held my hand.

"He is lovely Ish, I see why you are so fond of him."

I grinned at her, thrilled she liked him.

"Yes, he is a special man. You were great, I knew it'd be alright; how are you feeling?"

"Wonderful, but yes, you were right; I'm glad for that. Ish, he asked about my bruising, I struggled to answer so I didn't get the chance to explain; however, he was understanding. Ish, I picked something up from your house, I hope you don't mind?"

"Avraham certainly can be, it is clear he likes you Betty, he would have said otherwise. Right, now I'm curious again; what is it?"

She delved into her pocket, pulling out the paper for the competition; then looked at me encouragingly.

"I picked it up in the bookshop in town; I don't know why, it was in the window, I just had a moment I think."

"I guess you met my uncle then, he owns it?"

"Yes, although I wasn't aware at first until he said how proud he was of you, that you were a nurse; he seems a nice man."

"He is, he is my Avraham: he means the world to me. Ish, I really think you should enter, but I know it's your decision."

"We will see, come on shall we get something to eat? I've not eaten a thing today ."

"Give me a minute, Ish?"

"I can do better than that, Betty"

She laughed then rushed back into the hospital; she was gone for at least fifteen minutes, now I became slightly concerned. What if she was followed? What if Jerry knew more than either of us wanted him to? I felt very paranoid until she came back as if she had no care in the world.

"Betty, don't do that again, let me know where you are going."

"Ish, hey, it's fine. I never meant to worry you, I'm sorry I did."

"Betty, you're very important to me now, I…"

"I know, Ish, I know, I understand you're protective, same as Avraham is with you; I have arranged a couple days off, that's all; I didn't mean to alarm you."

"Betty, I know I am overreacting, but I just don't want

anything to happen to you; I couldn't handle it."

"I know, let's put our heads together; come up with a solution, we will figure it out, Ish."

I moved a hair from her face then kissed her head, she held my hand again; we then made our way to town.

"Where are we going, Ish?"

"There's a lovely cafe in town to have something to eat"

"No, I can't go there."

I became very perplexed, but she had that fear in her eyes again.

"Betty, why?"

"What if he's around, what if he sees us? I fear for you too; I couldn't handle anything happening to you either."

"Then let him see, I know you're scared but he will not touch you while I am there. I will look after you Betty, whatever it takes."

She hugged my arm, now looking more relaxed. We walked to the café and sat out on the veranda, where I had last seen Rabbi.

"My treat, beautiful, what would you like?"

"No, Ish, let me get it; you have done enough."

"We are together, Betty, get used to it."

"Okay, okay, well next time it's my turn; I won't take no for an answer."

"Clearly, hmm, it appears the menu looks as good as you do Betty."

"Ishmael, stop it; behave yourself."

"I'm trying, but I am struggling with that one for some reason."

We gawked at each other now, she wanted to laugh but stay serious at the same time; all the while, I was trying to stay serious but couldn't help smiling more than anything else. Moving some contents out the way, she then leaned closer to me over the table.

"Ish, there is a time as well as a place; we will find it, it's inevitable."

She winked at me now, not taking her eyes off mine; she

knew exactly how to get me going. I smirked at her.

"You tell me to behave? I'm thinking the time and place can't come quick enough; but I also know you will be worth the wait."

"Choices, choices, Ish, for now I think we should order."

Before I spoke, the same waitress I had seen the time before came over happily.

"Can I take your orders please?"

"As seen as Betty isn't on the menu, I'll have a coffee with a sandwich."

Betty turned to me with a slight smirk, blushing; and with embarrassment in her voice.

"Ishmael!"

She put her hands over her eyes, then pulling them away she turned to the waitress apologetically.

"I'm so sorry, I'll have the same; thank you."

"Okay, it won't be long."

She left, leaving us alone again, she had kept a level of professionalism, but she, too, had appeared to see the funny side. Betty did, too, partly, but she wasn't prepared to let it go just yet. I looked at her reaction then grinned cheekily.

"What? You started it."

"Oh Ish, no, I haven't even begun – yet."

"You know, I'm thinking I should have ordered something cooler: it would have been much more appropriate."

"I think you have scared the waitress enough for one day."

"I'd be more bothered about scaring you; but something tells me that wouldn't be the case."

"No chance, I don't scare that easily, besides, I can handle you Ish. Question is: can you handle me?"

I leaned in closer to her now.

"You're going to have to find that out, aren't you? I'm confident enough, when we find the time, the place, Betty, I will prove it."

"Well, just so you know, I will make sure of it, Ish. Here's the waitress, best behavior."

The waitress returned with our order. We changed the subject, chatting happily while tucking into our food. She spoke more about her words with Avraham until we both heard shouting. I spun around to see Jerry. Betty looked terrified once again, she was trying to pull back in her seat, but for me, enough was enough. I got up, annoyed now.

"Jerry? Betty, hey, stay here, don't move."

"Ish, no, don't go."

"It'll be alright; whatever happens stay here."

"Ish, no."

He approached us, screaming, throwing his weight around. People were stopping to look at all the commotion, while shop owners and customers who could hear the shouting out in the street, were coming out the shops very much bewildered. I was afraid to a degree, but he was a bully; even if I got a beating I was going to give him a piece of my mind now. He came towards me.

"You? Move out my way."

"I will not; back off Jerry, you will not touch her."

"Don't push me, I will hurt you."

"Do as you must, Jerry, I am not afraid of you; I swear, you will not hurt her again."

He stood in thought for a moment, then, as anger fell over his face, he pushed me hard sending me flying out of his way.

"Ishmael?"

"Betty, no, stay there, I am alright."

A butcher came out from his shop holding a meat cleaver and looking angry; he moved towards Betty. Standing in front of the steps leading up to where we were sitting he tried to protect her. He looked straight at Jerry.

"HEY, mister, I think you better leave now: I'm not afraid to use this in defense, don't let me tell you again."

A lady who was eating got up quickly then went over to Betty. Jerry, who completely ignored the butcher, now turned and shouted over to Betty who was huddled up.

"I want what you owe me, you won't always be surrounded."

Getting to my feet I stormed towards him; I was livid now.

"You will get it, but you ever try to hurt her again, I will kill you, Jerry."

He laughed at this remark then looked towards Betty. I was not aggressive, but I had anger built up for so long; he was going to be on the receiving end of it if need be. I tapped him on the shoulder forcing him to turn back.

"You are nothing but a bully, a coward. I know what you are, who you are. How you make your money through vulnerable girls; you absolutely disgust me. I promise you: if you ever go near her again then I won't be responsible for what comes next. If I were you I would leave this place quietly, you deal with me now. Mock all you want, Jerry, but let me tell you this: I would kill or die for this girl in a heartbeat. I have nothing to lose, so I'm warning you: don't force me to do something I will regret. You are not welcome here, so, leave now; there is no more to be said."

He looked around, unsure as to whether I meant it or not, but something I said ticked him. Looking flustered, he grabbed me by the shirt sharply.

"This isn't over, I'm warning you now; you will pay for this!"

With that he left. People started cheering then clapping, I just stared as he went: I was uneasy about his last words. Betty ran over giving me a hard squeeze, then started repeatedly kissing me.

"Oh, Ish, that was amazing; I'm not sure he will be gone for long, though."

"He won't touch you again, Betty, you can be sure of that: I meant every word spoken. I will pay him then he will be gone for good. Are you alright?"

"Yes, Ish, I am now."

People came over to us; soon we were surrounded. They

were patting me on the back or shaking my hand, also checking on Betty.

I saw Rabbi with some of the Jewish community around him, watching on. Some confused, some shocked, but only Rabbi stood smiling. I looked straight at him as he walked over. I called Betty, people were checking that she was okay still, she came over as Rabbi approached me.

"Rabbi, this is Betty. Betty this is Rabbi."

"Yes, my boy; you did a fine thing there, you should be proud, Ishmael. Pleasure to meet you, Betty, I hope you are alright?"

"Pleasure is mine, Rabbi, but yes, I am fine; thank you for asking."

"Ishmael, may I have a word?" Rabbi smiled at her as he pulled me to the side.

"Ishmael, what was that about? What is that man after?"

I told him the situation as he listened carefully; a look of concern was on his face now, I could tell he didn't approve.

"Son, you must not get involved; I am pleading with you?"

"Rabbi, Betty needs me, I can't ignore that, she has made me a better person: she brings the best out of me. She has brightened my life in so many ways; I know she has issues, but I do, too. We are right for each other, I want to help, for her to be safe; she is…"

"Say no more, Ishmael, I see you love her: you have proven that. I just hope you know what you are doing? You do have my blessing, so I want you to know that."

He kissed me on both cheeks.

"No, Rabbi, I'm not really sure what I am doing or what to do, but I will find a way. I appreciate the kind words, it helps."

"Yes, I know you will, Ishmael. I am always here, don't forget that. I will let you go, goodbye, Son."

"Thank you, Rabbi; yes, I know that, too, goodbye."

He wandered off, Betty, a little concerned, came back over.

"Is everything alright, Ish?"

"Yes, Betty, Rabbi is as protective as Avraham sometimes, he has given me his blessing, too."

Now she was puzzled, turning her head down in thought then back towards me.

"His blessing? For what?"

I laughed, her face was a picture, but I did not want her to know my plans for when Jerry was gone; I just had to get that out of the way first.

"There's a time and place for that, too."

I winked at her, leaving her in thought. We turned to see Betty's uncle running over, calling out.

"Betty, Betty, what's happened? Are you, all right?"

"Yes, Uncle, I am fine, it's down to Ishmael that I am. We bumped into Jerry."

"You…? Aah, now it all makes sense; Betty you're hurt: your face…? That man I will…"

Betty's face had become bruised enough to be more noticeable now; like me her uncle was outraged. I tried to give him reassurance.

"It's fine, sir, he won't bother her again. It's all under control."

He just glared at me in vexation. Somehow, I knew now he was going to make it difficult to get acceptance. My heart sank: I wasn't sure if he did not approve of just me or of us being together. He ignored me, turning back to Betty abruptly.

"I am not happy, Betty."

"Uncle? Wait!"

"No."

He marched off leaving Betty emotional, it was clear his reaction had really upset her: she was now in a dazed state.

"Give him time, Betty, I'm sure he will come around"

"I thought he would be happy? I don't understand, Ish; I must speak with him."

"If you must; but let him calm down for a while. You will not be able to talk civilized otherwise, he just needs space."

"I know you are right, I just hate seeing him upset; speaking will solve this."

"I know, Betty, if you want me to go with you then I will."

"No, you're a sweetheart but I must to do this alone: it's the right thing to do for now."

"Okay, Betty. What do you say to doing something fun tonight?"

"Fun, I've missed that; okay Ish, so what do you have in mind?"

"Hmm, five words, Betty, five words."

She looked at me in a seductive manner before walking up to me, making out as though she was going to kiss me. Intentionally missing my lips, she whispered in my ear.

"But only two are relevant, Ish, just two."

I stared at her, smirking at the comment, she always had a way to make me smile regardless; I loved her for that.

My life had been turned upside down since she entered it, but I didn't want it any other way now. With her I had purpose, reason to get up in the morning, with a potentially good future. The situation was one I did not know the outcome of, but I was now wanting to fight for her, protect her, love her more than anyone ever had. I had found passion for life, had the backing of Avraham as well as Rabbi now. I felt overwhelmed in a way, but I could take everything life gave me, I owed that to Betty.

Her ability to remain optimistic inspired me: she could laugh through her pain, put me before herself, accept me for the mess I was; she was incredible. Behind her laughter she was tormented in many ways; only I could see it, but she allowed me to, she wasn't afraid of that. I thought if I could make her smile inside, then I would use every breath I had to do it. I picked her up by complete surprise, swinging her around.

"Ish, put me down."

"I'm never putting you down, I love you, Betty; I will

until my last breath."

"Ishmael?"

I put her down as she looked at me again with a grin.

"You know, you will have to at some point: that, too, is inevitable. Come on; we've been center of attention long enough."

I pulled her closer towards me now, a smile spreading across my face.

"It is, but I have no problem with putting you down when it comes to it, nor do I have one of making sure you're centre of attention for a lot longer, that, too, is inevitable."

"Well, so you know, you are not the only one thinking that, Ish."

I just kissed her then, I didn't care who saw or how inappropriate it may have been: none of that mattered.

"Let me thank the butcher, Betty; I won't be a minute."

I walked over to his shop where he was now behind the counter, carrying on as though nothing had happened. He raised his head as I entered.

"Aah, brave thing to do out there, mister."

"It's Ishmael, sir, I'm not the only one, I wanted to thank you for what you did, that, too, was very noble of you."

"I have worked here my whole life, never have I come across such nastiness; I will not have it. I was glad to intervene, protect your lady; it was clear you couldn't in that moment. Ishmael, if that man had had a chance it wouldn't have been pretty; I'm glad she is alright, you are too, so it seems?"

"Yes, you were there when I wasn't, Betty could have been hurt otherwise: he is a nasty piece of work. I owe you."

"Nonsense, I am pleased to of helped, here take this?"

"No, you don't have to do that: you've done more than enough."

Betty came wandering in inquisitively, appearing eager to thank him, too.

"Thank you, sir, if there's any way I can repay you then let me know."

She walked to him gently kissing him on the cheek, he beamed, then looked at her kindly before turning to me again.

"Here, please take it Ishmael: I want you to have it?"

"Okay, well I don't want to upset a man with a cleaver, thank you very much; you enjoy the rest of the day, good day to you."

He started laughing now.

"Very funny, Ishmael, yes, good day to you both, goodbye."

"Goodbye, sir."

5 JERRY'S REVENGE

We walked out, he had given me a package with various meats in along with a big bone. I knew Jonah would be pleased with that. I had been caught up with all that had been going gone on so that I hadn't given much attention to him; I felt guilty for that. I did not want him feeling left out or abandoned, suddenly I felt panicked which didn't go unnoticed.

"Ish, what's the matter? Why are you so tense?"

"I don't know Betty, it's Jonah, I need to see him now: I'm feeling panicked for some reason, I…"

"It's alright, Ish; come on let's go to him, we can spend the evening together if you like?"

"I think he would like that, Betty."

"He's not the only one, Ish, come on."

We walked to mine, chatting, cracking jokes. The feeling of panic intensified as we got closer. We soon got to my road, then I noticed something lying on the roadway in the near distance. I saw my neighbour Jeremiah standing there. As we got closer I knew what it was; I froze on the spot just staring straight at it. Betty looked at me alarmed then glanced over to see what I was looking at.

"Oh no, it's not? Jonah? No, Ish? ISH?"

She shook me in panic, instinct forced me to dart over now; I had to get there straight away. As I approached, I saw him lying on the road, Betty became increasingly upset: Jonah was not moving, only looking straight ahead, paralysed with the shock and pain that had been inflicted on him. I knew it was Jerry that had done this to him; I just didn't understand why Jonah, he would not have hurt anyone. This was personal, my first thought was that I wanted to go looking for him, however, Jonah needed me now more than ever, he was my priority.

Every second that went by my heart felt like it was being torn in two; I lay down next to him.

"Jonah, Jonah, please don't leave me, I love you boy; I'm sorry, he will pay for this."

"He needs looking at straight away, Ishmael: he is not good. I tried to stop the man, but I couldn't. He has just left. I'm so sorry Ishmael; I promise I tried, I've never seen a man so angry."

I stood up to speak with Jeremiah, desperation now in my voice.

"What happened, Jeremiah? Please, tell me what you know?"

Jeremiah told me how he had heard banging, then shouting at my door. Startled, he came out to see what all the noise was about. In his anger, Jerry had kicked my door in, breaking the lock, only then he was faced with Jonah who had tried to fend him off. He was kicking him with great force, hitting him hard. Jeremiah told me that Jonah followed Jerry outside where Jerry continued to beat him, and, too weak to go back inside, he collapsed were he now lay.

Jerry had run off once he realised how bad Jonah was. I didn't understand how he even knew where I lived. Now I wondered if the attack was aimed deliberately at Jonah: especially after his last words in town, or whether it was meant for me. It played on my mind: wondering if he would come back, he didn't care for anything when he wanted revenge, that much was clear. I would have happily taken the beating if it would have saved Jonah.

That moment I felt tears falling, I was so angry, so devastated; my Jonah had defended me risking his own life, he was barely breathing now. He was so loyal: even in my absence he never thought twice. Betty touched me on the shoulder, she was anxious now.

"Ish, please, we need to get him to the vets immediately."

"Betty, how did he know where I lived? I don't understand."

"I don't know, Ish, maybe he followed me? Jonah needs you now, be with him."

"Ishmael, Betty, let me drive you; I want to help?"

"Yes, thank you, Jeremiah, we must hurry, come on Ish."

Betty wiped my tears before I went to Jonah. I picked him up gently, he yelped; seeing him in pain like that was too much to bear. I got in the car where I held him, hugging him gently; I whispered in his ears.

"Please pull through, Jonah, my brave friend; please hold on."

I put my head down on his head, now I really cried: something told me he wasn't going to make it. I really struggled to believe it; I couldn't, I could only hold on to what hope there was. Betty sat there quietly, I knew she felt responsible. I wanted to reassure her, but I was unable to: I didn't know how this would unfold or the effect it would have on us. Jonah, seeing me like this, tried moving his head to lift mine up, almost like he was saying 'it's okay, you are here now.' He had a look about him; like he knew his fate.

He looked broken both physically as well as mentally; he would never be the same after this if he lived. This only exasperated my emotions more, leaving me to hug him tighter. Betty put an arm round me, then one on Jonah.

"I'm so sorry, Ish, this is all my fault."

"Please, let's just focus on him now, I don't blame you, but Jonah needs us."

"I'm here, Ish, I'm always here."

"I know. Betty, I know."

We drove quickly to the veterinary centre. I hurried Jonah inside as quickly as I possibly could, trying to be as gentle so as not to cause any more injury to him. A nurse rushed over, taking him from my arms; she was horrified to see an animal in this way."

"Oh no, sir, what on earth has happened?"

"He has been… he has been…"

I couldn't say it, I somehow lost my voice, saying it so casually was not something which would fall from my lips very easily. He was everything, always had been, it made it seem much more real saying it aloud. I was broken-hearted seeing him like that: he was in agony. Betty, seeing my struggle, came to my aid.

"He has been viciously attacked, he's in a bad way, please help him?"

"Please, wait here, I'll take him straight in, what is his name?"

Betty went to speak again but I butted in.

"Jonah, his name is Jonah, please, will he be alright?"

"We will do what we can for him, sir, that's all I can promise for now."

The nurse hurried off with him. I tried to think of all the happy times with him, anything to take away the reality I was faced with. A short time passed by when the nurse came out looking serious.

"Sir, I'm sorry, but there's nothing more we can do for him."

For a minute, I thought it was a dream, echoes of her voice passing across my ears, but I could not accept it: I wouldn't, not my Jonah, that was just incomprehensible.

"No, please, no, there must be something, please?"

"I'm sorry, sir, there isn't: his injuries are too severe. He is in a lot of pain; the best thing is to put him to sleep."

"NO, no, not Jonah, not him; I beg you, he means everything to me. Please, he's not like other dogs; please help him, you must?"

"You can stay with him, I'm so sorry to give you this

diagnosis, he is beautiful, but it's the best thing for him now."

Betty started to weep: she could not contain her grief either. I knew she was extremely fond of him. Every passing second, I was wasting time not being with him. Jonah was dying so I had to be there no matter how hard it was.

"Sir, follow me: I'll take you to him."

I grabbed Betty's hand then followed her in. Jonah was lying still on the table, facing the other way. He couldn't see me, so I walked to him soundlessly. I watched him, it didn't seem realistic: he was at the last place I would see him, I would be leaving there without him, too. I wouldn't see his tail wag again or excitement on his face; I couldn't see a world where he was not in it.

"My Jonah, thank you for being in my life, for having my back, for all the memories. You've always been my best friend; I will never forget you, I love you. I will always love you, boy."

I sat next to him, giving him a kiss, then laid my head on him again. He was warm, his heart beating. I prayed for it all to be a mistake, but I was only kidding myself: he would soon be gone, the waiting was unbearable now. It was only a matter of time till the nurse came in and it would be over, at least for Jonah.

Betty, standing back a little behind me, came over.

She gave Jonah a kiss then hugged him gently before looking at him to speak.

"Jonah, I haven't known you long, yet you've comforted me, protected me and accepted me, I won't forget what a special dog you are, thank you, Jonah, I…"

She started crying again so I pulled her towards me.

"Betty, I know you loved him, the fact he did those things shows he loved you, too, he pulled me to you the day we met: he knew you were special."

"I'm so sorry, Ish, I have no other words."

"I know, Betty, but none are needed now."

We sat in silence, she held my hand trying to give me

some comfort as I did her, but I knew it wouldn't last long. A few minutes went by until the door opened; the nurse came in holding a tray which had the end written all over it for me. My heart was in a million pieces: I couldn't face what was coming.

"Sir, if you are ready?"

I looked at her thinking what a stupid remark, how can anyone be ready for something like this? I turned to her sternly.

"I will never be ready, never."

She walked over, then dosed up the syringe before she gave it to him. Jonah, not expecting it, gave a little yelp, I stroked him trying to comfort him, but I couldn't look; I buried my head in him, tears streaming again.

"I love you so much, Jonah; I'm so sorry."

"It is done, sir, stay for as long as you want to."

She left the room, but I didn't move. I felt his heart getting slower as the seconds ticked away; then it stopped completely. My Jonah had gone; there was nothing I could do. I fell on my knees crying harder than I ever thought possible; then I completely lost it.

"No, NO, JONAH, NO, NO, NO. Come back. Please come back. You can't go. AAAAH, I'M GOING TO KILL HIM, I…"

Betty gripped me, tears also flowing down her face. I fought her, but she refused to let go, holding me tightly. She struggled to stay strong for me, trying her upmost best not to lose it, too. She spoke softly while still holding me.

"Ish, I know he meant everything. I know this won't help much, but he is in no more pain; he is at peace. If you want a moment alone, I'll understand?"

I moved to look at her, she had as much sadness in her eyes as I could feel inside myself. I took her hand.

"No, please don't go Betty: I need you."

After a minute I closed his eyes; he looked like he was just sleeping. He was such a beautiful animal, his coat still shining, but he looked peaceful. The only comfort I had was knowing he was no longer in pain; the sorrow I would feel through not having him here was insufferable; I wondered how I'd ever move on now. I stayed with him for a while until eventually the nurse came back in.

"He's in a better place now: I see he meant a lot to you?"

"Yes, he meant the world to me, there will never be another like him; he was my best friend."

She looked at me with a smile only half there. She handed me his collar before placing her hand on my arm as a source of consolation. I held it tight, it was all I had left of him, besides the memories, now. I felt the anger come back, now I wanted revenge for him.

"I'll kill him, I'm going to kill him, Betty."

"Ishmael, no, don't do anything stupid; please?"

"He has killed my dog, Jonah. I can't accept that, I am sorry; I need justice for him, I'm going to get it, Betty."

"Ish, listen to me, please? I know you are hurting deeply, I know how angry you are, but acting on it will only create more chaos for you. Please, you've been through enough. I am going to report him, I cannot cower anymore; he will be made to pay for what he has done, I promise. Ish, just think about it, you are much better than this; it's not the way."

She stared into my eyes, I felt the tension melting away, but it left a feeling of numbness. I switched my thoughts; I could only think of Jonah, how I wasn't there for him when he needed me the most; I hated myself for that. I didn't understand how Betty couldn't see it too, she certainly seemed to know me better than I knew myself; that was so confusing. My issues seemed so much bigger now; my grief was blinding me as to what would be the right thing to do. It was the first time since I met Betty that I wanted to isolate myself, pick up a drink: I didn't just lose Jonah, I lost a part of myself. Now I just wanted to go home, alone.

"I need some time alone, Betty, I can't do this, I'm sorry."

"Ish, wait!"

I walked away, then went home, pacing myself as slowly

as possible: I was dreading it. Once there I saw the police were outside; I immediately wanted them gone. I started to walk into my house but was stopped by an officer who stretched his arm out in front of me.

"Sir, sir, you can't go in there: officers are searching."

"That's my house, I've just lost my dog officer; what are you doing here?"

"We need to take a statement, your neighbour called us; do you know who did this?"

I didn't hesitate, I gave him the name of Jerry with a clear description, I didn't care if any consequences came from it.

"That is the man responsible. Now if you don't mind I would like to be alone, please, officer?"

He gave the nod then they all started clearing out one by one, the officer turned to me.

"We will be in touch again, goodbye."

He got in his car and moved off steadily, I watched as he went.

Suddenly silence fell, another day that had changed my life forever; I felt so alone now. I slowly walked into my house, knowing Jonah wouldn't be there, knowing I would be surrounded by reminders of him. I had to live on without him; I couldn't get my head around that. I wished Betty was here now, I had left abruptly but I had needed to think, grieve on my own. Inside, I saw his empty bed, now only holding the half- eaten bone he never got to finish, the absolute chaos Jerry had left was clear to see; the place was a mess.

I started clearing up, fixing furniture; I put my hand on the coffee table to straighten it out, and as I did so I noticed blood on my hands. I looked down at them then flopped onto the chair, I screamed out as loud as my lungs would allow.

"WHY? WHY HIM? Am I really that bad? Why do you keep punishing me? Why not take me? WHY? AAAH, I

CAN'T DO THIS ANYMORE."

Suddenly there was a knock on my door, but I ignored it: I couldn't face Betty or anyone else, but the knock became persistent. I got up, then opened it; very much agitated now. I was completely astonished to see who was standing there.

"Rabbi? What are you doing here?"

To my surprise he just hugged me. His face was a serious, yet sad, one.

"I heard what happened, I am so sorry, Ishmael: I know you were very close."

"Rabbi, I'm not much company; I am not in the mood for talking."

"Then you can listen; come, I will make some tea."

He walked in and went, adamantly, to the kitchen, he said nothing else while in there. I sat down staring at my hands which were bloodstained, just waiting, wondering why he was even here. A couple of minutes later, Rabbi joined me; he saw my hands, now a look of concern was showing.

"Ishmael, your hands; what have you done?"

"It's Jonah's, Rabbi, I should have been here."

"Ishmael, I can only try to understand how you're feeling. I know you, always doing what's right, quick in helping others without regard to yourself. Now that has cost you something precious, but Son, you can't feel guilty over another man's actions, they were not of your doing."

"Rabbi, how did you know about this?"

"Betty: she was worried about you, she said you were in shock, needing some space. She knows how devastated you are. However, she felt coming to me was the best, why would she feel that, Ishmael?"

"Oh Rabbi, because I left her: I needed to be alone to think. I left without really thinking of anything else but Jonah, it got too much, I…"

"Ishmael, you blame her, she blames herself; neither of you are to blame. You love each other, grieve but don't push her away. Speak to her, avoidance or shutting yourself out will not help you. Jonah has gone, but, if you are not careful, Son, you will lose someone who makes you very happy, don't allow it, Ishmael."

"I feel like I abandoned him, I wasn't there when he needed me; I only blame myself. I hate myself for it: he was loyal till the end, Rabbi, but I let him down. Why does this keep happening?"

"You beat yourself up constantly, Ishmael. You have done everything for him since he was a puppy regardless of your issues, you gave him a wonderful life, you were devoted to each other until the end. I understand how difficult today has been; it will be for a while, but you are a good man. Don't let unnecessary guilt drag you down: you have come too far. It's not about you now, your girl will be feeling ten times worse, but, Ishmael, She has still been there for you; that took great courage, Son, under the circumstances."

"I'm a fool, today shouldn't have happened; not to Jonah. Jerry warned me, Rabbi, he warned me."

"Ishmael, I know, but you didn't know he would do this, of course things may have been different if you did, but by allowing someone to force you to change things, it would only bring misery anyway. Either way he would've won. But calling yourself a fool, Son is so far from the truth: you wouldn't have allowed it if you were there. But Ishmael, who says that even that would have stopped him? Don't beat yourself up, nobody is to blame but Jerry. Now about Betty? You will need her Ishmael; you couldn't save Jonah, but this? You know she understands."

I listened to him, took in all he had said. I admired the man: he gave me his time, his compassion, sharing great wisdom. He really cleared my head, made me see things from a different perspective; that helped enormously.

"Rabbi, did Betty say where she was going?"

"No Son, I also left in a hurry. That poor girl: seems

everyone has been running from her today."

I felt awful now, my actions in my grief were no excuse; if I wasn't careful, I could lose her too, as Rabbi had said. I knew, after Jonah, that would've been the final straw. Feeling sorry for myself was not going to do me any favours.

"Rabbi, if you're not too busy, would you do something for me?"

"Anything, Son, what is it?"

I grabbed a pen then got some paper that had been knocked over. I quickly scribbled a note.

"Would you go to the hospital? Give this to Avraham for me? I don't want him to worry, but I have things to take care of now; he will understand."

He smiled cordially at me.

"Of course, Ishmael, I will go now; you know where I am as always."

"Thank you, Rabbi, thank you."

He got up then kissed my cheeks, he opened the door, stepping outside, then turned to face me.

"Ishmael, remember what I said, I will come by tomorrow, help fix your door, take care, Son."

"Goodbye Rabbi, thank you again."

He left, putting his hand up in gesture; I shut the door slowly. I was alone again, but now what? It was near the time where I would take Jonah out for a walk, but he was no longer here. There would be so much I would miss besides just having him around; regardless of what Rabbi said, I would still feel the guilt, how could I not? I had a lot to be guilty for. Betty was another reason I felt bad, too, then Avraham. I had so much to sort in my head as well as in my life; I didn't know where to start.

I found myself being drawn to the notepad again: I had a strong desire to write, stronger than it had been before. Maybe it was grief, or it was the fact I felt so emotional; I wasn't sure. I picked the notepad up, grabbed a pen then started writing.

I wrote for a while without stopping: it was like I had so much to say with so little time that my hand could not move quick enough. Everything just poured out; I felt a release I had not done for a very long time. It had taken a great weight off my shoulders, I got up just staring at it; I felt satisfaction, but also thought it strange that something helped me that much; I had not experienced that before. For now, I could not read it: I couldn't bring myself to read my own deepest thoughts, that terrified me. I had got them out, but for now that was enough, besides, I had more important things to deal with.

Betty was a priority; I just hoped I hadn't blown it. I wouldn't have blamed her if I had. She may have understood, but her feelings mattered too; I knew that, I just hadn't thought at the time.

I decided to look for her, time was getting on now, but I had to speak with her as soon as possible; let her know how I felt, tell her that I didn't blame her or hold her responsible in any way. She was hurting in a lot of ways too, but if I wasn't there for her, then for me there was no point; I loved her so much. Inside it pained me, I knew we would get through this, but I wanted us to do it together. I grabbed my cloak then set off towards her house. I hoped she was safe; I couldn't take anything else now, not today.

It was a beautiful night, like the one when Betty had first kissed me; the one where Jonah was happily running around, confusion on his face as he sat there waiting for attention, wondering what was going on. The memory made me smile, my mind was filling with images of good times; but it wasn't to last. I felt a lump in my throat; I was really going to miss him, the memories could not bring permanent comfort, at least not yet.

I soon arrived at Betty's house, there was a light on. The house was silent, only the slight rustling of trees around could be heard. I felt relieved but also nervous; I knew Jonah would pull me towards the door now, so, I took a deep breath before I walked up slowly. I put my hand up to knock, hesitated for a second then knocked on the door.

"Who is it?"

"It's okay Betty, it's Ishmael."

I heard her coming quickly to the door, upon opening it she flung her arms around me.

"Oh Ish, I've been so worried, I wanted to come around, I…"

"May I come in, Betty?"

"Yes Ish, of course."

I walked inside, as she closed the door I turned to her.

"Betty, I am sorry: I have been awful today towards you, I'm so ashamed. I want you to know that I don't blame you for Jonah. Today was a massive shock, I was deeply hurt by him passing, but you were there. Without your support I couldn't have done it alone. It's no excuse, Rabbi came around, I…"

She grabbed me gently by the arm, smiling.

"Hey, Ish, you don't have to apologise, I know how hard today was. I know you would have had every right to blame me; telling me you don't says an awful lot about you. I just want to be there for you now: I've never loved anyone so much as I do you, I'm complete with you. Ish, we can get through this, you can get through this, but don't apologise, not to me; you've nothing to be sorry about."

I looked at her warmly, she always knew what to say to settle my mind, just as I did with hers; nothing could get in the way of us. Jonah was unique, but she made things easier, gave me the strength to cope better. I already had a lot I owed her for, but the fact we had each other was enough. I pulled her to me, not letting her go. I held her for a while then had an idea, I moved away gently.

"Betty, it's a beautiful night, why don't we go for a walk?"

She grinned at me, that twinkle was back; she looked just as beautiful as ever.

"I'll get my coat."

I gripped her by the arm gently.

"Betty, I had the police round, I gave him the name with a description for Jerry; I was angry."

"It's okay: I have given a statement, too. For now, let's just enjoy the evening; tonight, is for Jonah."

"For Jonah, I love you Betty."

"I know, Ish, I love you too."

We soon left her house; I was at peace with her, still, Jonah was evidently missed. Every lamp post every patch of grass, reminded me of him; especially seeing others with their dogs, no walk would ever be the same. I was so glad I wasn't on my own. Betty would squeeze my arm in comfort every now and then: she knew, too, that it wasn't easy. But the night was one that had to be appreciated, it was almost like Jonah had done it. Somewhere, in my own insanity, I believed Jonah was smiling down on us, confirming that everything would be alright. A sign for me to move on, because every moment should be enjoyed.

It was warm out, but I felt a chill over me; I almost laughed in disbelief. I had to be imagining it; I just felt he was here with us. I knew he had gone but I gained a feeling like wherever he was, he was alright; I was content to believe that, even for a moment.

"I will always love you Jonah."

Betty looked at me sympathetically.

"Oh Ish, he loved you too."

We stopped to just look up: the night sky was filled with millions of stars, twinkling, dancing in the sky, around the full moon which was beaming down. It really was incredible.

"I've never seen the sky like this, Ish, it's stunning."

"Yes, it really is something; I'm glad you are here to share it with me, Betty."

"I wouldn't want to be anywhere else but here: I could stay here forever."

From the corner of my eye I watched her looking up,

her face still bruised, but she was happy; I could not help but feel that too. Things were not over, but for those few minutes I allowed myself to enjoy them. We walked a while then I dropped Betty home. I was glad how the day had ended, it had been one of the worst days, but having Betty there, as well as Rabbi, I got through it much easier.

That night I slept better than I expected to. In the morning upon waking up, for a split second, I expected Jonah to come. I expected to see his face excited, ready to go out. I suddenly remembered yesterday, leaning back I sighed. I heard the door go a few minutes later. I shot up taking a top from a drawer, trying to put it on before I reached the door. I opened it, standing there was the officer I had seen from the day before.

"Good morning, Ishmael, may I come in?"

"Morning, officer, yes, please this way."

He smiled as he cautiously walked in.

"Thank you, I'm here to inform you that we have arrested the man, Jerry. We now have him in custody, he has been wanted for a while now; with your help we will keep him behind bars."

I didn't know what to say. I know Betty would want me to press charges for what he did to her, and especially for what he did to Jonah. I also wanted it for the two of them, but I felt it was something we should decide together: it was different cases, but it affected both of us.

"Officer, I need my girlfriend with me: I can't decide anything yet, you are aware of what he did to her?"

"Is this Betty, is it?"

"Yes, that's right."

"Yes, we know: Betty gave a statement. We are still making enquiries, nevertheless, your help will give us enough evidence to put him away for a long time: he is a foul man for many reasons, Ishmael."

He didn't have to tell me that, I knew it was the right thing to do; if I could help to stop him from hurting anything or anyone again, I would be happy to do that; so I agreed.

"Okay, Officer, I will help if I can."

"Thank you, Ishmael, may I?"

He pointed to the chair, I nodded to give him the go ahead, sitting myself down too. I told him what I knew; although I only knew what Betty had told me. Regarding Jonah, I wasn't there. I told him of the incident in town, all I had heard at Betty's, what Jeremiah had told me. I didn't feel I was that much help; but any evidence was important no matter how little the detail. I also told him that Jerry was the only one who had ever had a vendetta against me. Talking about Jonah, too, was difficult to say the least: having to relive it was hard. The officer looked up from his notepad, seeing my distress he stopped me.

"It's alright Ishmael, we have enough for now. Thank you for your help; I'll see myself out."

He got up, then left. I sat thinking before I was interrupted by the phone ringing; it was Betty.

"Ish, I'll be round soon; wait for me, I love you."

She sounded enthusiastic which got my curiosity stirring. I tidied round a little, starting with the table and around the couches, it was still very messy. I had only done as much with the time I had but I now had time to do a lot more. I then waited for her to come around. I started thinking about Avraham: I wondered if Rabbi had seen him yet. I knew I must speak to him soon, like with Jonah I hadn't been there for him as much as I wanted to be, but I knew he wouldn't have minded, considering. Nevertheless, that didn't take away the guilt I felt over that, too, it only added to it. I felt annoyed about that. Betty arrived a while later, giving a loud knock on the door.

"Betty, whatever is the matter?"

"My uncle, he wants to speak with you, please say you will go?"

"Yes, of course I will go, but…"

"Now? Can we go now? He is waiting."

I laughed seeing her so excited, it was a good sign, but anxiety was creeping in again; I wasn't sure why.

"Give me five minutes Betty, then we will go?"

"Four to get back here: I want a minute with you?"

"Hmm, I'll take that minute now?"

"It suits me, Ish, countdown has begun."

I grinned, then moved in to kiss her, if it hadn't been for the meeting with her uncle then I'd not have stopped. She soon pulled away from me.

"Minute is up, Ish."

"Seems so, but hey, I'm thinking it's just as well."

I winked at her, but she just smirked while staring at me. I then went to get dressed properly. No sooner had I gone into the bathroom, when she called me back again.

"Ish, what is this?"

I walked back into the lounge where she was holding the paper I had written on; I completely forgot I had left it there.

"Oh, it's nothing, just something I wrote."

She looked at it, reading it. I wanted to finish getting ready but couldn't drag myself away, she looked at me when she finished.

"That really is beautiful, Ish, just beautiful."

She stood with her hand to her chest, I could see she was moved.

"I'm glad you like it, Betty. However, to me it's just words. It helped to write it."

"Ish, you should send it for the competition."

"No, I couldn't: it's just scribble. Give me a minute, I'm almost ready."

I finished brushing my teeth then put my shoes on. We went to set off, but Betty held me back.

"Ish, it'll be fine, don't worry."

"I'm trying, Betty, but I know you'd say otherwise. Come on let's not keep him waiting."

"Exactly, but Ish…? I think it'll be alright; my uncle can fly off the mark sometimes, that's all."

I still had an unnerving feeling in my stomach, but she was happy; behind my anxiety, I trusted all would be well now.

We came to the town, it was busy as usual. Suddenly, from nowhere, people started running over giving their condolences for Jonah. I saw the butcher again, fixing something outside his shop. He turned around; seeing us both, he marched over like he was on a mission.

"Ishmael, oh Ishmael, we have heard what has happened from the bookseller. I am terribly sorry about your dog: we are told he meant the world to you? I hope that man gets the punishment he deserves for what he has done? How anyone can do that to an animal I will never know; no animal ever deserves that."

"I agree, but yes: they have him now, thank you. Jonah was my best friend."

"Yes, if there is anything we can do, the town is here for you; I'll let you go now, good day to you both."

"Good day to you, too. Wait: what is your name?"

"Oliver, some call me Olly."

"Well, it is much better than 'the butcher' I think?"

He now laughed wholeheartedly.

"Yes, I agree; you are a funny guy, good day, Ishmael"

"Good day, Oliver."

Betty hurried me along, eager to get this over with.

"Ish, come on: my uncle."

We said our goodbyes, then I followed her to the familiar bookshop.

I looked through the window; he was in there, busy like the last time I was here. I entered behind Betty.

"Uncle, Ishmael is here?"

He turned, putting down the books he was holding. Hastily moving towards me, he then shook my hand very firmly: like he had been on edge waiting.

"Forgive me, Ishmael, I was very rude to you; my behaviour was unacceptable. I wasn't happy I admit: it was hard to see her growing up, meeting someone. I felt like I was losing her, but I have never seen her happier. She truly loves you, so I won't stand in the way of that. I am also saddened to hear about your dog, Betty tells me you were joined at the hip?"

"Thank you, sir, yes; he was a very special dog. Betty was right there through it with me. I love her too, sir, more than you'll ever understand. I only want to make her as happy as she makes me, so your reaction is understandable. But you won't lose her sir, I know you two are close; I won't jeopardise or get in the way of that either."

"Bert, call me Bert, I am happy for you both now; you are good with a kind heart. Betty needs that in her life."

Betty stood there watching us, a bemused look on her face; she was unable to get a word in edgeways, until now.

"Hmm, looks like I am not needed now?"

I walked to her looking in her eyes.

"You are always needed, Betty, I would be lost without you."

She chuckled as she put her arm around me.

"That makes two of us, Ish."

"I can accept that, Betty; seeing as it's you."

"You haven't got a choice, Ish; seeing as it's you."

Bert put his hands to his face then pulled them away, sighing jokingly. He cleared his throat to remind us he was there, too.

"You two, there is a time and place for everything."

Both of us looked at each other, then burst out laughing. Bert was not impressed with us whatsoever, although he couldn't help but grin, too. Puzzlement on his face as to what was so funny showed. I turned to him, smirking.

"Bert, let's just say we know."

"Yes, we do, very well, Uncle. Come on, Ish, let us leave him be before he bangs our heads together; I love you, Uncle."

"Okay, yes, I must see Avraham soon: check all is going as planned. Goodbye, Bert."

"Goodbye, you two, enjoy your day. Oh, Ishmael, I'm glad we sorted things out, thank you for coming; stay distracted, that will help."

"As am I; for both of you. Thank you, I'm sure Betty will continue to do that, goodbye, Bert."

"Yes, he has no choice in that either, goodbye, Uncle, I love you."

We stepped outside, then Betty stopped point blank.

"Ish, give me a minute: I forgot something."

I was at a loss as to what she could mean, but waited patiently while she went back inside. A minute later she reappeared.

"What are you up to, Betty?"

"You will see, Ish, you were great in there; I think he really likes you."

"If you're both happy, that's all that matters, I can see why you're fond of him, too."

"No, Ish, you must be, too, that matters to me."

"I am, Betty, you make me that way."

I was delighted now things had been settled with Bert. I was happy she had someone else who cared for her as much as I did; having his blessing, too, was reassuring, something else I could put out of my mind.

I only knew by her comment that whatever she was up to, it had to do with me; she was a real mystery in her actions at times, but I found it enchanting. I knew that all would be revealed soon enough, whatever it was.

6 ISHMAEL AND HIS POETRY

It was still early so we strolled the shops. I saw Betty eyeing up a necklace in the jewellers. I had saved a lot of money since I had stopped drinking; I wanted to get her something special now, just for being there, for how I had been at times, for her just loving me.

"Betty, I must see Avraham soon, would you go and get me a couple of things? Milk and bread will do for now. There's something I must do; I'll wait for you here in ten minutes?"

"Sure, is everything alright?"

"Yes, everything is fine, ten minutes?"

"I won't be away any longer than I must be, Ish, I'll be here."

She winked then kissed me before she hurried off. I didn't really need anything, but I couldn't surprise her with me. I walked into the jewellery shop, stealthily, hoping she wouldn't see me.

"Morning sir, can I help you?"

I walked to the counter to ask about the necklace.

"This is our prized piece, sir, it's an amethyst; a rare cut."

"I want something special for my lady; I saw her eyeing it up, so I will take it."

"She is a lucky lady; I am sure she will love it."

"Yes, but I am the lucky one."

"You sound made for each other, would you like it gift wrapped?"

"Yes, that would be great, although not completely sealed thank you, but yes, she is special."

I paid the girl as she handed me the bag. I then thanked her before walking outside. I put the bag inside my cloak. Betty was not back yet; I saw her in the distance going into the greengrocers. A couple of minutes later she came over.

"Are we done?"

"We are done. Betty, I must go to see Avraham, he is coming home today; are you coming?"

"I know, Ish, of course, but I have a few things to do so you go; I will call you later, you don't have an option I'm afraid."

"Hmm, well, not unless I call you first."

"Oh, the suspense, Ish."

"Such a romantic, Betty."

We both laughed simultaneously, then I kissed her before making my way to Avraham's. It seemed ages since I had last seen him; I missed him just as much as I did Jonah. I hoped he was doing well. My turning up unannounced might be an inconvenience for him; I hoped that wasn't the case, but I also knew he would never turn me away unless it was necessary. I got closer to his house, only to see Rabbi, with a couple of others I recognised from the synagogue, standing outside. In a state of panic, I rushed over.

"Rabbi? What are you doing here? Where is Avraham, is he alright?"

"Aah, Ishmael, yes, yes, he is fine. Don't worry, he is inside; I only came to help him. Come."

"Thank you, Rabbi."

I went to walk in when he stopped me.

"Ishmael, how are you today? Avraham knows everything; he will be very pleased to see you."

"I feel much better today, Betty has helped with that, too, but I miss Jonah; I will always miss him. I'm pleased I can see Avraham, it seems so long."

"Yes, Ishmael, you will; but he will always be in there."

He pointed to my heart, I glanced at him to see him

smiling.

"Go now, he is waiting."

I was keen to see him; I went inside quickly, calling him as I entered.

"Avraham, it's Ishmael, can I come in?"

"Ishmael? Yes of course; please sit down. What are you doing here?"

"I had to come, Avraham: I said I would. I am so sorry I was not there earlier this morning for you."

"No, my heart broke when Rabbi told me about Jonah. I am terribly sorry, Ishmael, he was really something; I wish I could've been there, you had quite the day yesterday from what I gathered."

"I miss him terribly, Avraham, I will always feel something is missing, I know he was an animal but…"

"I know, but this is going to take time, you have me, Betty, Rabbi, too. A lot of people still care about you, Ishmael; they can't replace him, but they are just as important. You are strong my friend, I have always said that, somewhat a hero, too, so I heard."

"I only did the right thing, Avraham. Betty would have been hurt, maybe others. I never felt good about it but I…, well, I was angry."

"Yes, but you had every right to be, through his actions you lost Jonah because you stood up to him. I know you must feel terribly guilty for that as well as not being there, but you must not: it was not your fault. He is a man without thought or care for others, driven by money. But yes, you did the right thing, never doubt that."

"How are you feeling now, Avraham?"

"I feel proud, Ishmael: proud of you. I am fortunate to have you for a friend, blessed to still be here. What is this, may I look?"

He picked up the necklace, turned the box around, then opened it.

"I got it for Betty, she has been great even through my moments; I want her to know how much I love her."

"The fact she was there proves that already, she knows. You are made for each other; you deserve it. I know you won't believe me, but you really are some guy, Ishmael; I hope one day you will see that."

"The lady in the jewellers said the same thing, people say nice things, but I feel I'm expected to be something I'm not; I am not sure I am capable of it?"

"Ishmael, you are yourself; that's all that is ever expected, you're good-hearted, an honest man. That's why Betty loves you. Overthinking will do you no good; just stay as you are, that's all that matters to people close."

Rabbi came in that moment, overhearing Avraham's last bit of conversation.

"Wise words, Avraham. Ishmael, he is right: for a man to go through what you have, to still be as you are is not something we are all gifted in. You are what human is; you can do anything. I must go now, I am needed elsewhere. Call me if either of you needs anything."

"Thank you, Rabbi, I'm not quite sure what else to say."

"Yes, I can see: but that's because you are humble. It's what helps makes you who you are, not something we all have either. No words are needed, Ishmael, just stay that way. I really must go now, goodbye to you both."

He left before I could reply. My thoughts changed now, Avraham turned to me, also recognising this.

"Ishmael, Rabbi is also right, but I know you, there's something else on that mind of yours, what is it?"

"I want to ask Betty to marry me. I am not sure if the timing is right or if I should wait; what do I do?"

He looked me in the eye then put his hand on my shoulder.

"That is easy: just follow your heart, the stronger the feeling you have is what you go with; if you do that then all will be well."

"Avraham, I am so glad I still have you, thank you for always being there even when you're not; you are some guy too; I've missed having you around."

"Ishmael, no thank you is necessary: it's what friends are for."

"Avraham, I must go, I will see you soon. You know where I am, too, don't hesitate if you need me."

"I won't, Ishmael, I will see you soon."

I got up to leave. For some reason I felt really empowered, more than I ever had. I wanted to believe what they had said, to do something good with my life. I had been dealt a lot of misfortune, but I had been rewarded tenfold with the people in my life. Yes, I was still grieving over Jonah, but now hearing the words from both Avraham and Rabbi, it gave me inspiration for myself. I felt I had to give reason for the words, do something more to allow myself to accept compliments like that.

I still found that hard regardless, but doing something positive or meaningful would make it easier. I had to look at myself from inside: to find what I was good at, find a way to help people through doing that, too. I went to leave when Avraham called me back as though a matter of urgency.

"Wait, Ishmael, I almost forgot; could you take this to the carpenter in town when you get a moment please?"

He handed me a very small sealed envelope.

"Yes, I can do that, see you soon."

"Thank you, goodbye, Ishmael."

I thought it an odd request: he never said why, or ever rarely went there unless for something special. I thought no more about it, I would just take his request to the carpenter as promised.

I soon arrived at his shop, it contained an array of handmade goods. The man was a genius, a master of his trade; whatever Avraham wanted it would be a beautiful piece. This made me eager to see it.

I dropped the note to the carpenter before returning home. I was meeting Betty that evening so needed to change. I had been rushing round so much lately that time for myself was very much appreciated. It gave me time alone which allowed for thinking – reflecting on life, where it was heading, coming to terms with Jonah. I had taken the advice I was given: I started really thinking about what real abilities I had.

I was only existing now, but I needed more. Wanting to make people proud was never far from my thoughts, but all I was ever good at was writing, even then I was unsure whether I had talent or not. Doubting myself was not easy to ignore. I had enjoyed the moment when I needed to write, but I didn't think I could use that to help anyone. That seemed pretty futile for me, I felt I needed to do something more physical to help others. I just wanted to do more than sit at a desk writing words, for me that was more a hobby, a personal thing, just part of me. It had crossed my mind I was maybe supposed to write in a more meaningful way; but I had no idea how. I thought I'd see if I could get any ideas from Betty: she knew me better than I knew myself so maybe she could help me.

I had half an hour to go before I saw her. It felt strange having a girlfriend, I became used to just myself for company most of the time, with Jonah. Now I had a girl, but Jonah was gone. I still felt tremendous guilt over him, he gave his life to protect me, even though I wasn't there. However, he knew I'd be back; his instinct was to defend himself, his loyalty showed with his instinct to protect me, too.

He tried but Jerry was too big, too strong for him; Jerry didn't know how special Jonah was or would even care. He really was an amazing dog, being with him I found more joy than I ever did with people, now I was left with only people, part of me still felt completely alone. Betty and Avraham were brilliant, but I still felt an emptiness within.

Nothing could fill the void of Jonah; I struggled with it. I knew it was still early days, grieving would last a good while, but there would never be another of him. I was lucky I had him for so long, as Rabbi said, I gave him a good life, but he didn't deserve what happened to him, that's what got to me the most. I was bitter about it: I wanted that man to pay for Jonah's brutal end. Getting some justice would be a way to honour him; move on with some peace knowing that he didn't die for nothing. I really hoped I wouldn't need to go to court because I knew if I saw him I would not be able to contain myself. I didn't want to give him any satisfaction by being put behind bars myself, so not going would have been real benefit to everyone else there, myself included. But if needed I would do it; I would do it for Jonah.

I went to meet Betty, we were having dinner in a posh restaurant in town, I took the necklace I bought to give to her. I was excited to see her face, I was still wondering if asking her to marry me was right. I loved every inch of her, we got through a lot in the short time we were together, but I always knew she was the one for me. Maybe I was just nervous, or now wasn't the right time for it. I walked up to meet her.

I saw her standing there, fumbling around in her bag. I couldn't help but smile: it was like the first time I'd seen her, she looked stunning in a deep purple dress with heels, her hair tied back with a diamante clip. I still wondered why on earth she picked me. I tiptoed quietly up to her then grabbed her waist. She smiled as she turned around.

"Betty, wow, you look incredible, good enough, too…"

She stopped me, putting her finger on my lips, smiling.

"Ish, say no more."

"This second, Betty; no words are needed now."

She stared at me, a smile increasing. I leaned in then kissed her. Every time was like the first, making my heart pound. I could've stayed there all night, kissing her, those moments were like we were the only two in the world.

"I have missed you, Betty, these moments are timeless."

"We belong together, Ish. I know things have been difficult, but I love you; I always will. Now our hearts are filled, let's go and fill our bellies. I'm so hungry."

This made me laugh hard: poetry with a touch of

humour, only she could have pulled that off.

"Like I've said: such a romantic. I thought I was the poetic one here? I have competition I see"

Now she laughed, shaking her head.

"No, Ish, you're the true poet, I'll never be as good as you."

"True poet? I could never be that."

"That's something I must disagree with on this one; the way you put words together is beautiful. Ish, that is a true poet, you should not doubt yourself; you have a gift."

"Yes, you are my gift."

"Ishmael?"

"I know, I know, I just don't see what you do."

"Yes, I am aware of that, but I do; I'm here to make you believe, one day I think you will."

"I only know having you by my side anything is possible, Betty: you help me believe."

"I wouldn't do anything else but that, Ish, I know you could really help people, that I am certain. Shall we go?"

"I really love you; you're amazing Betty."

"No more amazing than you are, Ish."

This comment made me think. I've not seen my work as anything but jumbled up scribble. I saw it differently to Betty: self-doubt was maybe the cause of it, I wasn't sure. I thought that when I got home I'd try to read what I wrote from a different perspective. Maybe then there would be a chance of me trying to write again to help people; that was a long shot, but I felt much more hopeful now, thanks to Betty.

We soon arrived at the restaurant where we ordered dinner. I sat watching her, waiting for the moment to give her the gift. I started feeling jittery, it felt right to ask her, but I couldn't: my heart fought over my mind, which made me indecisive, this caused slight anxiety. It was as if I was being pushed to do it but being dragged back all at the same time; Betty noticed immediately.

"Ish, are you okay: you seem nervous about something?"

I reached into my cloak to pull the necklace out.

"Betty, I got you something, you've been right there for me; especially lately. So much has happened, but you have been so supportive; I just want you to know how special you are to me."

Her eyes sparkled like the night sky on a clear crisp night. She appeared dumbfounded but excited, too.

"For me? Ish, you didn't have to get me anything."

"I saw you eyeing it up, it's as beautiful as you are; I couldn't resist. I hope you like it."

She picked up the box containing the necklace, then slowly opened it. I saw her eyes filling up: her face amazed by what she was seeing. I never expected to see tears; I knew it meant a lot, I didn't realise just how much.

"Betty, I'm glad you like it."

"Like it? Ish, it's gorgeous, I adore it, thank you. I'm just stunned, nobody has ever given me anything like this before."

How could they not? She was kind, generous, beautiful, smart, wise, loving; she deserved that, plus so much more.

"Then they are fools, Betty, you deserve nothing but the best; you will get that with me."

I pulled her close and hugged her, I never liked seeing her cry, but this was different: she was happy just as her tears were.

Seeing Betty upset the waitress came over, she gave me a look as if to say, what did I do? I smiled but she didn't, she only turned to Betty.

"Everything alright, miss?"

Betty looked up, smiling awkwardly.

"Yes, he just gave me this, that's all. I'm just a little emotional, but fine."

She showed the necklace off to the waitress who admired it, also.

"Wow, that is an exquisite piece, your man has taste; I think I'd cry too. You're a very lucky lady."

She turned to me now with a regretful look.

"Excuse the look, mister; we see a lot in here."

"It's okay, miss, I understand that. She has never been spoilt, I am glad to change it for her."

"I am very lucky, he's amazing." Betty focused on me as she said this.

I winked at her. "No more than you are, Betty."

I thought how was it possible to love someone so much.

We decided to walk through the park beside the lake after dinner. It was Jonah's favourite place; I felt closer to him there. The night was calm and quiet, the sound of trees rustling gently as the wind went through them, was all that could be heard. I turned to Betty, curiosity setting in once again.

"What are your dreams, Betty? I mean if you weren't a nurse, what would you want to do?"

"I'm a nurse, Ish, I couldn't be anything else."

"I know, Betty, but there must be something else? I don't know why, but something made me ask."

"There was, but it's silly; it doesn't matter now. I'm a nurse; I always will be."

"It does matter, course it matters, please tell me what it is?"

"Well I loved to sing, I always wanted to sing but I don't get the chance anymore; that was my dream once."

I hadn't had the foggiest idea that she could or wanted to sing, although something told me she was a beautiful singer and the urge to hear her was so strong I had to ask her to.

"You have the chance now?"

"What? Here? No, I couldn't."

"Why not? There is nobody around?"

"It's been so long, Ish; I'm not sure I can."

"I know you can, it's quiet, just you with me; I'll beg if I must?"

She started laughing, I loved seeing her do that.

"Hmm, tempting, Ish, tempting; but that won't be necessary, leave that for another time. Okay, this is for you."

She winked at me then stepped back closing her eyes; I sat on a nearby bench. She started to sing. I was astonished: she had an incredible voice. People, who appeared to show from nowhere, stopped to watch, unbeknown to Betty. I had never heard the song before, but I knew it meant a lot to her. I felt my eyes watering; I felt so honoured to be in her presence. I listened, not taking my eyes off her. She finished her song then opened her eyes, a few people started clapping. She smiled shyly while covering her face, then ran over to me; the people started moving off, happily chatting.

"Betty, that was so beautiful, you must pursue your dream, you can still be a nurse but a talent like that… well!"

"Ish, I am not good enough for that, I am happy doing it just for you."

"Not good enough? Betty, you blew me away. You brought tears to my eyes, gave me goosebumps; that says it all. You say you're just happy to do it for me, but I know that's not true. I could hear it in your voice, you belong up there. Please don't give up, not yet."

"My mum used to sing me that song, I…"

She put her head down, the sadness still deep within her. I lifted her chin up then moved her hair from her eyes.

"Your mum and dad would be so proud of you, never forget that, you really are beautiful in every way; don't ever doubt that either."

She looked at me, somewhat doubtful at my comment.

"Ish, that's all I ever wanted, yet even though I've come far I still don't believe that I…"

"Betty, listen to me, we all make mistakes, but we learn from them. You don't need to have an amazing job or fancy things, you are a beautiful person inside; that's the important thing. I am so proud; your uncle is proud. I know your parents would be, too, you can do anything you want to do; I will help you achieve it."

"Oh, Ish, do you really think I am good enough?"

"No, I know you are: Betty the talent you've kept hidden? Just, wow, thank you for letting me witness that."

"I love you so much; have I told you that?"

I chuckled then put my hand on her shoulders playfully, I looked her in the eyes.

"You've showed me enough."

"Oh, not quite, Ish: there is still room for more."

We strolled for a little while longer, but it was getting late now. I walked Betty home at the end of the night. She was back in work the next day. I needed to think about how I could help her pursue her dream.

"This is me, thank you for my gift, Ish; it's beautiful."

"Suits you perfectly then, you're a superstar, Betty; just magic."

"When we find the time and place? I can't wait to be close to you, Ish; every inch. Do you know how hard it is to resist you right now?"

"Not as much as you are for me, Betty, I'm sure."

I gazed at her, she smiled then gave me the softest kiss while staring into my eyes.

"You drive me wild, Ish, goodnight."

"Funny that: I haven't even started yet, goodnight beautiful."

She drove me crazy; just everything about her. It made it hard to resist, but she made waiting fun. I knew the night with Betty would be like nothing else, something that would be worth the wait. She knew it, too. Betty was happy, but it was obvious she still felt incomplete.

Her fears and doubts had her forfeiting her dreams; I couldn't stand back and let her do that now. She had a stunning voice. Now I knew singing was what she really wanted to do, I wanted to make it happen for her. I didn't have a clue about how to do it, at least not yet. I could do everything except that, which bothered me: it was the one thing she wanted more than anything.

I hadn't written anything else, but I wanted to write her a song now. I thought maybe she would gain encouragement from that. I could only aim to do my best, hoping it would be enough.

My birthday was coming up. Betty and Avraham, who was a lot more functional now, wanted to take me to dinner. I had never liked fuss or birthdays since I was a boy, but I was looking forward to this one, and also dreading it in ways, too. It'd be the first without Jonah who I missed terribly, nothing would take that away. I still wanted to help people, do something positive with my life.

Helping Betty was also on my list of priorities, and I still needed to write her a song.

I had a slow morning, Betty was working so I decided to try writing again. I made a coffee before I sat down. I found myself focusing on her, then after a few minutes I started to write. They were only words to me, but I knew Betty could do something more with them. I got a phone call from Bert which I was not expecting; I instantly thought something was wrong.

"Hello, Ishmael speaking, can I help you? Who is this?"

"Aah, Ishmael, it's Bert, sorry to bother you, could you come to the shop? It's about the poetry competition; I have good news."

I breathed in relief, but was also surprised by the reason for the phone call.

"Poetry competition? But Bert, I never entered; you have the wrong person?"

"No, I haven't Ishmael; I will explain. Could you come now? I need to go out soon."

"Okay, yes, I'll be there shortly, see you soon."

I thought that it was very strange, until I remembered Betty had seen my poem. I hadn't thought to even look at it, so I hadn't noticed it was even missing. She had entered me in the competition; I was there when she did it, but she was an expert in mystery when she wanted to be. I put my head to my hands, chuckling, I pulled my hands away then muttered to myself:

"Oh, Betty, you really wait."

I walked up to the bookshop where Bert was waiting; I marched inside. I was still confused by it all, apart from the fact that I knew it was Betty who had entered me in it.

"Ishmael, come in, don't look so muddled: you won the competition, that is good news."

"Bert, why did Betty do that?"

"Ishmael, she rushed to me with it, said she thought it was the most beautiful thing she had ever read, she loves you, but you doubt too much from what I gathered; this is something to be proud of."

"I am not angry in any way, but I knew nothing; I thought we told each other everything?"

"She asked you, Ishmael, she couldn't not enter you. Betty asked if it was the right thing to do and I told her yes. You have a gift, but you waste it, Betty wanted you to see that; now you've won. Her intention was to encourage you."

Suddenly I stopped, those last couple of words hit me: I was doing the exact same thing with her. Bert was right, I had to stop doubting so much, otherwise I would find no peace or success with anything.

"I have been doing the same with her. I know she meant well; course I do. I'm just surprised I guess. Bert are you aware she can sing, incredibly? It's her dream."

"Yes, she has a beautiful voice, she can play guitar, too, but she also has qualms. You both have talent that you could both make people happy with; this world needs that, doubting gets you nowhere."

"I want to help her, but I don't know how, what do I do, Bert?"

"I'm not sure, but I am confident you will think of something, Ishmael. Here, this is your winnings."

He handed me a bulky envelope, tightly sealed and with fancy handwriting. It certainly looked appealing.

"Thank you, Bert; I hope you are right."

"Aah, don't you worry, you will think of something, now I must ask you to leave: I must go."

"Oh, of course, good day, Bert."

"Good day to you, Ishmael, congratulations, Son."

I wasn't surprised to hear Betty could also play guitar, it gave me more drive to help her: this girl had an amazing gift. I believed Bert when he said something would come up which gave me hope for her.

I walked outside, I opened the envelope I was holding. Carefully I started opening it. Three hundred pounds was inside with a note. It was neatly folded to perfection, it seemed a shame to spoil it, but my curiosity took over. I took the money out, then opened the letter.

"Dear Ishmael

Thank you for your entry.

We are happy to announce you have won first place in the poetry competition.

Your poetry is exquisite work; it is a pleasure to award you the three hundred pounds.

You must keep writing: I haven't seen talent like that in a long time.

In the future I hope to have the pleasure of reading more of your work.

Keep writing and keep believing, you are a gifted individual

Yours faithfully

Imelda Grace

The letter moved me: I never thought that her doing this would make me feel good, it really gave me a boost inside. Not only did I want to write a song for Betty, but I wanted to write even more now. It made me more determined to get her some encouragement, if it worked on me then it would work on Betty. I had three hundred pounds, I knew exactly what I was going to do with it. I was excited to see her face. I walked over to the music shop and strolled in.

"Hello, mister, can I help you?"

I looked at a girl standing there, she appeared to be about twenty, had different colours in her hair, tights with rips in. She wore blue denim shorts with a t-shirt which had a band name I hadn't even heard of. All the way up her arms she had tattoos with a lip stud on her left side of her lip.

She looked a little odd to me, I thought; but her smile was warm.

"Hello, yes, I am looking for a guitar for my lady, but I don't know what I'm really looking for: music isn't my forte?"

"Okay, we have an array of models, do you have a price in mind?"

"I have three hundred to spend, it must be something to encourage her to want to play."

The girl looked at me with confusion at the comment, unsure what to say.

"Not sure I understand, mister?"

"She has an incredible voice; her dream is to sing but she doubts she can do it, so she won't do anything about it. I want to get her something that can encourage that; I don't know where to start really."

"They are all lovely instruments, we don't sell anything specifically for that; but maybe the carpenter can carve something meaningful on it?"

"What a great idea: that would be much more meaningful. I'll look around, thank you."

"I'll be over here if you need help, mister."

I started looking around, they all looked pretty much the same to me, just different shades. Some smaller than others but all a work of art; something I didn't have much, if any, knowledge about. I was drawn to one straight away, it had angel wings on its body. It reminded me of the first time I saw her; I loved it. I called the girl over.

"Excuse me, how much is this one?"

"That one is two hundred and fifty, but new customers

get a discount; I can price up for you?"

"Yes please, that would be great, thank you."

She stood working out the discount, mumbling numbers to herself.

"That'll be two hundred and twenty today, mister."

"I'll take it, with a case, too, thank you."

"You get that free, mister, plus a few other things; I'll pack it up for you."

She packed it up then I paid her. I was pleased as it was a step closer for Betty. I just hope she loved it as much as I did. I thanked the girl again then left. I just had to see if I could get it carved now. I thought, as I slowly paced my way to the shop, about what to put on it. I suddenly had an idea – it was perfect. Quickening my steps I arrived at the shop. The carpenter was there, working on something.

"Aah, Ishmael, what can I do for you?"

"Good day, Isaac, I am hoping to get this carved with 'Don't Stop Believing' on it; if you have time?"

"Of course, I can do it now if you want to wait?"

"That'd be great, yes, I'll wait."

I handed him the guitar then stepped back so as not to get in his way.

"This is a beautiful guitar, Ishmael; may I ask who it's for?"

"It's for my girlfriend, Betty. I am hoping she will follow her dream of singing, that will help to take any uncertainties away, I want to encourage her. I just hope I haven't made a mistake by making her feel I'm pushing her."

"A mistake? Nonsense, this was bought with love, Ishmael; with great intentions. Whatever doubts she has she will see that, I am sure you have done the right thing."

He got to work so I wandered round his shop, it had been a while since I had looked around properly; the beauty and skill of his work was mind blowing.

"Isaac, your work is truly something."

He lifted his head up, smiling proudly.

"Aah, thank you, yes, I have great joy making them;

especially one specific thing which I've been working on."

He gave me a smirk like he knew something, I had no clue what he was talking about.

"Sounds interesting, what is it?"

"A carpenter never tells, Ishmael. I'm a lucky man doing what I love. We should all do something we enjoy: that's where great work is made. I am almost done now."

He had a point I thought, people do jobs yet are unhappy, others do what they love which leaves them content. I didn't want to do something for the sake of it: I wanted to enjoy it, do something worthwhile. I knew writing was it; I had a chance to do it anytime, too. I felt happy inside now, I could not ignore it any more. Isaac soon called me over.

"Ishmael, I am done, do you want to have a look?"

I walked over looking down over his shoulder, it was beautifully written with intricate details; nothing less than a master job. I was delighted.

"Isaac it's beautiful work, thank you."

"My pleasure, Ishmael. Oh, would you inform Avraham his piece is ready to collect? I have final touches but that won't take long."

"Yes, I will let him know; I must go, take care, Isaac."

I handed him some money; Isaac looked down then stopped me before I got out the door.

"Ishmael, this is too much?"

"No, it's well deserved, good day, Isaac."

"You are too good; thank you, Ishmael, very much. A very good day to you."

7 JUSTICE AND A BIRTHDAY

I felt good now. I was apprehensive still, but I knew deep down she would be grateful. I did feel that in some way I was forcing her to pursue singing which concerned me; but I also couldn't sit back without trying. If she still decided she didn't want to do it, then I would know I had really tried; I'd support her whatever decision she came to then. I went home, she would be finished from work soon. I would call to ask her to come around.

Opening the door to an empty house was still hard: I couldn't get used to it. I was hoping I would be able to move on but until Jerry was sent away I would not find peace. I owed it to Jonah; I hadn't wanted anything so bad in my life than justice for him. I got home then made a drink. I just wanted to write now; I grabbed some paper from close by.

I found the pen flowed freely, within minutes I had written a whole bunch of words. I only stared: I didn't know what to make of it, I didn't like it or hate it.

I tried to look at it from a different perspective, but I still couldn't see what Betty did; I felt nothing from it. I thought if Betty could bring it to life then I know it'd make me smile, maybe I'd see what the words mean to her that way. I folded up the piece of paper then placed it carefully in the strings, closing up the case. She would surely be home by now, so I went to the phone and started dialing.

I heard a knock which forced me to place the receiver down; I went over to open the door. It was the officer I had spoken to before now.

"Afternoon, Ishmael, may I?"

"Officer, please, what are you doing here?"

"Just to inform you that Jerry has pleaded guilty over your dog; among many other charges. He will be sentenced soon, he's looking at a long time away."

I just stared at him: dazed, I couldn't believe it. I somehow found some respect for Jerry, he could have kept lying; but he didn't, surprisingly. He accepted his wrong doings, was willing to pay for them. I could not forgive him for Jonah, I could only accept it was an apology to some degree. I was saddened to think he was still young: now he had thrown his life away. He was clearly troubled, a lost soul. Probably feeling so many emotions over different things that made him how he was. Maybe with time away he would see the error of his ways, have a chance to change in the future.

I hoped so for his sake; he would not hurt anyone or anything else anymore which was comforting. I could not be glad about the news: there was no joy in the situation. I was only glad that Jonah's death was acknowledged: he would now get the justice he deserved.

"Ishmael, are you alright?"

"Yes, officer, that's... well, that's good news. It just should never have happened; thank you for letting me know."

"I understand that; people are cruel, but your dog's death has helped to bring a dangerous man where he belongs: in jail. Okay, well I'll be off, good day to you."

"Good day, officer."

I closed the door then walked over to ring Betty again. I picked up the receiver.

"Hello?"

"Betty it's me, can you come over as soon as possible?"

"Yes, I was on my way, what is it, Ish?"

"Just hurry; I'll explain when you're here, see you soon beautiful."

"Okay, I won't be long."

I had a quick tidy round then put the kettle on. I hid the guitar behind the sofa; the anticipation of wanting to see her reaction, the right one, was putting me on edge. I kept looking at the clock until I heard a knock. I rushed to open the door.

"Hello, handsome."

"I'm nothing compared to you, beautiful."

"Funny, considering we are the same."

"Smart too, not sure I can compete with that one."

"I'm smart enough to not be fooled by that, Ish, I know better."

She winked then I grinned before kissing her on the cheek.

"Betty, the officer has just been here: he bought some news. Have you heard?"

"News? What news, no Ish?"

"Jerry has pleaded guilty to all charges; even admitted to Jonah. He's to be sentenced soon; I expect he will be away for a long time."

Her eyes widened, she thought for a split second before jumping up to hug me.

"Oh, Ish, he's really gone? I don't believe it: after all these years to be rid of him. That's fantastic news. I've not heard anything yet, only from you. Justice for Jonah, maybe now you'll find some peace?"

I looked at her, smiling unconvincingly.

"Not yet, look behind the couch?"

With confusion on her face, mixed with a wave of curiosity she got up, a glimpse of a smile also there. She went over then popped her head round the sofa; to say she looked shocked would have been an understatement.

"Ish, no, is that…?"

"Yes, I won the poetry competition you entered me in. I got you a guitar; but open it, there's more."

A look of excitement overcame her now, she brought it round by me where she kneeled to open it; lifting the case lid, she gasped.

"Oh, wow, Ish, you've done this for me? I really don't know what to say; thank you. But Ish, you have talent too, I had to do it. What's this?"

She saw the folded paper then eased it out gently; opening it carefully.

"I wrote you some lyrics to a song, Betty, I thought maybe you could put music to it; maybe sing it if you want to? I know you said you didn't want to pursue it but you're incredible. I had to encourage you like you did me; how could I not?"

"It's just beautiful, all of it, I won't stop believing, oh Ish, thank you."

She moved her hands up delicately along the neck, moving them back down the guitar, examining it; gently pulling on the strings.

"Good, you know I won't allow that don't you?"

"I should do by now, Ish. I love it, but, I love you more."

She looked at me affectionately then got up, putting her arms around me again. I felt her excitement, relief, new found belief. I always found myself loving her even more; it never stopped. I thought that now she was one step closer to fulfilling her dream; now I felt content. The day had changed things for me where I knew now I could move on: I had found some peace. I could start really enjoying whatever good the future had to offer me.

"I'm looking forward from now on, whatever happens we have each other; I am thankful for that."

"Never have I met someone like you, Ish, you've been amazing: encouraged me, believed in me, just loving in every way. Because of you I can now believe in myself, I am so blessed I found you."

"You should believe, do what you love, Betty. Isaac spoke of that when I was there for Avraham, he is right; now how about a coffee, grab some dinner?"

"Sure, but I am paying. I won't take no for an answer: you deserve to be spoilt."

"Okay, Betty, if you insist."

"I could insist a lot more, Ish; but that can wait."

She grinned cheekily; I loved the way she did that. I went into the bathroom to freshen up. A minute later I heard the guitar playing. I came out to see her eyes closed; she looked so peaceful, I just watched her, smiling. She started singing quietly, humming to herself. That was a great moment; I could've stayed listening to her for hours. She continued for a couple of minutes before slowly opening her eyes.

"You're going to be a star, Betty, people will love you."

"It's a stunning guitar: plays beautifully. It's been so long since I picked one up."

"You were fantastic, you belong right there with it, oh, Avraham."

"What? Ish?"

"The carpenter told me to tell him his piece is ready for collection, I've forgotten, oh no."

She stood up putting the guitar down gently.

"Ish, relax; he will understand. Ring him now, he may still make it in time."

I picked the phone up urgently to ring him.

"Yes, may I help, please?"

"Avraham, it's Ishmael, Isaac said your piece is ready to collect, sorry I should have called sooner but…"

"Aah, Ishmael not to worry: we are all busy. Perfect timing, we are still set for your birthday meal, yes?"

"Yes, Avraham, I'm looking forward to it; be good to see you."

"Likewise, Ishmael, well I must go to pick this up, see you soon."

"Are you sure you are well enough to do it, I can if need be?"

"No, you couldn't Ishmael, but thank you, goodbye my friend."

"Goodbye, Avraham, take care."

I placed the receiver down scratching my head in thought.

"What is it, Ish?"

"I think your mysteriousness has rubbed off on Avraham."

She smirked in amusement at this comment, then laughed.

"Oh, you do say some funny things, Ish. Me, mysterious?"

"Yes, beautiful, smart with a mysterious side; I've noticed."

"You wouldn't have me any other way."

I walked over to her then put my arms around her neck.

"Hmm, do you want to bet on that?"

She grinned then looked at me.

"That's not necessary, people only bet when they are unsure of the outcome, we have no doubt here."

"I've never been so sure of anything in my life when it comes to you. Okay, now, regarding Avraham, I know he's up to something?"

"Well I am sure if it's anything to do with you then you'll know soon enough, if not then it's not your business. You must stop allowing things like this to bother you so much, Ish. Come on, let's go out?"

"You're right; but I can't help it sometimes. Well, I'm ready."

"It's good to be curious but not to the extreme you go to; time will reveal all, Ish, think no more about it."

I know I was far too curious, but my senses would play on it sometimes. I would come across so many reasons for this curiosity; becoming stressed about each one. I know it is ridiculous, maybe it was paranoia or because I cared too much. Maybe I was just cautious after Avraham had been so ill; I didn't know. I am just glad Betty was there to pull me back: distract me from it. I couldn't escape my own mind, but I could focus on other things for a time.

We headed out; Betty carefully packed her guitar up

placing it on her shoulder.

"Ish, let me put this in mine?"

"Of course, but let me carry it; we can drop it on the way."

We dropped the guitar off at Betty's then walked to town. I was thinking that tomorrow will be my birthday; so much had happened since last year. My whole life had been turned upside down: I'd lost things, lost Jonah, gained people who have proven their importance in my life, found purpose in my life. It had been a roller coaster year, but I was happier now than I had been last year which was down to three people. I looked at Betty, she seemed deep in thought, was humming to herself, her artistic mind at play until she noticed me looking.

"That's an interesting tune?"

"It's just something I made up; Ish, do you mind if I go home earlier, I want to work on it?"

"No, Betty, it's so nice to hear them words. We can eat, then I'll walk you home after."

So as promised I walked her back after dinner. I was excited knowing she was working on something; I couldn't wait to hear it once it was finished, if she let me. She had changed a lot, she glowed with confidence yet remained humble, she had no fear of Jerry now; she was free. She took that and thrived, getting more stunning because of it; I was so lucky. Stopping outside her house she turned to me.

"It's your birthday tomorrow, Ish, my first with you."

"Three words, Betty: I can't wait."

"I'm thinking another number; it's going to be perfect."

"It already is beautiful; I'll see you tomorrow."

"Goodnight, Ish."

I walked home. I hated not being with her all the time: I missed her.

It made me think more about proposing, for now, though, I wanted to write. I'd put it off long enough; now I needed to see what I could do. Knowing Betty was working on her music gave me the nudge to do something, our connection was strong even when I wasn't with her. She was still able to push me which I couldn't discount anymore.

Once home I pulled out an old typewriter which had belonged to my mother. It had gathered dust over time as it hadn't been used for so long. I didn't know if it would even work effectively now.

I put the fire on, made a drink then grabbed an old rag from the cupboard. I began cleaning the typewriter gently until every part of it was carefully cleaned.

It was stunning, just as I had remembered it. I had done this, yet still had no idea as to what I would write. I put paper in to test it out, writing Betty and Jonah to test the keys.

Suddenly I had a brainwave: I knew what I was going to write. It was a challenge but with the idea came the determination to do it. I started writing and didn't stop.

I'd hear the chime from my grandfather clock strike each hour that passed, yet it was a distant one I barely noticed as I had become so absorbed with what I was doing. Completely in my own world, I was now hooked.

Not even the urge to go to the bathroom or the thirst I felt could stop me: not until I'd finished what I wanted to say. I was wriggling at times to get up but here I could forget everything except the words I needed to write. I looked at the clock; it was three a.m.

I hadn't noticed how late it was, I knew I must sleep but writing was a much better option. However, I knew the day would be busy, by having no sleep I wouldn't function or enjoy it. I was tired, so, reasoning with myself, I surrendered; I would get some sleep then come back to it when I could. I had written quite a few pages now, I surprised myself with the amount. I went to bed happy, with a smile on my face. Soon enough I fell asleep peacefully. I looked forward to telling Betty I, too, was working on something.

I got up a couple of hours later to see the postman had been. A few different coloured envelopes lay on the floor in a pile. Shocked, I picked them up then sat down to open them. There were cards from Rabbi, Isaac and Oliver; plus a couple of other people from town. I smiled, my instant thought being I must thank each one of them as soon as possible. It was completely unexpected, but my birthday morning had been filled with kindness. I felt very emotional about it all.

The phone soon rang; it was Betty.

"Happy Birthday, Ish, I'll be at yours in an hour; I have my first surprise for you,"

"Morning, beautiful. First…? What do you mean Betty? You don't have to."

"Ish, it's your birthday; as I said last night, you're first with me. I'm spoiling you whether you like it or not; see you soon."

I started to speak but she put the receiver down hurriedly; this made me laugh. I knew my day was going to be full of surprises, but nothing could surprise me more than what was to come. I didn't have time to walk to town before Betty came, so I took the chance to try and pick up where I had left off with my writing. No sooner had I got back into it when Betty, just as she promised, knocked an hour later. I opened the door and felt puzzled as, very oddly, she stood there with her back to me. That made me laugh, too.

"Betty, you look very odd, what on earth are you doing? I don't look that bad, do I?"

She laughed then turned just her head around, before facing forward again, I couldn't help but grin now.

"Of course not. Okay, Ish, I know how much you miss Jonah, nothing will ever replace him; but he needed a loving home, I knew you'd be able to give him that."

She turned around. To my complete amazement she held a husky puppy; he was gorgeous. He had colouring which was very like Jonah's; I fell in love instantly. I become emotional now, too: seeing him gave me a feeling of completeness. Since Jonah's death I had an emptiness inside which no human could fill. I smiled as she handed him to me.

"Oh, Betty, I… I… thank you, it was the last thing I expected; he is gorgeous."

"Aww, Ish, I know you miss your walks, everything Jonah gave you. I thought for days what to get you; it felt right."

"He's perfect, but you? You never fail to astound me Betty, he is the best gift I've ever had."

"You're the best gift I ever received, Ish, I know he will be just as much a pleasure as Jonah was, I'd bring Jonah back if I could."

"I know, Betty. The emptiness I felt over losing him? Already I feel that starting to fill, you did that, I…"

"No words needed, Ish: I know what it means to you. Happy birthday, my special guy."

"I'm nothing compared to you, thank you, Betty. How's your music coming along?"

"That you will have to wait to find out, so, what are you going to name him?"

I looked at him, he was tiny; Jonah would have loved him, we walked inside with Jonas before I turned to Betty.

"Jonas, I like Jonas. I know it's almost the same as Jonah, but he reminds me of him. I thought it'd be a good way to honour him."

"Ish, yes, that's a great name; it suits him. Oh, wait I've left something."

She opened the door, stepping outside. She brought a bag in with a variety of things inside for Jonas.

"A bed, a collar which you can have his name engraved onto, food, toys. Aww, Ish, look: he's trying to see, he's just as curious as we are."

He had been sitting quite happily while we chatted, but now he was keen to see what was going on. To explore his home which would help him settle in. I lay the bed down, he sniffed it, stepped in then out; then sniffed some more. Betty dropped a ball; he ran for it playfully. I sat smiling, thinking yes: we are going to have a lot of fun together.

She soon noticed the mail I left on the table.

"Oh, Ish, all the cards; that's so kind. A lot of people really care for you."

"Yes, it seems so; I must thank them. I've had a lovely birthday, Betty."

"It's not over yet, Ish, have you seen this?"

She was holding an envelope; I hadn't even noticed it. It was from the prison; she handed it to me, gesturing me to open it. I did so quickly, now I was confused again.

"Jerry? Why would he be sending me a visiting order?"

"I'm not sure, but you don't owe him anything: after what he's done? Ish, you don't have to go."

"I know how you feel about him, I won't do anything you are uncomfortable with."

"Ish, you do what you feel is right, I'll support you in whatever choice you make, but I cannot go with you I just…"

"No, I understand that; I wouldn't ask you to Betty. I do need to find out what he wants, we can both have closure then. I'll go tomorrow."

"Yes, I know that. Well, I need to go to work, I'm sorry I couldn't spend the whole day with you, Ish; I will see you tonight, I love you."

"I can't wait, see you tonight, beautiful, I love you too."

She kissed me then blew a kiss at Jonas; I could still hardly believe I had him. I needed to go to town: thank people for their kindness. I realised I'd suddenly become fearful of leaving him: the psychological effect of that day hadn't even been apparent until now.

I know he was safe, but after Jonah the fear was still present; I was angered by this. I decided I would take him with me. It was a nice day so getting him used to the area wasn't a bad thing. He was walking round the house sniffing things, just as Jonah had done when I first got him. I called him over.

"Jonas, come here boy, Jonas."

He looked at me with his big eyes, confused, he knew I was speaking to him, but the name wasn't familiar to him yet.

This made me laugh. I bent down before I stretched my arm out towards him. I clicked my fingers, calling him again; this time he came, wagging his tail. I picked him up to give him praise while he licked me.

"Good boy, Jonas, shall we go out, come on."

I put on the collar then grabbed Jonah's old lead; it was all I had for now. I felt slightly uneasy using it because it was Jonah's, it didn't feel right, but I had no choice. I could not take him without one: he was still too young. I was protective of him now, he relied on me to keep him safe. I picked him up then stepped outside.

It was strange walking the same streets; only this time with a puppy. Jonas seemed excited, too, but nervous: every noise he would look around or jump. He was a beautiful animal. I knew he would be as loyal as Jonah had been, and become just as trusting. I looked forward to every day with him.

We got to town eventually. I walked round thanking people who had sent cards. Jonas inevitably got admired and fussed. I turned to see Rabbi who was walking towards me, but had not seen me yet. I don't know what it was but every time I was in town he would appear; still I had the chance to thank him, too, it would also save Jonas from walking to far; I called him over.

"Rabbi?"

He glanced over putting his hand up in recognition of me; he then came over smiling.

"Ishmael, oh, he is beautiful. Happy birthday, Son. What's his name?"

"Thank you, Rabbi, for my card, that was very kind of you. I named him Jonas."

"Aah, yes, of course, I can see why; I assume he is from Betty?"

"Yes, she surprised me this morning."

"I have something for you, but I will give you it later?"

"Later? But Rabbi, I am having dinner with Avraham and Betty?"

"Yes, Son, you are, good day."

He walked off with an out of character smirk; I knew he was up to something now, too. His abrupt, odd comment had me curious again, Avraham was also the same. I just wanted to know what was going on; this evening couldn't come soon enough.

My thoughts now turned to Jerry again: why would a man who had done something like that want to see me? I was unnerved by not knowing: I thought I'd be the last person he would want to see.

Only part of it made sense. It was odd he would contact me after what he had done, I guess I'd have a chance to ask why he did that to Jonah, maybe he wouldn't say anything. Maybe he just wanted to apologise, for now I could only guess.

I didn't hate the man because he had accepted his ways, also because of the fact that he was prepared to take his punishment. But the circumstances when he took Jonah, it was in such a cruel way; that was something I could not accept, not ever. I had no sympathy for him, only pity: for a man to act in such a callous way showed how dysfunctional he was, it was clear how unstable he was, too.

I believed that in itself was something which he couldn't be fully blamed for.

There were so many questions that I had for him, I just hoped my emotions wouldn't get the better of me. For now, I had an evening of celebration ahead; I wanted to enjoy it.

I turned my focus to Jonas, he had enjoyed the trip, being fussed over and admired. He was so affectionate for such a little dog, I felt my life was complete, but Jonah would still always be a big part of it.

Time was getting on, I had been in town a while thanking people, chatting to them. However, Jonas was getting tired now, so we headed back home. I had a couple hours till I met with Betty, along with Avraham, at the restaurant. I was keen to do some more writing before going back out; it'd relax me, too. We arrived home, I fed Jonas, gave him some water then sat down after making a coffee. After eating Jonas came over to me, immediately he started whining; I looked down, his big eyes staring back.

"Jonas, what's up boy? Come on you can sit on my knee."

I picked him up gently, he fidgeted for a moment then lay down on my knees, within seconds he fell asleep. I glanced over to see where I was up to, then continued writing.

Next time I looked at the clock it was quarter past six. Completely lost in my own world, the panic came, disturbing Jonas: I didn't have long before I had to go out, I needed to shower then change.

I picked Jonas up carefully then put him down on the floor. Still half asleep he looked for the nearest comfortable spot to continue his dreams. He stumbled over near the fire then flopped himself down before closing his eyes instantly. I watched him, it made me chuckle: I thought to myself, if only I could fall asleep so easily.

Forgetting for a moment I was in a rush to go out, I quickly got ready, putting on my best clothes. I had fifteen minutes till I was expected. Grabbing my cloak and hat, I quickly walked to the restaurant.

I felt somewhat nervous: part of it was leaving Jonas, but another part of it was all the sneaking around, the mysteriousness; I didn't know what to expect. My senses were aware, giving me butterflies in the pit of my stomach,

I was unsure whether that was a good or a bad thing. I ran nearly the whole way there, but then I had to stop to catch my breath.

Leaning against a wall I put my head down against it: I felt so dizzy, everything looked fuzzy. The intensity of my breathlessness, now forced me to hold my chest. I tried to shake it off, I stared ahead trying to see if I could see which direction this would go, whether I would recover or pass out completely. I then heard a very faint voice calling my name but couldn't make out where it was coming from. The blurriness subsided, I could soon feel the cool air fall over me. I slowly got up completely baffled, looking around to see if anyone was nearby. There was nobody in sight.

What had just happened?

Was I ill without knowing it? Is there something wrong with me? Now I was tormented trying to find a reason for what had just occurred, not just the physical but the voice, too. That was a first for me. I managed to make it to the restaurant feeling dazed; I stumbled inside. Betty saw me when she heard the door opening, she smiled but seeing I wasn't quite right it quickly turned to a look of concern; she rushed over.

"Ish, you're here, whatever is wrong; you look awful?"

"I'm not sure, I had a funny turn, I've not had that before, I'm a little dazed but I'll be okay."

She turned to her nursing role straight away: checking my pulse, looking in my eyes, routine things she could do without necessary medical equipment.

"Ish, we don't need to stay if you're not up to it, I understand?"

"No, I'm fine, maybe drinking some water I'll be alright. Betty, I heard a voice, it was so clear but there was nobody there?"

"It could just be a hallucination, Ish, the body does strange things when it's under high level stress or strain, try not to worry."

I could take this explanation as she was a nurse, she

knew more than I did, but I couldn't help but still wonder; it was just so strange. I tried to put it out of my mind, I had looked forward to this evening; I was determined to enjoy it. I sat down while Betty got me some water. I heard someone speaking behind me and I recognized it as being Avraham arriving. Betty went to greet him before he hastily came over to me.

"Ishmael, my friend, are you alright? Betty said you had a funny turn?"

"I'll be fine, Avraham, it's good to see you."

"Yes, you too, happy birthday, Ishmael. Food then gifts I think; I have something special for you."

"You didn't need to do that, Avraham; your company is more than enough."

He just smiled, but I meant every word. I was blessed having him here still, especially looking so well; the evening was one I never wanted spoilt in anyway.

After some water I felt better, although everything seemed dreamlike for a while. I watched people enjoying themselves, but I felt disconnected, invisible, almost like I was going to be pulled away any moment.

I was torn between whether to go home or whether to stay: I felt safer staying in case anything happened, but I didn't feel with it at all.

I was in my own world, only whispers of far off voices from customers in the room passing my ears prevented me from wandering too far. I wanted to know what the meaning was behind the experience in the street, especially the voice: it seemed so specific. I felt the urge to run out of there, but only the fear of a repeat stopped me. I didn't notice Betty who came to sit down along with Avraham. Bert came with Rabbi, plus a few others, it was only when Betty grabbed my arm, that I was shaken from it.

"Ish, are you alright? You are miles away; do you want to go to hospital?"

Looking at her, I could see her eyes were still filled with worry. I'd always been well but now she saw me anything but; naturally, this caused her to be somewhat anxious.

"I'll be fine, honestly Betty; just in a world of my own, I feel better now than I did."

"I noticed, Ish, but I've not found anything alarming, if you feel bad again you tell me; promise me?"

"Yes, you have my word, I love you."

"Good, I've asked a few people to come; I had to make this night the best, I love you too, Ish."

"Yes, Betty, I noticed that; well eventually, thank you."

She laughed giving me a wink, her look was now a more relaxed one. I looked round, everyone's eyes on me. I felt somewhat embarrassed, but the sight was welcoming. They'd given their time to come here for me; I had to at least try looking a bit more appreciative. The shock of the moment had caused me to forget everything I should've already done, I hadn't greeted anyone or said anything, only to Avraham and Betty; that's what upset me the most. I stood up, I had to say something.

"Thank you all so much for coming. I had no idea you would all be here; it means a lot that you have all come. I had a funny turn on the way here but I'm feeling better now. Please forgive my ignorance. I hope you all enjoy the night."

I sat back down, the whole table went quiet for a moment. I waited before starting to speak again, yet Rabbi stepped in.

"Ishmael, I think I speak for all of us when I say it's a pleasure for us to be here; we hope you enjoy the night too, happy birthday, Son."

"Rabbi, thank you, I know I will."

Betty kissed me on the cheek then whispered in my ear.

"I have a surprise for you later, Ish."

I looked at her, I did not know what she had planned. The mischievous grin told me it'd be worth the wait; with her everything always was. I gazed at her then returned the same look.

"Really? Well, maybe I have one for you too: I've been

doing some thinking. You look beautiful tonight Betty, you always do."

I winked but kept looking at her, I then smirked; she knew exactly what I had in mind.

"Looks like you've only beaten me to that; but you won't always be so quick, Ish; you can be sure of it. Let's eat."

The feelings I felt at those moments were ones I couldn't describe; let's just say she was lucky we were surrounded. We ordered dinner, the night went much better after that; I felt myself again. After everybody finished eating, Avraham stood up.

"Ishmael, you've had a hard year; for you that's nothing new. Nevertheless, you push on, you keep fighting; I for one am proud to call you my friend. Now, everyone knows about Jonah, I know his passing has been devastating for you; we have all felt the effect. He won't come back, but I thought with my gift you would have something to remember him by; I hope you like it. Happy birthday my friend."

He bent down to pick something up. He handed me a gift, neatly wrapped. It had some weight to it; intrigued I started opening it. I couldn't believe my eyes, now it all made sense. It was a beautifully carved wooden figure of Jonah, every detail down to perfection. I was literally choked for words.

"Oh wow, Avraham, I don't... it's stunning, thank you so much, I am a little lost for words."

"Yes, Ishmael, I expected that, but it's not necessary: you are very welcome my friend."

Others handed me gifts too. Rabbi gave me a diary, it was very classy: leather with gold trim. I was grateful to be given anything, but I just didn't see why he gave me it: it seemed an odd gift. I was no lawyer or doctor, it puzzled me. Nonetheless, I knew he wouldn't give anything without a reason; so I accepted that.

I was overwhelmed with the generosity I received, it had been a day of love, filled with surprises. I soon learned it wasn't over yet. Betty stood up then turned to me.

"Ish, to end the night I have prepared something already for you; it's your song, but my way."

She went off to grab her guitar. The whole table waiting in suspense for her return. A minute later she returned, pulling a chair away she sat back down. People were still chatting until the second she started singing. Everyone in the room stopped dead to listen, not a soul blinked. She did not look down this time but straight into my eyes; she took my breath away.

She was amazing: the way she put it together in such a short time, perfected it. I'd never felt prouder of her, that song topped the whole day off for me. We never took our eyes off each other the whole time; until she sang the last word. Once again putting her head down at the end, she got a standing ovation, everyone was talking or looking over at her from around the room. She came over, humble as always, then gave me a kiss.

"Betty; that was amazing, I knew you'd make it beautiful, thank you."

"Happy birthday, Ish. No, we made it what it is, it would be nothing without the words."

I pulled her close to kiss her, we didn't care who was round: we never did. I for one could not hold back; neither could she by the passion I felt. During the embrace we were interrupted. Betty got a tap on the shoulder, there was a man in a suit standing there, he had a look of some importance about him.

"Excuse me, Miss, don't mean to interrupt but I had to: you have some extraordinary talent. I'm in town with some friends, this is my card. Give me a call, you belong on stage; I can make that happen for you."

For the first time her jaw dropped, neither of us could

believe it; she was lost for words, just staring at the card. I put my arm around her.

"Betty?"

She looked in disbelief at him before finding her voice again.

"Sir, I will, thank you, I apologise: I am just shocked. My name is Betty."

"Herbert Jenson, not at all; your voice pleasantly shocked everyone in the room. Good evening to you both, speak soon, Betty."

He went to join his friends while she looked again at the card she was holding.

BLUERAY RECORDS
AND MUSIC PRODUCTION
HERBERT JENSON
NEW YORK

HOME OF WHERE DREAMS ARE MADE!

Her face suddenly turned to one of despair; she looked at me clutching my arm.

"Ish, no, he's from New York: I couldn't afford to go there."

"Betty this is a massive opportunity for you, grab it with both hands. I will help if you need to go there, don't let finances get in the way. We will find a way, okay?"

She just threw her arms around me. I was standing there thinking, panic set in for me now. I couldn't help but think about what would happen if she did have to leave, how could I leave Avraham, my home, what about Jonas? I knew it was selfish; I was so happy for Betty, but now fears of me losing her were suddenly very real. Instinctively I pushed her away leaving her very much alarmed by it.

"Ishmael, what is it? What's wrong?"

How could I tell her my selfish thoughts, have her worry; I didn't want to put her in the position where she would have to choose between me or her dream. I avoided any of that; changing the subject quickly.

"Come on, we need to get back to the others."

She knew there was something but didn't push me, I just felt worse, I could tell she felt hurt. For now, I would enjoy whatever time I had left with her, let her decide on her own without me clouding her judgement.

"Sure, Ish, whatever you want."

8 A NIGHT TO REMEMBER

Everyone was remarking, praising Betty over the evening; she told them about Herbert, they were pleased for her, Avraham too. However, he never failed to speak up if he had concerns over something; this helped me instantly now.

"Betty, I am happy for you; but if you leave, what will become of your relationship with Ishmael?"

I know he saw my discomfort with the conversation. He knew this would plague me, he also knew how hard I'd find bringing it up myself. I just looked at him, I was uneasy at what she would say; I almost didn't want her to answer.

"This man has been incredible, he's my world. I love him with everything. If I leave I would want him to come, but I know he wouldn't want to leave you all. Ish, I won't let what we have come between anything: we will make it work. I don't know what will happen, but I know whatever does, we will still be together. I love you, Ish, I will always love you."

"Betty, you need to do what's right for you; everyone will agree you belong on the stage. I love you too, I will do what's needed to make you happy. I pushed you away because I thought I'd lose you, I..."

"Yes Ish, I thought that to be the case but..."

Rabbi tapped a glass then stood up. He started laughing, everyone looked at him a little bewildered by it.

"Forgive my laughing but you do not see, it's not what's good for you individually any more, it is about you both now. Ishmael, you write, yes? You have so much to give, you are afraid of leaving but ask yourself this: apart from your friends, what is keeping you here?"

I didn't see it from that viewpoint, thinking about it now there was nothing that really was, only the comfort along with the familiarity I'd grown to need; it was hindering me. My concern about going anywhere else was that I would not fit in. Before Betty I had no reason to think or consider it. Rabbi turned his head towards me nodding, and raised his eyebrow along with a smile: he knew he'd got me thinking. He looked towards Betty now.

"Betty, you have a beautiful voice, talent like that should be spread. This will be a journey for both of you, a choice to do it together because you belong together. Sometimes sacrifices must be made but it's worth the risk; things will work, or they won't, you gain from it or you learn from it. Whatever the outcome, you should always try; both of you."

With that he sat down. I felt so relieved about those words, Rabbi was a great man: his problem solving seemed effortless. He was inspirational; had become important in my life more than ever. I turned to Betty.

"We will see what Herbert says, Betty; if you go then I'll go with you."

"We are in this together, Ish."

Avraham stood up now. Picking up a glass he tapped it gently, everyone waited for him to speak.

"Time for change, Ishmael; for you it's a must. But whatever does happen, you always have a place here; now I think it time to call it a night."

I looked round as people started getting up, some I may not see for a long time, if so I knew I'd miss them a lot. Avraham was right, the time had come for change, but although I was apprehensive about it, I was excited too.

The fact I would be with Betty also alleviated my concerns. I knew I'd be alright with her, unfamiliar surroundings were what caused some of my anxiety, but she eased it dramatically. The not knowing where we would end up or what we were both letting ourselves in for was what bought it on. Whether it would be everything Betty had hoped for, I didn't know that either. I had no answers, so the risk was huge. Nevertheless, it was something we had to find out, which in some way helped settle my mind considerably.

Everyone lined up to say goodbye, wishing us well. Rabbi and Avraham were the last in line. Stepping forward, Rabbi placed his hand on my shoulder warmly.

"Ishmael, Betty, we are both very fond of you. Do not worry what lies ahead, enjoy the moment.

"Always remember we will always be there for you both. Betty, you will go far; follow your heart always, that will serve you well. This journey will test you both, so you will need the support of each other. Enjoy the rest of your night, happy birthday, Ishmael; I hope you have enjoyed it?"

"Thank you, Rabbi, yes, I have: it's been such a lovely day."

"I am very glad to hear that Son, goodbye to you both."

He walked away, leaving Avraham who stared at me with almost grief in his eyes.

"I will miss you, Ishmael, very much, but I don't want you to worry about me. I want you happy, that's all that matters, it's all that has ever mattered to me."

He said it as though I wouldn't see him again, like he was letting me go. I wasn't about to agree with allowing him to think that; he was so important to me. I had to settle his mind as much as I could; he had done it for me on many occasions.

"Avraham, listen to me, you're very important in my life, wherever we go I will be back as often as I can to see you. I made you a promise; it's one I intend on keeping. Don't worry about us either, we will write often, ring you. Avraham, this isn't goodbye, not for us: you don't get rid of me that easily."

I could see him relax a bit more, he laughed at my last words. Although he knew me well, I also knew him too; putting his mind at ease was important with his health being precarious. He wanted me happy, even if he had to let me go. But regardless of where I was, he would always be part of it; I would make sure of that. Betty, who was listening to us both, soon intervened.

"You two, we may not be going anywhere yet; Avraham, if we do I will make sure he comes to see you, even if I can't make the journey. Please don't worry, we will keep you informed of everything."

She kissed him on the cheek then hugged him, he showed a smile again.

"You make him happy, Betty; for that I'm very happy. You belong with each other; I know this, just never forget it either. Right then, I'll let you both go: I'm sure you both want some time together."

We both chorused goodbye to him as he started walking out. I hoped I could keep my word: that nothing would prevent it. It bothered me, too, that he wasn't in great health; what if something happened but I couldn't get back? What if that was the last I saw of him but barely said anything? My mind raced now, forcing me to call him back.

"Wait, Avraham!"

"Ishmael, what is it?"

I ran over to him, hugging him firmly. That was rare, for me to do that, but I couldn't let him go without showing him what he meant, this for Avraham said it all.

"Aah, I know Ishmael, I know, come on go be with Betty, it's not goodbye remember. Happy birthday my friend."

I let him go, he smiled squeezing my shoulder; I felt much better for it now, I stood watching him leave. Betty followed over.

"Ish, I know you worry about him with his health, but if you need to get back, then whatever it takes, I'll make sure you do so; I promise."

"I know you will, Betty, I never doubt it. It'll be hard for him: we've always been together. He doesn't show it; but I can see. Sometimes he just needs reassurance, I hope me giving him that wasn't premature."

"We don't know what will happen, Ish, but people who are important to us will always come first no matter what; Avraham shall always be main priority."

"How did I end up with someone as incredible as you?"

"I've thought the same, Ish, there will never be another like you, you're a one off."

"Well I hope not, Betty, one of me is more than enough in this world."

This sent her in fits now, forcing me to laugh too. She then stopped to think before she walked in front of me; with confidence oozing from her. Lifting her finger to my chest while staring at me, she dragged it right down to my waistline, inserting her finger in my pants she pulled me abruptly closer, before speaking in a sultry tone.

"Well, Ish, right this minute? One of you is all I want; do you know what you do to me?"

I grinned before whispering in her ear.

"Oh, I haven't done anything, Betty; yet."

"Well, we have the time, the place?"

With a sincere look I gazed at her.

"The time and place won't have any relevance soon, that I am certain of"

"After many birthdays that have been forgettable, this one will be unforgettable; I will make sure of that."

"I know with you; it wouldn't be anything else, Betty."

"We have all the time in the world, Ish, but I can't wait another second, my resistance is about to run out."

"Hmm, well that's perfect timing; because so is mine."

I winked at her, she didn't say another word, just took my hand, leading the way. Betty looked gorgeous in a short black dress with heels; she had the necklace on I bought her with a short multi-coloured jacket. Her hair was tied back but still showed her curls, while a loose bit fell over her face. She was a vision; I couldn't take my eyes off her. We soon got back to my house where I unlocked the door, before putting my gifts down inside. Betty went to walk in, but I stopped her before she had the chance.

"Betty, loving you has been so easy, but resisting you has been the hardest thing."

"That will no longer be an issue, you look gorgeous tonight, Ish."

She leaned in to kiss me softly while gazing into my eyes. I lifted her up then carried her inside. Jonas was fast asleep; our entrance didn't cause him to flinch. She took my hat off placing it on her head, with a lustful look that got my heart thumping. I eased her back down onto the floor by the door.

"The night is ours, Betty, I'm going to make the most of every second with you."

"Seconds start now, Ish, I can't fight it for a minute more."

"Betty, I…"

Grabbing my shirt, she pulled me as close as she could.

"Ssh: just kiss me, Ish."

Even then the energy I felt was strong, I smiled at her just let myself go: kissing her passionately. I couldn't stop myself now, neither could she. Moving onto her neck, I removed her jacket before feeling her body with my hands. My senses where tickled by her sweet-smelling odour; I couldn't get enough. I moved her head gently to the side to dive in deeper; that really stirred her up until she pushed me away. I kept trying to kiss her, yet she pulled away some more: teasing me. Once I stopped to look, she came at me to kiss me again with the same passion; she now felt my body while trying to say my name.

Releasing her audacious side, she gripped my arms before flipping me around, pinning me against the wall, just smirking at me.

"Do you remember when I said you wouldn't always be so quick, Ish?"

"How could I forget?"

We both grinned before she started kissing me more softly; my heart raced even more now. Immediately, I scooped her up, then moved us towards the bedroom. Lowering her down onto the bed I removed my cloak, she leaned back with an inviting look, just watching me. I stared into her eyes without blinking, I wanted to explore every part of her; I leaned in close, forcing her to lie back.

"Ish."

I kissed her once on the lips then looked at her again.

"Remember what you said about every inch, Betty?"

She started to speak but I put my finger on her lips before she could say anything, then kissed her eyes tenderly before cementing my lips back onto hers.

I slowly started touching her body again, gliding my hands all over her gently now, feeling every part of her. I moved onto her neck, softly biting it. She moaned throughout, trying to push me away; then grabbed my hair to push my head in again. Using her strength, she rolled me over, placing herself on top of me. Looking in my eyes she came in close, whispering in my ear.

"Every inch is a line I must follow through with, too, Ish."

She gave me a provocative look before taking my hands, pinning them behind my head. She bent down, lightly bit my bottom lip, then focused on my neck, intensifying every bite the more I moaned. She moved her hands over my body, signaling her enjoyment vocally with low moans too. Slowly, my shirt buttons were undone one at a time, each one unfastened would have her putting her hand inside, grasping my skin while squeezing it; leaving me moaning with her as she continued. I called her name out now softly; she looked at me with a smile, then started kissing me again.

She gained pleasure from hearing me, too; this aroused me even more. I pulled her close then reversed position. I lifted her up to face me, both of us now breathing more rapidly.

"As gorgeous as you look in that dress, the desire to know what's underneath is growing rapidly."

"Well remember when I said curiosity can be a good thing? This is one of those times."

I moved hair from her face then put my hand behind her head, before kissing her again lovingly. The energy increased substantially as every second passed.

Laying her down I slowly started unzipping her dress from the side; only revealing bits of her little by little.

"I've found an inch of you, Betty; you know how curious I get?"

"Not as curious as I am of you this very moment."

I grinned at her then looked at each part I had revealed, acknowledging it with a kiss. Unzipping it all the way I then softly kissed, then bit her sides which caused her moaning to increase. Gradually, I began to peel the dress from her which was clinging to her perfectly shaped body. Sitting her up, I removed it altogether before laying her back down. She grabbed my chin.

"I told you you'd have to put me down some time, Ish."

I kissed her again before I pulled away; she opened her eyes.

"I told you that I'd make you centre of attention for so much longer; that time has come, wait for me, beautiful."

"Ish."

I kissed her neck then moved my hand down, lightly moving it up her side in soft strokes, making her flinch with pleasure. From her neck down, I began to explore her whole body, with a kiss or a gentle bite. Moving my tongue up her sides, then down from beneath her bra to the bottom of her stomach. I blew on the wetness my tongue had left, leaving her twisting, touching the parts after I'd moved on, groaning all the while. I slid my hand under her bra, caressing her breasts, squeezing them gently, as I continued kissing her body.

I then put my hands under to lift her up, then fixed my lips onto hers. She grabbed my head with both hands as I moved my hands right the way down from her underarms, down her sides, then back up before undoing her bra. She laid herself back, bringing me with her; I pulled away to gaze at her.

"I don't know what it is, but I just can't get enough of you, Betty; I think you're my new addiction."

"I have just the right medicine for that, Ish."

I smiled at her then moved down again. I began kissing her breasts, I moved my tongue in circular motions around her nipples until they hardened, then softly nibbled them.

She watched me while running her fingers through my hair, grasping it firmly then releasing it. She pushed my head in more while moaning my name. I grabbed her hands then put them down on the bed, continuing. She relaxed as I moved onto her bottom half; starting with her inner thighs, kissing them with gentle bites, cooling down the warmness of her skin with cold blows, while stroking her vagina tenderly.

Moving her knickers down slightly, little by little, I softly kissed each bit of her, then sitting up I removed them altogether. Glancing at her I saw that her eyes were closed; now she was writhing around while touching her own body, excitement in her voice as she moaned.

"Ish, I can still feel you, Ish?"

I pulled my body over hers, enveloping her. Opening her eyes she looked at me, now with breathlessness creeping in. Moving back down, I continued to kiss her, then moving onto her vagina I ran my tongue in the middle of it before exploring the inside, rotating my head slowly in circular motions on her clitoris; blowing there too. Quickening my movements, she began lifting her body then bringing her legs up then down, grabbing my head with one hand then using her other to touch herself, calling out to me in-between.

"Ish, mmm, Ish."

Gliding myself back up, I kissed her while touching her body again, moving my hand down lightly over her vagina, then looked at her as her breaths eased.

"My hand is wandering, Betty?"

She smiled then moved her hand down my arm towards my hand, then kissed me once before whispering in my ear:

"Maybe it needs some guidance?"

She kissed me fervently then felt for my hand. I pulled slowly away to look at her. As we watched each other, we both inserted my fingers inside; she gasped, lifting her body off the bed, then back down again while sighing with a moan. Gently I started to move them quicker; in then out.

"Ish, mmm, Ish"

She felt her breasts then moved her hand down again to her clitoris, rubbing it while moaning until I pushed it back out of the way. I kissed her again, then felt my way to her clitoris which I began to rub quicker, before slipping my fingers back inside. She pushed her body into the bed then upwards, repeatedly, saying my name over again. She tried to push me away until she could only grab me, using her nails to press into my back. I moaned then moved my hand focusing just on her clitoris, moving my fingers much quicker now. She started becoming emotional, holding onto my neck, squeezing me, giving herself no option other than to really call out to me now in breathless bursts.

"ISH? Ish, I'm... I... Ish?"

"I'm here, you're amazing."

"Ish… I… mmm."

I placed my lips back on hers but was unable to, she pulled away then tried kissing me again between breaths. I slowed right down then eventually pulled my hand away before kissing her gently. She then moved, looking at me with a wild look before pushing me onto my back, rolling me into the same position as before. She sat up, loosening her hair which had curls falling around her shoulders. Removing the pin from her hair, I closed my eyes as she ran it down my body causing me to sigh with pleasure; I then fixated my eyes back on her: she was stunning.

"Those warming moments we spoke about? Well it's about to get a whole lot warmer, Ish, especially for you."

Just as I went to speak she stopped me.

"No more words, Ish, just you, I've been centre of attention long enough."

She grinned then kissed me softly, feeling my body before moving onto biting my neck. I started moaning which she imitated in return, as I was trying to move her out of the way she grabbed my hands, locking her fingers then holding them down. It wasn't just what she did that got to me, it was seeing her enjoyment doing it; her confidence mixed with sensuality. We knew exactly what each other wanted without saying a word, it was breathtaking – literally.

She started to kiss my chest, then moved to lick my nipples, softly biting them while gently running her nails down my side at the same time. Using her tongue lightly, she started moving it down towards my navel, blowing on the wetness she now left. It sent a chill right through me, I murmured her name as she loosened my belt, then she moved up to kiss me before sitting up again.

Removing my belt, she then ran the buckle down my body, with the coldness increasing, she went over it with the warmth of her tongue. She then stripped me of my pants before moving on to my lower body. Gently she started biting my inner thighs, kissing them while using her hand to rub my penis. She then held it, moving her tongue all the way along, making me groan loudly. She blew on it before moving her teeth up then down gently, squeezing my testicles softly throughout. I was so aroused that I went to sit up, but she prevented me.

"Every inch, Ish, remember?"

I surrendered, lying myself back down. Moving to kiss my navel, she went back to repeat it all again, only this time putting it in her mouth moving in upward, then downward strokes getting faster, then slowing down only to increase speed as I relaxed. I started calling her now while trying to catch my breath, gripping the bed tightly.

"BETTY, I ca… I… mmm, Betty."

She pulled away moving back up towards me; I sighed before she lay her naked body on mine. Now she kissed me like her life depended on it. I pushed her upwards sitting her on my knee, she gently rubbed her body against me, we just gazed into each other's eyes before she spoke.

"I'm in danger of igniting the world up for what I feel now."

"I have a solution for cooling you down only?"

"That's the only solution there is, Ish."

I picked her up, moving us towards the wall. Leaning her against it, she took a big breath followed by a moan as the coldness touched her skin. I aimed for her neck again before pulling her away for a split second, then forced her back gently; this sent her wild. She gripped my hair forcing me to face her, panting more rapidly.

"I don't know what's stronger, Ish, the passion or the love."

I smiled then stared into her eyes.

"That's because like us, they are the same; although I think love wins this one?"

She gave me a kiss before staring deeply at me again.

"It will always win, Ish, that I am certain about."

The energy we both felt was like a drug, it was so addictive. We were completely satisfied but we still couldn't get enough of each other: the passion in the room was indescribable, stripping each other to the soul still wouldn't be enough.

I grabbed her wrists, lifting them behind her head.

Kissing her affectionately now, I released my hands from hers, touching her again.

She reversed me round, pushing me against the wall; the coldness of it making me gasp, then she felt my body with her hands. With one kiss on the lips, she began to move downwards, kissing my body, then coming back up slowly until she came face to face with me again.

"We are connected in so many ways, Ish."

"All except for one, Betty?"

She smiled then leaned in to whisper in my ear.

"I know we can do better than that, Ish."

I pulled her close then kissed her before I started walking her back towards the bed, gently laying us down again. Easing myself onto her body, using mine to rub against hers, she clenched my buttocks pushing me against her more. While watching each other, I moved her hands behind her, holding them there with one hand, then using my other to slowly penetrate her; both of us inhaling with one big breath.

An instant tingling sensation ran straight through me: almost as if my soul was dancing because it had found its other half.

I leaned in to bite her lip lightly, before blowing some air on her.

Quietly moaning while holding onto me she pulled me closer, then moved her nails along my spine lightly, before pushing them in harder; both of us moaning now, I watched her before I called her.

She kissed me lovingly, then wrapped her legs around me, using them to push me deeper; we both groaned loudly.

She opened her eyes trying to fix them on mine, but closing them as my body went inwards. Slowly I began to thrust back, then forth; she began constantly calling my name in a whispered tone.

I thrust harder now, gaining more speed, then slowed down only to do the same again, more groans came from us both at the same time.

She grabbed me trying to push me away, only to pull herself back again, becoming even more emotional now.

"ISH? oh my... Ish? I... ISH?"

"Betty, Betty."

"ISH, I... Ish?"

"Hey; I've got you, you're so beautiful, Betty."

She held onto me tightly, now I began slowing down more. She kissed me while grabbing my neck with one hand, using her other to grab my buttocks, pushing me into her gently before opening her eyes.

"Ish, I don't want this to end, don't let me go."

"Up until I met you, until tonight, I didn't know what real love was, because of you I do. I'll never let you go Betty, I love you so much."

"Up until I met you, until tonight, I didn't know how incredible a man could be in every way, you've shown me that. I love you, Ish; I will love you always."

Still inside her, we just continued staring into each other's eyes as I gently moved my body. I smiled at her then leaned in to kiss her again; that's when everything just went black.

9 A WORLD OF CONFUSION

I gradually opened my eyes to see a doctor standing over me, next to a nurse. They were mumbling things, voices echoing around me; I couldn't grasp anything they said. Opening then closing my eyes, barely conscious; I became panicked quickly, trying to escape the bed.

"Where am I, what's happened? Betty, where is she?"

They looked at each other, somewhat confused: not knowing what to say, the doctor hurried over.

"Woah, easy, Ishmael, welcome back, you've been in a coma; you're very lucky to be here."

"Betty, where's Betty? Please I need to see her, Jonas, he's just a puppy? Please."

The nurse looked at the doctor who walked towards me; he sat on the bed.

"Ishmael, nobody by that name has been to see you, only your friend Avraham who came with the rabbi. He brought you in after finding you by a puddle; you were face down in it. They mentioned your dog Jonah barking, but didn't know how long you had your head under water; that's why you were comatose, you were in a very bad way."

I lay there when suddenly the reality hit me. I had dreamt the whole thing, I couldn't contemplate it. I completely panicked now, desperation taking over.

"NO, NO-O-O-O! BETTY? Please, it's not true? Doctor, she was my world; Jonas, no, will be alone, I don't understand?"

"Ishmael, easy, I'm sorry, whatever happened during your coma it was just a dream. Today is November 14, 1957, this is reality."

"NO, I DON'T WANT THIS REALITY, TAKE ME BACK, I DON'T WANT TO BE HERE!"

The doctor got up to put his hand on my shoulder firmly.

"Ishmael, I can't, go easy, Son, you mustn't over exert yourself."

"I don't care, doctor, I have nothing to stay here for."

"You've had a shock, I see that, but you will get through; your friend will be here soon, he's arrived the same time every day. You have much to be here for, I must go but someone will check on you often."

He got up, then spoke to the nurse before leaving. She looked at me before also leaving the room; now I was alone.

I was so mixed up, feeling so many things. Absolutely devastated knowing Betty, especially, wasn't real. I was so angry because it felt so cruel: I had been in another world where I had everything, only to be pulled back to face a reality I didn't ever want to come back to.

Why? What was the point? I started thinking about my life, comparing it to my dream. I was confused because I had dreamed how close I was with Avraham, but in real life, it wasn't the case.

We were close once, but due to my behaviour, my drunken ways, I constantly let him down which caused distance between us.

Yet he had still been there while I was in here: he obviously cared. There was one thing which rang true, something that stood out a lot more for me. That was the fact that I hadn't been there for Avraham, just like in my dream when he was in hospital. There was so much to get my head around; I didn't know where to begin.

I wondered why I had dreamt all I did; all I knew at that

point was that I badly wanted the life I had in the dream. I knew that wasn't real, but I had to change if I was ever to have even a small part of it.

I never believed dreams could happen, but I could try to make my life better.

I couldn't control what happened, but I realised I could control myself which empowered me; for the first time in my life I wanted to take back control. The nurse came back a couple of minutes later.

"I'm finishing now but Essie will be in to take over. Hey, it'll be alright."

I only smiled at her as she walked out. I felt completely alone now, I didn't feel great physically, either, or any way for that matter; my mind was in overload. I lost complete track of time as I stared up at the ceiling. Soon there was a tap on the door, I glanced over; it was Avraham.

"Ishmael, I am so glad you're awake, how are you?

I just looked at him then turned away.

"Ishmael?"

"I am not quite sure, Avraham; I had a dream, another life I didn't want to leave. I don't understand why, I should be grateful to be here but I'm not; I'm so confused. Wait, Jonah, is he okay, are you okay?"

"All is well, Ishmael, but yes, you're lucky to be here; saying you don't want to be, alarms me. I can't comment till I understand why you feel that, but it was just a dream, Ishmael. However, it's obvious it's had a strong impact on you."

"It was a dream, but I want it, Avraham; I want that life. Oh, I don't know, I only know that I must change now; would you help me?"

"Yes, I'd be happy to, you don't allow anyone in but I'm your friend, Ishmael; trust me?"

"I've been a terrible one, I've been selfish, I've not thought about anyone; I hate myself right now, I know that much."

"That's not going to help, you've been through a lot,

you've lost a lot, but you're a good man underneath."

I looked over at him, stunned: it was very like what he had said in my dream. I felt freaked out by it; in a way I was scared. I was moving my head side to side, it was too strange for me to comprehend. Avraham looked concerned now.

"Ishmael, what is it? Are you alright?"

"I dreamed you said almost the same thing; what is happening to me, Avraham?"

He sat in thought for a moment, not sure what to make of it either. He knew I was disturbed by it, but he hadn't come across it before, either; he turned to me.

"Maybe the dream was trying to tell you something or show you things you needed to see? Telling me about it may help me make some sense of it for you; I'm at a loss otherwise."

I took a breath, I thought maybe it'd help us bond better; it would certainly explain my confusion to him. Also, being able to talk would help put things into perspective even a little, he always made sense to me; so, I told him everything. His facial expressions changed. He laughed, was empathetic, amused with some parts; he listened to others with a serious expression on his face. I didn't, however, tell him of the night I shared with Betty: that was irrelevant, plus I wanted to keep that part to myself. When I finished, he pulled his chair close to my bed.

"That was some dream, Ishmael. I see your confusion. Hmm, it occurred to me that maybe it's a look at what you could have, what you're capable of in all areas of your life. Change for you seems urgent now, I know Rabbi still cares; he was good to you when we first arrived. Ishmael, you don't have to throw everything away; make changes, only then will your life get better.

"You almost died, Ishmael, through loss of control, there is so much more to you inside. Take the chance; people are here to help"

I sat thinking now, taking in all that he had said.

"You're right, maybe it'll help me too, would you bring me a pen with some paper in tomorrow?"

"Yes, that's no problem but why?"

"To make some notes, I meant what I said about changing; it starts now, Avraham"

He laughed, patting my shoulder.

"Yes, Ishmael. Well, visiting hours are over; I must go. I'll be back tomorrow. Don't dwell on what's gone, look to the future now."

"Thank you for coming, Avraham, see you tomorrow."

"I'm always here, Ishmael; always, goodbye."

I soon fell asleep again; I had no dream of Betty or any idea how things would turn out, but I still slept peacefully. It had been a long time since I had that in real life; I was grateful for it.

I was soon awoken by Essie coming to do her rounds. Slightly groggy with blurry eyes, I sat up. I couldn't take my eyes off her: not only because she was beautiful, but she looked a lot like Betty had done; the resemblance was uncanny.

I was drawn to her, she glanced over often with a smile while preparing to do my checks. I became aware I was staring; feeling slightly awkward I looked away.

"Hey, I'm Essie, I'll be looking after you; arm please? I noticed you staring at me?"

"I'm sorry, you just remind me of someone; she was beautiful too."

She blushed by this, trying to keep a professional attitude.

"Well aren't you the charmer, were you two very close?"

I didn't know how to answer this, I put my head down. I missed Betty painfully; even though it was a dream. I felt it

153

was real in my awakening, I felt genuine grief over her. Essie appeared to see my awkwardness; she spoke quickly.

"It's alright, you don't have to tell me anything; looks like you are on the mend, you'll be right in no time."

I felt the urge to explain things now, she would probably think I was crazy, but that didn't faze me; I grabbed her arm.

"It's a long story; a crazy one too. As for being right in no time? I'm not convinced."

"Well, for now, you are my last patient as you were sleeping, I have some free time?"

"You don't want to hear it; I know you will have better things to do."

She put her hand on my arm, smiling warmly.

"No, not for a while, we can chat; I'd like that. I can listen too, it's part of my job."

She was persistent, so for the second time today I talked about my dream. She seemed fascinated by it, she never once looked at me judgmentally; just had her hand on my arm while listening. We talked for a while, but I knew I was keeping her from her work.

"Essie, I know you will think me crazy, I just can't make sense of it; do you have to go?"

She looked at me then sighed, taking my hand.

"Ishmael, I can't comment on your personal life, but I may be able to explain your reason for staring at me when we first met. See, all the time you were sleeping, I came to talk to you. Perhaps you heard my voice subconsciously, for I have told you all my secrets. This may seem unprofessional, Ishmael, but, well, I feel like I know you some way, I don't know why I did it either; I was just drawn to you, for me that is a first."

"Yes, it would explain why I stared, I knew it was more than your looks, the resemblance. My subconscious will know you; I, however, don't, it is very peculiar."

She just smiled at me. I couldn't help but feel a connection with her; now I knew why. She was so like Betty; I was intrigued by that but also by her, too. For her to sit listening to my dream, to give support along with encouragement, that must have meant something, right? Maybe I was overthinking things. I was desperate to have what I did in the dream; perhaps it was just fantasy having her there. I wanted her to go, but at the same time... I didn't, I wanted to know her.

Everything had changed since I woke up, now I needed to think, it seemed to get more complicated with her there; this caused me to become stressed. Essie became aware of it.

"Ishmael, are you okay?"

"Essie, thank you for listening, for your words, but I need you to go; I'm sorry, I..."

"It's okay, Ish, I understand. I'll come back to check on you in a while; it is still my job after all."

"What did you just say?"

"Sorry, what?"

"Only Betty called me that, I'm sorry Essie, I didn't mean to sound aggressive. But I just found it strange; everything is right now."

"It's alright I can appreciate that, but I won't call you it again; I just have a habit of shortening people's names."

"No, I don't mind; you just caught me by surprise, that's all."

"Well, I'll leave you alone for a while, see you later, Ish."

She gave me a wink then left the room. I felt a warmness in me I hadn't felt before; at least not in the real world. I couldn't wait till she came back; possibly in time I could ask her out. I knew that I wanted to, although whether she said, yes, was another matter.

In the morning the doctor came back. I was feeling much better now; I was sitting up in bed. He assessed me while writing things down on his clipboard.

"Things look good for you, Ishmael, we may be able to let you go home in a day or two; we just need to do a few more tests first."

I just looked at him; anyone would be pleased by this, but I wasn't, far from it. I wouldn't see Essie; I didn't know her well enough to ask her out yet, especially based on feelings I didn't know were real or not. I was embarrassed too: what was once a nice home had gradually become a dump now. It only inspired me to do better, but I couldn't do anything till I got out.

I looked forward to Avraham coming in soon, getting his side of things always helped; maybe he could give me some light as to what to do regarding Essie. She was due to come to work soon; I hoped I would have a better outlook than I did yesterday. I was given some breakfast, I didn't know coffee and toast could taste so good: I couldn't eat them quickly enough. While I was stuffing my face, Essie walked in, very much amused by it.

"Morning, Ish, you haven't lost your appetite I see?"

I laughed at this, while trying to swallow the bit of toast I was eating. Wiping my face, I then turned to her.

"This is so good, I didn't know I was so hungry."

"Well you've been comatose for over five months, Ish; you're going to be."

"What? Five months? I need to go, why didn't anyone tell me?"

I went to get up, shocked by hearing that, but she hurried over, placing her hand on my shoulder gently.

"Woah, because you still need to rest: it's important for your recovery, please, Ish?"

I sat back down, I knew she cared, that was obvious; I just didn't know if it was professional, or because she liked me.

"Why do you care if I go or not: that's not your job?"

"No, but I would lose my favourite patient. Okay, Ish? I probably shouldn't say this, but I sensed something yesterday. I want to get to know you, help you; think it's something I am meant to do."

I was taken aback by this, she likes me but thinks she is meant to help me, but is that it? I felt confused again: she was gorgeous, but I would be nobody's burden. I didn't hesitate to say so.

"I felt a connection too, Essie, but I won't be a burden to you; I can manage on my own."

"No, Ish; you don't seem the type that would want to burden anyone. I want to because I like you more than anything; it is something that I can't explain. I've haven't stopped thinking about you, Ish; that's strange for me, too."

We just stared at each other now. I saw passion in her eyes, I knew then that she meant what she said, she didn't see me as a charity case; she, just like Betty, saw more.

"Essie, I may be allowed home in a day or two; I won't see you for you to do anything."

"You can leave your address, I'll come to see you, check you are alright?"

"No, I mean, well, my place is a dump, Essie. I wouldn't have you there; I couldn't."

"I don't care about that; I will help you sort it out, that is if you would like me too?"

I wanted to just kiss her at that point; I thought she was amazing. Now I couldn't wait to leave here to spend some proper time with her, even if it was just sorting things out.

"Yes, I'd like that, Essie."

She gave me a kiss on the cheek; I closed my eyes as she did it, I felt a tingling right through me. I couldn't help but compare it to the dream: I questioned whether she was the same as Betty had been. My instinct told me she was, but my head told me to not be too hasty. I didn't know what to think; I could only wait now in the hope that my instinct was right.

"Me too; I'll see you later, Ish."

She left, and I sat in thought for a couple of minutes. Soon Avraham came knocking on the door.

"Ishmael, you are looking a lot better; how are you feeling?"

"Fantastic, I can't wait to get out of here, Avraham."

"Ishmael, I was thinking about something: have you thought about your alcohol issue? Perhaps some help will keep you on the level?"

"I haven't thought about it, but I meant what I said about changing my life; I will have to deal with what comes, maybe it's something to consider, although I am not an alcoholic."

"You were dependent, Ishmael, denial won't help; life is a lot different out there to in here. I just fear for you again, you really scared me, I didn't think you would ever wake up. I'm trying to be your friend, that's all."

"I can see that, you're right, Avraham; if it eases your mind I'll see what's available. I feel good for now; maybe I'm over the worst?"

"You have come from a coma; another world where everything was wonderful to a degree. You have only faced that reality in here, you still need to face it at home; you must prepare yourself. I won't go through that again, Ishmael, but if you do not care then why should I?"

"Avraham, I do care. I just, well, I don't know how to show that. I have asked the same question, but a second chance has been given to me; I won't waste it. I don't know what the future holds but any negatives will not beat me down again."

He looked at me, unconvinced; but he knew it would be hard. Being a strong person to just thinking you was; well that was entirely different. It did get me wondering: would it be so simple just to stop the drink? Walk out of the hospital almost a new man? Seeing it from that point made me comprehend the fact that it was not realistic: I had a struggle ahead, but I didn't know how I would face it. That's why Avraham was so concerned, I was grateful for his honest view; I saw things clearer because of him.

"You are deep in thought, Ishmael, I…"

"I see your point of view; I have been unrealistic that is clear, but maybe that will help me? I don't know what to do; I just don't want this life anymore."

"I won't abandon you, Ishmael; I will help as much as I can, but you must not shut me out. Whatever you need just ask. I've bought you a notepad with some pens."

"Thank you, Avraham, I may be out tomorrow or the day after."

"Well, I will let you get some rest. I'll come back tonight; remember what I've said, that's a start. Jonah misses you."

"I miss him too, it'll be nice to see him again; goodbye, Avraham."

He put his thumb up while walking out. I was left with my thoughts again. I reached for the notepad but started feeling somewhat fearful: everything I did, or things that were said, were so like the dream. I sat there in a daze, not sure what to even write now; only the feeling of anger building by the second was clear, the extent of it was unexpected. People acted normally; but for me inside my head, normal was so far from my reality. Frustrated, I pushed the paper to the side then screamed out.

"WHAT HAVE YOU DONE TO ME? ENOUGH IS ENOUGH, DO YOU HEAR ME? I CAN'T DO THIS, I TRY, I TRY BUT FOR WHAT? Why bring me back? WHY?"

I threw my hands over my face then heard someone hurriedly come to the room; it was Essie. I had no idea she was still around; suddenly I felt idiotic. I saw the shock on her face, my first thought was that was it: there is no way she would want to help me now.

"Ish? Hey, whatever is wrong? Come here."

I was as shocked as she was when she gave me a hug, it

was clear I was distressed, but she never hesitated to give me some comfort. However, I pushed her away: even that had a too familiar moment, I felt like I was losing my mind.

"Essie, I'm out of the dream but I feel I'm still in it: everything I do, things people say. I don't know what's real or not anymore; I just feel so angry, people acting normal but for me nothing is. I…"

"Ish, I know, you are seeing it all as a negative but it's not; you are realising your fears. You've had an unusual experience; you're bound to feel highly emotional, as well as unstable. Hey, but it will be alright. All this is real, me, Avraham, hospital; that's your reality, it will take time to adjust."

"What about when I leave? It's all going to change again; I am not sure if I will handle that alone. I want to change, Avraham said I must, and he is right; I'm just not sure I am strong enough."

"Things will change, Ish, that's why I want to help you; you're not alone, not anymore. Have some faith, you are much stronger than you think; you will get through this"

"You are amazing, Essie: I haven't known someone like you, well, other than Betty."

"Ish, that's sweet, but I'm no more amazing than you are crazy."

"To me you have been, thank you for coming; I feel so lost, I just snapped."

"Oh, Ish, it's my pleasure; you're only human, remember that."

She winked at me again then gazed into my eyes, I couldn't resist the next move or know why I did it. I moved in to kiss her, but to my embarrassment she pulled away.

"Ish, not here, I'm sorry; it's just I could lose my job. I am still on duty for a while."

I felt myself going red, lost in the moment I hadn't give it a thought. Seeing my humiliation, she grabbed my chin, turning my head towards her.

"Ish, don't be embarrassed: it's fine. I am not saying I

don't want too, it's just not the right time, not here."

"I didn't think, nor could I help myself, I'm sorry, Essie: I never meant to make you feel awkward."

"I don't, I just like my job as much as I like you; listen, when you get out we can do something if you want too?"

"Are you asking me out on a date?"

"Yes, something like that."

She looked at me, grinning, then thought for a moment before turning her head away; she looked up.

"It looks like our date may come sooner, Ish: you're doing great."

"Yes, I feel it: thanks to you. Oh, it's a yes by the way."

She looked at me then smiled again.

"See you later, Ish."

She had almost walked out of the door when I called out:

"Gee Gee"

She popped her head back in looking amused.

"Gee Gee? What's that?"

"Goodbye gorgeous, it's a habit I seem to have."

I winked at her as she walked away laughing. I couldn't believe she asked me to go out; she was so calm about her feelings compared to me. She captivated me; I hoped I would get the chance to express my feelings, feelings that were growing considerably more.

I was on cloud nine for a while after that, I saw Avraham that evening, then Essie popped in to say goodnight later on. I thought of everything they had both said to me; I felt much calmer now mentally. I figured I needed to enjoy the moments life gave, to not overthink situations which would send me on a downwards spiral again.

I had to take each day as it came; to make the most of it. My dream would always be a part of me, it'd come to light when I had to change something in my life. The dream wasn't real, but my reality now was. I had to want it, be willing to work for it, too; but I wasn't afraid of that. Only fear of the unknown had caused instability before; but I had to control that by whatever means necessary now.

I was afraid of losing more people, of letting anyone in then having them taken. But I also knew that by not doing so I wouldn't make it next time; I knew there could've been a next time. Now, though, I had Essie. I knew she would keep me on the right path, help me conquer my demons, but I was still unsure of how things would turn out between us.

I just had to take a chance like Avraham had said; to try without messing things up again. I had had no more flashbacks yet, but I didn't know if that was because I had so many other things to think about, or whether what had happened since had healed me in some way. I could only wait to find that out.

In the morning the doctor came back, smiling and looking pleased.

"Well, your results have come back clear; you are good to go home today. However, I must stress: the alcohol is having effect on your liver, you must stop. This is no joke Ishmael."

I didn't expect this, but it was no real surprise either. I had drunk whiskey as well as vodka straight for a few years, now it had taken its toll. Avraham was always there, I owed it to him to make up for my ways or I would lose a very good friend; I didn't want to lose anyone else, not ever.

"I will do what it takes, doctor, I'm not going to mess this up."

"I'm going to refer you for some counselling, Ishmael, it may really help."

I wasn't as quick to accept this: I never liked speaking to anyone about my issues, especially with people I didn't know. I knew it wouldn't help me because I would not be comfortable; I wasn't going to waste his time.

"Doctor, I appreciate it but it's not really for me, I have

people who will help; I really think I will be alright now."

"Ishmael, I can't let you go until something is in place, it's my duty; just think about it, let me refer you. If when the time comes you still feel the same, then that's fine; but, Ishmael, it will be there if you need it. Give it a chance: you just never know, it could turn out to be very important for you?"

He made sense when he put it like that, everything could turn upside down again leaving me with nothing. If I was really going to change regardless, then it would be sensible to accept this; so, I did.

"Okay, doctor, you can refer me; thank you."

"It's the wise choice. Right then, you are all set: you will be discharged when Essie does her last checks."

"Thank you for everything, doctor, I won't forget it."

"It's my pleasure, you take care of yourself do you hear me? I don't want to see you back here, Ishmael. I wish you the very best."

"Yes, I hear you. Thank you, doctor. Goodbye."

I was excited to be leaving but also nervous, I had to speak to Avraham who was due in shortly, let him know my feelings, keeping them hidden was not going to help me. I knew if he was to help, he needed to know these things. I was busy packing when Essie came in.

"Morning, Ish, how are you doing? I'm discharging you."

"I'm doing okay, hmm, can't get rid of me quick enough I see?"

She started laughing at this: it was obvious she didn't expect that reply. She turned to me.

"Of course, I'd have got you out quicker if I could, Ish."

She winked again, making me grin now. It distracted me for a moment from the anxiety which I felt, I sat in thought as she did her last checks. However, she noticed I had gone quiet.

"Ish? Hey, you've gone quiet on me?"

"I'm sorry Essie, I'm just, err…"

"You are nervous?"

"Yes, I am not sure what to expect, other than seeing my dog."

"It'll be fine, Ish, don't allow this to stress you before you even leave. I'll tell you what: I'm free tonight, why don't we do something if you're up to it? It'll help with your first night back. You have a dog, what is his name?"

"It's Jonah, my husky, don't you have anything better to do?"

"Ish? I wouldn't ask if I did, meet me at the pier about seven?"

"I'll be there. Essie, hey, thank you."

"What for? I'll look forward to it, Ish."

"Not as much as I will, see you tonight."

"See you tonight."

Avraham arrived a few minutes later, surprised to see me packing the last of my things.

"Ishmael, what's going on?"

"I'm being discharged, Avraham: they are letting me go home."

"You seem saddened by this, what's wrong, Ishmael?"

I pulled him towards the bed then sat him down.

"I'm not sad, I'm nervous: scared I'll mess up, worried I'll lose people, start drinking again, I don't know what to expect, I…"

"Ishmael, yes, you will be: I know this isn't going to be easy. But I'm there anytime, day or night; don't forget that. If things become too much you call anytime, you aren't alone. Come, I will take you home; try to not stress otherwise its beating you already."

"I know I am overthinking, but I can't help it; I am glad I have you by my side, Avraham, I appreciate that."

I patted his shoulder, and he looked at me sternly.

"You will get through this, Ishmael, I know you will; you need to believe it too."

"In time maybe I will, but thank you for the encouragement."

Avraham picked up the notepad, staring at it for a moment before looking up at me.

"Ishmael, I remember some of the things you wrote: they were very moving. Perhaps writing again will help too, you have great potential."

"I have thought about it; I tried but became angry, my mind went blank. I don't know, maybe I can't anymore."

"You have a natural gift for it, maybe now you can't but that is understandable: you have had so much to adjust to, still have. But Ishmael, just don't give up trying. Finding your writing again can inspire many people; it'll also keep you grounded."

His words made me think, especially with the dream touching on it too. I used to love writing but life separated us. I had forgotten about it, maybe it was a way out for me; but possibly, it could do me more harm. For now, I was happy not knowing either way. I gathered my things taking a last look around. Avraham touched me on the arm gently.

"Come on, Ishmael, if you're ready let's go?"

"I've been here for five months, I'm only aware of the last couple of days; so much has happened, it's so strange, Avraham."

"Yes, Ishmael, but this is only a small part of your life, you don't belong here; we must all move on, we have to."

"I can only aim for that, Avraham. Okay, I think I'm ready."

10 ISHMAEL FINDS PURPOSE

It was a bizarre feeling: I had been there for months with no idea about any of it. I had felt somewhat glad to be there upon waking, I felt safe under the watchful eyes of the doctors; but now I would be left alone somewhere I hated. I didn't want to go back, but it helped knowing I wasn't alone. I had accepted I needed to change; I had been through enough now. My thought was: surely my life would continue to get better from this point?

We left the hospital; I was blinded by the natural light, the room I was in had given barely any. It was raining hard, but I just laughed as I walked out into it without a care, arms stretched out. Avraham glared at me.

"Ishmael, whatever is so funny?"

I turned to look at him with an eyebrow raised.

"Do I really need to explain?"

"Aah, no Ishmael, I don't think you do; I'm glad the dream can give you good reminders, too. Come on we can grab a taxi."

We headed to one that had just pulled up. Hurrying over we soon got inside; we were soaked. I was so excited to be seeing Jonah, just as much as I was Essie. I hoped the rain would ease by the evening.

Driving home, I was familiar with my surroundings; it was so different to my dream with dark and derelict areas even the sun couldn't brighten. Grayness overshadowed everywhere giving the streets an uninviting look.

My only thought was that I had to get out of here. We stopped at some lights and, turning my head to wonder around, I noticed a homeless guy sitting there. He looked so cold, almost beaten, yet he was smiling at people passing who ignored him, just hoping for a coin or two.

That second changed my whole perspective, I had a very strong urge to go over to him.

"Driver, pull over here for a minute, near that man, please, it's important."

Avraham was confused by this sudden outburst, his annoyance becoming obvious.

"Ishmael, what are you doing?"

"Just give me a minute, please Avraham; I'll explain in a minute."

I jumped out as the driver pulled over. I ran to the man sitting there; standing over I bent down to him.

"Sir, how do you do that?"

He looked up at me, then turned away.

"Do what?"

"You manage to smile, even though you are on the streets? Why is that?"

He looked up at me again; he must have thought I was insane, but he laughed shaking his head. Now he looked at me solemnly.

"Son, I am alive, I see the rain, I feel the wind; I am still luckier than some. We must all count our blessings, I never lose hope; that's why I can smile."

I was completely overwhelmed by this: those words hit me hard. He was amazing. I thought, here is a guy with nothing other than his blessings grasping onto hope, and that was enough to make him smile and get him through the hard days on the dull streets. He completely knocked me for six, I rummaged around in my pockets.

"Sir, what is your name?"

"Richie."

"Richie, you are so inspirational: you blew me away with those words, thank you so much. I will never forget them or your name. Here, I only have some change, but you can come by mine anytime for a coffee; it would be my pleasure."

He looked shocked by this offer; but I was drawn to him instantly. I felt the need to help him; it was a risk as I didn't know him, but he had touched me inside in a way nobody had, possibly changed my life. I felt that I was in debt to him.

"Son, don't worry about me, it's a kind offer but I am nobody's problem, I will cope on my own."

"Richie, I know; it's why I offered. Look, take my address, I only live down the road, if you change your mind then you're always welcome. I was told to take options today as you don't know when you'll need them?"

Now it was his turn to look surprised by my bit of wisdom; he gave me a smile.

"Okay Son, I will, thank you."

"No: thank you, Richie, goodbye."

I give him my address then ran back to the car. I was soaked but I didn't care, my thoughts had changed. I felt inspired to help: change how people were living. I had no idea how, but maybe Richie was a start if I saw him again. But if I never did, then he had given me reason, purpose; I was determined to do something good. I got back into the car; Avraham did not look amused.

"Ishmael what on earth has got into you?"

"That guy, he is remarkable; I want to help him as well as others like him. He smiles because he's thankful for his blessings, he still has hope; he has nothing, Avraham. That man did something for me, my whole perspective has changed; he has potentially changed my life."

He stared at me amazed by this, for the first time he was speechless; I spoke again.

"Avraham, you know how you said to believe in myself?"

"Yes, Ishmael?"

"Well now I do: for the first time in my life I believe I have a purpose. I don't know where to start, but I will fulfil it."

He looked at me warmly now, he saw my passion along with determination I didn't even know I had till that point. I had a long way to go personally, still needing to fight my own issues, but I had reason to get up. I had a real focus now; that was a surreal moment for me. I was no longer worried about going home, or what would happen next: I was ready to take on anything life threw at me now.

The driver pulled up to my flat; I looked at it. It was tired looking, worn out, but I felt so lucky now to even have it; I smiled at Avraham as he got out of the car.

"Shall we go in then?"

I think he found my enlightening moment comical: giving a little chuckle. He followed me up the steps then inside, I was stunned. I stared around for a minute before I turned to him.

"Wow, Avraham, what have you done?"

"I cleaned a little, Ishmael, I know you were nervous coming back with the state it was in; well it was easy to see why. I thought it would help?"

I just gave him a hug now, I couldn't help it; a smile became apparent, too. Avraham had his annoying moments, sometimes too serious, but he was a true friend. I was dumbstruck by his kindness for me, his passion for wanting to get me on my feet. I guess his seriousness at times was another blessing, he motivated me which I needed, especially now.

"You're welcome Ishmael, you have some things in; I will bring Jonah round tomorrow. I'll let you get settled, do you need anything else?"

"No, Avraham, this is great, I'm very lucky, thank you."

"Yes, things will be fine; but you know where I am if you

need me. Ishmael? I mean it, call me anytime; see you tomorrow."

"I will, Avraham, see you tomorrow; thank you again."

He left, leaving me alone. I looked around in disbelief: he had really worked hard on this, my respect for him shot right up. Even if I hadn't met Richie, this would have lightened the mood for me considerably; I recognised that. I was blessed having someone who cared so much: he proved it by his actions. I started to think about writing again, I had a few hours to spare before I met Essie.

Now with a calmer mind, I thought about giving it another go. I made a coffee before I rummaged around in my bag for the writing material; digging it out, I sat down. Sitting in thought with the pen to my lip, daydreaming, I wondered about what to even write.

Going through things in my mind, I knew I only wanted to write about a specific thing. It would be a challenge, but I also knew in my darkest days it would bring some comfort, even give me some real light. So, with a smile spreading on my face, I began writing.

I chuckled to myself: thinking that I wished I had that typewriter, it'd be so much easier on the hand now, but I wasn't going to let that put me off. After a while I noticed just how much I had missed it. The words flowed easily this time, almost like I was meant to do this now; it was odd. Conscious of the time, I found myself not wanting to stop: I was enjoying the moment, getting everything off my mind. I felt so relaxed, I knew I was at the place where I was meant to be right then.

I glanced at the clock; it was five thirty now. I reluctantly put the pen down before I looked to see how much I had written; I even surprised myself at the twelve pages. It would soon be time to meet Essie, if not for doing so, I would have written so much more. However, the excitement to see her soon dragged me away. I went to get a shower; tidy myself up before I headed out.

I put on my good shirt along with my pants, I had some

aftershave my parents got me for my sixteenth birthday before they died; which I sprayed on sparingly. I looked up at the ceiling as I put it on: thanking them. I really missed them a lot; I hoped that one day I would be able to make them proud.

I was finally ready, so made my way to the pier; nerves were now setting in. I wondered if she would turn up, whether the connection would still be strong. If what happened between us at the hospital was real; my feet couldn't take me there quick enough. I arrived, and turning around a corner I saw her; it wasn't seven yet, but Essie was looking around, waiting.

She looked beautiful with a black dress on, now much taller with the heels she wore; her hair was falling on her shoulders, over a little jacket. My first thought was the dream: how Essie looked brought back that night Betty and I had spent together. I started feeling an array of emotions as I stood looking over, only the squabbles of birds nearby forced me out of it. Composing myself with a breath, trying to push it all aside, I walked over, quietly tapping her on the shoulder. She turned around quickly, laughing to see it was me.

"Ish, you made me jump."

"Sorry, Essie, you look gorgeous; have you been here long?"

"You're sweet, no, I just arrived a couple of minutes ago; how's your day been?"

I pulled her to a nearby bench, sitting her down. The rain had ceased but there was still a chill in the air, nevertheless, it was pleasant enough.

"Interesting, very interesting: things seem good up to now, it's been quite a day."

She looked at me curiously, so I told her about Richie first, then about me starting to write again. I also mentioned what I wanted to do next; she stared at me admirably.

"Ish, that's fantastic, you can do anything you put your mind too; just don't give up dreaming, having a focus will get you far."

I stared into her eyes, listening to what she said, I knew we would go the distance even then. I was falling for her too easily; it scared me, but it felt right with her. I had wanted to kiss her since I laid eyes on her, the hospital was inappropriate but I felt the moment to do it now was perfect. However, I still hesitated: I wanted to be sure of it, but bringing it up would've spoilt the moment. I put my head down, becoming quiet again.

"Ish?"

I looked up to see her smiling.

"I have wanted to kiss you for a while, Essie, ever since I got here. I know it's the first date, probably much too soon, but I'm so drawn to do it, I'm sorry I…"

"I feel I have known you so much longer, Ish, in which case we are late for it, I think?"

She grinned at me; I didn't think twice now. I leaned in to kiss her; she put her hand behind my head to kiss me back, another familiar moment. There were no stars or clear skies, but I felt the same feeling I had in my dream, just as much passion. It was just as magical; just as strange. I knew without any clouded judgement she was very special. I continued kissing her; I didn't want to stop, only for the sound of voices coming did she pull away.

"Not all urges are wicked, it wasn't bad, Ish."

She winked at me as the people strolled past, she stood up wandering out a little. I laughed at this comment. I knew she was only teasing, but I was more than happy to tease her back.

"Oh really? Well I'm sure we can do better, Essie?"

She put her arm out, so I took her hand. Pulling me to her, she did another all too familiar Betty thing: whispering in my ear.

"Not sure that's possible really, Ish."

I beamed at this, I couldn't help it; she didn't hide her

flirtatious ways, she used them just at the right time, too. The moment felt just as good as the kiss did. It was really quick to have happened which gave some doubt; but it still felt so right. I knew it was just me. I was confident that if she was in my life, then things would always be good; just as it had been with Betty.

"So, what do you want to do, Essie? It's becoming colder, shall we go somewhere for a coffee or…?"

"In a minute, kiss me again, Ish?"

Standing there I smiled, before I kissed her again. I soon forgot where we were, even though the chill that was lingering had increased a lot more now. She made me feel special; it felt like we were the only two people in the world when we were close. Pulling away I noticed her shivering: the coldness was very apparent now, so we headed to a late-night cafe. Walking I was thinking: she was so like Betty, her looks, her words, her ways too. Part of it was hard, but having someone resemble Betty so much I knew I was incredibly lucky. Deep inside I thought that God, or some higher power, had stepped in: by bringing her just when I needed it. I thought that the dream regarding Betty, specifically, was to help prepare me for Essie. I thought it crazy in one way, but I didn't believe in coincidence either: I thought there was always more, I believed it to be the reason. She was the perfect person to help me, along with Avraham; in time I knew I could really love her, just as I had done Betty.

I told her about my life, all that had happened. I wanted to give her reasons why my life had turned out the way it did. We spoke for a couple of hours; she just listened. I knew I could tell her anything; I felt such a release knowing that.

I needed to get everything out: I could start to heal then, eventually put the past behind me. It was small steps but it helped massively. Suddenly I was aware it had all been about me up to now; as much as she didn't mind, I did. I wanted to know more about her, about her life. Once I started talking I couldn't stop, but I felt slightly guilty; I quickly turned to her.

"Essie, what about you? I suspect you must be fed up listening to me."

"No, Ish, I'm not, really. I can see you needed to but it's okay, I don't mind. Well, my life has been eventful too, I don't know my father, he left when I was three; he never returned. I don't speak to my mum, she abandoned me in my teens, but she was never there either. I brought myself up really, I got involved with drugs heavily when I was younger; I wasn't a nice person. It was only being admitted to hospital for an overdose, where I almost didn't make it, that I decided I wanted to change, too, become a nurse. They are the only ones who ever really cared what happened to me; life is hard, but we can get through it."

I knew she hadn't had it easy, her eyes showed the sadness within, all the wisdom she possessed told of many experiences; I came to realise just how extraordinary she was. I wanted her to have the best of everything; I wanted to love her, not ever let her go through something alone again. She was special, but until now I had no idea just how much.

"Essie, you're incredible, but I care now; I will always be there for you, you're not alone anymore."

I took her hand: giving it a kiss. She gazed into my eyes then smiled. Her shoulders relaxed like a weight had been lifted.

"I hate what you've been through but I'm so glad I met you Ish; without you being admitted we may never have crossed paths."

"No, Essie, I'm honoured to have met you; to have the chance to get to know you. I think you're an inspiration, really. I'm stunned you are so beautiful inside, after what you have been through; I want you to know that."

"Oh, Ish, you're a sweetheart, I have learned from my

lessons, grown from them. I didn't have a choice, but I am thankful for them: it's made me who I am, but I'm not amazing, just me."

I knew she found it hard to take a compliment: that was clear. I also felt saddened that she had been through that much, yet she could still doubt herself. I knew there was more she hadn't said, but I didn't want to force her; I just wanted her to see what I did in her, for her to be happy. I knew being back in the real world it would take time, but I vowed to help her just as much as she had me. The waitress came over informing us it was time to shut the café. Finishing our coffee we hurriedly stood up; I grabbed her, giving her a hug.

"Whatever it is, Essie, you can tell me; I just want you to be happy, I will help if I can."

She hugged me harder then pulled away, tears now in her eyes which alarmed me.

"I'm sorry, Ish, I am alright; come on we must go."

I followed her out, now concerned about her; she was really hurting about something, but I felt hopeless. I couldn't let her go without knowing she was going to be okay.

"Hey, I'm sorry, Essie: I can't let you go so upset, please, what is it?"

"I have kids, Ish, or rather I did; I don't blame you if you don't want to bother now, I just…"

"Essie, are you serious? I am not going anywhere. I see how troubled you are, but I am too. I meant what I said: if I can help anyway then I will. Now, put that gorgeous smile back, it will all work out you'll see."

She flung herself at me, almost knocking me over, details could wait. I knew now she would confide in me, but I wasn't going to press her for any more. I just couldn't let her go home so upset. I hoped now she would sleep well:

she was tormented with the issue, as well as having to tell me. Nonetheless, she had some peace, at least for now anyway. I walked her to get a taxi, I was reluctant to let her go but it was getting late; she had to work the next day. I hadn't enjoyed a night so much for a long time, all thanks to Essie. We arrived at the taxi rank; I opened the car door.

"Hey, I have Jonah back tomorrow, you're more than welcome to come around after work; we could go for a walk?"

"I would like that, thank you for tonight, Ish; it's been great."

"That's because you're great; come here."

"You're still as charming as ever, Ish?"

"Might have to prove that one, a kiss should do it?"

She grinned at me then, for the last time tonight, I kissed her. It was Essie who didn't want to let me go now; I held her until the driver interrupted us, sounding fed up.

"Are you getting in or what?"

She let me go, then got in the car.

"Goodnight, Ish."

"Gee, Gee."

I winked at her then shut the door, she laughed while waving until the driver pulled away. It had been a long night, but I was happy. I knew Essie was much happier, too; this eased my mind considerably. I walked home deep in thought: thinking about all that had happened. I tried to decide what to do next, but for now I had no answers; I was content with that. I soon came to the spot where I first saw Richie; I saw no sign of him. The streets were completely derelict now as darkness had descended, shadows had covered every crack, cradled every tree that was around, too. I hoped he was alright, that he had maybe found a bed for the night. but again, I could only wonder.

In the morning I was up early, I contemplated the night before. Wondering how Essie was feeling, I felt distracted now which was, to me, a good thing. She was a priority now; I wanted to really help her.

For a mother or father to be pulled from their children, for whatever reason, would be the most heart-breaking thing to go through. The guilt as well as the sheer sadness she must have felt which was still so visible, that was so difficult to see.

She had come so far yet was still so tormented by her past. I vowed to do all I could to make the situation better, although I had no idea of how. It would be something which we would have to sit together to discuss if she wanted to, try to work through it. I was willing to do that, just to see her happy.

I decided to do some more writing before Avraham arrived; it would turn my thoughts from overthinking to being productive, it was a blessing for now. Without it, there was a chance I could easily have gone down another path where I would be no help to anyone. I was distracted by Essie, and had also found a focus, but I had by no means recovered from the dream. I was still adjusting to the reality I'd come into. After a while I heard Avraham knocking at the door. I got up and went to answer it. Opening it I was very surprised to see who was standing there, completely soaked through.

"Richie?"

"You said I could come for a coffee if I needed to?"

I stood there a bit shocked: I never thought I'd see him again. Unfortunately, he saw my reaction which led him to think he was in the way.

"I shouldn't have come, I'm sorry."

"No, don't be, honestly. Please, come in; I didn't expect to see you again, Richie, that's all."

He looked around, wondering if he was doing the right thing and if he could trust me. His eyes seemed weary and an almost questioning look showed on his face, was he wondering why I was being so kind? The smell of coffee I made earlier came wafting out; he smiled.

"If it's alright, sir; just for a little while, it's too cold now. I'm not feeling great and I remembered what you said, about taking the option if needed?"

"It's Ishmael, come in, you're soaked through. I'll make some fresh coffee then find you something dry."

"Thank you, Ishmael."

He strolled in, I wondered if I had done right: I didn't have much of value, but I didn't know him or anything about his past. My heart ruled now but I had a feeling it would be alright. I just needed to chat to him, that would help ease my mind. Avraham would not be impressed I had let a stranger in, but I would have Jonah back soon so I put it to the back of my mind. I made some fresh coffee, then found him some old clothes; he changed, then eventually came to sit down. Unintentionally I stared at him as he was sitting there, he looked lost, beaten down. The days on the streets had made him age, he looked down on the floor while holding a coffee to warm himself. His fingers had blackened and looked very worn, the hardships out there on the streets were obvious by that alone. He lifted his head, thinking for a moment before speaking until the silence became uncomfortable.

"Can I ask you something, Ishmael?"

"Yes, Richie, anything; what is it?"

"Why have you done this for me?"

He caught me off guard, I wasn't sure what context he meant it in; I had to choose my words carefully now.

"Well, I told you you've inspired me: you did something with those words. Meeting you made me want to help people like you. You gave me purpose, I can always offer a listening ear or a chat now. I was drawn to you, Richie, but I don't know why. I just know after seeing you my life has become better. I wanted to offer you a chance to have somewhere to come, make your day better as you did mine."

He listened carefully, he showed no emotion

whatsoever. I didn't know what he was thinking, he took a sip of his coffee then sat up looking puzzled.

"Ishmael, I could've been anyone, words mean nothing without actions; some would say your actions towards me were careless, but I can't have any opinion of that. You say your life has become better, how?"

"Yes, I have not had it easy either, Richie. I have just come out of hospital after five months. I was in a coma where I nearly died. There I had a dream, another life. Waking, I came to the realisation it wasn't real but I had to change my ways. Now my actions speak louder than mere words which I was used to doing before. I saw you, and instantly I knew I had to help the homeless somehow; I believe that's why I am still here."

"You have passion along with a determined mindset but, there are so many of us out there, you can't save everyone, Ishmael, at least not alone."

"Then help me, Richie? I know you're a clever man, this would help both of us."

"I don't know where I'll be one day to the next, that won't work; it's kind but I can't help."

I sat in thought for a moment; I decided to do something very risky now, but for some reason I knew he was the one that could help me regarding the homeless. I turned to him.

"Okay Richie, what if you stay here? I'll fix you a bed, help you get back on your feet. I can't send you back out there: I just can't. If I am to help, then helping you first is a start?"

"What? Are you serious? You want me to stay here? I have nothing to offer, Ishmael; I must pay my own way."

"You will: I have a dog who is due back soon, you can walk him while doing other things for me. It'd help me a lot, that can be your keep. It will be company for us both too, just till you are on your feet again."

He looked at me admirably, just looking at me. I knew that everyone deserved a chance; Avraham had given enough of them to me. But there was something about him

I couldn't put my finger on, he was a man of intelligence who had gained wisdom through his experiences. Underneath I knew he had a good heart behind his appearance, as well as the trust issues he seemed to have.

"Ishmael, I don't know what to say besides thank you, thank you very much; I will never forget this, I will repay one day."

"Richie, it's my pleasure; I ask nothing, other than to just not let me down."

He nodded his head in agreement. I got up to clear the coffee away, walking past he touched my arm.

"Ishmael, please may I get a bath? It's been so long since I had one."

I laughed at this, I was happy he felt comfortable enough to even ask.

"Yes, of course, Richie, there should be hot water available; I'll grab you some towels in a second. If you hear the door go, it's just my friend."

He got up then went to the bathroom, I got him sorted before leaving him to soak in the bath. No sooner had I sat back down when the door went again; it was Avraham with Jonah.

"Morning, Ishmael, how are you? You're looking very well."

"I am great, Avraham, come in."

Jonah popped his head round the door, as soon as he saw me he jumped all over me excitedly, with his tail wagging frantically. I had missed him something rotten.

"JONAH, hello, it's so good to see you boy, I am so glad you're back; thank you for having him, Avraham, I really appreciate it."

"He was no trouble, pleasure really. Ishmael, is there someone here?"

He noticed Richie's bag then heard someone in the bathroom. I told him about my offer to help Richie. As expected he didn't approve, but he could see I was trying. Nevertheless, he still had a few things to say regardless.

"I hope you know what you are doing: you don't know him in the slightest. I know you are keen to help, but this is your home; please Ishmael, just be careful."

"I know you mean well, but he is a good man, just a little lost. He helped me Avraham, so I want to help him, it's only temporary. I could not throw him back out on the streets, I just couldn't."

"I know, Ishmael, I am not saying to not help: only to just be aware of the consequences that may come from this. I am your friend; you have been through enough, people are not always what they seem."

"Avraham, I know but yes, I will be careful, but thank you for your concern, please, don't worry."

"I always worry, you are a really good person, Ishmael; people take advantage of kindness too easily, then leave others to pick up the pieces when they have finished with you. I fear what will happen if this should backfire, you are still not fully recovered, far from it."

Richie came out at that moment, you could see he felt awkward because he was being discussed. Jonah went to him immediately, sniffing him, just checking him out. Funnily enough he sat by him in a protective manner; no barking or warning sign, he did the complete opposite. Richie stroked his head.

"Ishmael, he is beautiful. Look, if it's a bother me being here I will go; I don't want to cause any trouble."

"No, it's fine, Richie. I want you to meet Avraham, the one person who has always been there for me; he is just looking out for me that's all, he always has."

Richie walked over then shook Avraham's hand firmly.

"Pleased to meet you, sir, I won't let him down, you have my word; I have learned to appreciate everything. I know Ishmael is a good man."

Avraham seemed surprised by this, he looked kindly at him now.

"Yes, one of the best. Ishmael? Rabbi has been asking about you, he is glad you are recovering."

"You know where I stand, Avraham, it's nice he cares but the Jewish way is not my way anymore. I need to go my own way now, getting involved would stray me from that. Thank him but that's as far as it goes."

While waiting for him to comment, Richie stepped in.

"Ishmael, it is none of my business but if I may? He sounds like he cares, don't push good people away for the sake of getting involved. Nothing can come between something if you want it enough. He may just want to be a friend; you can still have that, you may need that in the future. At least think about it?"

I was astonished by this, even Avraham looked shocked; he stared at Richie for a moment, disbelief on his face. Without a shadow of a doubt now, I knew I had done the right thing with Richie. It seemed Avraham would accept this too. He stared at him for a few seconds more before putting his head down shamefully. He put his hand on Richie's arm.

"Richie, I was wrong about you, I am sorry for being so presumptuous; that was wrong of me."

"No, Avraham it wasn't, you did the right thing; I understand that. We aren't all bad: some of us have just lost the way, but Ishmael has given me hope, I could never repay that back. I am very lucky, I'm not about to mess it up."

"Okay, Richie, remember that if you do, there will be no second chances, certainly not with me."

"Yes, I can see that, Avraham, that I understand too."

"Ishmael, I must go, Jonah seems pleased to be back; it will be strange not having him around."

"Yes, but Avraham you know where he is, where we both are."

"I do, Ishmael, I do."

11 ISHMAEL'S IDEA

Avraham seemed gloomy about bringing Jonah back. I knew he was lonely; the time I spent in hospital, Jonah had given him company.

He was such a good man; it was hard to tear them apart. Jonah had always been in my life; he was my best friend. It was only clear now that Avraham would undoubtedly have a bond with him as well, which made it even harder. We had not been close as we were in the dream, even though we had known each other years. I learned to appreciate him, to give the respect he deserved; I hoped in time, we would become closer because of it. I wanted him to know that Jonah was as much his as he was mine, I didn't want to get in the way of the good bond they had. I was happy to share Jonah with him, I wouldn't have him if not for Avraham getting him in the first place.

"You are always welcome to take him, you know that; it will be strange for him, too. You have been good to us both, Avraham, I know he will miss you, I also know you care for him."

"Well if either of you need anything then let me know. I am off to see Rabbi before I run a few errands. Oh, Ishmael? I appreciate that too."

As Avraham went to walk out Jonah followed him, he bent down stroking the dog fondly.

"Jonah, this is your home now; I will see you soon. Goodbye, Ishmael, Richie?"

"Goodbye, Avraham, nice to meet you."

He got up then left. I hadn't had a chance to welcome Jonah back so took the opportunity now to do so. I called him as he stood whining by the door after Avraham.

"Jonah, hey, Jonah; come here boy."

He came over looking at me deeply. It was a questionable look as if to say, "where have you been?" I stroked him, trying to reassure him I was here to stay. I had abandoned him in his eyes, I could only hope he would forgive me for it in time. I had been so selfish, I let him down; now I had a lot of making up to do. He moved towards me a bit more then lay his chin on my lap. Richie sat watching now; he seemed to be settling in well.

"You have a way with animals, Ishmael, that's a rare thing to see that."

"I have let him down, he has always been loyal. I abandoned him through my ways, I know he feels that. He saved my life: barked for help when I fell. I owe him everything too."

"Ishmael, you could not prevent what happened, given a choice you would have done things differently, we all make mistakes. I see the bond you have; in time he will see you still care. Changing will prove to him you're sorry; don't be too hard on yourself, maybe a walk will help?"

"Thank you, Richie, yes, that sounds like a good idea; will you come with us?"

"Oh, I'm not sure, maybe it's better you go with just you two, for now?"

"It'll be better than sitting round here all day; I will make lunch when we get back."

"Okay, Ishmael, you're right, a walk will be good."

"I'm not asking because I don't trust you; I want to be clear of that?"

"I know, Ishmael, it's nice of you to say anyway."

"I'll grab my coat, I may have a jacket while yours dries."

I dug out a spare jacket I'd been given a few years back, yet never worn. I handed it to Richie then put mine on, and put the lead on Jonah. His tail was wagging, he had a familiar look of excitement on his face; this bought the dream back. I looked at him, losing him in the dream had made me wary of putting him in any danger. I had to protect him by any means possible, always put him first. When I thought of losing him, I didn't think I would have handled the guilt as well in reality, as much as I did in the dream: he meant the world to me.

I had realised my ways, I had to recognise his importance; I now believe that's what the dream was showing me when I lost him. Like Richie said, I couldn't prevent things happening but I could help important people in my life, as well as Jonah, from suffering in any way.

We headed out, the sun was shining; but my area looked no better in the day, than it did in the night. I don't remember it being like this: maybe I was too drunk or wrapped up in my own troubles to notice. But it was tired looking, not been touched for years. It was awful to look at, it had been completely abandoned as the years passed. There were many empty buildings scattered around, which had rusted over time; such a waste when people needed somewhere to live. It gave me something to think about: there seemed a lot of homeless around the area who needed help. I suddenly stopped dead in my tracks: I had a brainwave. I found myself grabbing a very much surprised Richie.

"Ishmael?"

"Richie, we should open a shelter?"

"A shelter?"

"For the homeless, it will be hard work but it's possible, isn't it?"

"I'm not sure, Ishmael, that would cost a lot of money."

"It's worth considering, surely? It would be a start?"

"Sure, we can do that, just don't build your hopes up: it only sets you up for disappointment."

I stared at him as we walked. He wasn't very tall, average build with short brown hair, now turning grey with time. He also had an untidy beard which also had grey flecks scattered around. His skin was an olive colour and he had fine lines around his face, wrinkles were becoming noticeable over the bags under his piercing blue eyes. Now he had a much friendlier look than when I first saw him. He certainly looked like a man of great interest, which led me to a certain question.

"Richie, what's your story? How did you end up on the streets? I am only curious; you don't have to answer."

"I have made a lot of bad choices in life, I was a carpenter years ago. I tried helping someone, but it cost me my home, my family, everything. I've been homeless since. Not everyone wants to be helped, Ishmael; you must realise that too."

He looked off into the distance, he was so solemn. I wished I hadn't said anything, but I wanted to find out more about him: I could learn a lot, not just from him as a person, but from his experiences in life.

"I didn't mean to pry or upset you; I just want to get to know you a bit more, that's all."

"It's nice someone wants to know: it has been so long since anyone cared enough to even ask. I guess if I am to stay then you need to know about me; I just need time Ishmael, understand this."

I looked at him, he too had the world on his shoulders; my issues were nothing compared to others. I wanted to help him; I just hoped I had not got myself in too deep. I was happy knowing he had somewhere to stay: it would help even if only for a while. I wondered about his family, maybe that was something to consider, although it was a delicate issue which needed to be dealt with sensitively. For the moment, I didn't want to burden him with anymore worries; changing the subject quickly seemed very logical now.

"Richie, I have someone round tonight; will you be alright with that?"

"Yes, but I don't want to be in the way: I can go?"

"No, I wouldn't have asked if it was an issue; I'm just letting you know. She is lovely, Essie."

"Aah, it's a she? You seem fond of her: just by the way you speak about her, if I may say?"

"Yes, I am, very; she is special."

He only smiled at this, I didn't know what he was thinking, he only said things when confronted or a subject was bought up. He seemed interested in me just as much as I was in him; it would help if I needed to reverse the conversation. However, I had to tread carefully: being on the streets for so long, even being as wise as he was, underlying issues could be bought to the surface. I was still unsure I could handle the fallout from these. We continued walking, Jonah was happy enough. I had missed our walks. He was sniffing around, checking regularly that I was still there.

"Ishmael, I do have a daughter, I always think about her."

This came out the blue, I wasn't sure what to say; I gave it some thought before saying something random. Something untoward that didn't help.

"Have you not thought to look for her?"

I knew that was a stupid question which I regretted instantly: it sounded insensitive, but the words just fell from my mouth. He looked at me like the question was a joke.

"Of course I have, Ishmael; it's not that easy, do you think because I am homeless I don't care?"

I could've kicked myself, I thought he would storm off at that point, not look back. I had gained his trust to some extent, I thought I'd probably blown it on one careless question.

"Richie, I know you care, I am trying here, it was a random question. Forgive me, I wasn't implying anything, nor did I mean to sound so insensitive."

"I'm sorry Ishmael, I know you care; but you have much to learn. I didn't mean to snap it's just, well…"

"It's hard to talk about, I know, Richie, but if I can help in any way with it; then I will."

"Thank you, Ishmael, I am sure it will be too late now, some things are best left buried."

I wanted to tell him how much I disagreed with that remark, she would obviously be hurt, certainly angry after so long; but to do nothing would bring more regret. I knew it was not my place to push him, this had to be something that he wanted to do on his terms; I said no more about it. He was now thinking, so it was best leaving it at that; at least for the time being.

We had covered some distance, got lost in conversation without noticing. We decided to walk back to grab some lunch. On the way back Jonah started growling. Without thought as to why he was becoming aggressive my instincts, as well as my fears, came full force. I started having flashbacks of the dream where I lost him, which threw me into a state of panic.

"This isn't happening, they are not going to touch him; I'll kill them I swear. I won't let them hurt him, Richie."

I had my hands to my head pacing on the spot. I then moved to stand in front of Jonah: my protective mode taking over. Now I was becoming increasingly anxious. Richie saw I was distressed, instantly he tried to calm me down.

"Ishmael, it's alright: it's just another dog, nobody will hurt him. Come on, let's get you back."

He pulled me back where I composed myself, the realisation that situations I came across would have that control over my emotions wasn't something I could accept. I hated that I was going to be affected, unable to stop it. I knew I needed time, pretending everything was fine would eventually prove otherwise. I had to do something about the dream: come to terms with it so I would be able to take control in the future.

I didn't like the fact that Richie had witnessed me in that state: I was meant to be helping him, only now it was the opposite. It was something I was uncomfortable with: I barely knew him. This made me wonder if he would see me as too fragile to be able to help him. Richie knew nothing of the dream, to him it must have appeared like I was overreacting, just having issues. Something which would've caused doubt for him, but also doubt for myself. The dream had such an impact; I would not be able to see when another occasion like that was coming.

Yet, I was adamant it wouldn't stop me. I couldn't hide behind the comfort of my home, this had a hold, but I wasn't beaten yet. Walking back home he kept looking at me, I know he was just checking but it was the wondering about his thoughts which unnerved me significantly; I wasn't sure I wanted to know anyway. I felt so inadequate as well as embarrassed; the walk back was one of complete silence. When we got home I went straight over to where I had started writing, sitting down without moving. Richie walked over then put his hand on my shoulder.

"Ishmael, if you need to talk, please know I will listen."

I turned around to look at him. He had compassion in his eyes, he didn't want to force me to speak, but he seemed to know words chosen carefully, but said at the right time could be a comfort. This I appreciated, more than he ever knew. I felt I had a duty to tell him in depth about my dream: give him some understanding about my recent reaction to something that others wouldn't even bat an eyelid at.

"Yes, Richie, a chat would be good: I want to tell you about my dream, it'll explain why I reacted how I did. I feel it only fair, maybe it will help."

"Sure, Ishmael, I am sure it will."

So, I told him everything except, again, the one night shared with Betty. Jonah's ears where pricking up when he was mentioned; he sat very close to me now. I wondered if he understood some of it based on my emotions; and whether he had forgiven me, too. The way he was now, was like it used to be before everything had happened. I stroked him to let him know all was going to be okay. I am glad that I had him there, Richie too, otherwise I may have hit the drink again. I sensed maybe it was why I did what I did for Richie,, that there was deeper meaning behind it.

Richie sat listening to all that I told him; I felt much calmer telling him, a connection was there: like he knew what I was going through in some way. He, too, had faced a lot, he still had many fears which haunted him to some extent. Knowing he didn't judge me or ridicule me was going to be something to really help me in the future, strengthen the relationship.

I sat staring into the now empty coffee cups, it always seemed so surreal talking about it: it seemed it was more of a story than actual events, the feeling was bizarre.

"I don't know how I'm going to overcome this, it worries me, how can I help anyone if I can't help myself?"

"By having faith, Ishmael."

"I lost that a long time ago: I can only help myself now."

"Sometimes you just need to trust things will work out; I did, I am here now because of it. Things will get better; you've been through an ordeal, that will take time to adjust."

"I know that but what if I can't, Richie? Then what?"

"Then we will deal with it if it comes. You can't live in fear or keep wondering what if, Ishmael: that will drive you crazy. The good news is you are aware of the impact it can have now. That will make you able to deal better if there is a next time."

"Richie, thank you, I really needed to hear that; maybe you're right, I need to prepare rather than hide."

"Hiding won't solve anything; you have people who care, you don't have to face this alone, you know this."

"Well, Essie will be round soon, I think you'll like her. You know, Richie, I still don't understand why the dream ended how it did: it was unfinished."

"Ishmael, take from the dream what you need to, don't waste time dwelling. The dream shows you that you need to do better with your life, it is telling you there is more to you inside. You've wasted years drinking, you put your life on hold because you feel guilty, allowed anger to consume you. What happened was not your fault, only how you dealt with it is. The dream is unfinished because it's not over yet.

"Richie? I…"

"Let me finish, Ishmael; you have had it rough, done things you're not proud of; you have a chance to change now and you're doing it. You can be what you want to be, aim to have the things in the dream. It shows you that nothing is impossible, Ishmael: you can create your own ending because now you are possible yourself, good things return to those who are good."

He left me with a lot to think about. I had been so confused about the dream: mainly its meaning as to why. I now saw it in a different light: I could learn from it to better my life. I was ready for that now. Things were getting better already; having three important people there I knew it was very possible I would make it. I had such a positive feeling inside; I'd never had that before.

I couldn't wait to see Essie again. She was one person I really wanted to help; although the dream had a major impact which would still influence my life, it wasn't going to define me. After what Richie said I knew that I could do that myself. I had to focus on helping those close to me, just as much as those many others who were in need. That would keep me occupied, preventing me from potentially spiraling out of control. I believed there was a reason for everything; that would help me accept whatever came, no matter how bad things may become.

I had a quick tidy round whilst Richie was fiddling round with some paper, then I had a quick wash. I started feeling nervous for some reason; it wasn't because Essie was coming over, I was excited to see her, but there was something. I tried ignoring it, putting it down to having her over, regardless. Shortly after I had got ready, there was a knock; I went to open the door.

"Hi, gorgeous, come in."

"Hi, Ish."

She gave me a kiss then walked in, I pulled her back gently as she began to head towards the lounge.

"Essie, I have someone staying with me; I'll explain later. You don't mind that he is here, do you?"

"Well, Ish, hmm? No, that's fine, come on, he will feel awkward with us standing out here."

I smirked as I followed her into the lounge. Richie moved to the kitchen. Jonah ran to greet her, checking her out just as he had done with Richie.

"Oh, Ish, he's as gorgeous as you are."

I started laughing before turning to her.

"No, I think Jonah wins that one."

While she fussed him, Richie came back out of the kitchen. He had decided to make something to eat for us. Essie stared at him, the nerves I had felt became more intense now; why was I feeling like this? I didn't understand. They were both staring at each other now, so I pushed to get us out of the awkward silence.

"Essie, this is Richie. Richie, I'd like you to meet Essie."

Both realising they were staring, they moved in to shake hands, neither taking their eyes off each other. Richie went back into the kitchen hurriedly, but Essie kept looking towards it.

"Essie, what's wrong?"

"I'm not sure, Ish, he seems familiar, but he can't be? I don't know, or have ever known, a Richie."

"He was homeless; so, you may have seen him around. I was drawn to him on my way home from hospital. When I got out of the car to ask him how he still managed to smile, his reply did something for me: changed my whole outlook, I found purpose. I told him if he wanted to come for a coffee then to knock anytime. He turned up, but I've decided to let him stay: he is going to help me to build a shelter. I have a good feeling about this."

"Oh, Ish, you're lovely, he seems to have had a good

influence on you."

"Yes, even Avraham likes him. I want to do something for Avraham, he has always been there, Essie. I feel awful, he got close to Jonah but now he is left alone again; I know he is alright but…"

"Well there's your answer, get him a puppy or even a bigger dog: it will be company for him as well as a friend for Jonah?"

"I'm not sure, something like that I need to know he would be happy taking one on full time. He never speaks of that part of himself, or gives much away. It's hard knowing what to do for him."

"Then ask him; that's all you can do, Ish. Can I ask, has he no family?"

"No, his family met the same end as mine. He's never married: I am not sure why. I feel all the years he has watched out for me I've denied him that. I know I shouldn't think like that, but I can't help but blame myself for him not pursuing a family. I had nobody, I was a wreck; I wouldn't be here if not for him, Essie."

"Oh, Ish, listen, the fact you have changed will prove that to him; what's done is done, it's what happens from now on that is important. He believes in you, we all do; make him proud, show him he did the right thing."

"I have no problem doing that, I just hope I can."

"Ish, I know you can, believe it too."

She leaned in to kiss me just as Richie walked in. I laughed seeing him with an apron on; Essie was also amused by it.

"Ishmael, do you both want this when its ready? What are you laughing at?"

"I'm sorry, Richie, you look very funny with that on; I didn't expect it."

Essie had her hand over her mouth trying to hold back now, too; the puzzlement on his face also adding to our amusement. He came out not bothered in the slightest, it was hilarious; he really was a picture. Now, putting his hand on his side with a smirk appearing on his face, he turned to us.

"Well, I am glad I amuse you both, I'll return to the kitchen before I give you both aching sides; it will be ready soon."

He went back into the kitchen, I watched, chuckling, before I turned to Essie.

"Essie, something has been on my mind; I don't want you to take it the wrong way, I don't think you will but I…"

"Ish, I won't know unless you tell me? What is it?"

"Things have moved very quick between us, I am thrilled; but I want to get your opinion on it. We have such a connection, but my feelings…? Well, I want you to know they are separate to the dream, I don't want you to doubt that."

"Ish, I know, I have thought about it too; but this is meant to be, you're bound to feel other things besides what you feel towards me, especially after your experience. We don't need to rush anything, neither do I doubt that what you feel is genuine."

"It's just bizarre, I know it's meant to be; I believe that, it's…"

"Ish, relax, I know more than you think I do; we both deserve a chance, whatever happens I will always be there for you. Now are you going to kiss me, or do I have to make the move?"

"Hmm, I don't know, but either way, Essie, you're not going anywhere without one."

She started laughing, leaning in I kissed her.

Richie came in clearing his throat to interrupt us. He carried out a potato gratin; it smelled delicious. I thought it strange from someone who was a carpenter: to make it as well as he did I thought he must have trained. Essie seemed to be somewhat in a world of her own now: she barely said a word whilst eating, it felt difficult in a way. I couldn't understand why but I knew by what she said she didn't know either. I felt it better to ignore it, turning to focus on the dinner that had been made for us.

"Richie, this is great, have you trained?"

"No, I just made it a lot years ago; I haven't done it in a long time."

The comment was an abrupt one, I could tell straight away that this wasn't something he really wanted to discuss; he had to want to in his own time, so, I said no more other than to thank him. I thought here was a man who probably had so much to tell, yet hardly told a thing. It worried me he kept so much in, very like Avraham, but I knew Avraham had overcome much that had happened. I didn't know that with Richie; whether he was a ticking time bomb that would go off at any moment, or whether he, too, had dealt with much in his life, during his time on the streets. Richie also seemed quiet around Essie, I began to wonder whether having her here was a good idea, even though she had every right to be. I had the right to bring anyone back here, too. But I wanted to help him, not stir things by my actions or wants. He was still here so I had to consider that, until he was ready to say more. I was done with being selfish; I cared now. I knew that if I was really going to help people, I had to put them before myself; and I was willing to do it.

After dinner we took Jonah out; it was raining quite heavily and my thoughts were averted back to the dream, reminding me of the part where I first met Betty; part of me felt terrible. I didn't know if I would ever disconnect from that, or if I would always be comparing Betty to Essie unintentionally. They were very similar both in looks as well as in their ways, but it was Essie who was real, so why couldn't I focus on that? I had to find a way otherwise it would come between us eventually, and that was the last thing I wanted. Essie was understanding but even she would have her limits, and quite rightly so. I was aware now that my dream could catch me off guard at times; I knew I had to speak to her about it, as I hadn't yet told her about the episode with Richie, at least then she could understand.

It wasn't because I couldn't, but just the fact I didn't want her to worry every time we went out, or were going somewhere. However, I felt I should be honest about it now, especially as she picked up I wasn't quite with it at the moment.

"Ish, is everything alright, you seem a bit off?"

"Do you remember the dream I told you about?"

"Yes, of course, what about it?"

"You are so like Betty in many ways, but there was an incident with Richie regarding Jonah when we went for a walk: my dream seemed to take over and I reacted badly. I want you to know that I can't stop comparing yet. It makes me feel awful, but I must be honest. I know you're real, I've said my feelings for you are real, but I'm caught off guard at times, I just…"

"Ish, it's alright, I understand. I know this isn't something which you can just sleep off or forget, you must deal with it however you can. Now you've told me I can help too, I spoke to you during your coma. I feel responsible in a way; if I hadn't…"

"If you hadn't, we may not be here now; Essie you've been amazing, during my coma then after I woke, I just want to thank you for that."

"You don't need to thank me, Ish; so, have you given any more thoughts to the shelter?"

"I'm not sure where to even start, I want to help but I'm…"

"You are doubting yourself: I see it. Ish, you can do this, you will find a way, don't give up."

"I won't give up, I just need a plan."

"That's a start, don't stress, it'll happen in time."

She always made me feel good: she was so optimistic, and I needed that, someone who would believe in me, who would push me when I needed it. I wished my parents could've met her. I had learned that dwelling on the past would only put me back into darkness, I never wanted to go back there. I had much to look forward to now. I began thinking about Avraham: about getting him a puppy. He had gone above what any friend should have for me; like I said, I owed him everything. Perhaps a puppy would help show my appreciation.

"Essie, I've been thinking about what you said about getting Avraham a puppy, I think it's a good idea; would you help me pick one?"

"Ish, I'd love to; I'm sure he will love it."

"I hope you're right, he is a caring man; he loved having Jonah."

"Don't worry, Ish, come on you can walk me back; it'll be fine."

I walked her back home; we were both drenched by now. Jonah seemed happy enough, sniffing around then shaking himself every so often; he didn't have a care in the world. Watching him always made me smile, the dream made me appreciate him so much more now. He was dependent on me, his loyalty was above average. I was looking forward to seeing Avraham's face when I give him the puppy. I could almost picture it, but he wasn't a man who showed much emotion, so that part was unclear. I could only wait now, in the hope that I was doing the right thing.

I headed back home, I was geared up to speaking to Richie about making plans for the shelter. I knew I didn't have the funds to just open one; I didn't even know how to do it, but I was determined nonetheless. I was banking on Richie having some knowledge of anyone or anywhere that may help; I didn't know. I just trusted I hadn't set my goals to high, that would lead me to potentially failing in the end.

I got home, then changed. I had a sense of optimism which I knew was because of Essie. Richie was cleaning up in the kitchen but popped out on my return, his apron now taken off.

"Richie, have you got a minute?"

"Sure, Ishmael, what is it?"

"About the shelter, I really want to get moving but I

don't even know where to start, have you any ideas, thoughts?"

He took a deep breath then sighed, looking straight at me. He turned away then dried his hands on the tea towel he was carrying; chucking it in the kitchen, he then sat down.

"Ishmael, I don't know what you're asking me? I have been homeless for years. I don't really have any information other than you will need money a lot of it; nothing is free."

"Richie, that's it, you're brilliant."

"Ishmael? Whatever are you talking about; what is?"

"Donations, sponsors; I can ask people, businesses. We can even put up fliers; we can't do it alone, but we may not have to."

"But Ishmael?"

"Richie, I know it's a long shot but that's all we have for now; I must try, this could work?"

"Just be aware that it may not; don't build your hopes up. I know this means a lot to you, Ishmael; I will help of course, it's the least I can do after all. I just know what disappointment can do."

I glanced up at him, his mixed messages about it were disheartening but I knew he had his reasons. I got up to grab some writing materials; I knew I was onto something, regardless of Richie's doubts. I had a burst of energy; excitement rippled through me, it felt like he had hit the nail on the head. I was almost convinced it would work now.

His words did grab me, but I ignored them to an extent too. I knew passion, along with hard work would pay eventually. I did see concern in him, but I needed to understand why. I knew disappointment too, but this was different.

I was aware it could all fall flat, but it's something I could push for. Maybe seeing one guy doing something would give more people the urge to help? I knew not all would, but a lot might; perhaps just enough to get this going.

"Okay, Richie, what concerns do you have? We cannot go into this with any doubts; I may be able to ease any uncertainty for you. Please, let me at least try?"

"The world is cruel, but people are much worse, you can't rely on people to just help. I know some do, but so many won't. The odds are against you; that's my concern. Tell me, Ishmael, do you know what people think about the homeless?"

This put me right on the spot once again. I now understood he had been treated badly, that he had lost faith in humanity; he had a real concern which made me think once again.

"Richie, I saw many walking past you that day, the ignorance, the cold glares. All the whispering from small minded people, but I saw different in you. I saw a man who has had it tough, done what he could to survive. In you I saw a fighter, all you are with what you've been through may help. Let us tell people, make them see it from your eyes; maybe then they will have more compassion?"

"No, Ishmael, I see your point; but it will not work."

I was beginning to become agitated now. I was really trying, but he was coming across as stubborn. Perhaps there was more reason behind it, but once again he would not say. I had to push now, he was either with me or not.

"Why are you so convinced, Richie?"

"Because they just don't care. The world doesn't care; people that do are far and few. The homeless are strangers to everyone; we are caped in dirt, many use drugs or drink, we are just rejects to them, a waste of time. They see it as our own fault; they are blind, but that won't help. Ishmael, I do believe in you, but this isn't the way."

"No, Richie, I know it is; even if a couple change their views, that'd be worth it, wouldn't it?"

"Yes, course it would be worth it; but for what you want it just isn't enough. Look, Ishmael, you have my view on it, I will help, but please, be prepared for the outcome like I've said; it may not be what you want."

"Well I respect that, more so your honesty. Still, I have a good feeling about this: I can't figure out why I can only trust. I will be prepared, Richie, I know how vital that is."

We sat for a while writing down ideas; names of businesses we could ask, possibly where the best places may be. Richie started getting more into it, for a while he seemed to forget his worries; I admired him for that. Regardless of his views or feelings, he still wanted to help; my respect for him was growing for that alone.

"Richie, tomorrow we can make fliers, I am out with Essie in the morning, but would you help on my return?"

"Yes, Ishmael, no problem; I can do that."

"Right, well I'm off to bed, I have an early start, thank you for your help, Richie, goodnight."

"Ishmael, thank you for allowing me to meet Essie; Goodnight."

"Oh, sure; not at all, Richie, see you tomorrow."

I thought it an odd comment but maybe having her there had helped him after all; I didn't think much of it as I went to bed.

Richie did not go to bed straight away, he sat up for hours working with designs he created for the fliers. He set a couple aside which he thought were the best, before finally going to bed himself.

I woke up the next morning, still half asleep I stumbled into the lounge. Neatly placed on the table were his designs; I noticed them briefly, whilst going to the kitchen to make coffee. After making it I took a sip and headed towards the table. I was shocked to see what he had done. I picked them up carefully, scouring each one.

There was one which stood out to me; it was of a man on the streets, people walking past but he was invisible, like a force was separating them. It blew my mind: it was a very powerful drawing. I wasn't aware he could draw, the man had talent, yet he did nothing with it; it had me thinking about him now. I soon heard him getting up then coming down the hallway.

"Morning, Ishmael."

"Morning. Richie, these are amazing drawings, you have real talent."

"Bah, it's just scribble; nothing special."

"Isn't that what every creative mind says?"

"What difference does it make? I can't do anything, I know you mean well, Ishmael, but just... I don't want to talk about it. I did them to help you, nothing more."

I heard the passion in his voice, the annoyance that he was almost forced to hate the talent he had. Convinced he couldn't do anything about it because of his situation. In a way it made me chuckle because he was a man of wisdom, yet he couldn't see that if he wanted something, he could pursue it regardless.

"Richie, you can, regardless of your situation. You have real talent; people will want that, don't give up if you have dreams. You can make them happen: fight for them if you have too, this is not over if you don't want it to be. Please, just think about it; you say you believe in me, well I believe in you. This is exquisite work whether you think it or not."

"Do you really think that?"

"I don't say anything I don't mean, Richie; you're a good man who has had a hard time, but that isn't who you are, you are who you are."

He sat thinking now, almost like he was questioning everything he had believed in or thought. A look of confusion fell over his face, and I said no more. I finished my coffee then went to get ready. I was meeting Essie soon, so I couldn't be late: she had work. I hoped I hadn't said too much, or stuck my nose in where it didn't belong. I marched back into the lounge; he hadn't moved an inch. He looked like he was in a world of his own; I wanted to check he was alright before I left, but I didn't want to interrupt his thinking. I walked over, gently I put my hand on his arm.

"Richie? Are you alright?"

"I… yes, I'm alright, I have an idea, Ishmael; I don't know if it'll work but it's worth a go. I need some money, I hate to ask?"

"Okay, what is it?"

"To create then sell art. You need to go, we can talk about it later. I have some planning to do, but, Ishmael, thank you."

"Not at all, Richie, if all your work is as good as these, then you will be alright; don't stop believing."

Those words, they fell from my mouth effortlessly without thought, but took me right back again. It made me want to laugh: déjà vu always at play. I found it strange that life was becoming very like the dream some ways, yet it was still all so different to how things had been panning out. It was a constant reminder to keep changing, keep doing better; for me it was becoming normal to do that. I hadn't drunk since I left hospital, not even had the urge. I knew that was down to three people who cared: they believed in me which made me so driven to make them proud.

I missed my parents very much, I knew that dwelling on it wasn't healthy; I had to try accepting what had happened, but this would still take time. I could begin to see what Avraham meant about things happening for a reason; this was my comfort now, this was my reality.

12 ISSY AND AVRAHAM

I gave Richie some money then went to meet Essie. She was wearing her uniform but still looked gorgeous. I had much to tell her; I was feeling so positive now, more than I ever had, it seemed to show.

"Someone looks happy?"

"Hello gorgeous, yes; it's been an eventful morning I must say."

"Really? Come on then, tell me about it?"

"It turns out Richie can draw, extremely well too. He is talking of creating then selling his art: to help towards the shelter. I'm now thinking to write more so I can do the same. I need to make my own living, I can't rely on others anymore."

"Ish, that's great, I am sure people will be interested in Richie's art just as much as your writing; it's a very positive step."

"Yes, we have some plans to also ask businesses to help; I know it's a long shot, but that, too, is worth a try?"

"Ish, yes, of course it is, you never know otherwise. I know you will get there, just keep trying; that's all you can do."

"I know, I can't help being excited, but I can't help not being either: listening to Richie, I know this isn't going to be easy. He believes people don't care and part of me knows there is much truth in that."

"Ish, if you have real beliefs, if you think you can make

a difference then you will. Nothing worth doing is ever easy; but perseverance pays in the end. Don't let people's opinions cloud your goals; Richie is bound to have negative views, but it's you that can push for what you want, no one else."

"Come on, or we will never get there, you have work soon, I know you're right, negative or not he meant well, I just need to prove him wrong."

She kissed me on the cheek then we strolled towards the dog's home. My heart sank seeing so many abandoned animals, all desperate to be loved but confined to cages. I wanted to stroke every one of them; some were barking, some were just lying there, almost like they'd given up.

"Essie this is awful, look at them; I don't see any puppies here."

"I know, Ish, and no, you may not do here; but I'm sure even a bigger one will be okay. They need a home; Avraham can give at least one of them that. Come on let's look around."

We went to every cage. I was then drawn to an Alsatian, she was sitting there, looking straight at me; curious, I went over."

"Here girl, it's alright, come?"

She didn't trust me that was clear, I bent down as an almost surrender to her; now she came over slowly, step by step. I reached into the cage to stroke her, she was weary but liked the fuss. Soon a lady came over who worked there looking very much surprised.

"Aah, she seems to have taken a liking to you. She rarely does that, in fact, I've never seen her so at ease with anyone."

"Does she have a name?"

"We aren't sure, she was in a state from neglect when we got her, no collar or anything to show her identity. She is healthy now, but she has been through quite an ordeal; I must make you aware of that."

I stood up, I knew this dog was the right one; I knew the

search was over.

"I want to take her, what do we need to do?"

"She needs her checks which won't be till tomorrow, you can take her then."

"Surely, I can get her checked? Can I not take her now?"

"We can't let her go until then, sir: its procedure."

"Ish, we can get her tomorrow; she will be alright till then."

"Fine, we will return tomorrow morning for her."

"She will be waiting sir, goodbye."

We started walking out when I turned to Essie.

"I'd take them all if I could; it's heartbreaking seeing them that way."

"You're too kind-hearted, Ish, I know you love dogs especially, but even though it's hard, they are better there: they are at least out of harm's way."

"I know, but every animal, just as much as every person, deserves to be loved. They shouldn't be caged like this, no animal should; it's something I'll never understand. Anyway, someone needs to get to work, you will be late."

"That is something we both agree on there, but yes, I better go; have a great day, Ish. Hey, no dwelling either; see you in the morning."

"No time for that, I have things to do."

"Go on, I'll see you tomorrow."

"It can't come quick enough, have a great day, Essie."

"Something else we agree on, Ish."

She winked as she walked off. Grinning, I headed back; keen to know what plans Richie had. I had to alert Avraham to be around mine tomorrow. My mind was busy for once, but it was filled with optimism. Ideas were filling my mind instead of the negative thoughts I used to have. That was a good feeling: I had things to look forward to. I had a focus that would keep me going for a while; that made me feel good too.

I soon arrived back to a now empty place, I saw a note on the table. Nervously, I paced myself towards it. I really hoped he hadn't left, or I hadn't upset or unnerved him in any way. I got to the table where I picked up the note; it felt ominous that's for sure.

Ishmael,
Popped out
Few things to take care of
Don't worry, Back later
Richie

I breathed a sigh of relief, I would have hated pushing him away through my tongue. Whatever he was up to he seemed jolly enough, so, I thought no more about it. I was tidying up when I heard the door going. I knew it to be Avraham: just by the soft firm knocking. I was surprised as it was unannounced; I went to open it.

"Avraham, I wasn't expecting you?"

"Ishmael, no, I wasn't planning on being here."

"I am glad you're here, I was coming around to see you."

"Really, why? Is everything alright?"

"Yes, it's fine. Avraham, I have done something for you; I just don't know if you will accept it? It'll be my way of saying thank you for always being there. I want you to know I am grateful; even if at times I haven't shown it."

"What is it, Ishmael, what have you done?"

"I have got you a dog?"

"What? A dog? Why, Ishmael?"

"Because I know how much you miss Jonah, I know you are close with him, I thought having your own would be a good move, but it's no problem if it's not; it was meant to be a surprise."

"Ishmael, yes, it's a good move; I really don't know what to say, just thank you."

"She is an Alsatian; I get her tomorrow morning. But Avraham, you have nothing to thank me for, ever, it's nothing compared to what you've done for me. What is it you came around for?"

"It doesn't matter now, I can take Jonah for a few hours if you like? I must go, I have a dog to prepare for; I'm meeting Rabbi, too. I will come around tomorrow morning early."

"Avraham, of course you can take him; if you still want too?"

"Yes, okay, I can take him; I'll bring him back in the morning, thank you, Ishmael. There's no Richie about I see?"

"Of course, Avraham, but no, he has gone out; I'm not sure where to until he comes back, he asked for some money earlier then left a note."

"Ishmael, I know you care but you don't know him, what if he's in trouble or brings it here? I like the man, but you must still be cautious."

"I am not worried, Avraham, the man has given me no reason to be. I see your concern but it's not necessary; he will say when he is back I'm sure. Come on let's get Jonah."

"Okay, I will trust your judgement, you know where I am if needed."

"Yes, I know, I always appreciate that, Avraham."

As soon as Avraham stepped into the lounge, Jonah raced over to greet him. He fussed him as I watched. I could see he had something on his mind besides wanting to take Jonah, but he seemed to perk up once I mentioned the dog; he was taking Jonah, too, which cheered him up.

"Right I shall leave you to it, I will see myself out. I shall bring him back early; have a good day Ishmael."

"Yes, you too, bye, Avraham."

I patted Jonah fondly before they left. I began to be convinced he was lonely. Seeing me getting on now, making my way, may have made him think he wouldn't have been needed as much anymore; this really bothered me. I had always relied on him; thinking about it, in some ways, he had relied on me, too. We didn't have anything to keep us together in our friendship other than the need, but now that was fading. He had been more like a father figure than a friend, due to what had happened in our lives. With him being older and having great wisdom, we never got the chance to be just friends, or develop that as it should've done. I knew a dog would be company, but I knew he deserved so much more: I wanted him to find someone, to settle down. Maybe that was selfish because it would settle my mind, but regardless of the way we were, I still valued him in my life. He was important; his happiness mattered to me, too. I decided to speak to Essie, then convince Avraham to start dating: he deserved someone special too.

I decided to try my hand at some writing, it had been a while since I'd done any more; I had time whilst waiting for Richie. I didn't know if I was up to the standard of Richie's art or whether anything I wrote would sell, but he was making the effort so it was clear I should, too. It was the only thing I knew I could do; spending time seeing what I could create would at least tell me if I had anything which would be even possible to sell. I sat down, forgetting all I had written before. I knew that what I wrote now would have to be something that people would want to know about; it would also be something which may help others. With many ideas flowing through, I began to write. First it was a page; then it was two. By the time Richie returned, I had quite a bit done. Distracted by his entrance, I hesitantly put my pen down. He had his arms full of stuff.

"Richie, what have you got there?"

"Ishmael, I have art supplies; I can make art. I also have a suit."

"That's great, you have been gone ages? What's the suit for?"

"Well, if we are to go knocking on doors, I need something to look a bit respectable; it's only charity shop but it will do for now. I see you've also been busy?"

"You've done good today, Richie, and yes, I have. I've started writing which may help fund the shelter, too; however, that isn't a guarantee."

"May I look?"

"I don't know, it's just drafts for now."

He came over, then picked up the paper I had been writing on. He turned to look at me, I gestured with my arm to give him the go ahead. I felt uneasy waiting for him to read it: I knew I would have to overcome that otherwise it would not help me if I wanted to publish or sell my work. A few minutes had gone past when Richie looked up.

"Ishmael, wow, this is really good work, you have a great mind, your talent is special; you will finish this, won't you?"

"I want to so I must try; you made me realise that using our talents could help make this shelter a reality. We need a property but…"

"Aah, yes, we do; there may be a place available cheap, but it needs a lot of work doing to it."

"Richie, that's fantastic; how do you know this?"

"We homeless get around, we see all sorts; come to know things, especially about properties. We see who goes in or out of them, the knowledge is rarely useful to the likes of me. Ishmael, I think I know the fella we need to see: I recognised the name, although I doubt he would want to see me."

"Richie, you're going to need to tell me what's going on, why would you say that, who is he?"

"I've done things I'm not proud of in the past; I've hurt people, been selfish, done whatever it's taken to survive. I hurt this fella so that's why he will not involve himself with me. I can't blame him but this part you're better off doing yourself."

"No, Richie, this is your chance to apologise, make amends. I don't blame you because you haven't had it easy, but running away isn't the answer. You cannot hide or fear bumping into him; if we get involved then you will for sure. You need to face up to this, do the right thing; if it falls through then you've tried. We are in this together, Richie."

"You're right, Ishmael, I need to face up. I just don't want to cause you any bother; I want to help."

"This is the right thing to do regardless. I know too well what fear can do; you must do what's necessary when you get the opportunity, this will be a chance to make some wrong doings right."

"Right, well I'm going to start some drawings if I may? They won't buy blank canvases."

"Sure, Richie, maybe we will find this man soon, for now I'll leave you to your creativity, I'm going to do some more writing."

He looked at me with a smile, he seemed much more content now. I knew that the first meeting, if it came about, would be a difficult one, especially with the history. It's something that would have played on his mind which I understood; I just hoped our chat had eased it even a little bit. He started carefully arranging pencils, along with the coloured pencils that he had brought, in a line, sharpening them to perfection. The usual preparations before an artist starts work. It was enthralling to watch. He then sat down, got himself comfortable, thought for a few seconds then put pencil to paper. I twisted myself back around to focus on my writing. We spent the rest of the day in silence, the only interruption was for refreshments. Time was getting on; next time I looked up I saw Richie rubbing his chest. I restlessly kept glancing over for a couple of seconds: wondering if he was alright. He leaned back looking uncomfortable, so, I intervened.

"Richie? Richie what is it?"

"I'm fine, Ishmael, I just need some water."

Startled, I got up to get him some water, my concern was growing by the second. I had to convince him to get checked over; I was in no position to give medical treatment, or even know what to do if someone needed it. This worried me substantially, I wished Essie was here.

"Richie, you must let me take you to get checked: I am

very concerned about you."

"No, don't trouble yourself; it'll pass."

"I can't leave you like this; Richie I am not trained, please, let me take you?"

"If I worsen then yes, for now I am alright; relax Ishmael, it may just be indigestion."

I wasn't convinced: his facial expression told me otherwise. But there was no more I could do, I made it clear I was worried; he gave me permission to get him help if needed. I could only wait to see how he progressed now, hoping he would be alright. I saw he had done a few drawings already; they were beautiful.

I stood in awe looking at them: I felt really privileged to witness it. I was glad that I had given him the chance I did. I was sure that his work would sell, but I wanted him to reap the benefits. Now it felt wrong asking him to sell it for the shelter: he had put all his emotion, all his feelings into this. It was obvious how personal it was. It was his right to do with them what he wanted; I knew I had to let him know that. He seemed to look a little better now, which I was relieved about; he was no longer rubbing his chest, he had gained his colour back, too.

"Richie, whatever you do with these must be your choice. They're amazing, I think it only right you reap the benefits; you deserve it. I don't want you to feel obliged to do anything you're not happy with, we will find another way."

"I don't, but no, I have much to make up for, Ishmael. If my work can be used to better people's lives, then I will do it. I've never had much, neither do I ask for much; you've given me more than I could ever repay. Helping you would mean a lot to me."

"You don't owe me anything, it's been a pleasure having you here: you've helped me, too. How are you feeling?"

"Ishmael, whatever happens, make the shelter happen; finish your writing, if my work can help in anyway then please don't hesitate. Promise me that?"

"Richie? That's an odd thing to say?"

"Promise me, Ishmael?"

"Okay, Richie, you have my word. But why are you saying that? Is there something you want to tell me? Please, I can't deal with any more shocks; why do I feel I am going to get one?"

"We don't know what the future holds or how long we have left. I am telling you this because if anything does happen you will have peace of mind. Don't let my words worry you Ishmael; what will be will be, everything has been taken care of."

He completely baffled me with this; I slumped onto the couch, so many thoughts going around my head. I had an uneasy feeling about Richie's reassurance, and it wasn't reassuring me. I had become fond of him in the short time I knew him; I couldn't bear to see anything happen.

He soon went to bed, but I could not: I became more restless as time got on. I had to check every so often he was alright. I had major paranoia; it was the first time I wanted a drink because of it. Knowing that if I got in a state I would not be able to help him if he needed me was the only thing that swayed the temptation. I fell asleep after a while, only to be woken by Richie the next morning.

"Ishmael, why have you not gone to bed?"

"I was worried, I couldn't sleep, how could I after what you said?"

"You can't carry on like this, neither can you prevent things from happening. Ishmael, I know you've lost a lot, but you're still healing; think logically for your own good."

"I know, Richie, I panicked; it reminded me of the dream, like so many other situations. I am trying; it would be so much easier if I didn't care, but I do."

"Yes, I know, sometimes too much, but you need to think with your brain at times, too, not always with your heart. Ishmael, do not forget that."

"I need to get ready: I'm picking up Avraham's dog in an hour. Thank you, Richie: you make sense, but I find it hard at times, that's all."

"And yet you do it; you really are some guy, Ishmael, whoever has you in their life is blessed. Thank you for everything you've done for me."

"You're always welcome, Richie. Right, I need to get a move on, Avraham should be round soon. Would you open the door if he knocks?"

"Sure, Ishmael, I will make coffee?"

"That will be great, Richie, thank you."

I went to get ready, Avraham arrived shortly after. I finished cleaning my teeth then went to greet him. I stopped abruptly before I got to the lounge door: I heard them both talking very quietly. I couldn't catch what was said but it made me feel really agitated. I marched straight in.

"What are you whispering about?"

"Ishmael, I told Avraham about yesterday: he should know so he, too, is aware."

"Why the need to whisper? I am not a piece of glass, I thought you would know me better than that, Avraham?"

"Ishmael, Richie just cares, we both do. I know you well enough that whatever happens you will need the support. Don't be angry, I know you're much stronger now, but you are not fully recovered."

I glared at him, exasperated now; I could feel it building until I couldn't contain myself. Once again I lost it.

"Avraham, I appreciate you both; but sneaking around, all the whispering behind my back, I do not. I watched my parents being shot before me, I fled my home, turned to drink which almost cost me my life. Then I fell into a coma; I ended up thinking a dream was my reality. I believed people were in my life that weren't, grieving for people I thought were real. I thought I'd lost Jonah; you almost died twice but that wasn't real either. Yes, I may be adapting, but I'm still here. I'm trying but you are not making that easy by doing things like that; you're holding me back."

"Holding you back?"

"YES, you're not helping: you are making things harder

I…"

Richie stepped in now: seeing the tension growing worse by the second.

"Ishmael, easy."

"NO, Richie, I will not, it needed saying; enough is enough."

For the first time ever, Avraham snapped.

"ISHMAEL, ENOUGH! Do you not think I don't know what you've been through, are still going through? Do you really believe I think so little of you? I have only ever tried to help, but I can see I haven't. I will go, maybe that dog will be better with someone who cares, it's obvious you don't think I do, or that I ever have."

"Avrah…?"

He blocked me with his arm, completely ignored me. That was also the first time he had ever done that too; he then stormed out. He looked broken after my words; I now felt so much remorse. I allowed my anger to take control again. What's worse, I didn't know if this was ever reparable; I hated myself. I didn't need to throw that in his face: he had been there through it all, I always knew that, too.

"AAH, I hope you find this amusing, I hope you're SATISFIED. DO YOU HEAR ME? Call yourself a God?"

Richie grabbed me firmly, Jonah came over whining.

"ISHMAEL, stop: that's enough. What is wrong with you? You need to control your temper. Avraham is really upset, you know he cares."

"Yes, Richie, WELL SO DO I. People need to stop pussy footing around me; do you and Avraham not realise how that makes me feel? It doesn't even matter. I need to meet Essie, she will be waiting."

"Do the right thing, remember that one, Ishmael?"

"MAYBE THAT WILL NEVER BE GOOD ENOUGH? Perhaps I'm just not good enough, I didn't ask to come back, Richie, it would've been better I didn't."

"ISHMAEL?"

Infuriated, I ignored him, stomping out then slamming the door behind me. I knew I was over reacting, but I also made a point. I just went about it the wrong way which may have cost me the one person who I trusted, admired, as well as respected the most. I knew I was a fool: I had proved them right. If I can't handle a bit of private conversation, anything more serious I certainly wasn't going to handle well. I soon met Essie, now much calmer; however, devastation was filling me instead. She saw right through me.

"Ishmael, something is wrong?"

"I think my friendship with Avraham is over."

"What? Ishmael, no, what has happened?"

"I am a fool, I have been unforgivable. I lost my temper, Avraham snapped; Essie he looked broken. I've never seen him like that. Walking here, I knew he only cared but he thinks he's been nothing but a burden; I feel awful, it's the first time he has ever ignored me or lost his temper. He put his arm up to block me, then stormed out."

"Oh, Ish, you can fix this: he will understand."

"Why should he? Essie, he has been there always, no questions, no complaining. I just lashed out; I wouldn't blame him if he didn't, he hadn't even done anything. They were whispering about me; I just lost it but can't explain why? I saw him yesterday when he came around. I told him about the dog; he was coming with us, but he said to give the dog to someone who cares. We have never fallen out like this even at my worst moments, I don't know how to fix this."

"Okay, Ish. Give him time, he will be upset because he does care, he wouldn't be bothered otherwise. We will still get him the dog. Hey, words are said in the heat of the moment, but perhaps this will bring you together more? Come on, the day is still early. I will help you mend this: you two are inseparable, even if it doesn't feel like it."

We went to get the dog, I was glad we didn't have to go through the row of cages again: I was in no mood. We arrived at the reception where we were greeted by a different lady; we went over to give our details in.

"We are here to pick up the Alsatian?"

"Okay sir, if you want to take a seat I will go to check whether she is ready or not."

We sat down in the waiting area, my first thought was Avraham: I felt so ashamed by my outburst. I whispered to Essie.

"Avraham should be here; Essie what have I done?"

"Ish, don't beat yourself up, we will sort this out I promise. Even after what's happened, you're still doing right for him."

I took her hand, squeezing it gently. I turned giving her a smile, I was grateful for her support; even though I felt very undeserving of it. A couple of minutes passed until the lady came out with the Alsatian on a lead. She seemed excited to see us again, desperately trying to pull towards us. The lady gestured to me before speaking.

"I need you to sign a couple of papers before you leave, please; this way."

I followed the lady as she handed the lead to Essie. Essie fussed over the dog immediately. After the paperwork was signed we thanked the lady then headed out.

"I must see Avraham now: the dog cannot get too attached, that wouldn't be fair."

"Ish, maybe it's too soon? Give it a while."

"No, I must do this, even if he slams or doesn't even open the door; I must try, it's the least I can do."

"Let me knock first, I can explain things? It could become worse otherwise: ruin any chance of reconciliation."

"You haven't even met him, Essie?"

"I have, Ish, while you were in a coma; only a couple of times briefly, but you are in no position to do it yet, it must be me?"

"You're amazing, do you know that?"

"I care, Ish, I know this would devastate you both; I have enough with one, let alone two."

She winked at me making me laugh. I knew she made complete sense, with my tendency to have explosive outbursts at any moment, it was the logical thing to do. I didn't want to jeopardise any chance of making amends with Avraham; I would do anything to make it up to him, I wanted the dog to be a start.

We arrived at Avraham's house. I stayed back as Essie went to knock; part of me felt like a coward, just like I did in the dream. I should've been able to confront him myself, but I knew at this moment I couldn't. I saw Avraham open the door, he bent down to stroke the dog as Essie spoke to him. He looked over towards me after a minute. Waving his arm, he encouraged me to go over; I didn't hesitate. I just had to try to remain calm.

"Ishmael, you still got her? She is beautiful, thank you."

"I am so sorry, Avraham, you didn't deserve that: I know how much you care, I just lost it, please forgive me?"

"Yes, I was hurt but I know you too well. Stop seeing me as the enemy, Ishmael; I am not. We have been friends how long? Sometimes remembering I know what's better for you than you do will help us get along? I don't think it is because you are weak; it's because I know how you feel, how you will react to things. Please trust me to know."

"Yes, I know that now, Avraham; I've been a fool, you are the most important person in my life. I thought I had blown it, that will never happen again."

He stared into my eyes for a moment, then with a look of amusement at my comment, he put his hand on my arm.

"No, Ishmael, I am sure it will, but now you know there is a lesson to be learned from this. Maybe it's a good thing to have happened? Please don't push me away."

I laughed hard at this. They both looked at each other in confusion; Avraham interrupted.

"Ishmael, what are you laughing at?"

"Well, Avraham, let's just say I won't ever do that."

He clicked on to what I was laughing at now; smiling while shaking his head. I had almost lost him in the dream and could have lost him in reality through my actions. It was clear Avraham recognised the deeper meaning behind my comment, which I hoped would give him reassurance I would be more trusting of him in the future. I had an amazing girlfriend, as well as an amazing friend; he was like a father in my life, yet never tried to be. He was always my friend first. I was so appreciative that he did know me well enough: our friendship may not have been so easily resolved otherwise.

"Avraham, the dog has no name, have you thought of one?"

"Issy, yes, I will call her Issy; after you, Ishmael."

"Aww, Avraham, that's sweet; isn't it, Ish?"

"Well, I don't know whether to be honoured or insulted?"

I raised my eyebrow making the pair of them laugh.

"Oh, Ish you are funny sometimes; I am so glad you two have sorted things out."

"I am too. Avraham, why don't you bring Issy to meet Jonah? Spend the day with us; have lunch?"

"I don't want to be any bother, Ishmael"

"Avraham, what…? You are never a bother, come on we would like that; we will do it more often."

He smiled, then went to grab his coat before he locked the door behind him. I gave him a hug, catching him off guard, , much to his surprise.

"Thank you for everything, Avraham; whatever happens I am always there for you."

Essie interrupted us, turning to Avraham.

"No, Ish. Avraham, we are both here for you."

Something clicked in him then, and pulling away he wiped his eye. I had never seen him emotional, but that told me everything except why? I sensed there was more to it, just as I had when he was at mine, but he was a private man,

I didn't want to make him uncomfortable by asking questions. I thought maybe if there was more to it, then he would tell me in time; it wasn't my place, or the right moment, to push him. I now felt that from then on, our friendship would become what it should always have been; I really hoped that to be the case.

Perhaps he would open up, confide in me in time, let me help him, like he had always done for me. I knew he didn't have that with anyone; he was brave, extremely selfless, so much more of a man than I could ever be. I thought that what had happened was the best thing to have happened now: things had turned out better than I had ever expected. Essie was right, if Avraham hadn't been who he was I was convinced I would never have rekindled our friendship. I would never question his motives again: I knew he never had anything but good intentions for me. He was just Avraham, that would always be enough.

13 A MASSIVE SHOCK FOR ESSIE

We headed back to mine. Issy was a fine dog, she had beautiful markings on her, black with tan patches; she was just as curious as my Jonah. Her eyes were brown, but had a deep sadness to them; it was heartbreaking, I wondered what type of person could do that to such a beautiful animal? Regardless, she seemed to be happy walking with Avraham, who also appeared a lot happier: it showed in his face. I was glad I had got her for him, at least if we ever fell out again he would have her. We soon got back, only to hear Jonah barking; he never barked. I knew straight away something was wrong. I thought someone had broken in; flashbacks of seeing Jonah lying there started to pour in again.

"Please, no, not Jonah, I can't lose him."

"Ishmael, calm yourself, let me go; stay with Essie."

"No, Avraham, we will both go, you may need me; I won't let you go alone. I swear, anything happens to him; I will not hold back."

"Ish, relax, you will only make things worse; it'll be alright."

"Ishmael, come, hurry."

We both raced up towards my door, surprised to see that it hadn't been disturbed in any way. We both looked in confusion at each other, then cautiously I opened the door. Jonah was sitting by Richie, who was now lying on the floor. Jonah was barking to alert help. Although I had made up with Avraham, it still wasn't the case with Richie. I was beside myself.

"Oh no, Richie, Avraham get Essie, quick."

I kneeled beside him, he was still breathing but barely; he kept falling out of consciousness. I placed a cushion under his head, trying to make him a bit more comfortable; I felt completely helpless.

"Richie, hang in there, Essie is coming; we will get you to hospital. I so sorry about earlier, I was a fool."

"Ishmael, it doesn't matter: I understand. But my daughter, if you ever see her, tell her I love her; promise me?"

"You will tell her yourself, be still now, save your energy."

"I need your word, all I've said to you; please, Ishmael?"

"I promise, Richie, look, here come the others; don't worry, please say no more."

Essie came hurrying over, she did various checks as we waited, Avraham came over to me.

"Ishmael, I remember Jonah did the same with you: when you fell he barked for help. You have a very special dog. This may be a hard day for you."

"I know Avraham, I can understand this is hard for you too, I pray he will be alright."

"Ishmael, we don't know, be prepared for any outcome, that is so important for you; you have a good heart. I know you are troubled deeply by bad events, but I am always here; I know you know this now."

"Yes, if not for you I wouldn't be, Avrah."

At that moment Essie came over in a state of panic.

"Ish, we need to get him to hospital now: he is in a bad way. I can keep him stable, but not for long. You must find help quickly; go, I'll stay with him."

We both rushed out, banging on doors. We almost lost hope that anyone would answer, until a man came out. I knew he had a car, but I wasn't sure he would help.

"Eh? What are you playing at? Is everything alright?"

"I'm sorry, it's my friend: he needs a hospital immediately. We have no transport or time to wait; please, can you help us?"

"Yes, of course, hang on, give me a minute."

He came out a minute later, we then rushed back to where Essie was waiting. She was in tears now: yet I didn't know why.

"Essie? He hasn't?"

"No, but he's close, looks like it's a heart attack. We must hurry."

She got up, now in professional mode. I couldn't understand why she was so upset; I had to speak to her even for a second. Avraham and my neighbour went over to get Richie. I caught Essie by the arm.

"Essie? Hey, what is it?"

"I'm not sure, just something he said; let's leave it for now. Please, Ish, we must go."

Whatever it was I had to leave it: she was needing to do her job first. If I got in her way, then it would not be doing Richie any favours; he was priority now.

They got Richie up gently, he made it to the car; we then raced to get him to hospital. The man who drove us was called Alfie, I thanked him before he left for work. We rushed in where Essie converted into medical language: telling doctors of his condition.

He was carted away. I gave in what details I knew of him and we were then left waiting. I couldn't even guess the outcome, I knew I had to prepare for the worst as Avraham warned. A good hour later, a doctor came out looking serious; I just knew what he was going to say.

"Are you with Richie?"

"Yes, he has been staying with me: he was homeless."

"I am afraid I have some bad news, he suffered a massive heart attack. We couldn't do anything for him, I'm very sorry."

The doctor just stood there, not knowing what else to say, waiting for a reaction. He touched Avraham on the shoulder.

"He has a couple of things, I will bring them out to you soon as I can?"

"Yes, thank you, Doctor."

He left us. I had known Richie wouldn't make it, part of me was hoping I was wrong; I only blamed myself. Essie stood right by me with Avraham, awaiting my reaction. I just slumped down, no amount of screaming would change things now. I was heartbroken for him, shocked it was so sudden. I became wracked with guilt: wondering if I had added to his passing. My outburst wouldn't have done him any good which was at the forefront of my mind. By his words, he now seemed to know it was coming, yet I had ignored it hoping for the best. Avraham sat next to me.

"Ishmael, my friend, do not blame yourself: he would not want that. After all you did for him? You made his last days good ones."

"I can't agree: I screamed at him on his last day. I ignored his pains. I should've done more; this is my fault. I won't forgive myself for this, Avraham. He was a good man; I failed him."

"Ish, you weren't to know. What happened this morning couldn't have predicted this outcome; you can't feel guilty. Avraham is right, please don't do this to yourself."

"I don't know what to feel; I have a numbness, yet I want to react in so many ways? Some emotions are stronger than others, he knew what was going to happen: the things he said. I know this could have been prevented."

"You haven't failed him; how many people would do what you did? Yes, you had your outburst, but that was meant to be; the same with Richie, it was just his time. I know that doesn't help, but you're in shock; you will see that in time. Ishmael, believe me when I say you are thinking too much into this."

I sat there not knowing what else to say, we all just sat in silence before Essie went to get some coffee. She soon came back. Avraham kept looking at me, I was in my own world with so many thoughts going around my head still; the silence didn't help. Essie was holding my hand every so often for comfort. A while later the doctor finally bought out some of Richie's belongings, puzzlement now showing on his face.

"Ishmael, I'm a little confused; you say his name was Richie?"

"Yes, that's right, why?"

"Our records show that he goes by another name; his ID badge confirms it. Henry, Henry Jacobs? I…"

Essie dropped the coffee she was holding: her facial expression now looked one of horror. All eyes turned to her; Avraham rushed off to get some towels. I jumped up to her.

"Essie, what is it?"

"No, it can't be; Ish, please?"

"Essie, hey; you are not making sense, can't be what?"

She stared into space: thinking, squinting her eyes with every thought. She was as white as the walls around us. Pulling on my coat she then moved her head towards me, looking me straight in the eyes.

"Ish, I… I… I think he may have been my father; oh, I don't know. He told me he knew who I was; he was glad he saw me again. I became emotional: inside something just clicked. But I don't remember how he looked now, my memory of him is different. I only recognise the name for certain. This makes no sense."

I didn't know what to say; seeing their reaction when they first met, her feeling like she knew him, it would make sense. I thought maybe this is the feeling I got at the time, too: it was telling me something. If that was the case, then this would be devastating for her; in more ways than one. It wouldn't be me that needed the support but her; I could do that.

"Okay, Essie, it's alright, we will sort this out: I can help you. Things will make sense eventually; you will get closure."

"I won't ever have closure: he's gone. Doctor, may I have those things? Ish, do you mind?"

"No, Essie, of course not; please."

She got his things then sat down. He had a little address book, his ID badge, his jacket, along with a bit of change. You could tell he was from the streets: he had nothing in life, on his last day he died with nothing, too.

"Ish, why would he have an address book?"

"I don't know Essie, the man becomes stranger by the hour; we knew very little of him, maybe that will help you to find out more?"

"Doctor, did he have no pictures on him?"

"I don't know miss: the nurses gathered his belongings. Please, I must get back to work; are you wanting to see him?"

I wasn't sure I wanted to; but I had to be strong for Essie. I wasn't convinced I could handle it. Essie thought differently, she turned to me.

"Ish, I need to see him; will you come with me?"

"I'm concerned I may freak out, I can't fall apart, you will need me Essie; I can't say I won't."

"I can't do it alone, Ish; whatever happens I am with you, we will deal with whatever comes together; please?"

"I am with you, Essie; always. Yes, Doctor, we want to see him."

Avraham barely said a word. I had no idea how he was feeling: worried for me, concerned for Essie, maybe he too was feeling some remorse, I couldn't say. I had to make sure he didn't feel alienated, this affected him, too; I wanted to be certain he was alright.

"Avraham, will you come with us?"

"Me? Why, Ishmael?"

"He thought highly of you, you're just as involved as we

are; but you are not obliged to do anything you don't want."

"No, Ishmael, I will come: I should pay my respects. I didn't know him as well as you, but he was a good man. That's always worth respecting."

The doctor led the way. I was dreading it: I didn't know what to do or say, what I would think or feel. I paced myself as we got closer to the room where he lay; the whole time I was telling my mind to remain calm, praying it would listen. I needed to sway any impulsive actions or emotions arising: Essie needed me now.

I saw the look on her face; what she must have been feeling, I couldn't even imagine. I had to push my own fears aside, just be there for her, make an effort to control anything that tried to surface.

We came to the door, but Essie stopped; hesitantly she turned to me again.

"Ish, I...?"

"I'm right here, I'm not going anywhere. You don't have to do this if it's too soon, Essie; I know it's difficult under the circumstances."

"No, I must: I will regret it later. Ish, if he's my father then at least I've said goodbye."

The courage she displayed was remarkable: how she kept her emotions back like that, I could never know. She was so calm on the surface, so composed. Behind that, I knew she wanted to lash out: I sensed it, her emotions would have been everywhere. Yet to look at her, you would never have guessed her turmoil; she really was far more extraordinary than I had ever thought.

I felt for her deeply. To realise that the man I had picked up off the streets could in fact be her father, after so many years, then to not even know him till he passed, must have left her so confused to say the least. She was also in shock;

I knew it was only a matter of time before she let me know just how she really felt.

Essie gripped my hand tightly then opened the door. We went inside. Avraham followed, closing it behind us quietly. The room was small with whitewash walls. It had been made up to be a little chapel of rest, surrounded with different sized white candles, all of them burning. A large gold cross hung on the wall above where Richie lay.

He was lying in a coffin, laid with satin. He had a suit on the hospital must have donated. He looked so different to me now, clean shaven and smart. Essie seemed to recognise that, too. She hesitantly took steps towards Richie, her eyes now fixated on the coffin. Standing over it, she stared at him for a moment. I looked at Avraham, who was watching her, before I turned away ready to step forward. I went to move, but Avraham stopped me; he whispered to me.

"Ishmael, give her a moment; you will know when to go to her."

I just looked at him, he stared ahead. Before I could even speak I realised he was right. Essie now started becoming more vocal.

"Dad, is that you? No, it can't be? Please? DAAAAD, NO, DON'T LEAVE ME AGAIN, PLEASE, DAD? DON'T YOU DARE, COME BACK, PLEASE?"

She started shaking him. I dashed over to grab her. I could feel tears forming in my own eyes now. Essie was completely hysterical, trying to collapse, then stand. Wanting to turn back towards him; she didn't know what to do. I could feel her shaking uncontrollably. She looked at me; her eyes were soaked from tears, a look of complete bewilderment on her face.

"WHY, ISH, WHY?"

She started punching me with her fists, the anger she released was so intense; I just held her tightly as she sobbed. It was so hard to watch: I could relate deeply with her.

Avraham came over, placing his hand on her shoulder.

"Essie, I'm so very sorry."

She pulled away to look at him, but she had no words. I wiped her face.

"Why didn't he say? If he knew, why, Ishmael, why?"

"Essie, I have no answers; I'm sorry, all I can tell you is he told me if I ever found his daughter, to tell her he loved her very much. He loved you, Essie, never forget that."

"He could have told me himself: he had enough chances. I don't understand why he didn't and now he's gone; I can't forgive that."

Avraham stepped in to put his hand on her arm gently.

"Essie, he had his reasons. I know that will be hard to accept but, whatever they were, he was a good man. I believe he did it to protect you in some way. I know you're angry; you have every right to be, but don't hate him. He loved you, in time you will see that; we are both here for you."

"Avraham, he abandoned me. For years I wondered where he was, if he would come home. Praying I would see him even once: just to get some answers. He was at Ishmael's for a while, knowing yet saying nothing; would you forgive that?"

"Essie, listen to him: he speaks more sense than I care to admit. He spent years on the streets; perhaps he spent years looking for you, but when he found you he couldn't bring himself to say anything? Maybe just seeing you often was enough. I don't know; none of us do, but we know there was so much to this man. Essie, he was good, so his intentions would have been too."

"Do you really think that? I don't know what to think; why would he punish himself like that?"

"I know he wanted to make a lot of his wrongdoings right; it would make sense he tried to find you, especially to do that. You were loved by him, Essie, even though he wasn't there."

She turned, then walked back over to the coffin. She

fixed his hair before stroking his face; reluctantly, she then leaned over to kiss him.

"I love you, Dad, I always loved you. I know you suffered, but you could have just said. I need answers, I want to understand."

She started sobbing again, I took her hand pulling her to me; never had I seen anyone like that. No hug could take away what she was feeling; I could only let her know I was there, offer as much comfort as I could. She stood there for a few minutes, the silence was deafening, but peaceful now; it was only interrupted by her occasional sobs. She pulled away, wiping her eyes.

"Thank you for being here, I... I couldn't have done this without you both."

"You could, Essie, you are much braver than you know."

Avraham touched her gently on the arm.

"Essie, we will help you through this; he would've been very proud of you, any father would."

"Oh, Avraham, you will start me off again; you really are a lovely man, thank you. Any lady would be lucky to have you."

She hugged him then gave him a kiss on the cheek, both exchanging smiles. Essie put her head on my shoulder to rest. We stood there for a while. Avraham to our surprise walked over to the coffin. I watched him. He put his head down for a moment in respect, then patted Richie's hand.

"We will always watch out for her now, she will always be safe with us; rest in peace, Richie."

Essie lifted her head up, I was gob-smacked: he didn't often display emotion or how he felt, but you knew about it when he did. The words were powerful: he thought a lot more of Richie than he ever let on. Not just Richie, but Essie, too. They had never had a proper introduction, he just accepted her, was willing to help her, as well as protect her. He told us that through the least amount of words; he was very extraordinary at times, this was one of those moments.

"Ish, let's go, I am done here; there's no more to be said."

"Are you sure? We can stay for as long as you need too?"

"I'm sure, Ish. Avraham, may I have a moment with Ishmael alone?"

"Yes, of course, Essie; I'll be outside?"

"Thank you."

He left, shutting the door behind him quietly.

"Essie? What is it?"

"Ish, I learned today that important things should be said. You've been amazing today; you always are, but I can't hold back my feelings any longer: I love you, Ishmael, I really love you. I don't, I…"

I lifted her head as soon as she dropped it; I smiled at her and for a split second it took me back. The similarity to the dream, again, was so creepy, but she hadn't been beaten or broken like Betty had, yet, the situation Essie was going through very much caused just as much devastation for her in other ways. She was just as remarkable as Betty was. Those words warmed my insides; I had no problem telling her my true feelings for her, too.

"Essie, hey? One thing the dream told me was that we can't change how we feel, that there is nothing wrong in feeling what we do, no time will change it. I'm not going anywhere: you complete me, I feel that. Apart from Jonah, Avraham too, you're the best thing I woke up to because you're real. We spoke of our connection, things moving quickly, even then I knew how I felt. From the moment we met I knew I would feel this way. The dream clouded me but my feelings have always been clear, I just couldn't fully trust them; I didn't want to scare you off. We can't help how we feel, nor should we fear to speak or express ourselves; I don't. When you know, you know. Essie, I love you, too, part of me thinks I always have. You're beautiful in every way."

"Oh, Ish"

I kissed her before she said anymore. Knowing how she felt now, was the best feeling I had ever had awake. I felt so privileged to be there with her. I knew I was loveable; I was capable of it, now I would do anything to make her happy.

"Ish, Avraham is waiting, come on."

She took my hand as we opened the door, she looked back one last time.

"Sleep well, Dad, I love you."

"He loved you too, Essie. Never forget that: it will help you through."

She looked at me warmly; then we strolled over to Avraham who was waiting patiently, looking tired now. The whole day had tired us all out, it would be odd going back without Richie being there. I was concerned how Issy would fair with Jonah, wondering if they were getting on. Through the mayhem of the day, they had just been left. Essie turned to me.

"Ish, may I come back to yours? I don't want to be on my own tonight, I…"

"Essie, I won't leave you on your own if you don't want me to. Of course you can, come on."

"Ishmael, I can leave you both if you want: I know you will want some time."

"No, Avraham, we would like you to come; I know Ish will, won't you?"

"Yes, Avraham, we are family; we stick together now, you are always welcome regardless of what goes on."

He just patted me on the shoulder; never said a word. We headed back to mine, where all was quiet now. We walked into the lounge where Jonah came running over, followed by Issy. They were both fussed as always by Avraham then by myself. I was pleased as they seemed to have got on well. Looking over to where Richie was last nothing had been moved, his pencils were as he left them as well as his cup. It was hard: I would miss him very much, as well as his company. Essie, who seemed to be in a world of her own, went straight over to his drawings, understandably forgetting to greet the dogs.

Issy was fussing around her, but Jonah seemed to know: he just sat watching her, he seemed to sense her emotions. He stared then put his head down a moment, lifting it before staring at her again. A sad look now appeared. It was a powerful moment that only I seemed to notice. Essie picked up the pictures and the tears began to fall again.

"Ish, did he do these?"

"Yes, he was talented wasn't he?"

"They are amazing; what are you going to do with them?"

"Essie, that should be your choice, he did ask me to sell them, as I said, and put the profits towards the shelter. But he was your dad so I haven't got that say any more, that belongs to you."

"No, if that's what he wanted then you must do it. I know people who may buy these. You must open the shelter; please don't lose focus of that, promise me, Ish?"

I laughed without thought: I could see the resemblance, it was crazy. Essie, even Avraham, glared at me now.

"Ishmael."

"Ish, what are you laughing at?"

"Sorry, Essie, he said the same thing exactly how you said it. You're certainly his daughter; I will miss having him around."

"I know, Ish, we all will; I wish I had got to know him more. I should've came around more often, I just... well..."

She broke down again, I put my arm around her as Avraham came over.

"You didn't know Essie; it's clear you would have done, but what happened isn't your fault. We must accept his reasons; take comfort knowing you did see him, even if it was blindly. Remember that he loved you, that's enough. I know this is difficult, but dwelling won't help things now.

Essie, put that smile back while I make us some coffee, it will be alright."

As much as she didn't want to, she couldn't help but smile by this: the fact that it was coming from Avraham was the reason why. He was showing a completely different side of himself now, it was so nice to see; his way with words, on top of his soft voice, was reassuring. Nobody could ease people's minds the way Avraham could.

We had coffee while we spoke of Richie. After a while Essie got up.

"Ish, may I see his room?"

"Yes, if you're sure? Do you want me to come with you?"

"Yes, I'd like that, Ish."

"Come on. Avraham, we won't be long."

"Ishmael, it's fine, go; take all the time you both need."

14 RICHIE'S LETTER

I nodded appreciatively towards him, then took her to Richie's room. For a man who had lived on the streets, he hadn't forgotten how to keep a place tidy: his room was spotless. Essie walked round slowly, picking up things then putting them back. She then sat down on his bed looking around. He had a little wooden unit with a drawer, by his bed. Essie kept touching the handle then pulling away.

"It's okay, if you want to open it you can."

"I don't know, it feels wrong, Ish; I'm scared too."

"You don't have to do this now; you've had a massive shock today, it can wait."

"No, Ish, I felt drawn here, there must be reason?"

"There's no rush, take all the time you need; do you want me to wait outside?"

"No, don't go: I need you here. Would you help me open it? I…"

"You know I will Essie, we are in this together."

"Together."

I kneeled by the bed and slowly we opened the drawer. The relief on Essie's face was clear. Inside there were various things along with a letter. There was a photograph, too. She picked it up then clutched her chest; her jaw dropped.

"Ish, I think this is me, when I was a baby; I can't believe he's had it all these years?"

"Oh, Essie, that says it all: he really loved you."

She looked at it for a moment before picking up the letter. It had both my name and Essie's on it. We just looked at each other simultaneously, puzzled: not sure what to do or who should take it. I immediately handed it to Essie.

"Essie, go on, he was your father; you should open it."

"No, I… I can't; please Ish, you read it."

I opened the envelope, not knowing what to expect. There wasn't just a letter but a key for a property of some sort. I was curious by this, as well as confused: why would a homeless man have a key? I handed it to her; then got up to join her on the bed. I held her hand.

"Essie, are you ready?"

"Yes, Ish, I'm ready."

"Dear Ishmael, my dear Essie.

If you're reading this, then I am no longer here. I have written many letters in my life, but this one is the hardest I've ever written; but necessary.

I want to thank you Ishmael for what you did; you have proved there are great people around. But I can't say I am one of them: I have not been as honest as I wanted to be, I have exaggerated everything, done what was needed. Ishmael, Essie, I made things up to pass as a homeless man; it is truly unforgivable, but I did not want to lose contact with my daughter, especially when I finally found her after so long.

I have not been living on the streets as you thought, but Essie, I have searched for years trying to find you; to tell you I didn't want to leave you, to let you know I never stopped thinking about you. I always loved you from the minute you were born. I saw all the love between you both, something I never had with your mother; we were both miserable, to the point where I had to go. That was the hardest decision of my life; but Essie I knew it was right, for you mainly.

Every day I prayed you wouldn't be angry or hate me. I vowed to make things right from the day I left. I am not a poor man, but seeing you open your property when you have little yourself, Ishmael, now knowing what you want to achieve, I will be leaving you enough money to do that along with a car. Ishmael, no isn't an option. My Essie, you too shall receive my inheritance, my house is yours; do what you will with it.

My lawyer will take care of it all. I could not tell you; I would never have made things right with you otherwise. Above anything else, that was my lifetime goal. I have not been a well man for many years, I had nobody I could leave my fortune to, I couldn't give you much when I was alive but through my death I can give you a better quality of life. I hope you accept it, as you are all deserving. I know you will feel like you don't know me at all; but if there was another way, I would have done it. I never wanted to cause problems or cause any issues for anybody, that is why I did not say, Essie; that too was so hard, but you may see why.

I just wanted to be close to you Essie, seeing you happy I couldn't say as much as I wanted too: it may have caused problems between you and Ishmael, I couldn't be sure it wouldn't, so it was a risk I couldn't go through with. I hope you both forgive me one day.

I want to also leave Avraham something: he is a better man than I ever was, extraordinary I would say. He was quick in protecting you both; I must honour that. I know, Essie, now I am gone, you will be safe with them both.

Ishmael, from the bottom of my heart, thank you, go out there now, live your dreams; be happy. Please don't let my ways stop that; that is my last wish.

You all made my last days precious. Ishmael, your wisdom you don't even realise you have, that has helped me see things clearly. I could find some peace, and for that I am forever grateful. I wasn't deserving of what you did, but you never judged the person you thought I was.

That is a gift no money can repay or buy; it makes you special, it will take you far. Buy Jonah a bone and give him one last stroke from me. Keep writing, Ishmael, use your gift; make people see that through darkness there is always light. This I know you can do: you've proven it. My intentions were always good even if my ways proved otherwise; I hated having to do it that way, but it was the only way. Finally seeing you, Essie, after so long made it worth it. Maybe you will see that now, if not then one day; I pray you will.

Thank you for allowing me to be a part of your lives even for a short time. I love you all.

Till we all meet again.

> *All my love*
> *Richie/Dad*
> *Henry Jacobs*
> *Xxx*

Essie, I know you have children, my grandchildren; they, too, will be taken care of. I wish you to hold them again; don't dwell on what's happened, they belong with you. My last bit of advice? Look to the future now, always do what makes you happy, fight for what you want if you need to. Follow your heart; let nobody stand in your way. I love you always, my beautiful daughter.

p.s. The key is for the house.

Essie went quiet, I took her hand then she looked at me.

"Essie, I don't know what to say; it is a lot to take in,

especially for you."

"I want to be angry, Ish, but I can't, I only feel sadness. I understand his reasons, but I wish I had the chance to tell him he was wrong."

"I know, Essie, I can only imagine how hard this is for you but, regardless of his ways, he showed just how much he loved you; through all this, that stands out the most. It is okay to feel how you do, but I know dwelling on it is not going to help you; you will get through this."

"I know, Ish, I am so glad I have you here, he thought highly of you, he proved that, too, by the letter; I hope you can start to fulfil your goals now, he knew how much it meant to you."

"It feels wrong, Essie, it isn't right taking anything, I…"

"Ish, look at me, it's alright: what you did for him deserves rewarding. He is right, you are such a good man who has been through so much. My father wants you to have the money because he knows good will come of it; you must accept it."

"I made him promises, Essie, I will keep them, but okay."

"Oh, Ish, I know this is as hard for you, you're a man of your word; my father knew that too. Come on, let's get back to Avraham, we've been here ages."

We walked back in to see that Avraham had fallen asleep. It was late now, he looked so peaceful; I didn't want to wake him, so I just got him a blanket then left him where he was, I looked over at Essie.

"Will you stay, Essie? I just… well, I find myself not wanting to be alone tonight."

"Me neither, Ish, I would love to stay; there's no place I'd rather be right now, I love you."

"I love you too, I'm exhausted; time for bed I think?"

"The day has been a long one; I'm tired too. Ish, be quiet: don't wake Avraham."

We went quietly to bed. To have her in my arms that night was something else, she fell asleep almost instantly. I savoured the moment a bit longer, until my eyes could no longer stay open. I thought: if I had this coming out of my coma, I would've woken a lot happier. But having it here for real was indescribable. I realised just how blessed I was; my stubbornness was holding me back, not to mention my pride.

I fell asleep knowing I was wrong to turn my back on Rabbi: he had been extremely good to me over the years. All that Avraham said rang true, it wasn't God who did all this, and even if it was it brought me to where I was now. I had to be thankful; more importantly, I also had to thank Rabbi, I hoped he could forgive me.

I woke up remembering yesterday's events. Essie was lying there awake; again, in a world of her own.

"Morning, beautiful, how are you feeling?"

"I am not sure, but I am okay, Ish"

"You will be, Essie, it will take time, coffee?"

"I know, but yes, I would love one, Ish; you slept well?"

"Yes, very; how could I not?"

I gave her a wink then kissed her before getting up. Jonah came running in excitedly then jumped on the bed startling Essie; she only laughed.

"Hi, Jonah, time to get up is it, where is Issy?"

He put up his paw panting excitedly, looking round like he understood her. Essie started tormenting him, pretending to get up then laughing; giving him a stroke until she did get up. Avraham was up, too, he had already made breakfast for us and the aroma was wafting in the room. Only he could have let Jonah into us, but I didn't mind; those few moments seeing her playing with Jonah were priceless. He called out to us.

"Ishmael, Essie, I have made breakfast, come while it's hot."

I walked into the lounge, he had really gone to some effort; I smiled.

"Avraham, you didn't have to trouble yourself, thank you."

"Nonsense, Ishmael, it was a pleasure."

Essie followed in a minute later, we then went to the table. Sitting down, I turned to Avraham.

"Avraham, Richie left a letter, he wants to leave you something; Essie, maybe you should explain?"

"Ish, maybe letting him read the letter will be better, would you get it?"

"Yes, give me a moment."

I got up to get the letter, Essie turned to Avraham.

"Avraham, thank you for yesterday, you didn't have to do what you did."

"Essie, not at all, you are very important to Ishmael; I meant what I said to your father."

She smiled as he turned away, she put her hand on his then he looked at her again.

"Avraham, thank you, but you are very important to Ishmael, but also important to me, too. I want you to know that."

He only smiled at her as I came back in. I handed the letter to Avraham, he took it from me then began reading it; we waited for him to finish. A couple of minutes later he looked up at us both seriously.

"Essie, thank you, but I cannot accept anything: I see his point, but that's just my ways. I can't accept this for doing that, it's not right."

"Avraham, you have been an incredible friend to Ishmael, you are not being rewarded for your ways: you are being rewarded because you deserve to be, it's what my father wanted. It's time you found some happiness; his gift may help with that. I know you're a proud man, but Avraham, you are the most deserving one I've ever come across; please accept it."

"Avraham, it's time to think about your dreams, what you want to do; we are always here for you, but you have given enough of your life for me. It's important you do something for you now."

Avraham sat back in his chair, you could see he was overwhelmed; I couldn't have wished this to happen to a nicer person. I was so lucky having a friend like him, we had become a lot closer. The dream didn't touch what we had now; it had turned out so much better. I had come far, but I wouldn't have without him. He stayed quiet throughout breakfast, as if he was going through everything in his mind. After a while he sat up then put his hand on my arm.

"Ishmael, your parents will be proud of you now, as am I. I am glad I stayed all those years ago."

"I am too, Avraham, I wouldn't be here if it wasn't for you."

"No, Ishmael, I think you would; I cannot take credit for everything. It's you who chose to become who you are; remember that."

"Avraham, I've been thinking: I want to see Rabbi, I need to make things right with him, he has been good to me over the years. I have been wrong to push him away; would you ask him if you see him?"

"Ishmael, you know I will, he thinks a lot of you, regardless. He is an understanding man, especially when it comes to you."

"Ish, you lost your way, turned your back, many would've done the same. However, it's never too late to change that too. Like my father said, follow your heart: that way you will be happy. Whatever you decide now will be right."

"Essie, yes, I know I can change some things, this is one I must; I need to make amends, too, just like I told Richie. Avraham, I know he is understanding but I won't take that for granted, not anymore."

"Ishmael, he will be pleased so do not worry. I will take the dogs out; maybe I can see Rabbi now, let him know what you said."

"Avraham, maybe I should go with you?"

"No, Ishmael, be with Essie today; I can go alone."

"Thank you, Avraham; I will see you soon."

"Yes, I shall get the dogs then be on my way, goodbye, Ishmael, Essie."

"Goodbye, Avraham."

"Goodbye, Avraham, thank you for being there, see you soon."

"I am glad I was, Essie, goodbye."

Avraham left while Essie started sorting through the rest of Richie's things; I cleared the breakfast dishes away. As I walked into the kitchen, Essie called me.

"Ish, what do we do with these? I am not sure selling them is right, now?"

"Keep them if you want to, they will be more sentimental value to you; it would be greedy profiting I agree, it's not necessary."

She picked one up clutching it with sadness against her chest, putting her head down in thought; taking a moment, she looked up.

"Ish, I…"

That moment I heard a knock on the door. We looked at each other baffled.

"That can't be Avraham back already, hang on Essie, I'll answer it."

I hurriedly went to open the door. A man was standing there, all suited with a smart looking briefcase. He was a chubby fellow with an untidy moustache which matched his grey hair. He seemed friendly enough; he looked important, yet he was certainly no snob.

"Yes, can I help you?"

"Perhaps? Are you Ishmael?"

"Yes, that's right, you are?"

"Mr. Joshua Samble, Henry Jacobs lawyer. May I come in, please?"

"Yes, of course. This way."

I led him into the lounge where I introduced him to

Essie; she was inquisitive now as to whom I was talking to.

"This is Essie, Henry's daughter."

"Aah, yes, he mentioned he found you. I'm sorry for your loss, miss; it must have been quite a shock."

"Thank you, sir; yes, it was. Please, have a seat?"

"Thank you."

He sat down then started organising papers from his briefcase; he pulled out glasses along with a pen.

"I believe your father left you a letter?"

"He did sir, how do you know? Are you needing it?"

"He mentioned he wrote you one. But no, don't trouble yourself for now: we have much to get through. Are you aware your father was wealthy? In fact, very wealthy; a millionaire if you please."

"What? No? His letter just said he was not a poor man. My father said he had left us money, but he made no mention of that; we had no idea."

"Aah, his wealth was one reason why he found you, he had people searching for you for years, miss. He came to see me the day before he died, his fortune is to be shared between you, your children, Ishmael. Avraham will get something too; where is he?"

"He left earlier, he does not live here, sir, he's my best friend; he stayed last night as it was a long day."

"No explanation necessary Ishmael. Essie, your father has a five-million-pound fortune; I see money will no longer be an issue for all of you, congratulations."

I didn't know who was more shocked, I was speechless; Essie, she couldn't take it in either.

"What? Five million? No, this isn't happening, Ish, I…"

Mister Samble started laughing: he seemed to take pleasure in giving good news.

"Yes, it's real alright, your father certainly had a way of surprising people. I have some things for you to sign then it can be released. I know he left a key to his house, yes?"

"Yes, he said nothing else except he was leaving it to me; I don't even know where it is."

"It's in America, miss. Beautiful it is. He spent years looking for you as you know: mainly because he had a bad heart, besides the fact he loved you. This was the case for as long as I remember. Once he knew where you were he came straight over. He never stopped speaking about you: wondering, questioning where you were, whether you were happy. I never saw him so excited the day he got the call about your whereabouts. Anyway, Ishmael, he left you a car; that's on its way here, the car was of great importance to him."

"I will take care of it; you have my word."

"Would you sign here please, Ishmael? Essie could you sign these too, please? I will give you papers for Avraham, he must also sign them; may I leave them with you? They can be dropped in my office when done. Well, I will leave you to it then."

"Yes, I will ask him to sign soon as possible; they will be returned to you."

"I will be returning to America in a couple of days, I am here specifically to make sure your father's wishes are met."

He handed us the papers to sign; after doing so we gave them back. Then with precision, he placed them into his briefcase before taking off his glasses then standing up.

"Well, nice to finally meet you both, if you ever need a lawyer; give me a call."

"Wait, I may need one?"

"Essie?"

"Ish, my kids were taken, placed with a family to look after, they don't belong there, I want them back. Please sir, can you help me? I don't think I'd want anyone else to do it, not now?"

"If I can help I will, call me when you're ready; we will go from there. Remember I'm only here for a couple of days, please let me know your decision. I will see myself out; good day to you both."

"Thank you, sir, nice to meet you, too. Goodbye."

"Thank you, I will be in touch soon. Bye, sir."

Her face lit up; we had become millionaires within a day, but all she wanted was her kids. I wanted that for her more than anything now, she was so like Richie in some ways: her devotion to her children was all that mattered, just as she had been so important to Richie. It was humbling, she had the opportunity to get them back, an opportunity she took without thought.

"Ish, this is so surreal, I…"

"I know, Essie, I don't think it's quite sunk in yet. But you have a chance to get your children back; I know you will be happy then, I'll support you all the way."

"I really love you, Ishmael, you've been brilliant, thank you."

"I love you too; but Essie: you're everything to me, I want to see you happy, I will do all I can to ensure it."

"I know, Ish, I am so lucky. I've been thinking about the house; America?"

"Yes, it's a long way, but if you decide to move or sell, I will back you. Essie like I said: whatever makes you happy, that makes me happy. We can visit sometime, it may help you to decide for definite, there is no rush."

"You are incredible, I am so blessed having you, Ish, but this will be a decision we do together; I won't do it any other way."

I really admired her: she had the whole world on her shoulders but to look at her you would never think it. Only I knew her pain; she looked so vulnerable, yet she was so strong. Looking at her, I wanted to make the proper commitment: I wanted to ask her to marry me. Years ago, receiving money like that I would have been ecstatic, but I now knew there were more important things in life, the money would help but without it I'd still have Essie and Avraham. Part of me still didn't think I deserved any of Richie's money, I wouldn't see it as mine either. I had a chance to really help people with it now; it was what Richie wanted.

We spent the day looking through Richie's things while we chatted. He didn't have much for a millionaire; but what he did have, Essie examined carefully. She was asking questions, which I could not answer, leaving us both wondering. A while later, Avraham knocked on the door.

"Essie, break the news to him gently: this will really shock him."

"I know, Ish, don't worry, go; don't keep him waiting."

I let him in, then gave him warning we had some news.

"Avraham, we've had the lawyer round, you may want to sit down."

"Ishmael?"

"It's okay, Ish. Avraham, you know my father was leaving you something? We've just learned he has a five-million-pound fortune; you will be receiving a share of it."

"What? No, no: that is too much, I won't take that, I… I…"

"We know it's a shock Avraham; but you deserve it, the amount makes no difference. You must have dreams? What's one thing you would like to do?"

He gave it a minute before he looked at me, seeming to be unsure of whether to say what was on his mind. I moved closer to him.

"Avraham? You can say whatever is on your mind?"

"Yes, I have a dream; I want…? No, I would like to go to see the place we fled from; Rakira, our home. I've wondered about it all these years; I guess part of me missed it, but I won't go alone. It's silly I know."

"No, Avraham, it's not; I've often wondered about it too. I just, well, I've always been afraid to go back; maybe we should?"

"We? Ishmael?"

"Avraham, I know this is important to you, it is for me too. We fled together; we should go back together. I will go with you, we all will."

"Ish, you're so sweet."

"Yes Ishmael, never did I think I'd hear you say those words; for me it would mean a lot, thank you my friend."

I patted him on the shoulder fondly, he turned showing a smile.

"I'd be honoured, Avraham; I wouldn't have it any other way."

"As will I, but only when you're ready. Oh, Ishmael? Rabbi will be happy to see you; he said to go whenever you can."

"That I can do alone, Avraham."

He looked at me then started laughing, Essie too, he then turned to me.

"You can do anything you put your mind to, Ishmael, I've always known that."

"I will make the arrangements, thank you Avraham."

"Likewise, Ishmael, likewise."

I had a lot to plan and organise; I didn't know where to even start, or what to start with. I felt somewhat overcome, like things were coming at me in all directions. I didn't want to cause worry for Essie or Avraham by telling them. I had been cooped up inside a good while, so I decided a walk might help put things into perspective; it would at least clear my head a little. Avraham was chatting to Essie; I was in my own world, for a few moments at least.

"Ish, are you alright, you're quiet?"

"I'm good, Essie, I am thinking of going for a walk; would you like to join me?"

"It's a good idea. Avraham will you join us?"

"Thank you but no, I must be going: I have things to do. Jonah enjoyed his walk with Issy, they seem fond of each other."

"Yes, they get on well, I am glad for that."

Essie turned to Avraham, picking up the documents the

lawyer had left.

"Avraham, before you go, we were asked to ask you to sign these then return them; they are for the lawyer."

I knew Avraham would find that hard to do so casually, so I stepped in: hoping to unload the burden.

"If you sign, Avraham, we will take them: you've done enough for me."

"Okay, Ishmael, yes; that will be easier if you could."

I grabbed a pen giving it to him. I could see his hand shaking: it was obvious now he was struggling, Essie noticed too. She put her hand on his warmly then smiled.

"It's okay, Avraham, take your time: I know this is difficult, but it is what my father wanted. Please, don't forget that; you deserve this."

He glanced up at her, took a deep breath then signed them like it was no big deal. Essie looked at me; we could only smile at each other now. He had always put on a brave face, but seeing him like that, then reversing back, was endearing. He wasn't afraid to show that side, but he did take to a little reassurance. He signed them swiftly, handing them to me once done.

"Avraham, I hope the money brings you at least some happiness."

He looked at me with a serious expression, staring for a moment then took a breath.

"No, Ishmael, only my friends can give me that: friendship is far more valuable than any money could ever be. Right, I shall be off again. Essie, thank you."

"You've nothing to thank me for. Goodbye Avraham."

She chuckled shaking her head: it was humorous as well as humbling, the man had become a millionaire, but to him, it was just another day. We took the papers, handing them in to Mr. Samble's office. From there we walked round the shops, it was strange now: just knowing I could buy anything, yet I could only focus on the shelter. I wasn't materialistic whatsoever; I could do without lavish things, the money was to do good for others, not myself. One thing that did cross my mind was that a typewriter would help me. I promised Richie to finish my writing; it was something I wanted to do, although that would have to wait. I decided to sort out the shelter first, that was the main thing. I would then be able to arrange a time where I could propose to Essie; maybe then I could focus on my writing. I was aware I had promised to help Essie get her children back, so that was on my list of priorities, too.

15 RABBI AND A PROPOSAL

A few weeks had gone by. We'd had a small memorial service for Richie. His lawyer told us his wishes: that he would be taken back to America, where he had made funeral arrangements for after his passing. Essie was understandably upset by this, but she could also see the reasons as to why.

So, considering all that had happened, she felt it right to do what he wanted, but having something private for him was something she had to do, too. I could understand her wanting to say a proper goodbye, she knew I'd never got that chance with my parents which made her more adamant to do it. She knew the importance of it. The day was emotional but pleasant, I believe Essie found a lot more peace afterwards.

Not long after, we all received Richie's gifts; the car was beautiful, a Chrysler Imperial I was told, maroon red. I fell in love instantly when it arrived; it turned a few heads, too. I was close to being able to drive it after taking lessons. I decided to get a runaround once I was able to drive legally. Driving about in Richie's car was not really my way, I'd use it for special occasions only. That way I could keep my promise to Richie's lawyer in looking after it.

Jonah was still Jonah, I hadn't spent a great deal of time with him lately, our long walks seemed to become more of a chore. I know he was happy, but I missed it. It had been so busy lately; I hoped things would calm down enough in time when I could spend more time with him. Avraham saw him more, but I was glad for that in a way as he was with someone who loved Jonah just as much as I did. He also had Issy who Jonah really enjoyed being with.

Essie was told I was taking driving lessons, but not how far I had got: it was all part of the plan to turn up unexpected then drive her somewhere to propose.

I had bought a building for what would be the shelter; I had builders working on it, too. Essie had been to see about getting her children back; we had barely seen each other lately due to focusing on our own things. I had still not been to see Rabbi, due to other things which seemed to pop up at the times I wanted to and kept preventing me. Essie rang in excitement this one morning as I was waiting in for Rabbi, and I was unsure if I'd see him now at all.

"Ish, I… I…"

"Essie? Are you alright?"

"Ish, I've just been informed I'm getting the children back, I have a date; I can't believe it, they are coming home."

"I am on my way round, this is brilliant. Essie, I'm delighted for you, I won't be long."

"See you soon, Ish, I love you."

I put the receiver down quickly then grabbed my coat. I almost ran to her house. She was standing outside waiting when I arrived. I ran over then picked her up, spinning her around. She laughed, smacking me on the shoulder playfully to put her down. Hesitantly, I did, I looked her in the eyes before taking her hands.

"Things are going to be perfect, I promise; how are you feeling?"

"I can't explain, Ish: it's all I've ever wanted. I wish my dad was here."

"He is, Essie, he is in your heart; that will never go."

She threw her arms around me excitedly; it was lovely seeing her so happy.

"What are your plans, Ish, let us do lunch?"

"Well I must see Rabbi, I can't put it off any longer. Come back with me, he is due to come around soon? We can go afterwards?"

"Yes, I understand that, Ish. I'll grab my coat."

We headed back, Essie talked excitedly about all the things she wanted to do, places she wanted to go with the kids. It was warming to see her finally able to do that. She could plan or buy what she needed, too. I was looking forward to meeting them, although I knew that wouldn't be so soon.

I was happy for her to do things her own way; she would allow me to meet them when she was ready. Giving them time alone to adjust together was far more important than my needs or wants. We got back to wait for Rabbi; I made some coffee in the meantime.

Rabbi was due anytime within the hour, part of me was nervous. I knew he would tell me not to be, but it wasn't that easy: it'd be awkward in a way, that was my own fault because of how I had treated him. I had to make things right even if we never spoke again. A good half hour passed until the knock came. Essie saw I was nervous, so took it on herself to answer it; I was grateful for that. I heard them talking.

"Good morning, I'm here to see Ishmael?"

"Morning, Rabbi; I'm Essie, his girlfriend. Please, come in, he is through here."

"Pleasure, Essie, thank you."

Rabbi walked in followed by Essie who went to make some fresh coffee.

"Good day, Ishmael, I hope you are well? Avraham said you wanted to see me? This was some time ago, why?"

"Yes, Rabbi, I apologise: I've not had the chance to, I have just been so busy, it's no excuse but... well, I got you here because I want to make things right with you. You did so much for me when we first arrived. I was so selfish, thought about nobody, I know you came to see me in hospital."

"Slow down, Son, it's alright; may I sit?"

"Please do, Rabbi."

"Ishmael, Avraham has told me everything that has happened, I can't be angry with you: you have been through much in your life, but you seem to be making up for that now. You may have lost your faith, but it seems faith has got you here. Ishmael, you have done yourself proud to get where you are, I'm not saying to come back to the synagogue or follow the tradition, but you still have friends. I know you feel they let you down, but they only wanted to help: they are good people, but you were blind through your troubles. Ishmael, you are always welcome; just, don't think you can't if that's what you want."

"I have been through a lot, learned many things; my dream also teaching me so much, one being that the people in my life are the most important thing, and that includes you, Rabbi. Neither me or Avraham would be here if it wasn't for you doing what you did. I can't say what I will do regarding the synagogue or my faith, but I do want you in my life. I have become so much better now, I won't let anyone down again; I am truly sorry for my behaviour."

"Yes, I can see that, Son. I know with you there was never anything to forgive: I always knew you would come good in time. I've always had much faith in you; I was right to do so. So long as you are doing the right thing, you can't do much wrong, Ishmael."

"Rabbi, you were in my dream, it was like it has been now: the distance between us. Yet I saw you, but you were so much older? You helped me to become a better person; but in real life, that hasn't been the case because of the distance between us. I don't know the relevance to it?"

"Aah, Ishmael, I see the confusion, but you didn't appreciate I was always here, maybe the only relevance of the dream was to draw you back to me? You pushed people away, myself included. I can understand that because I know what you've been through. However, besides you wanting to make amends, maybe there are other reasons I am here now? The dream was showing you something, Ishmael, maybe it was just the fact that I won't always be around; I cannot say for certain. I know from Avraham that it had a big influence on how you've come to be now, but it's also shown you how important people can be, too. I don't know your dream, Ishmael, only you can decide that. You have embraced much of what the dream has shown you, now you can achieve anything you want to. Ishmael, until you're happy with yourself, you can't make others happy; only by accepting things can you really move on. I could be wrong with my assumptions, Ishmael, but there is a reason for everything; time will tell what those reasons are. It did give you a choice regarding myself; I am glad we have come to this point now, without it the distance may have gone too far."

"Yes, what you say makes sense, Rabbi, in some ways, but I can't say for sure either. I only know for certain that I want you in my life. My stubbornness got in the way, but after Richie passing I knew I had to try to make amends with you, even if you pushed me away. Based on the dream alone, that wasn't enough to convince me, but with that happening, too, it told me for sure. For whatever reasons, you are meant to be in my life, Rabbi; but that is your choice now, I know that too."

"Ishmael, I won't ever turn my back on you, sometimes situations or events teach us the most valuable things, but sometimes not having people around is the only way we realise the lessons, your dream has proven that with us. We are fortunate, Ishmael, some people never realise those things, and they are left with much regret. If anything happened to either of us, then we would have had that remorse always; I am glad we have spoken now."

"I, too, am glad you gave me the time, the chance to say what I needed to, thank you for that, Rabbi."

"No, thank you, Ishmael, you certainly have changed, I can see you're happier with who you are now; as for Essie, she, too, seems to make you happy?"

"Rabbi, she has been unbelievable, she is a beautiful person; she has helped me, too. I love her."

Essie came out then carrying coffee, she had been in the kitchen a while: I assumed it was to give me time with Rabbi. Now, hearing her name mentioned she came out.

"Rabbi, we make each other happy, we are a team; I'd be lost without him."

"Yes, I can believe that, well I will let you go; I know you are a busy man, Ishmael. I am very proud of you, I am always there if you need me; come around anytime, just don't leave it so long next time. Goodbye Essie."

"Goodbye, Rabbi, nice to meet you."

"Likewise, Essie."

I walked him out, closing the door over to Rabbi's puzzlement.

"Ishmael, what is it?"

"Rabbi, in my dream you said I should follow my heart: to not worry about the opinions of people? I told you I wanted to marry a girl who wasn't Jewish, but I was told it may cause problems because of my faith.. Rabbi, Essie is not Jewish either, but I want to ask her to marry me; I'd like you to marry us? It still concerns me."

"Ishmael, I would say the same now; people won't approve you doing it in the synagogue the way things stand now. However, I can marry you if you want that, it would be an honour to."

"No, Rabbi, it is me who would be honoured after everything; it would mean a lot."

"It is done then, let me know your plans; I will see my availability but, also, I can let you know if I can marry you in your chosen place. You know there are places I won't be able to do it, Ishmael, but this is your day; it must be somewhere you both want, regardless."

"Yes, I know that, Rabbi, but please, not a word if you see Essie from now on: she has no idea of my plans."

He put his finger to his mouth, then gave a coy smile

while patting me on the arm. I shut the door behind him. I heard Essie pottering about which I was relieved about: the surprise would have been ruined if she had heard our conversation, I did not want that.

We went for lunch before I checked to see how the shelter was coming along, it was odd seeing a dream of mine come to life; knowing I could help make a difference was a great feeling. The building manager came to greet me, he was called Samuel; a nice chap, tall with a stocky build, he had a very bubbly personality. Seeing that I had walked in, he approached me smiling.

"Ishmael, it's coming along, I think we are almost done."

"Sam, you've done remarkably well; thank you for all you have done, it's looking great."

"Not at all, it's my job."

"Heart has gone into this Sam, that should be appreciated. How long are we looking at till completion?"

"Two days, it will be ready for furniture, then the opening."

"Sam, I didn't realise it would be so soon: I thought a few weeks at least."

"Things went better than expected, Ishmael; you seem a bit disappointed if you don't mind me saying so?"

"No, Sam, I am pleased, I just have much to organize; I thought I had more time."

"You have, Ishmael, there isn't any rush; open when you're ready, don't stress."

"Sam, I have a name for it, can you see to it? Here."

"Of course, leave it with me, Ishmael."

He looked at the paper I handed him.

"Richie's hope for the homeless? Ishmael, that is such a great name, I'll see to it immediately."

"Well, I thought it appropriate, thank you; I'll see you, Sam."

"You will, goodbye, Ishmael."

I stepped outside, I had so many things to organise, I was becoming stressed, only then to laugh: I knew Avraham would help if I asked. Essie would have helped too, but I knew she was busy herself with work, besides other things. I went straight home to call him.

"Avraham, I need your help, are you busy?"

"No, Ishmael, is everything alright?"

"I've just been told that the shelter will be ready in two days, I'm not prepared; I don't know what to do next, I need staff, I…"

"Woah, calm yourself, of course I will help; Ishmael, you are worrying over things that are not necessary, there is still plenty of time."

"I'm sorry, Avraham: it was just unexpected. I know things will be alright; could you come over now?"

"Yes, Ishmael, I am on my way."

"Thank you, see you soon."

"See you soon, Ishmael."

I put the kettle on then waited restlessly. He soon came knocking and then we got to work immediately. We arranged the furniture needed, put adverts in the local paper for staff, set up the opening; we covered everything. Avraham wrote times down along with all the dates; I knew exactly what was going on now.

"Avraham, I couldn't have…"

"Aah, no, you could Ishmael, you just need to relax more; stop fretting so much."

"Thank you, Avraham, I shall arrange our trip this week, I should have already done it."

"You would have if you weren't so busy with other things, some things are more important. I know the shelter means a lot, that is okay, you can't do everything all at once; don't be so hard on yourself. However, yes, I think we could all do with a break, but Ishmael, you must be comfortable with this; it won't be an easy trip."

"I know I'll be fine with you there, Essie too. I think I, too, need to deal with it: until I face it I can't heal fully. Avraham, I don't want that always on my mind; I need closure."

"Yes, I believe you will get it. Ishmael, as I have said before, I think your parents would be very proud of you now; that's what matters. Jonah is looking somewhat fed up?"

"I have been so busy lately, I don't seem to have the time for anything."

"Ishmael, my friend, listen to me; you are doing good, it's something you must keep on doing. However, Jonah does need your time, you need to make it. Your bond is a strong one, don't get so carried away that you risk losing it."

"I know, Avraham, I have given it much thought; he is so important to me, but I know he is happy. I am working towards giving him the attention he needs. I appreciate your concern, but I will give him back the stability he is used to. Avraham, am I really that bad?"

"No, Ishmael, of course not; I just know it would be devastating for you both if you lost the special bond you have built up. He will be happy; but that is by no means a replacement. I'm telling you this because it is important, Ishmael. I know you adore him, I am not trying to put pressure on you in any way; I am just stating my concern, that's all."

I knew better than to argue this with him, or argue anything for that matter: he was always right. My life had changed dramatically, but it wasn't of benefit to everything or everyone. Jonah did need prioritising more; after what we were able to sort out I did have some free time, I was going to spend it with him. I decided I would take a trip to town: to buy a ring for Essie. Jonah would come with me, then I would get him a bone off Richie; just as he had asked in his letter.

"Avraham, I'm taking him to town: there's something I need to do."

"Ishmael, I am sure he will appreciate that. Please, don't allow what I say to trouble you, I know you're doing your best; I just had to make sure you knew the consequences. I need to go, too; but as ever, you know where I am if I am needed."

"I do, but likewise, Avraham, thank you for your help today; I will see you soon."

"Anytime, goodbye, Ishmael."

With a lot of weight off my mind, I headed to town. Jonah kept staring up at me, wondering why our usually brief walks were taking longer. He seemed to relax the further we went, eventually enjoying it as much as I did. It wasn't the same as going to our usual places, but it was time with him; for now, we both valued it. I had the opportunity to organise how I was going to propose, a new restaurant had just opened where I went to look around. I left Jonah waiting patiently outside. I got an engagement ring, then a bone for Jonah, I also bought a suit. It wasn't what I usually wore, but I wanted it to be special; that meant dressing appropriately.

Now I just had to be able to drive legally, but I was almost ready to do that; I could then plan the actual day. I was excited but also nervous: I was sure she would say yes, just unsure of the timing, with her getting the kids back. I hoped in this respect, I was doing the right thing.

The day came when I was finally able to drive legally; it killed me not telling Essie, but I was pleased I had done it. I avoided her that day because she would've known something then I would have been forced to tell. The shelter was fully furnished now, almost ready to open. I had planned our trip back home. Avraham was still deciding what to do with his money; he hadn't spent a pound of it yet that I was aware of, but I knew he still found it hard to come to terms with. I wasn't totally sure whether he just didn't know what to do with it, or it was because he just didn't want it. I knew for certain that whatever he decided to do it would be the right thing. If he was happy then it was all that mattered. I went back to the restaurant to book a table, and I left flowers along with a card outside Essie's just a couple of minutes before she was due home.

"Hey beautiful,
Be ready at seven,
I'll come and get you
Love you
- Ish xxx"

I drove round to Avraham's as I wanted him to be there with Rabbi when I proposed. I knocked on the door excitedly, I heard him coming down the hallway then he opened it. My feeling switched to instant concern: he didn't look too well, one bit.

"Ishmael? I wasn't expecting you? Please, come in."

"Avraham, you're not looking too well, are you alright?"

"Yes Ishmael, I… I am alright."

"Avraham are you sure? I…"

"I am fine, come."

I followed him inside; I got a feeling he wasn't being completely honest, but if he was feeling worse than he said, then my nagging him wasn't going to help. Knowing he wasn't well I would ensure to keep my eye on him whether he liked it or not.

"Avraham, I'm here because I have a table booked tonight at the new restaurant; just opened. Would you be there if you're up to it, ask Rabbi? It would mean a lot for you both to be there."

"Aah, so, tonight is the night I presume?"

"Yes, I just hope I'm doing the right thing."

"Ishmael, if your heart says so then yes, it's the right thing; timing or worrying won't change that."

"It's just with her getting the children back soon, part of me thinks it's wrong asking her now; I love her so much. I just want her to know how committed I am; oh, I don't know."

"Ishmael, you're doing it again, you forget proposing or marriage is a big deal; you are bound to be feeling emotional, you are an emotional man anyway. But it is normal, don't let those fears spoil your night. You were made for each other, you know this; you won't stop caring, Ishmael, but not everything needs that attention. This is about love, how you both feel; it will all work out."

I just stared at him with a chuckle, he gave me a funny look back.

"Ishmael, what?"

"I used to hate your way with words, I hated you were always right, but Avraham, I don't know where I'd be if it wasn't for you. All that's happened so far: my behaviour, my ways, which I knew you also hated, you still stuck by me regardless. I know I've said it before, you will say it's nothing, but Avraham, you're wrong: for the first time I can say that, because to me it's everything. You are very important to me, you always will be; never hesitate to ask if you ever need me for anything at any time, give me your word?"

"Ishmael, I…"

"Please, Avraham?"

"Okay, Ishmael, you have my word, you better go to prepare; I will be there with Rabbi this evening. Oh, don't forget the ring."

"No, I won't, see you tonight."

"Goodbye, my friend."

I turned to look back at him; now smiling.

"Yes, Avraham, you're my best."

I went home to get ready; I was very worried about Avraham, wondering whether to cancel till he felt well enough. I knew he would have been annoyed if I did that: he hated fuss, but I hadn't seen him looking so unwell before. Essie, too, would have said to wait, but she had no idea what tonight was about. I got on my knees to pray for him, I rarely prayed but I could do nothing else; I felt he was hiding something which bothered me even more. I knew tonight I would have to ask him again; I could not let this go.

I was soon ready. Now it was five to seven, so I got into Richie's car, then drove round to Essie's. Early as usual, she was standing outside waiting. I pulled up outside then got out closing the car door delicately.

"Wow, Ish, you look sensational. I can't believe you have passed already; why didn't you tell me?"

I laughed seeing her face, she was certainly surprised; it had been worth it just to see that reaction.

"Yes, I passed a few days ago, but I wanted to surprise you, of course. You look very beautiful, Essie."

"Thank you, Ish, I'm so proud of you. So, where are we going?"

"You will see, come on?"

"So, you're a man of mystery tonight then?"

"It looks that way, but you will love where we are going."

"That makes me even more curious, Ish?"

"Well that's not a bad thing; really, come on."

I winked at her with a grin on my face, then put my arm out towards her, she took it slowly; with a smirk on her face, before finally getting into the car. I drove to the restaurant, nerves again becoming more apparent. I did have a trick to play first: driving past the restaurant once we arrived, I then reversed back outside it. I saw her look at it, almost disappointed as I drove past. She was thrilled when I stopped outside. I started laughing, much to Essie's annoyance; I opened the door to let her out.

"Ishmael, that wasn't funny."

"Sorry, Essie, I couldn't resist: your face."

"Yes, that's obvious, I will get you back, Ish; you wait. This place looks fantastic, but a park bench would've done me."

"Yes, I know, but you deserve better than that, Essie."

"Ish, it's just as well that you're a real sweetheart really, thank you."

"Essie, before we go in, whatever happens tonight; go with what you feel?"

"Ish, course, but why are you acting peculiar?"

"Don't worry, it was just important to say that."

"Let's go in, Ish? I'm so excited."

I really wanted to comment what I was thinking, but I just smiled at her then took her hand in mine. We then made our way inside. It was a very luxurious place: red walls with gold furnishings, lit by candles which were placed on the tables. Gold wall lights were hanging around the room. There was a very romantic feel in the atmosphere. Tables were perfectly set with a single rose, and surrounding the rose chocolates had been scattered on the red tablecloth which also with a gold trim. There were neatly presented gold plates with matching cutlery. Essie loved it.

"Wow, Ish, its gorgeous; it's good to see your romantic side come out."

"Only for you, Essie, you better get used to it."

I winked at her, she looked at me curiously with a grin. I was certainly impressed, just as Essie was. It was completely different now from when I had seen it during the day, it changed entirely at night; it really was stunning.

Avraham had already arrived with Rabbi, Essie figured something was going on straight away.

"Ish, why is Rabbi here; Avraham too? Is something wrong?"

"No, Essie, everything is fine; I asked them to come, let's go over to greet them?"

They both stood up as we approached them.

"Avraham, Rabbi, it is great you could both be here; thank you for coming."

"I wouldn't have missed it for the world, Ishmael, we have not long arrived. Evening, Essie, you look lovely, Ishmael, you certainly scrub up well, too."

"Thank you, Rabbi, Avraham, it's good to see you, both of you."

"Ish, let's sit down. Hang on? Wouldn't have missed what? Ish?"

I gazed at her then put my finger to my mouth, I again just winked at her. Rabbi was quick to distract her, I was preoccupied now with Avraham. He was much quieter than usual, so I took the opportunity to speak with him while I got the chance.

"Avraham, you are very quiet tonight; are you alright?"

"Don't worry about me, Ishmael, this is your night; enjoy it."

"You didn't answer my question? I'm very worried Avraham, I can't help that."

"Yes, Ishmael, please, I will be fine; how are you doing now?"

"Nervous still, but I am excited too."

"All will be well my friend, you will see, let's order?"

We ordered starters, but I could not wait any longer, I got up then knelt in front of her; she started laughing nervously. Only now could you see the lightbulb moment in her: realising the actual reason why she was here now.

"Ish, what are you doing?"

"Essie, I've never loved anyone so much in my life. Without you in it, I couldn't imagine it to be what it is now; you light up my world. I want to love you, support you; just as you have done for me. I promise to do all I can to make you happy, be there through the good, pick you up during the bad, until my last breath. I will always love you, Essie; you complete me. Would you do me the honour of becoming my wife?"

I opened the box with the ring then held it up to her; people around us were anticipating her reply, just as much as I was. She looked at me in thought for a moment, then a smile fell on her face.

"Ish, hmm, I'm not sure?"

"Essie?"

"Putting up with you, I don't know?"

"But I…"

"Ish, Yes, YES, of course I'll marry you; I love you; I'm sorry; I just couldn't resist that one either."

She winked at me then started laughing, the whole restaurant clapped now. Rabbi laughed along with Avraham at her joke too. Still kneeling with my hand on my head, I looked at her then chuckled while shaking my head; she certainly got me good. She flung her arms around me, then kissed me for a minute or two. Pulling away from me a moment later; now with a solemn look, she walked over to Avraham.

"Avraham, as you know, my father is no longer here. When it's time, I really want to ask whether you would do me the honour of giving me away? I couldn't think of anyone else I would want more."

I think we were all shocked by this, none more so than Avraham who seemed stunned. I looked at him just grinning; I couldn't think of anyone else I would want to give me away either. He turned to her.

"Essie, yes, I would love to, I am just a little surprised? Why me?"

"You were there through one of the hardest times for me, Avraham, just as much as Ish was. I know we are not as close as you are with him now, but you are just as important to me like I told you that day; I would be truly honoured for you to give me away."

She leaned over to kiss him on the cheek, he smiled warmly at her but could say no more; however, it wasn't necessary, enough had been said, especially for him. I thought her even more amazing asking him to do that, it showed just how much he meant to Essie too. When it came to the day itself, it would be hard; but she knew Avraham would help her through it. As tradition was, I wouldn't see her for a while until she walked down the aisle, but he would calm her, give reassurance, make her day special until we were together. He was an advisor, a father figure at times as well as a friend; we had the full package with Avraham, he really was a special man.

16 SOME DEVASTATING NEWS

Essie kept looking at her ring; I kept looking at her. All the worry had been evaporated instantly the moment she said yes, now I was very excited. I was happy; and it was clear she was too. Avraham was right: love conquers all, we certainly had that, I felt so blessed for it. Rabbi congratulated us, then Avraham did, too. We settled down to eat dinner then, it was enjoyed immensely, but Avraham barely touched any of it. As we were finishing he stood up.

"Ishmael, Essie, forgive me, but I am going to call it a night, congratulations to you both; I hope you have a lovely evening. Rabbi?"

"Avraham, please let me take you home?"

"No, Ishmael: I can manage, goodnight to you all."

I stared at him as he left. I vowed to myself, to check on him in the morning. I know he didn't want to spoil this evening, but there was something wrong; I could always tell that with him by how he brushed things off. He was unwell, but he had persuaded me it was no big deal; it was clear he wanted no fuss, but my concern only grew. The dream came into play where he was in hospital and had almost died; for some reason I believed this would soon be a reality. I prayed so hard that I was wrong with the assumption, now hoping that it was just my mind racing as it always did.

Rabbi also went home shortly after, congratulating us again; I was now alone with Essie. Lots of people; including staff, came to congratulate us, too. It was nice, but my mind was elsewhere through most of it, Essie did notice but she said nothing at the time. I turned to her once it had quietened down.

"Essie, why don't we go for a drive?"

"Yes, sure, Ish, that will be nice, but I know something is on your mind; what is it?"

"I'm not sure, surely you saw Avraham? He doesn't look well at all, I'm so worried about him, Essie, but he will not say what is wrong."

"Yes, he did look tired, I'm sure that's all it is, Ish; come on, we will check on him if you want to?"

"I want to spend time with you, but I can't stop thinking about him. I don't have a good feeling, Essie; I don't understand why? It's unnerving, I can't settle until I know all is well."

"Right, we are going to see him, put your mind at ease; then we can spend the rest of the night together. Avraham always takes priority first, Ish, come on."

We drove over to his house. We saw there was a light still on as we pulled up. I got out of the car then stood there for a moment just looking over. Essie touched me on the arm gently then took my hand. She had been surprised tonight by me, but I was in for the biggest shock of my life; I was not prepared for what was about to happen.

We tapped gently on the door; he answered, looking somewhat startled.

"Ishmael? Essie? Why are you here, what is it?"

"I'm sorry, Avraham: I could not leave it, I know there's something wrong. I've tried to ignore all you have said, but I can't; please, what is going on?"

"He's been terribly worried, Avraham, you know how much you mean to him."

"Yes, it is why I haven't said anything; I know I should've but I…"

"Avraham, whatever it is we can sort it?"

"No, Ishmael, we can't."

I looked at Essie who was just as puzzled by the remark as I was, Avraham walked into the lounge, Essie and I followed behind him quickly. I turned to him as he sat down.

"Avraham? What do you mean?"

"My friend, there is no other way I can tell you this, but I'm dying Ishmael, there isn't anything the doctors can do. I was afraid to tell you: I could not bear to set you back, I knew this would be a massive shock for you."

I couldn't believe or accept what I was hearing, Essie went white. Panic engulfed me now. I bent down by him clutching his hand, tears starting to fall.

"WHAT? NO! Avraham, no; there must be? You can't leave me, please, I can't lose anyone else, especially you. This is not happening, Avraham?"

"Ishmael, I know, I am sorry; I have all that money in the bank, but it is useless. Don't be afraid my friend, you have Essie now; I know you will be alright. It's my time, and God's will, that's how it must be."

I shot up, hands to my head then pulling my hair with frustration, turning in circles. Anger was brewing so fast; forgetting everything for a moment, I just screamed out, I couldn't hold back now.

"AAAH, WHY DOES THIS KEEP HAPPENING? WHY HIM? WHY? I HAVE LEARNED MY LESSONS, WHY IS THAT NOT ENOUGH? ARE YOU HAPPY NOW? ANYONE ELSE YOU WANT TO TAKE? I will not accept this, I can't, DO YOU HEAR ME?"

Essie was silent while she just stared at him, tears also falling slowly down her face. My instinct had been telling me something bad was going to happen; I just knew, but I wasn't prepared for this. It's what I was always afraid of; I was losing him, but I just couldn't accept it or change it. It was my turn to break down now; I was inconsolable.. I was so angry: we had finally got the relationship to be a good one, but now he was being taken from me. I could not fathom that or understand why. Avraham stood up to grab me, now having to raise his voice to calm me down.

"ISHMAEL, STOP, please, that won't change things. I know how incredibly hard this is for you, I always dreaded the day when I had to tell you. My friend, the doctor said I have a few months, so let's make them good ones; it will make my passing easier. I know you're angry but that won't stop what is going to happen. I'm glad I got to see the man you've become, and that you have found someone who makes you happy."

"Avraham, no, you should have had that chance, too, why couldn't it be me? This is so unfair. I'm sorry, but we should have had good years ahead; you should be there if I have children, I should be there to see you marry. Avraham, this is not right?"

"Ishmael, I know how much of a shock this is for you, no words I can give will bring you comfort now, but this is how it's meant to be. I don't know the reasons but in time my friend, you may."

Trying to hold back tears was a losing battle, they were flowing now. He put his hand on my shoulder reassuringly, I looked at him then put my head down, covering my face with my hands, then I just wept. Essie came to me.

"Ish, hey, Avraham is right: we must make these last month's memorable ones, do it for him."

I looked at her, drying my eyes; she had the same sadness in them as she did with Richie, but put a brave face on for me, I found strength in that. I turned to him now, determination in my voice.

"Avraham, write down everything you want to do, it doesn't matter what it is or where it is, we will do it. I will ensure these last month are your best, I promise you that."

"Yes, I know you always do your best, Ishmael, that is always enough for me. I knew I'd have to rely on you at some point; the fact I can now shows the person you have become."

"Avraham, how long have you known?"

"A while, since I came around for Jonah that day. I knew if I told you earlier you wouldn't have been able to focus on what you had to do. I guessed at some point you would know something was wrong; that's now come so it had to be the right time. Ishmael, promise me that however hard things get, you won't go back; you will keep moving forward?"

"How can I go back? Everything you did would have been for nothing, I couldn't do it; not now. I promise you, I will spend the rest of my life honouring you Avraham, you have my word."

"I don't doubt it, Ishmael, it was just something I had to say. However, you don't need to honour me, you must honour yourself."

Essie turned to me, putting her hand on my arm.

"Ish, I want to bring the wedding forward? I want Avraham to give me away while he can."

"Yes, it wouldn't be the same without you there Avraham; we can make the arrangements straight away."

"Ishmael, Essie, this is your day, it should be when you want it. I won't be around long, so it must be memorable for you both, this isn't about me."

"Avraham, it will be memorable having you there, it wouldn't be the same without you. Please, I want you to give me away, for you to be able to enjoy the day, too. Timing is irrelevant, especially now."

"Well you know where I…"

"YES, we know."

Both of us interrupting him abruptly only made him laugh. You could tell he wasn't well, but as ever he didn't change. I was broken-hearted by the news, I was really going to miss him; nothing would ever be the same again. I was just so glad I had Essie now: I knew when the time came I would most likely lose it again, having her there so close would make it less likely to send me back to that dark place.

I also questioned whether this was the reason why I wanted Rabbi back in my life? Again, it seemed ridiculous but, in my head, it also made sense in ways, too. It appeared to fit with what Rabbi had said, especially about possibly needing people in the future. It was clear now I would need him more than ever, but again, I had no definitive answers, in my mind, it was almost to coincidental. Part of me felt it was some kind of prediction, but it couldn't be, could it? It was very strange but, as Rabbi had mentioned, maybe the dream was trying to tell me something? I was unsure what would happen now; I just knew I was dreading the future a lot more.

"Avraham, we will leave you to rest; if you need anything you know where we are, anytime?"

"Yes, Ishmael, please enjoy your night, both of you; goodbye, Essie."

I walked over giving him a hug, I started feeling myself welling up again. He pulled me away before looking me in the eyes.

"Ishmael, don't cry for me my friend, it really isn't necessary."

"Avraham, I…"

He stopped me before continuing.

"You will understand one day, please, go, Ishmael; enjoy this night, for me?"

"Ish, come on, we must let him rest, goodbye Avraham."

"I am here anytime, Avraham, goodbye my friend."

"Yes, Ishmael, my best too."

He smiled before closing his eyes; I would check on him tomorrow. I hated leaving him, but he insisted I spent some time with Essie which was ironic under the circumstances. I left him to it, he knew to seek help if it was needed. We went down to the pier where we met on our first date, I had become a lot quieter now, going over everything in my head; Essie put her arm round me.

"Ish, I know how devastating this is for you, but you aren't alone in this; I will help you through it. I know how much he means to you, how hard it'll be. But don't let the knowing of what's going to happen spoil the time you have left; these moments with him are precious now."

"I just can't believe it Essie, inside I'm screaming, but as Avraham said, it changes nothing. I am so angry, worried I won't be able to keep his word after he has gone. I knew, Essie: I knew something bad would happen, I just never expected this, he has always been there."

"Hey, I know, but I'll be there to help you however I can, I am confident you will keep your word to him. Please, you must stop worrying so much, Ish, you are not the same person. I can't wait to become your wife, everything will be alright in time; I promise."

"I was so happy when you said yes, I can't wait to marry you as well. I just don't feel much like celebrating tonight, not now; it doesn't feel right."

"The night is beautiful; we have each other, we don't have to do anything but sit here. I love you, Ish."

"I love you too, Essie."

We sat there for a couple of hours, barely speaking a word. Tears falling through most of it. I knew things would be alright; I just didn't want to lose him, that's something I didn't think I would ever get over. I wouldn't be able to share with him good or bad times, get his advice or laugh with him; he knew me better than anyone, and that had proven to be of great value sometimes. I could only hope Avraham had got through to me enough to allow me to know myself; I was still uncertain this was the case in some ways. I could handle some things the way he would, I just couldn't handle my emotions as well as others which proved to be a dangerous thing.

I exploded when he told me, but that was just a snippet; he was still here so it didn't seem real in a way, but I was afraid now: it wasn't going to be that way much longer.

Essie started organising the wedding, involving Avraham as much as she could. He was deteriorating each day, but that didn't stop him. Avraham was always a true fighter, even now it never left him; in fact, it came out of him more. It was as though he had a point to prove, he was acting normally but in a way, it worried me. He had said all he had for my sake, but I knew him enough to know he was scared, and this made him fight back; it was hard, but leaving him to do things his way was what he always wanted whether sick or not.

The shelter opened which turned out to be a great success. Essie broke down when she saw the name of it, but was very proud, too. I started taking Jonah round, he was well loved by the staff as well as the people who went there. He bathed in the attention, was spoilt with treats that were given to him. Sam volunteered on some days; just to help us out. We had become good friends lately, although he did not, and would not ever replace Avraham, because nobody ever could; he would always be my one true friend.

I was very busy constantly. Any spare time I had, when I wasn't seeing Essie or Avraham, I wrote. That helped me, besides the fact I was also keeping my word to Richie. I hadn't seen Rabbi since that day; but I knew he was always there; he would also be a great comfort. Thinking about it caused Avraham's words to come flooding back about making time. I respected Rabbi immensely but only seeing him when I needed to was wrong; I had to do better, I had to make time for him as a priority, not a necessity.

I dropped everything one morning then drove round to see him. His garden was beautiful, filled with flowers of many colours, and he had a perfectly kept lawn with a small fountain. I saw him sitting outside reading, it was a beautiful day, warm. Rabbi stood up as he heard the car door shutting.

"Ishmael? This is a pleasant surprise, are you alright?"

"I said I would come, didn't I? I'm sorry, Rabbi, I'm just so busy I don't get a minute. Avraham said I should make time for Jonah, it made me remember I should for you, too."

"Aah, Avraham, I heard the news; I'm terribly sorry Ishmael, he is a great man. I have not seen him for a few days, how is he? Please, sit down."

"Oh, you know him, Rabbi, carrying on as normal, being the fighter, he always was; he gives nothing away. I am at a loss to know how I feel, I just know I am really going to miss him."

"Yes, he has always watched over you, he will still do so even in death, Ishmael; I have great belief in that."

"Rabbi, I know things happen for a reason, I know Avraham was brought to me to help me get to this point, but why take him now? I can't contemplate that. He deserves to live, find some happiness after all he has done; him of all people?"

"Ishmael, Son, I know, but listen to me for a moment, do you know what he said to me a couple of weeks ago?"

"No, Rabbi, what?"

"He told me that although his life hasn't been great some ways, he is blessed he had you in his life. He said even though you went down a bad road, you didn't give up on him; you proved to him that he was valued. Ishmael, you made him a happy man regardless: you gave him purpose. He always felt although you hated some of his ways, you made him feel he was a good person, because of that he is who he is. He taught you many things, but Ishmael, you taught him a great deal, too. Avraham thinks the world of you; just don't tell him I said so."

"Wow, Rabbi, he really said all that?"

"Yes, Ishmael, although he wouldn't tell you himself; he will leave this earth happy. I'm telling you this because it is important you hear it. That will make his passing easier to grasp; every second with him he truly values, that will help now. Make sure you have no regrets with him for you will regret it always."

"The thing I regret the most is not getting to know him as much as he knows me. I was so selfish, yet he persevered with me, there will never be another like him; sometimes I wish things were different."

"But what if they were? Do you think things would have really been different? We can't change what the future has in store for us, all that happened was for a reason; you know this now. If things were different, you may not have had Avraham, met Essie or Richie, you wouldn't have been brought to me; Son, you may not even have been here now. I know bad things have happened Ishmael, but they have made you who you are now, there is reason for that, too; that's what's important. Your bond with Avraham has become very strong lately, I know it is difficult, but maybe you're ready to take on the world yourself? Avraham was always meant to help you because you were destined for great things, which you're doing already. You make him so proud, Ishmael, I know you will always continue to do that."

"Rabbi, I'm just afraid, my best friend is dying yet I am helpless. I don't think I'll ever get over his passing. I'm trying to be strong, do what I should. Maybe I just wish I didn't know, this is so hard."

He put his hand on my arm as I sighed, putting my head down dispiritingly.

"Son, hard times are ahead; you won't ever get over it no, it would be foolish to think otherwise because he is a very special person. I know you're struggling to come to terms with the news, but Ishmael, you must think about the time you have left now, you will become unwell thinking like this. He is still here with us, but you are living in the future. Yes, we know his fate, but it has not happened yet. You are not helpless, you can make the times you have left happy for him, Ishmael? Enjoy them."

"I know you're right, course you are; you have helped massively, thank you, Rabbi. I shall let you get back to your reading; I've taken enough of your time."

"No, Ishmael, you could never do that, in the words of Avraham: I am always here, anytime you need me."

"This I know, thank you, goodbye Rabbi."

"Goodbye, Son."

As I left him I felt completely stunned over what Avraham had told him. I hadn't realised I'd had such an impact on him, saying that to someone else may have come across as selfish, but that wasn't Avraham. He was there because he wanted to be, I don't think I admired the man as much as I did now, he never ceased to amaze me. I promised myself to make the moments with him the best he had.

17 AVRAHAM'S DEPARTURE

Essie was very busy while awaiting the children's return, making many preparations for them. I decided to bring the trip home forward as Avraham was getting weaker. He barely left the house now but was so keen to go home that he still fought his illness. I really wanted this one thing for him more than anything, I just had my concerns now, but telling a man with such a determined mindset would have been a waste of time, he would have fought it more. It would be a hard trip for both of us, I had to make it as easy for him as I could.

Rabbi went to see him every day, both of us had keys to get in to his house now and we did all we could to make him comfortable. Each day got harder to see him but anytime now could be the last time, that was clear.

I was at my desk writing one morning, a couple of days before we were due to go, when the phone rang; it was Avraham.

"Avraham, are you alright? What is it?"

"C-could you come a-round Ishmael, w-when you have a m-minute?"

"Yes, I'm on my way; I won't be long."

I put the phone down then rushed round to his house. I had the same feeling in my gut again; I knew to expect bad news. I wasn't sure I could take anymore, but he needed me; my feelings had to wait. I just hoped it wasn't what I was expecting, although I couldn't be sure what that even was. I only knew that my instincts had been right before; so, naturally, I was nervous. Once there I opened the door where Issy greeted me.

"Issy, hello, come on."

I went into the lounge where Avraham was dozing. He looked so frail now, worn out, it broke my heart seeing him like that when on the inside he was the complete opposite. I went over to him.

"Avraham, it's Ishmael."

"Th-thank you for coming I-Ishmael, I, I know you're b-busy."

"I'm never too busy for you, Avraham, not ever. What is it?"

"I... I am not going to make the trip: I am too w-weak. I'm s-sorry Ishmael, I want to ask that you g-go? When I pass, scatter my ashes in... my h-homeland? Go to my house? W-will you p-promise me? I will always be with you."

"Avraham, I... it is not right I go without you; I'm not sure I can?"

"Ishmael, I kn-know you c-can, it will be h-hard, but you don't have t-to do it s-straight away. But one day, p-please g-go back; take me h-home. I... I am close now."

"Yes, you have my word, Rabbi told me what you said to him. I will never forget you Avraham, all you've done for me, the sacrifices you've made. You are a very special man, there will never be another like you. My children will know who you are, you will always be a part of our lives. Thank you for being you Avraham, for helping me become me; you are a real inspiration, forever my best friend."

"I... I die h-happy Ishmael, I... am... p-proud of you."

"You're very loved, Avraham, I've never said but you are; you always will be."

"I... I... love... you... Ishmael, y-you... m-made me happy, goodbye... my... f-friend, I..."

I looked at him stunned, he then closed his eyes, took one last breath, then it all went quiet. The reality suddenly hit me.

"Avrah, AVRAHAM? No, PLEASE, NO, not yet, Avraham, you what? Avraham? AVRAHAM?"

I shook him in complete panic, calling him but without avail; he had gone. I looked at him again, I felt anger building, consumed with grief I didn't hold back, yet again.

"AAAAAAAAH, WHY HIM? WHY NOW? IT SHOULD'VE BEEN ME! PLEASE? Bring him back? HE WAS everything, I CAN'T HANDLE THIS, NO, NO, not Avraham please?"

I was beside myself; I fell to the floor on my knees not knowing what to do. I looked back over, crawling towards him I began to fix his blanket, I kneeled by him then took his hand; now I just sobbed. My heart felt like it was breaking, no amount of screaming or shouting would bring him back as Avraham had said. The one person who had always been there had gone; it struck me like a bolt of lightning, straight through my core. I couldn't bear to leave him, but he couldn't stay there, people needed to come for him but I couldn't face that, not yet. I stayed by his side for a few hours before ringing for assistance. I watched as I saw my friend go, that was so hard: knowing I would never see him again. I rang Essie, I only asked she came here, but she could tell by my voice I was upset; she rushed over. I sat in his chair holding his blanket; tears still falling as I waited for her. I didn't know how much time had passed till I heard her voice; she barged in panic stricken.

"Ish, I'm here, where's Avraham?"

"He's gone, Essie, I saw him take his last breath, I can't…"

"NO, no he can't have? Oh Ish, I'm so sorry."

She broke down now, it was hard for both of us. I took her in my arms holding her.

"It's alright, Essie, I know he meant a lot to you too. He told me I made him happy, that he loved me; those were his last words. I never thought I would ever hear him say that. It doesn't seem real, Essie, I'm going to miss him terribly, how can it end like this?"

She looked at me now, with my head down, she then lifted my chin up to look at her.

"Ish, I know, he really was amazing; I'll miss him so much too, but it's not the end. He would have agreed with me, he will still be with us always. I know it isn't the same; but Ish, nothing will be now. In time it will get easier, you were a great friend to him in the end, that would have meant the world to him, you showed courage, gave him strength an…"

"I didn't do anything he wanted to do: the trip especially, I can't forgive myself for that. He wants me to take him home, Essie; it was his last wish."

"Ishmael, look at me, none of that mattered: you were there for him. Don't torment yourself over things which were out of your control: it just wasn't to be. We will take him home, it was important to him, you were too. That's what life is about, you gave him the most precious thing which is time; he will have been grateful for that. You parted as best friends; let that give you comfort now."

I broke down now; Essie just held me tightly. She, too, started becoming emotional again. After all that was said, all I knew about how it was right to let go, I still couldn't. I had to acknowledge my feelings, for Avrahams' sake I had buried them, now they hit me like a ton of bricks, more than they had ever done.

What I couldn't comprehend, was the fact I had turned my life round, learned the lessons I needed too, but I was still losing people. I was still being tormented, tested, but I didn't know why. Now I couldn't even ask Avraham; that was so hard. Even though he had been here for me, and got me to where I was now, I would never understand why he was taken. He wasn't old, he always looked after himself, too; it didn't make any sense to me. I didn't want to lose him, I wanted him here, I wanted to see him find happiness, fulfil his dreams but he never would now. He was the bravest person I had ever known, now there was a big gap in my life that nobody could fill ever again. It was almost like he had been there till I learned to appreciate him then, once I did, he was taken; it just didn't make sense, but nothing really seemed to now. I knew I was grieving, all the doubts, the questioning was normal, but this was too much. I wanted to stand at the top of the highest mountain to scream with every ounce of my being until every morsel of anger had left me, my last tear had been shed. But I couldn't; after all, what was the point?

Learning to appreciate people was one lesson I was glad I had learned: I could now allow people to be there, especially Essie; I was so grateful for that. She knew what I was going through, she knew what to say or do, she could calm me, too. Without her or Rabbi there I wouldn't have coped with Avraham's death at all; this was one thing I knew confidently. In my dream, I had wished Betty would become my friend if we became nothing more, I'd have another Avraham, but that wasn't real; Essie, however, was. Although not the same, she was just as amazing as him. Through my losses I had gained some very special people. I was distraught over Avraham, I always would be, but she was my future, I had to remember that.

I had to continue on now, not forget her importance or allow my feelings to consume me as they did before. I was able to control them to a degree, but now I had to fight them more than ever. I knew with her by my side I would; it was something I promised Avraham, too. I didn't want to let him down now. I had to prove that after losing him, although it was the hardest thing, I was strong enough now to cope. I could only take each day as it came but I would fight, I wouldn't give up either; I had to do it for him, just as he had done for me for so long.

We stayed a while, the cup he always used was sitting there. He was a simple man, only had what he needed although his home always felt welcoming. I was going to miss his home just as much as him. I did not know what would become of it, I just hoped that it would be looked after. I picked up the cup to take with me: it would sit on my desk now, remind me of all I had promised him, most importantly to always keep going. I would look at it often, remember all the memories we shared, the words of wisdom he gave, but especially the good times we had. However, it gave little comfort, but it helped in a way, too.

The days after were somewhat a blur, I arranged Avraham's funeral along with sorting other things out. Keeping myself busy helped but Essie was concerned I was so quiet, yet she knew how I felt to a degree, too. She was there for comfort and support when I needed it the most, but I knew she wouldn't have had it any other way; I really was blessed having her.

The day of Avraham's funeral came; part of me felt awkward being back in the synagogue, I was uncomfortable, but I was there for him. It was difficult because part of me still couldn't say goodbye; I knew I would never be ready for that, but I was forced to be. I didn't know if I would even get through the service, but for now, I could contain my emotions; I just didn't know how long for. Many people turned up to pay their respects, most I didn't even know. Rabbi came over to me, kissed me on both cheeks then hugged me. Essie was by my side but went to greet people while I spoke to Rabbi.

"Ishmael, I am so very sorry, Son, he will be at peace now, he was well loved."

"Yes, it seems so, I didn't know he had so many friends, Rabbi?"

"Yes, but Ishmael, you were always his best. He was well respected among the community, but you were very much loved by him."

"He told me, Rabbi, his last words to me were what you

said: I made him happy, that he loved me. Those words will stay in my thoughts always."

"Yes, it will help you through today, as well as times ahead Ishmael. You will grieve but don't forget you still have your life ahead of you, too?"

"I made him a promise, I intend on keeping it. Rabbi, thank you: today would have been harder without you, too, I must acknowledge that, especially after what was said."

"Aah, Ishmael, yes, it is clear now that is what I'm here for, just don't forget that, Son."

"You know, Rabbi, I don't think I will."

He looked at me then laughed, before touching me on my arm fondly. He then moved to greet other people who were turning up. I called Essie over then went to find us a seat.

"Ish, are you going to say anything?"

"Essie, I haven't thought about it, I don't…"

"Ish, you don't have to, I only ask just in case you do. I thought it may help, I can be with you if you need me to be. Ish, just don't feel you should do anything if you can't, you may be glad you did if you decide to do so, either way is okay, Avraham would understand."

I sat in thought about it, people were taking their seats while Rabbi was looking ready to start. Essie took my hand then Rabbi gestured for everyone to stand; it had begun. I sat in a world of my own. I could hear Rabbi's voice, but I wasn't taking in what was said. All I could think of now was the dream: wishing I was back in it were Avraham pulled through, how I felt overjoyed, the relief of getting that second chance. Now I could only feel myself welling up, but I couldn't lose it, not now.

Essie glanced at me then squeezed my arm, distracting me from my thoughts. I put my hand on hers then looked at her. Towards the end of his speech Rabbi asked me if I wanted to say a few words. I knew then I would regret it if I didn't, so I got up and slowly made my way to the front. I was so nervous my stomach was in knots. I took a deep breath and fixed the microphone before I looked up at everyone in the room. A lump forming in my throat was now becoming more apparent. I looked at the many faces staring back at me; I just wanted to run. Rabbi came over to me, whispering:

"Take you time Ishmael, you can do this, Son; we are all here for you."

He smiled then stepped back, I looked at Essie who also smiled. Taking a breath, I then began one of the hardest speeches of my life.

"Avraham, wow, where do I begin? He was truly an exceptional man, my best friend, selfless with wisdom beyond his years. He was brave, kindhearted, so compassionate, always ready to tell me when I was wrong, but there to help me see the right way to go. He was there to pick up the pieces which I always dropped without care. Always with me through the good times, more so through the bad. He was someone who always believed in me, helped me become the person I am today; he knew me better than I knew myself. Anyone who knew him was blessed to have him in their life. I... I... he gave me the strength to cope with his passing as well as I am doing, also to Essie; Rabbi, too, who have both been there; but it is down to him mainly that I can. The one person who has always been there for me has now gone, but he will never be from my thoughts.

"He will never leave my heart. Avraham should be remembered by all for who he was, anyone who got a kind word or a helping hand from him was blessed. He really was an amazing man; I... I will miss him so much. He made my life easier; I would not be here now if not for him, but he never did accept

that fact; it was just his way. Avraham, my friend, thank you for being all that you were, for choosing to be my friend when at times I was undeserving. I hope I continue to make you proud, just as much as you did me. It is so hard to say goodbye, but I know you would want me to, you would make me see sense like you always did, tell me to move on with life, to be happy, because that was just you. We fled our home together, you bought me to a better life. I was so fearful, yet you reassured me, grabbed my hand, pulled me up when I didn't think I could go on.

You watched your parents murdered, the same as me, yet you didn't leave because you knew one day I would need a friend. Maybe you knew more than you ever said, but because of your selflessness I ended up here. We fled together as I said, but we should've gone home together too, now that's up to me to do it for you. I promise you Avraham, I will do that; but I know you will be with me, just as you promised. Thank you for all you did, all you sacrificed, for leading me to this place where I've learned so many valuable lessons, met some amazing people. Every step you have guided me, given encouragement, made me see I needed to change, now because of it things have only got better. I lost my faith, but you never did, that, too, I am so blessed for. That is something that has helped me see things much more clearly, helped me become a better person. Now you take your place up there with your family, also with mine. Your last words before your final breath were that I made you happy and you loved me. Well, you made me happy in every sense even when I didn't show it, for all I have lost in my life, I know how truly blessed I was having you there from the start. We fought, then we became distant because I didn't appreciate you. I was agitated at times because you were always right, but you made me see in a caring as well as a loving way, I know without that I wouldn't have the people who are in my life now.

You were always there, through my coma, sorting my home so my spirits would be lifted, you worked so hard when I couldn't to get me that home in the first place, along with Rabbi. I hated what I put you through, but I know now you grew from it, too. It doesn't excuse it, I know I put you through a lot, scared you at times through my actions, but you never gave up on me. You calmed me, taught me so many things; you were such a wise soul, Avraham.

"Your wisdom has been so valuable for me, you have been amazing through our journey together. I know how special you were, but you always will be to me. I love you Avraham, my advisor, my teacher, and most of all my best friend. May you rest in peace knowing how loved you always are; I want you to know that you will never be forgotten. I will continue to make you proud, whatever that takes, you sacrificed so much for me; I don't feel worthy of that, but you proved I was; it just shows what an extraordinary man you really were. Thank you for being everything in my life, there will never be another like you, you truly were unique in every way. G, G, goodbye Avraham, till we meet again my friend."

I left the altar, the whole synagogue was in silence; some people had tears falling, putting handkerchiefs to their eyes.

I managed to hold myself together, but the tears were falling silently now, too. Essie stood up hugging me tight, one man got up then started clapping. As I moved myself from Essie, more stood up to do the same. I was truly touched: I never expected that. Rabbi's words of him being loved were proven; I couldn't help but feel it, and it now brought a smile.

"Ish, that was so beautiful, you've always done him proud."

"I miss him so much, Essie, I wish I could have said it to him."

"I know, Ish. He knew how you felt I am certain of it, you showed it to him these last months, I'm so proud of you too."

I squeezed her hand then glanced over at Rabbi, who looked at me warmly while people took their seats again. The curtains were soon drawn on Avraham, then the service came to an end. Rabbi came over as I had my head down.

"Ishmael, I want you to know: in all my years of doing this, I've never heard a speech like that. It was incredibly moving; straight from the heart. Never doubt you didn't do enough for him, it was an honour to witness that, thank you."

"Rabbi, I'm so sorry, may I have a moment with Ish?"

"Essie, of course."

I turned to her, this was unexpected behaviour: she never asked for a moment; so, I assumed it was of great importance.

"Essie?"

"Ish, I've been thinking: you know I love you, I adore you, but I don't want to marry without Avraham, it doesn't seem right now. I know we will not enjoy it without him being there; I don't want anyone else giving me away, oh this is so hard."

"Hey, no, it is simple: we don't have to marry to prove we love each other. I will do what it takes to make you happy, Essie, so if getting married means that you won't be, then we won't do it; I love you."

"Ish, if we don't marry, there is nothing to stop us moving in together? I hate being parted, we want to be together, so what do you say?"

"Exactly what you said when I asked you to marry me, without the joke this time. We will be together in a way we want to be, whenever we want to be."

"Ish, what about Rabbi: I know he was looking forward to marrying us."

"Yes, but he will understand. Essie, you tell me to stop worrying or overthinking; I should return the favour?"

"I know Ish, I just… it doesn't matter; this is Avrahams day; it should be about him, after your speech I just had to say it."

"Essie, relax, come on, we should find Rabbi: we should let him know. It will be fine."

We walked over to Rabbi; I tapped him on the shoulder, the person he was talking to moved away so he turned towards us.

"Ishmael?"

"Rabbi, we have decided not to marry, we…"

"Aah, something told me that may be the case. Ishmael, you don't need my permission; that's your decision."

"No, we know, but…"

"But nothing, Ishmael, do what makes you happy, both of you must stop worrying so much. I must admit that I'm disappointed I won't marry you; but I know you wanted Avraham there, I understand that. So, if it is right for you, then that's what matters. It's not about me, it's your life."

Essie took Rabbi's hand in both of her hands then smiled at him.

"Rabbi, if you wouldn't have been a rabbi I would have had you walk me down the aisle now instead. It's just: it would've meant a lot to Ish for you to marry us."

"I, too, would've been honoured; but Ishmael, Essie, sometimes things don't always work out how we want them to, but life goes on."

"Things have worked out in a lot of good ways; I am luckier than some for that."

"Yes, we all are, Ishmael, you both have a promising future ahead; enjoy every moment of it, I will be retiring soon, my time here is almost up."

"What? Rabbi? Your time is almost up here?"

"Yes, Ishmael, don't worry: I'm not going anywhere just yet. I've been here forty years now, it's time for someone younger to take this synagogue forward."

"Where will you go, Rabbi? What will you do?"

"I will live a little, Ishmael, while I still can. I will be fine."

I knew I had to do something for him: he helped me get a property, then paid for me to live when I first came here. He looked after me knowing I couldn't pay him back. I also knew he wasn't a rich man but, thanks to Richie, I now was. I took out my cheque book then turned to him.

"Rabbi, I want to do something for you, to help you do that. I know like Avraham you are a proud man, but please, let me do this? You have been of great importance to me in my life, you've been generous as well as kind, I want to make sure you can do anything you want to do."

"Ishmael, it's not necessary I…"

"Yes Rabbi, it is, it is a gift; a thank you. You deserve it; please, it would be my pleasure, please accept it."

"I don't know what to say, Ishmael, thank you."

"Now do what makes you happy, Rabbi: you've made so many others, it's your time now. Thank you for everything, you also did Avraham proud. I know you were a great friend to him, too."

I leaned in to give him a hug, he squeezed me then patted me on the back; he was unmistakably moved by this gesture, but he had given me so much. I wasn't greedy; helping him have a good retirement was important. Money wouldn't make him happy, but doing the things he may have always wanted to do, giving him the means to do it, would. I could give him that chance; so of course, I took it.

"We were great friends, but you and I always will be, too, Ishmael. I, too, am proud of you: how far you have come, this world is better with you in it. Now go: I have much to do, oh, Ishmael? Thank you. Goodbye Essie."

"You are very welcome, Rabbi, see you soon."

"Goodbye, Rabbi, have a safe trip. Oh Ish, that was a really nice thing you just did."

"It was necessary: he is a good man, very deserving. Anyway, come on."

"Yes, people are waiting, let us toast a coffee to Avraham."

"Of course; what else?"

She laughed at my comment as we headed out.

"That's not even an option, Ish"

"Yes, thank you to three people, Essie, but something I'm more than happy with."

"Or without. Ish, you've done Avraham justice today, you moved a lot of people, too, including myself. He would have felt that, knowing how you feel to that extent, the fact you can stay away so easily from drink now, too, shows what he did for you. You are inspirational; really. No matter how hard things get, drink will never be the answer; I do know you know this, Ish."

"Yes, I know but I'll never go back there, Essie."

"I know that too, I just don't know your every thought, Ish, so, it's going to cross my mind; doesn't mean I think you will, because I know you won't."

"I understand your concern; I am always grateful for it. I don't need anything that will jeopardise us, drink would; you're worth more than any drink could ever be."

There was no chance of me drinking anything else other than coffee, that would've sent me on a downwards spiral once again. Avraham was gone, now Rabbi was leaving, I would not have got through it again without them; so, it was reason to steer well clear of it. I could understand that, although Essie knew I wouldn't, times like this could easily have had me picking up a bottle again: my emotional state was unstable, so I could erupt at any moment. That in mind, her concern was understandable, even the strongest could fall during difficult times. It was the impact Avraham, plus the others, had on me which meant I knew better now. I didn't need it; sometimes being reminded was a good thing, I much preferred coffee anyway now.

The gathering afterwards was pleasant. We didn't stay long, people came over to comment on the speech, gave me their condolences; all the usual things. It was strange not having Avraham there; the fact of it being his wake, too. I had got through the day more easily than I thought possible; inside, I believed he was right there with me the whole time.

Getting used to not having Avraham around was not easy: just spending time with him having one of our talks or asking him about things I knew he could help or advise with. It put into reality just how much I had relied on him, how much he did for me, just how much I missed him. I soon got his urn; it was black with his name engraved around it, surrounded with doves. It had angel wings too: it represented him, his peacefulness, all he did for myself as well as so many others. We were due to fly out the next day, I was so glad for Essie: I knew I would be alright with her with me, but it was still unknown how I'd feel going back. It would certainly be a test but one I wanted to pass more than anything, for myself as well as for Avraham. I would prove to myself that I could leave all that happened in the past permanently.

Essie stayed at mine that night as we were up very early. I was restless; feeling anxious too. I stared at the clock watching each second go by until I fell asleep. Essie woke me up the next morning.

"Morning, Ish, today is the day; how are you feeling?"

"Morning, beautiful, I am not quite sure: I'm feeling many things."

"It will be alright, Ish, you'll see; I'll make coffee."

I dragged myself out of bed, then got a couple more things together. I sat down on the bed, looking out the window; I took a moment to reflect before muttering under my breath.

"Avraham, the day has come my friend: I'm taking you home. I will do you proud; be with me today, I'm not sure I can do it alone."

Next thing a bird landed on the windowsill, it took a couple of steps, then glanced inside towards me before flying off again. I thought it quite bizarre: I wasn't one to believe in signs or anything but that was too coincidental. I had never witnessed it before, so I was unsure whether it was a coincidence, or something more, but I felt a sense of peace around me. I got up quickly then went to the lounge, quite bewildered.

"Ish, what's the matter?"

"I'm not sure, Essie: maybe nothing. But something strange just happened, almost too strange, I'm not quite sure what to make of it. I've never seen a bird land on the windowsill, the whole time I've been here."

"Ish, why is that so strange?"

"I spoke to Avraham aloud; I asked him to be with me today. Then it just appeared from nowhere, it seemed almost to coincidental, I know it's silly."

"No, I don't think it's silly, Ish, it seems too odd not to be a sign. I believe it was, but it's not about what I think or believe, go with what you feel. I know either way he will be with you today; that may have just been confirmation for you, whether you believe it or not. It's a good thing, Ish; regardless."

"Maybe you're right, who knows. We better be getting a move on, we won't make the plane otherwise."

"I'm ready when you are. Ish, wait: today is massive for you, if there is any day Avraham would be with you it's today, I am with you every step too, I love you, Ish."

"I know, Essie, I really couldn't do it without you: I know my fears would have got in the way. Thank you for being here, Avraham was very fond of you, I know he would have felt happier with you being here with me, too; especially today, I have learned to take nothing for granted so it needs to be said, I love you."

"Oh Ish, I'm honoured to be; for both of you. Right: now we really need to go?"

"Wait, before we do? I just need to kiss you."

She came closer with a smirk, then kissed me once on the lips.

"Like that?"

"I'm thinking more like this."

I kissed her more passionately, but not for long: she pulled away then looked at me.

"I like your way of thinking, Ish, but we really must go."

She winked at me then we finally made our way to the airport. I felt nerves coming again, but I didn't feel too nervous, not like I should've done. I thought maybe Essie was right: that it was down to Avraham, that I didn't feel as bad as I could've, that he was there with me. I had other thoughts that the feelings were of something unexpected that was going to happen, like I had had many times before; or maybe it was the fact I had never flown which was giving me an unsettled feeling. I was hoping they would settle when I was in the air. I was more at ease knowing Sam had the dogs, I was glad they didn't have to go to a home, those places I knew Jonah would hate. It was good of Sam to do that, but I knew he, too, wouldn't have allowed them to go to a home anyway; it really made me appreciate him even more.

In a couple of hours, I would be in the place I had once fled, the place where it all started. My greatest worry was that I didn't want the flashbacks to return; I hadn't had them since the coma, but this could be a trigger for them again. I tried to relax, avert my thoughts elsewhere. Essie was reading quite happily. Part of me couldn't wait to get there now: I knew it would either be the worst decision I had made, or the best one. I prayed it would be the second one, but again, time would tell.

Avraham was persistent about telling me to go to his house which had me eager to know why. It had been so long, I hoped it would still be there, but I had no idea what to expect. Thinking about it had me fidgeting in my seat. I wanted to see it as I had remembered it, but I had no clue if anything had happened to it once we fled, what had become of it. Whether anyone stayed or moved in after the war, and had turned it into a place of living again. I wondered if it lay abandoned all these years, become a ghostly place over time that would be beyond recognition when I saw it; I knew they were things I would get answers to, I just had to wait. Diverting my thoughts, I sat thinking about where to scatter Avraham's ashes; I decided to do it by the river where we used to once play. He loved it there, so I think he would have liked that. Avraham had mentioned no specific place, but maybe he knew I would know where to put them. I don't think he would have minded where I did it: he just wanted to be home. I felt so many things but I was glad I could do that.

18 A LAST WISH

During the flight I realised just how far we had travelled all those years ago; it was astonishing, a small part of me still wondered how we even made it.

We soon landed, then headed towards a car I had arranged to drive. Uncertain of how I'd react once I got there, I didn't want to be with someone I didn't know, even with Essie there. It had to be just us because it was quite a drive, too; having someone else with us would have only increased my anxiety, that was never a good thing.

Essie stopped me before I got into the car, grabbing me by the arm.

"Ish, are you ready to do this?"

"Yes, I think so, Essie, come on, thank you again for being here."

"I wouldn't have missed it, Ish, you have done amazing getting this far, even if we went no further, Avraham would still be proud."

"Yes, we must go to Avraham's first, I promised him I would. But before we do: I'm concerned about the flashbacks returning. Essie if they do then just let me be. Please, give me your word?"

"Ish, take this slow, I am right here with you; whatever happens, I know you can do this, you have that control."

She hugged me which always gave comfort, her words gave

me empowerment too: I was so busy worrying about the flashbacks returning, I hadn't realised that I had control. I had the choice to let them overtake me or to fight against it; I felt such determination now, they were not going to have that hold over me again. That was the choice I made right there.

We soon approached a field I was familiar with. There was a scarecrow on it, but it had aged considerably. I remembered how, just before we fled, it looked brand new, no rips or broken parts, no holes or dirt. It had vibrant colours; a happy look to it. But now all that had wasted away, leaving it a shell of what it once was. The fields were unkept; they hadn't been used in years, I then knew the place was abandoned. This saddened me: before the war, it had been a lovely place. People were happy then, there was laughter from children, a sense of peace in the air; it was a place which prospered. Now it was just a shell, with memories of what was appearing round every turn. We soon came to the pathway leading to Avraham's house, Stopping the car before we got out, I just stood staring at it: the place didn't look much different to how it was, just unused now. Essie took my hand, I turned to her.

"This is Avraham's house, Essie, I…"

"Slow, remember: take your time."

"I'm fine, really; I must do this."

We walked inside, everything had been left as it was, it was once a nice place, bright with an airy feel, now it was filled with darkness, only light from the open door beaming in. There was a musty smell lingering in the air too, the once yellow walls had cobwebs on them. Burned-out coal lay in the open fire where the last fire had been lit. Many times I had sat in front with Avraham playing, it seemed so long ago; looking at it now you would never have thought there had been happy times once. I went to the windows to pull the curtains back. We walked around a while then suddenly heard a knock on the door. Both of us were completely surprised by it, the village was derelict, or at least it appeared to be. I hastily walked back towards the door.

A man stood there dressed in a ragged shirt; his pants were moth eaten. He had a hat which had a hole in it with nibbled edges from the many field mice I knew made their homes there. His brown hair was long, untidy looking; he had a long beard, too, which was going grey. He held a staff but had a twinkle in his eyes, he was a curious man; upon first look I had no idea who he was.

"Hello, can I help you?"

"Ishmael, is that you?"

"How do you know my name? Who are you?"

"Ishmael, it's Benyamin? You do remember me; don't you?"

"Benyamin? Is that really you? I... I don't believe it; why of course I remember. What are you doing here?"

"I never left here, Ishmael, everyone left after you did but I could not: I wouldn't have made it on my own. This is my home; it's by the faith of God I am still here, it was just meant to be."

"Benyamin, I can't believe you stand here before me after what you just said; so many years have passed, did you know I was coming?"

"Yes, Avraham sent someone here a while back, he asked me to come when you arrived here."

"Avraham? Okay, Benyamin this is my girlfriend Essie, Essie please meet Benyamin; we were childhood friends, used to play at the river. I remember when you pushed Avraham in it, he was not best pleased."

"Yes, I remember, neither was his parents if I remember correctly; they were good times, now only a distant memory. Pleased to meet you, Essie."

"Likewise, Benyamin. Ish, I guess you now know why Avraham was so persistent you came back?"

"Yes, I guess I do. Benyamin, would you not come back with us? I feel it's what Avraham may have wanted me to do."

"No, Ishmael, it isn't. I don't belong in that world: I

belong here, I cannot go. I'm guessing this letter he asked me to give you will explain anything necessary; go on, open it."

I started opening the letter, as slowly as I could, my hands were shaking now. The amount of faith Avraham had in me was astonishing; he never ceased even in death. Essie moved in closer to me as I pulled the letter out.

"Ishmael, My Friend.
If you are reading this, I know you got me back home where you found our friend Benyamin. I never doubted you would get here; even though you did. I want to thank you from the bottom of my heart for doing this for me.

I wish I could've been there with you, but getting here shows how strong you have become. I know how incredibly difficult it is for you coming back here, I hope by doing so you find the closure you have wanted for so long. I know the person you now are, so; what I ask of you next, I know you won't hesitate. Ishmael, I have all that money, but I only used some to get this letter here to you now. My dream was to always have our home back to how it was; to have our community together again. I want you to do this in my passing; I want you to prove that evil will not conquer, show others that good can come from all the horror we both experienced. I know this is a lot to ask, Ishmael, to take on especially, but I knew it had to be you that did it.

This is our home; I want the sun to shine on the golden fields, for children to laugh again. For them to play by the river we once did; for the fires to be roaring while the animals graze once again in the fields. This is all I've ever dreamed about, Ishmael; telling you sooner would have been a distraction, I knew the timing was not right. I always knew, underneath, you would one day prove that you would be capable of anything. I always knew you were destined for greatness. I hope you see we can't live in the past or allow fears of it to shape our future; your future. You can change what was into hope for many, into something many will be proud of. You can bring that to others, to our culture, because that Ishmael, is what you're about.

My friend: I know my mission was to help you, all we went through together, was how it was meant to be. You may feel you didn't do enough: that you put me through a lot, but, my friend, I also was meant to have that in my life. What happened made us who we are; it gave me the knowledge as well as the wisdom to help you. I am so happy that I got to see you as you are now; never doubt you didn't do anything worthy for me, because you did. I could sit at night, reflect on my life which many times I found myself doing. That made me smile, you made me smile; you also know that takes a lot. I can't be with you in body, but I am always with you. Ishmael, I know you know this deep down whether you admit it or not. The strength you got from me, you can now find within you; whatever happens you can deal with it in the right way. The fact you're here reading this proves I didn't ever need to worry, although I never did. I believe in you; now you must believe in yourself, trust yourself, but above all: love yourself. You can make a difference, which you have already done.

Go forward now, do not let my passing stop you achieving what I know you can do. You are a very special man, Ishmael; it was an honour having you as my best friend. My passing means I could not walk Essie down the aisle; that is my one regret. I know you both well enough to know you might not go ahead with the wedding; if this is the case then why? I know it meant a lot for you to have me there, but, to the both of you, it's not about who is there. Ishmael, Essie, it is about you two, your love which is a rarity to see. Do what makes you happy, because that matters, remember I will always be there with you. Please don't allow situations to bring regrets later on. After everything, you both deserve a happy day, a day to celebrate you both, all you've achieved. Go with your hearts; take whatever comes as the right choice.

Enjoy your lives now; live it to the fullest. Allow yourselves to remember the good, as much as the bad times: they will help you heal, to grow as people. Life is too short, so you must make the most of it; leave the earth knowing you made a difference, that you did some good, for that is what makes life worth all that we go through. Life is about love, you have much to give inside you, Ishmael; keep giving it, keep showing people that regardless of our bad times we are still capable of it. Situations don't define us, you have proven that; now you must teach others. This is something I also know you can do.

Never stop fighting for what you believe in or for love; never give up no matter how hard things may get. You have come so far, my friend; I now see a bright future, one with much happiness you were always deserving of. But without the hard times, you wouldn't have become the amazing man you now are. I have said this before, Ishmael, but I really am so very proud of you. I know your promise to me is one you will naturally keep, but with every day you got through I felt proud, Ishmael, every dark moment you fought I was proud of that too. Remembering how you used to be, to seeing the man you are now, has been a truly amazing transformation. Your coma in my eyes was the best thing that could've happened: I can see you asking why, but Ishmael, without it you would have still been as you were.

You went from a terrified boy to a man of strength, one of courage, but especially one of love. The person you are now is a testament of your fighting spirit, of a man who never gave up; that my friend is truly exceptional, anyone that knows you now is blessed. The world is yours,

Ishmael, spread love wherever you go. I know this will be effortless now, the world will be a better place having you in it.

Ishmael before I finish; I have one last request. I ask that you do something in honour of our families, to show the strength of our people, to remind others that we can get through anything.

Somewhere people can come to pay their respects, to find the peace many will want, just like you do. I saw you build the shelter for the homeless, so I know you can do this too. I want to thank you for all you have done for me, for so many others also. I never said this to you enough, but I love you my friend, I always did. Be at peace now, keep moving forward; never look back because you no longer belong there. I will be watching while smiling down on you always.

Goodbye Ishmael; my best friend
I will see you again one day
I leave the last of my love with you
Avraham

The one place we were happy the best
Is the place I want you to scatter
my ashes to rest
I am free, for I am home
Remember my friend
you are never alone.

Before you read on Ishmael: Benyamin has something for you?

I turned to Benyamin somewhat puzzled, he then placed something in my hand. Looking down I saw a marble; I quickly looked at him again, he smiled at me.

"Read on Ishmael."

I fixed the letter then continued to read it.

"Ishmael, do you remember when you gave me this? You were seven, your father brought you back a gift one day. I never got much as my family were poor, but through your excitement, you forgot this. However, when you saw my face you stopped. Then you looked at me as I had my head down, you then said my name. As I glanced up, you reached into your pocket then pulled the marble out. Do you remember what you said to me? You said:

"I have this new gift, so you can have the marble, Avraham; now we both have something, and I can let you play with my gift too."

Ishmael, you made me smile that day: you gave me happiness, showed me my worth. We played for hours afterwards, it was one of my best-ever memories.

I give it back to you now: it's a reminder of the good times, the memories we had. Cherish them my friend, as I have done over the years, nothing can take them away if we remember. I leave it there; but again Ishmael, thank you for being my friend, for all you gave me, for being my inspiration all these years.

Avraham

I looked up, completely choked by the words, tears now streaming down. I don't think I've ever been more astonished in my life. Essie turned to me.

"Ish? Hey."

"I have no words, Essie, except wow: just all of it. I miss him so much; it gets harder. I remember that day; yet I had forgotten until now. I can't believe he still had this; after all this time?"

"I know, Ish, but: he was, as you put it, a very unique

man. The marble is a symbol of all you shared together. Avraham kept it because he saw value in everything, whether the good or bad happened it would always be a reminder of you, the good times. Like my father: he had his surprises, but this time it's a very special one. I can see why he did that Ish: he knew one day that you would need reminding, he was right?"

"Yes, I have forgotten so much, Essie, I can see why he did that too, I must do him proud: fulfil his wishes. I just have one question going around my head: how am I going to do this? I…"

Benyamin touched my hand warmly just then; I turned my gaze to him.

"Ishmael, if I can be of any help, then I will help you, whatever it takes; he was incredible that's for sure. But you, Ishmael, you are too; just as much. Avraham told me about you, I know our community would have been proud of you both. I promise: we will get this to how it almost was, for Avraham."

"I would be honoured having you help me Benyamin, thank you; I just don't know where to start."

"Ish, this won't be done overnight; small steps mean success, you will figure it out, both of you."

"Benyamin, Essie, let's take a walk, that may help?"

We left Avraham's then took a walk around, the houses wouldn't take much to fix up, but I had no experience in getting a community together on such a large scale. I had to stay focused: this was massive, but it was the one thing Avraham wanted more than anything, I had to pull it off. It made me realise his love for the place; having to leave here was much harder for him, he kept so much hidden, bottled so much up but he did it for me, because he had too. I had so many mixed feelings about so many things, but now I had to put that to the side; I had to do this for him.

We soon came to the bend where my house was, I stopped for a moment to take a breath. Not knowing what to expect, almost not wanting to go any further, I started telling myself I could do it, but my stomach was in knots; inside the panic slowly arising. I grabbed Essie's hand, she then looked at me reassuringly.

"Come on, Ish, it will be alright, hey, I've got you."

"I know, I'm ready, Essie."

We turned the bend then I saw it: my house. I expected to see my parents still lying where they fell; but there was no sign anything had happened there. I turned to Benyamin.

"Benyamin, my parents fell here; what happened to them, do you know?"

"Yes, Ishmael, I buried them, along with many more. You left so suddenly; I had no choice. Did I do the wrong thing?"

"Benyamin, no, I am stunned you did that, I know that can't have been an easy thing. You don't know what that means to me; thank you. Can you show me where?"

"Of course, this way."

He led us to a hill, it overlooked the whole village. There was a big oak tree on top of it; it was very old, yet still very beautiful. As we moved closer, I could see he had built a small graveyard, being such a close- knit community everyone knew everyone. Benyamin knew family names of those he had buried. I looked at him admiringly as he pointed to my parents' graves.

"Ishmael, they are here; come, it's alright."

"Go on, Ish, I am here."

I took small steps over. Looking down I stared at their graves; I didn't know how to feel. I had no flashbacks, no anger, no emotion whatsoever; I just felt sad. I wished they were here but I knew that would never happen, I just accepted it. I don't know what I expected or if how I felt was even right. I stood there for a couple of minutes then bent down.

"I'm not sure what to feel or say: you were there one minute then gone the next, it affected me badly. I went down a dark road, but I am getting better. It is so strange being back here now, I don't know why that day happened,

I only know I love you Mama and Papa; I hope I make you proud one day. I'll never forget you both, you will always be in my heart, rest in peace now until we meet again; look after Avraham for me."

Essie walked over, she had flowers in her hand; I hadn't even noticed she had walked off to find some. I took them from her hands, and she kissed me on the cheek before I placed them on their grave, I felt a sense of peace then. What Benyamin did was more than a good gesture: if he hadn't of buried them, then they would still have been on the ground, I know I would not have handled that. He saved me from potentially losing it again in a big way, that was something I could never repay. I turned to him.

"Benyamin, I suffered flashbacks for a long time, they sent me down a very bad road which almost cost me my life. I was so worried to come back: thinking my parents would still be where they fell. You stopped me from potentially going down there again; I cannot repay you for that, thank you so much. I want you to know that I am always here for you; if you need anything, I will always help, I want you to know that."

"Ishmael, you do not need to thank me, they were your family; but we were all family at one time. I could not leave them there: they were good people who deserved to be treated right, I'm glad I could do that."

"You're a good man, Benyamin, a very good man."

"Come, Ishmael: we have much to do."

"Benyamin, wait: I want to see my house?"

"Of course, but I'll wait here, Ishmael, please take your time."

I went with Essie towards it. I opened the door, shutting my eyes. Essie touched me on the arm, I reopened them then looked around. I was shocked to see it as it was, it wasn't like Avraham's, dark or dull, it was bright with a pleasant feel to it, just like I remembered. I knew exactly who was responsible; I could only smile, Essie also smiled holding my arm.

"Benyamin did this for me. Essie: it's like I remember, why would he do that?"

"Probably because he knew Avraham, Ish; this was his doing too, he never stops surprising me that man. He is just like my father, again; death doesn't appear to stop him either. That's why Benyamin didn't come in."

"I wish Avraham was here, I wish I could hug him, thank him. Why did he have to go? I know all that's been said, but I really miss that man. We must scatter his ashes by the river; they were happy times."

"I know, Ish, I know, but he is with us: I can feel it. Let's do that for Avraham first: that is important, then you can show me your village."

Moving around, I started to tell her the stories of me watching my mother do her work, how I sat on the table eating snacks or bits of fresh bread or treats she had cooked. How she always made me laugh, then lifted me down on the floor kissing me when she had finished. We would then sit waiting for father to return from market after a busy day.

Before that fateful day, it was always exciting to see him arrive home, showing us both what he had bought back, lifting his goods up proudly with a big smile on his face. He would come over to me, then shake my wig affectionately; mother always got a kiss on the cheek. All that had been forgotten because that day had changed everything: I had lost all that was good until now. I had memories flooding back; some which made me laugh loudly. One memory was where my father banged his toe; he shouted blue mercies, only to notice me standing there. He looked at me then smiled, slapping his own wrist. He put his finger to his lips then, which I found very funny at the time. Then to pick me up, telling me sternly not to repeat them; but I never did. They were fond memories; that was what I had to remember too. Essie sat there very amused, listening contentedly then looked straight at me. I looked at her then smiled curiously.

"Essie? What?"

"It's so good to see you laughing; I'm thinking now you will be at peace, too. Ish, these are what you should carry with you; now I think you will."

"I am glad I came back: I know Avraham knew it would be good for me, now I can see why. I do feel peaceful now, the most I've felt in a long time."

"Everything will be fine, Ish; you will be too. You can rebuild this place knowing people won't go through what you did. I know it'll be hard, but it will be worth it too. There are so many of your parents' things; what are you going to do with them?"

"Leave them, Essie, I don't want to sell or let someone in this house. I want us to have it: we can spend holidays here, if we have children then they, too, will learn Jewish ways. I know I don't follow the traditions, but I won't deny our children the choice if we have any."

She walked over to me, grabbed me by the shirt, before kissing me on the lips.

"Ish, you've been amazing today, but I have a question now: how much closer can we get?"

I smiled at her then whispered in her ear.

"I would have to show you now I think?"

"When we get back: that is what I want."

She was so sincere with those words; the temptation to throw myself at her was hard to resist, she went to walk away but I grabbed her.

"When we get back: I want to show you exactly what you mean to me Essie, words aren't always enough."

"I've never loved anyone as much as I love you, words aren't always enough but coming from you, to me they're everything, you are my everything. Ish I…"

"Hey, I know: I can feel it, you were always worth waiting for Essie, I'll always wait for you."

"Yes, I know that too, but will Benyamin?"

Catching me off guard again, I could only laugh at this while shaking my head, I kissed her again.

307

"It was good to come back in here, but I'm done; we should get back to Benyamin."

"That's a wise choice, Ish, a very wise choice."

She winked at me then stretched her arm out, I took her hand then went outside to meet Benyamin. We spent the day walking round, making plans while taking notes. I wanted Benyamin to come back with us but now I knew his place was here; it always would be. Getting our village back to how it was would be repayment for what he did for me; I could make him happy, give something back to him. He had no phone, so I couldn't contact him, but I promised to get him one straight away. He could keep me up to date when I couldn't be there, or would be able to let me know what was needed.

We went to scatter Avraham's ashes by the river, it was a proud moment in a way, but one of immense sadness too. Benyamin said a couple of prayers. I stepped forward while opening his urn, I looked at his ashes, took a breath then released them.

"You are home my friend, you will always be loved, you will always be remembered. You will always be my best friend, I love you; be at peace Avraham, thank you for everything."

Benyamin turned to me then smiled.

"You've done him proud, Ishmael, you should be proud of what you did today."

"I am just glad I could do it for him, Benyamin, it is all he ever wanted."

"I know, Ishmael, but that is the point: you've done for him something that was incredibly difficult for you, especially so soon after his passing. He would have been deeply grateful for that, he always did love this place."

"Thank you for your words, Benyamin, but yes, it is only recently I realised just how much. Come on, I would like to look around our village, I know Essie is keen, too."

We looked around, taking notes, discussing plans, it soon came to light just how challenging this would be; but I was determined nonetheless. We needed to leave to get back, but just before we were about to set off home Benyamin pulled me to him while reaching into his pocket; he then put his head down and sighed.

"Benyamin? Are you alright? What is it?"

"Ishmael, I did something; although I'm not sure if it was right? All the people that died, I removed their jewellery just in case people came back, so they would have something to remember them by. I have your mother's wedding ring as well as a chain I took from your father. I thought you could keep them as they are sentimental? I hope you're not angry, I had nothing when my family passed because we were poor, but my parents taught me the important things. I knew things like that would be valuable to people who were close; Ishmael, I am no thief or…"

"Benyamin, I know you are no thief, neither am I angry; I'm speechless you even thought of doing that, it was a very lovely thing to do. When our village opens again I'm sure people will come looking. You did the right thing, so, don't doubt it. Can I ask Benyamin: what was a favourite thing your mother loved? Your father too?"

"Ishmael, I… well, I know my mother loved roses, she would speak of them often, telling me of the fragrance, the colours, the shapes. She warned me of the sharpness of the thorns, but she never had any. My father gave her one rose when they first met, she fell in love with them. My father loved to fish but he worked tirelessly, he never got the time, why do you ask?"

"This is where I can do something for you, Benyamin: we will build a fisherman's hut by the river, it will be named after your family. We will plant rosebushes of every colour, so you will always have something to remember them by. You have always put others before yourself, even when you have been alone, grieving; your strength is truly something else. I want to thank you for all you've done for me; also for all you have done for others. I can see why Avraham was your friend; he would be proud of you."

"I don't know what to say; just thank you Ishmael, thank you."

"It's my absolute pleasure, Benyamin. It is important to you; so now it is important for me."

"Ish, we need to make a move, I'll be sorry to leave this place: it is beautiful."

"We will be back very soon. Benyamin, it's been a blessing meeting you again. Here, this is my number; please call me when the phone is fitted. Take care, remember if you need anything at all, then let me know."

He grabbed my hand placing the ring and chain into it then put his hand onto my shoulder.

"I will, Ishmael. You have a great man there, Essie. Take care both of you. Ishmael, thank you again."

"Yes, like Avraham once said: the best, goodbye Benyamin, you take care too."

"Goodbye, Benyamin."

19 RABBI'S RETURN

We got into the car then waved to Benyamin, I watched through the mirror as he headed away; I was sad to be leaving, too. I knew he would be a great friend; I also knew Avraham knew that. I believed it to be the reason he brought me here: not just for me to fulfil his wishes, but for Benyamin too. As we got to the bend just before leaving the village, Essie turned to me.

"Take a last look, Ish: it will all be different next time you come."

"It will always be the same to me, Essie: I'll remember it for what it was, but yes, change must come."

"Yes, that's beautiful, you have that now; things will change, but not everything, not memories, they'll always be with you. Remember what's important, it will help you move on."

It had been some experience today, very emotional too; a day I certainly won't ever forget. I turned to look one last time.

"I love you Mama, Papa; I always will."

Things started moving back home, Benyamin saw over everything that we planned. Like Essie said: things would change, but in a good way. My village was becoming much livelier looking: things were taking shape, houses were done up. The fisherman's hut in the village was built which

Benyamin was ecstatic about. I put adverts in the paper looking for families of the relatives lost; some came forward that wanted to move back, however, many didn't, so they were kept for other Jewish families. Benyamin listed all the family names that lived there or died there too, I had them put on a large slate hanging by a large statue, which was placed by the village entrance. After a while Benyamin told me it was looking as it once was. I arranged to go back one day, I could not resist seeing it now. Benyamin was there to greet me.

"Ishmael, the work is almost done here, come: I have much to show you. Did you have a good trip?"

"Yes, it is great to see you again, Benyamin, you have done amazingly well."

"No, Ishmael: we have both done well, that is something you should accept, why don't you?"

"I find it difficult, Benyamin, I feel I have so much to make up for; I don't do it for myself, I…"

"Ishmael, you have nothing to make up for, the horrors which happened here were not of your doing, you were only young; you watched your parents murdered in front of you, that would send anyone the way it sent you. I know you feel guilt for your mistakes, but Ishmael, like Avraham said: they made you who you are. All you've been through, then gone on to achieve is truly inspirational, many people are so proud of you, Ishmael, be proud of yourself."

"You remind me of Avraham, I am so blessed having you in my life, Benyamin. I have learned over the years that things must be said; people must be acknowledged for all they do, no matter how small that may be. You have been there for me; even when I wasn't even aware of it. Everything you did here for me, for my family, right up to today. Benyamin, thank you, if our work brings you some happiness then that is something I can be happy with: you are so deserving of it, your family would also be very proud of you."

"I am happy, Ishmael, never did I think all those years

ago you would be back doing all this; life is so mysterious, it isn't all bad either, especially with people like you in it. Thank you, Ishmael, from the bottom of my heart."

"Anytime, Benyamin; anytime."

We took a walk to where my parents lay. We stood looking down on the area, I smiled.

"We did it, Avraham, my friend: we have our home back."

"Ishmael, I know he will be smiling down."

"Yes, Benyamin, I believe he will be too."

Benyamin said nothing more, only patted me on the shoulder, chuckling while nodding his head. I knew I had another Avraham for a friend, the feeling inside was one of complete harmony. I had to be getting back, the visit was a brief one, Benyamin came to see me off. Before I got into the car he touched me on the arm.

"Ishmael, never forget all that's been said or that I am always here for you; if you need me anytime, please do not hesitate to ask? You always have a friend in me."

I chuckled at this comment before staring at him

"Very much like Avraham, Benyamin. But no: I won't forget either of them. If you need me then you know where I am, too. However, I will be back soon with Essie, maybe we will have a chance of sitting down for a meal next time?"

He laughed at this, nodding in agreement.

"Yes, Ishmael, that will be good; I will make something traditional for us. Goodbye, see you soon."

"I look forward to it, goodbye, Benyamin."

Back home things were going well too, the shelter was becoming even more successful, I am glad we could help so many people, it was down to the dedication of the staff. I wasn't around there much but everything was taken care of, the staff were doing a great job. I had no concerns about it, so I could focus on other things. Jonah and Issy now, too, were there a lot, Sam would come for them when I couldn't take them there. I barely saw them, but they loved to go, they were comforting to the homeless, too, which I would never stop. I could only make the most of the time when they were here.

I also went back to the hospital to see the doctors and nurses who had helped me through my coma. Sitting there waiting to see the doctor I was appreciative that I had the chance to. I soon saw him approaching me, a smile on his face.

"Ishmael, it is good to see you, you are looking very well."

"Doctor, I felt it necessary to come back to thank you. When you said I had much to be here for? Well you were right, you really helped me. I must confess I never did need the counselling doctor, but you taught me a valuable lesson."

"It is my job, Ishmael, but I, too, appreciate what you have said. How is your friend, Avraham, is it?"

"He passed doctor, not long ago."

"I am so sorry, Ishmael, he seemed to be a good man, as well as a friend; he was very concerned about you during your coma."

"Yes, I know, doctor, he was a great man, I was lucky to have him in my life. I am grateful for everyone who has played a part in it some way, it was important I came back to see you. Thank you doctor for all you did, to the nurses too."

"I am just happy to see you looking so well, Ishmael, I said I didn't want to see you back here, but this is a pleasant visit, I am relieved about that."

I started laughing, he also chuckled as he looked at me. He then put his hand on my shoulder.

"Ishmael, I am sorry, but I must get back to work, it has been great to see you again, you really are one of the lucky ones, not everyone leaves here."

"Yes, I know, doctor, it has been good to come back too, you do great work; I am proof of that."

"Thank you, Ishmael, take care, goodbye."

"You too, goodbye, doctor."

Essie was due to get the children back in one day; she was cleaning, cooking, preparing for their return. She was very excited which was really nice to see after so long. As for Rabbi, well, he retired to go travelling; he would send postcards or ring every so often, keeping me updated on his adventures which I was thrilled about, I was so happy he was doing something for himself. He promised to come back to see us all, I, too, was looking forward to seeing him, but I knew it would be a while away yet.

I continued to write, every chance I got. If not for my promise, I may not have done it: I was busy most of the time, but it was also the one thing I enjoyed, it was something for me, too. I had been writing a book about all that had happened in my life: in honour of Avraham. It wasn't easy to do, but it was necessary: it helped me to show all the good people who came into my life my side of the story, what went on in my head throughout. Avraham was there through it all; so, it would be dedicated to him. All that I am now was through his belief, his loyalty, but his love above all else.

I missed him so much every day, but having things going on around me helped. Every time I sat at my desk, I would look at his mug, speak openly to him, tell him about my day, about all that had gone on. Some may think it was crazy, but it helped me deal with his passing effectively, especially when I had something good to tell him. It was my way to deal with it all which worked; so, I stuck to it.

I finally finished my book, then had it sent off. A few weeks later I was sent a published copy.

I sat staring at it just chuckling to myself: all I had been through was now in this book before me, it seemed as unreal as the dream was. I was glad I did it: I hoped it would inspire people to be better, to not give up, to let them know that people understood what they were thinking or feeling, and to let them know that they weren't alone.

Essie came in one day absolutely soaked: she had taken the dogs out for a walk. I was at my desk.

"Ish, I'm making coffee, do you want anything?"

I stood up then walked to her putting my arms around her neck.

"I have all I want here."

"Hmm, are you sure about that, there's nothing else?"

"Some things I can wait for, especially someone as beautiful as you."

I winked at her; she gazed into my eyes, then smiled.

"Things have been so hectic lately; there's many things I can resist in life, but you are not one of them, not any longer. I don't want you to wait, Ish, I don't want to wait."

I leaned in then and kissed her passionately before I pulled away.

"Then we won't?"

"After that? I will make sure of it, Ish."

I grinned at her, just before I replied there was a knock on the door. We looked at each other puzzled: we were not expecting anybody. I quickly went to answer it. As I opened it, I was stunned to see who was standing there, I was also very much alarmed.

"Rabbi?"

"Hello Ishmael, terrible weather; may I come in?"

"Please, you're always welcome, I can't believe you are back."

Essie, who followed me out, also stared at Rabbi, taken aback too.

"Rabbi? Is that you?"

"Aah, Essie, yes, you are looking very well."

"Thank you, yes, I am doing great, it's lovely to see you,

please make yourself at home. Ish, I'll make that coffee."

"Likewise, Essie; thank you. Ishmael, we need to talk."

I had a sudden urge to fling my arms around him, he was surprised but welcoming of it, he laughed then patted me on the back. He looked as he had done in my dream: much older, frail looking. His hair had greyed considerably; along with his beard. I had an uneasy feeling creeping in; even more so now since he said he wanted to talk. For the moment I said nothing. I had missed him, but it didn't seem the time to bring it up. After removing his wet garments I took him to my study where we sat down.

"Ishmael, I see you have become a much greater man since we last saw each other: you have exceeded all my expectations, you should be incredibly proud of yourself."

"Rabbi, no: I made promises. I owed it to Avraham to fulfil them; no matter how hard, it is he who should get the credit, I cannot take it. All he wanted was to go home, for it to be returned to how we remembered it, that was his dream. I had to do it for him and our people. That doesn't make me great, just a friend. Rabbi you have changed considerably, it is alarming?"

"Aah, but Ishmael: even friends can say no, even friends can turn their backs when difficulties get in the way. After everything you've been through, you didn't hesitate; you would have had every right to have done so, you don't see, do you? That's not just a friend, that is extraordinary, you have great resilience which has led you to do great things. Avraham would have said the same. I know you feel guilt, remorse about so many other things, but Ishmael, you have more than made up for any wrong doings you think you've done. You must allow yourself to take some credit; you deserve it, Son. I know you won't forget the people who touched your life, they will be part of you always, myself included. But I am old, Ishmael, your comment doesn't surprise me. Age catches even the best of us, those who see that are privileged. I can't be around forever, you must prepare for that too."

"You know, Rabbi, everyone I lost I learnt something from. I didn't understand it; I got angry which almost cost me my life, but I was blessed having any of it. I'm glad I became better, could change my life around, I may not be here now otherwise. I have special people close; my whole life ahead of me, I couldn't have got where I am without you all. Whatever I have achieved, it has been because of the people who never gave up on me. I didn't deserve any of it, but it never stopped you or Avraham. I look back, it's so confusing much of it, yet I learned valuable lessons; I came to know what is important. I just can't make sense of everything still. I know in time things will give reasons, it's times like this Avraham always shared his wisdom. Rabbi, I'm so thankful you're here, I know I said nobody would replace Avraham, but you are right up there with him, you will always be very important to me. Thank you for everything you've done."

"Ishmael, you're doing it again: overthinking things that don't need any thought. Son, the past is the past, you don't need to make sense now, it's also why you can't. You have learned from it; your knowledge gained, you will take forward with you. I saw a terrified young boy when we first met, yet you ran towards me almost fearless, then you stopped to figure me out. That second: I knew there was something in you."

"That's why you smiled; the reason you waited that day?"

"Yes, Ishmael, that's a rare thing to see. I knew you were special; Avraham being so close to you, as wise as he was, he knew it too. But you question everything; sometimes you just need to trust."

"That day, I had panic attacks coming down the mountain, we waited behind shops in fear of seeing soldiers. I was scared but then I saw you; instantly I felt the sudden urge to go to you, that's why I ran: in case you disappeared. Avraham was skeptical because he was afraid too, he just hid it well. However, he sensed we should come here, and we did it. I've met some amazing people because of his trust. He said we were led here, part of me believed it but…"

"You both took a leap of faith, Ishmael, you threw yourself into the unknown, do you really believe that was just coincidence? There was a higher power at play here; I don't say it because I'm a rabbi, I say it because you could have gone anywhere, yet you were led straight to me. I know you believe this, you turned your back on your faith, but it never turned its back on you. Maybe after all that's said, all you've done now, you will see why? I always said you were meant for great things, but I'm certain now I wasn't the only one. There's a reason things happened; there is a reason life turned out how it did, denying faith won't change that. That will always be there with you, Ishmael; you can trust it. Just like Avraham knew what was best, don't you think faith does, too?"

"Rabbi, I do believe something got us here, I'm just not sure what anymore: I have sensed when things would happen, bad things, but I can't make any logic of it at all? I just feel I should be following a different path, maybe that's why I've been forced from the Jewish ways? I am not sure if you will be offended, or know what I mean, I'm sorry, Rabbi."

"No Ishmael, please don't apologise, it seems you are describing something spiritual; your sensing is intuition, maybe foresight. That is a very rare thing if so, it's not always good, but if that's how you feel, then perhaps it should be explored? I have said to do what makes you happy, that means with everything; we will always be friends regardless, Ishmael. So, maybe this is the next path you must follow: bringing it up means it is of some importance to you. I will always respect that; I will still be there if I can. Do what's right for you; go where your heart takes you, use that intuition and it will show you the way."

"Rabbi, thank you, you never fail to ease my mind. I guess whatever path I'm meant to lead, I will know soon enough. What about your path? Where will that be taking you next; why come back so soon? Some things you have said are unnerving?"

"To put it bluntly? It was to say goodbye, Ishmael. After what you've said, I believe you knew that deep down, so, it won't be as much of a shock. I don't know how long I have. I just know I had to come back: to spend some time with you while I still could. We both know how precious time is; it was important to give us both that, you have lost many people, so I know as hard as it may be, you will appreciate it."

"Rabbi, I should be shocked; but I don't feel anything, why? I just feel I can only accept it. Rabbi, that doesn't seem right; I'm somewhat confused? I don't know if it's hit me yet, or it's down to something else?"

"Ishmael, Son, with experiences we gain wisdom; you have gained much of it. Please, don't feel bad for not feeling more: I know you care. By acceptance: you prove that you are strong enough alone. Everyone who comes into your life will not always stay, no one stays permanently either, Ishmael; that is just how life goes. Remember, it's not about people being there, it's about what you do while they are, making memories while learning from each other. Going forward you will only get stronger, in the time we have together now we will create good memories. That is what you will remember; it is also something that will help, too."

"But Rabbi, I…"

"No buts, Son, you have come far; anything we lose in life, we gain something from it. We spoke of things happening for a reason, but people also come into our life for a reason. With Richie you found purpose, Avraham got you to where you were meant to be, I helped you both to do it. We all had purpose; you did too, but you gave us all purpose, Ishmael, together we all became better people. Don't be afraid to let people in: they will add value to your life, or give you lessons which will be important for you. Now you help people, inspire them, that's what you're here for. Ishmael, we have become close this past year; but like Avraham, I am not meant to stay in your life either. We have learned much from each other, we will part as friends. I am grateful to have you in my life, I am proud of you; however, it is God's will when my time is up, we cannot change that."

"You, Avraham: both of you were my teachers, you were both there during my hardest times. When Avraham passed, you helped me through it. Rabbi, I know I have gained much strength, wisdom too, but I will never be as wise as you both, I still have a lot to learn. Losing you both worries me: who do I go to now?"

"Aah, that is simple, Ishmael: you look to yourself. You must, you have enough life experience now to know what to do in most situations. You have been at rock-bottom, but come through it. You watched your family murdered, yet you came through it. Son, you lost your best friend, were forced to live in a world that was not real, yet you got through it. You've battled with grief every day since you were seventeen, you have had so much anger, confusion, been living with so much uncertainty, but again, you fought it and won. Son, you wouldn't need any of us even if we were here: you are your own teacher now, rely on yourself because that will take you far. Realisation along with acceptance, you will thrive by yourself. You've relied on others your whole life which was necessary, but not now. If you had kept your tradition, your faith: you would've made a great rabbi one day, you can teach many. That, too, may be a path to take in some way."

"You know, Rabbi, that's the advice I speak of, you make sense always, but coming from myself I constantly question it; that will never go, how do I know it's going to be right?"

"Ishmael, Ishmael: all experiences so far have an answer, you won't know everything, because you have yet to experience so much still. That intuition you have? Use it, go with what feels right; whether right or wrong you will learn, but that is the point. I know you will know what to do, those feelings you have? Listen to them; do that then all will be well."

"I'm really going to miss you, Rabbi, it's so strange we are being so casual about it. I've pushed you away when I shouldn't have, I will always regret that. I am forever grateful it was you we were led to. I'm so thankful you didn't give up on me, blessed having you in my life for so long. Thank you for being a friend, a teacher, but most of all for giving us a chance in life."

"No thank you necessary, Ishmael, don't regret what has already gone: that has helped shape you. We are all very proud of you.

"I hold no remorse towards you, don't let little things niggle away: they will hold you back. You must always keep looking forward now; you have much to look forward to. Ishmael, I must rest if I may."

"Of course, but Rabbi: I won't forget all you have taught me, I may doubt myself at times, but I've never doubted you. I'll show you to your room."

"I know that, Ishmael, I know."

"Yes, course you do."

He smiled fondly at me, then I took him to rest while I went back to my study. I sat in thought, thinking over all he had said, Essie walked in a few moments later.

"Ish, you have that look again when you have received unsettling news, what is it?"

"Essie, Rabbi didn't come back without reason: after his time here, we won't see him again."

"What? No, you mean…?"

"He came to say goodbye, he knows my feelings or lack of them, after everything he's done I just accepted it. He says it is a good thing; but it doesn't feel right, he is just as important as Avraham was. I can't help but feel bad, regardless of what Rabbi said. He doesn't know how long he has, but he wanted to spend time with us while he could. That is why he came back early."

"Ish, I know how hard this is, everyone you have got

close to has been taken from you; but you are not alone. Don't let your experiences stop you from getting close to people, nobody will take Avraham's or Rabbi's place. Ish, you can't deny anyone a chance to be a good friend who comes into your life: you will never be happy otherwise."

"I'm so fortunate I have you Essie, it doesn't bear thinking about if I didn't."

"Well don't think about it: that is pointless Ish, I am here to stay, I am not going anywhere. What will be will be, we will get through anything together."

"You really are a rare one, Essie; how did I get so lucky?"

"That's not the question, Ish, the question is, why shouldn't you be? You've bought much happiness to so many people; all the bad doesn't make you undeserving, all you've done does. Love yourself as Avraham said, allow yourself to find peace within you now. You must stop thinking like that: you are amazing, Ish. I know you won't believe that; but many of us know it to be true."

"I look back, Essie, I never thought I would get where I am or have the life I have now. Never did I think my life would be like this. I don't feel I have had control over any of it, I can't feel like that or believe myself to be: if it wasn't for three people then, like Avraham said, perhaps I would still be where I was. After the coma, life was out of my control which turned out to be the best thing; but I am not amazing, I just wanted better. I wanted to give back to the people who were always there for me. Rabbi thinks divine power has been in play, part of me believes it, but my brain can't process that. All the feelings I had when bad things happened or feelings I got from people like your father, I knew taking him in was right, my intuition helped me throughout, yet I haven't become aware of it till lately; I can't help but think things may have been different if I hadn't ignored it."

"Ish, your intuition is there to guide you only, you can't be sure things would be different: you are only in control of your life, not others. The things that happened were supposed to. As for divine power: that's something you must decide yourself. But ask yourself this: apart from that once, all the other times you were alone in a drunken state, anything could have happened, but it didn't. Have you asked yourself why? Ish, inside myself I truly believe you were protected by something, but I can't be definite on that: it's what you believe that will help you now as you move on."

"I have learned anything is possible, sometimes I just know things; maybe going forward I will be more aware, perhaps I can use it for good. Rabbi believes it to be a gift, if that's the case it should be shared."

"I know you will share it, just don't put too much thought into it Ish: you just need to listen sometimes. Just remember: your intuition won't change things, it will prepare you for good or bad events or people you meet; that is a good thing so don't fear it."

"Rabbi said the same, but I don't fear it; I just need to try to understand."

"Ish, you will; just give it time, divert your thoughts to something else."

I looked at her now with a smirk.

"That's simple enough with you standing there."

"Well, I'm sure they won't be as complicated as the ones you've just had?"

"Hmm, they are certainly not as bad; in fact, far from it. I love you, Essie. When I get the chance I will show you just how much."

"Well, if you can drag yourself away from your study tonight, you may just get that chance?"

"It is a date."

She gave a wink then left me to my thoughts again. I sat thinking about what they had both said. I knew Rabbi had chosen to do things this way because we had become close; him leaving in his usual way would be easier to deal with, than him sticking around. I accepted it: I would deal with it better that way, but he knew I'd seen enough death, he had the choice to allow me to see that or not.

I'd have been there if he wanted, but he didn't and wouldn't allow it either; I had to respect it. None of it was an easy way, but he thought it to be the right thing to do, especially without Avraham now. I knew he was wise enough to know what was best, because I wouldn't have him either if I was in the same situation. I could have seen the negatives to it, usually I would have, but after listening to Essie I wanted to be more positive, try to change my way of thinking; use that intuition.

Those goals wouldn't be reached overnight, but this was a start; I was trying now so I had to acknowledge that. I started making plans for things to do, I suddenly stopped: a switch in my head turned on, I questioned myself now, asking what I was doing. I didn't need to plan anything: just being there with Rabbi was enough, just being in the moment enjoying it. That would be more important to him than any planned-out day or trip, we didn't have much time left so it had to count. I put my pen down then chuckled to myself: he spoke of living in the moment before, but only now did I realise the true meaning of it, this helped alter my way of thinking. I had spent my life worrying or doubting. I tried being positive, which in a lot of ways helped me achieve what I did, but personally, I was negative. Now I had to change that, change my attitude, too, because that was holding me back. I sat there taking a good hard look at myself, I didn't like myself, but I never had. Everything which had been said about me, I knew I should appreciate myself more; maybe in time I could love myself, find the peace within, for myself. I was uncertain of that but inside I hoped it would be a reality.

Sam soon brought the dogs back; they greeted me affectionately, excitement on their faces but looking tired too. They fed then went to lie in the lounge in front of the fire. I made my way to the kitchen where Essie was cooking dinner, I came up behind her then wrapped my arms around before kissing her on the neck.

"Something smells as good as you look."

"Well I'm hoping it tastes just as good too."

I spun her around before looking at her.

"I'm going to have to find that out; aren't I?"

"When it's time; you will, Ish."

I smirked at her, just then Rabbi came in looking tired, yet cheerful as ever.

"Evening, Ishmael, Essie, something smells lovely."

"It will be ready in five minutes, I have coffee made Rabbi?"

"Yes, thank you, Essie, that will be nice. Ishmael, I will be staying out tonight, I hope you don't mind?"

"Rabbi, not at all; if I can give you a lift anywhere, I will?"

"Aah, no, Ishmael, that is not necessary: I am getting picked up. I have some things to take care of while seeing a friend, but thank you."

"You will stay for dinner first, won't you?"

"Ish, let the man be, Rabbi you aren't obliged to do anything."

"Yes, Essie, I know; but if there is enough then I will stay for dinner."

"There is plenty, if you would like to sit at the dining table I will bring it in, you too, Ish."

I helped Rabbi to the table, the change in him since I last saw him was upsetting: just like Avraham, he was full of life, but on the outside, you could see his time was coming to an end. That was hard to ignore, but having the chance to help him now, even in small ways, just as he had done for me all these years, gave some comfort. It was moments like this that mattered.

After dinner, Rabbi helped me clear away whilst Essie continued her preparations; she didn't stop. As I went to collect plates, he grabbed my arm gently.

"Ishmael, I want to thank you for allowing me to be here with you both; it means the world to have people around me, I…"

He sighed heavily then put his head down in an awkward fashion: he looked troubled, his eyes were glistening from what appeared to be the start of tears. With uncertainty in my voice I placed my hand on his shoulder.

"Rabbi?"

That was the first time I'd ever seen Rabbi emotional; he was always so strong on the outside, always ready to give advice or share his wisdom. He could express what he felt, but coming from him they were just words, only had meaning or bought comfort to people he spoke too. I knew behind his ways he was fearful: I saw it in his eyes, now I had to try to bring him some comfort, like he had done for me so many times.

"I am fine Ishmael, I…"

"Rabbi sit a moment, please, listen to me: you are welcome here for as long as you want, you are very loved here. I know you are worried about staying around, but you don't have to be Rabbi; I want to be there for you as you were for me. I would insist on it: we are family, we stick together. Please don't worry about me, you've done that long enough. In your words, do whatever will make you happy now; we will support you all the way."

"I never had children, Ishmael, or married, that was one regret until you showed up with Avraham. Although, he didn't need the guidance you did, he was wise, fair and headstrong. But, you have been like a son; you gave me a chance to know what that was like. I'm very privileged to have had it. I cannot stay however, it must be this way. But I want you to know that you made me happy, too. You have gone from the frightened boy I first met, to a man of courage and integrity who has great strength within. You are selfless as much as you are generous. Ishmael, when I leave: be at peace. I did much for you, but you have given me so much, too. Thank you for what you said, although some things aren't meant to be, becoming family was; even in death that shall remain."

"Rabbi, anyone would've been blessed having you as

their father, I'm so glad I got to have that too. When you leave, I want you to also be at peace knowing I'll be fine, like Avraham, you will always have a place in our hearts."

"Yes, as you all will in mine, right we best get clearing."

"You know, Rabbi, Essie has the children back tomorrow, she will be glad you got the chance to meet them, they will be your family too. I know Essie will agree with me, no matter how many children we have, or how many people come into our lives, you as well as Avraham will always have a special place in it. That, too, shall always remain; nothing can ever take that away."

"Hmm, you say you will never be as wise as we were? Ishmael, I don't believe that for one minute: you already are. You don't even know you're doing it. Trust yourself Son, I am positive you will be fine, even more so now. Right we should clear away, but Ishmael? Thank you."

"Like you said to me, Rabbi, it's not necessary."

We cleared away then he left for the evening a short while later. I sat in my study where I found myself talking to Avraham.

"Avraham, my friend, I wish you were here: to advise me, tell me what to do. I am worried about Rabbi: I know he is afraid, I'm certain he feels he is alone. Avraham if you can hear me then please look after him in the times I can't be there. We both know the man he is; he showed real emotion tonight, yet I cannot offer him comfort. He is dying Avraham, he will not allow me to be there; I must respect that for him, but after all he has done for us, I cannot accept it deep down; he is very important just as you are. I worry how I may react, I still worry I am not strong enough to handle his passing, I worry everything will come crashing down again, please give me guidance, please keep me strong. Thank you, my friend.

I sat for a moment, the room was deadly silent. I stood up, after taking one step, I suddenly had a strange feeling overcome me, it was one I had never felt before. I couldn't explain it, but instantly I knew things would be alright; it just made me smile. I thought it very odd, it didn't feel like it was even me doing it. Part of me was almost in disbelief, but I couldn't deny that it had happened, much as I wanted to. I went to call Essie who came downstairs.

"Ish? What is it?"

"Avraham, being amazing as he always was."

"Ishmael, that doesn't make sense?"

"How do you explain chatting to him about my worries, my concerns, then a sudden feeling overcame me, a knowing that everything will be alright? That was very bizarre, Essie, I want to believe it was Avraham but I'm battling to know if it was or not."

"Ish, I can understand that, but you have your answer, that is all you need to know. If you want to believe it's Avraham, then you can; it doesn't matter. Like I've said before: go with what you believe. It confirms my thoughts of you always having something around you, that really does prove it, Ish; but it seems you may have more than just Avraham with you."

Putting my hands on her waist I grinned at her.

"Yes, I have you; but now I do? I'm not letting you go anywhere."

"In that case, Ish, I'm thinking I will have to take you with me; won't I?"

"Hmm, well I'm thinking: that kiss before, it was unfinished."

"So, kiss me, Ish; I'm not going anywhere until you do."

I moved in to kiss her just like before, she then pulled away gazing in my eyes. Smiling, she then led me upstairs. Before we went into the bedroom I stopped her.

"Essie, we have been through so much together, yet, we haven't had a chance to be together. I should never have waited this long: you're beautiful, you are my everything. After tonight, I hope you feel that regardless of how things have turned out, you are wanted in every way. I will spend every second proving that."

"I do feel it, Ish, I know it too; but as for you spending

every second, I wouldn't be so sure: I will prove that."

She winked at me before grabbing my shirt, then pulling me inside the bedroom, slowly shutting the door behind us.

20 JOSEPH SPEAKS

That night was more than I had ever imagined it to be. Essie had a hidden side to her, which she was not shy to reveal. The best thing about the whole night, was the fact it was real; there was no fear that I would wake up from it. Inside, I was haunted by the night with Betty some ways; even though it was just a dream. I worried it would hold me back, or worse: that it could leave Essie deeply upset; but she seemed to sense it. She was amazing in reassuring me without saying anything, relaxing me, then making sure I enjoyed every second; which I did. That night made me see that, although Betty had taught me many things; she couldn't be compared with Essie. I could put her in the past now, she would only be a memory; but Essie was my life, my future, as I said to her; my everything.

In the morning Essie woke as I lay next to her; just watching as she slept, she smiled every time she saw me, no matter the mood I was in, I couldn't help but return it. She stretched before sitting up.

"Good morning, my gorgeous man."

"Morning beautiful, today is the big day."

She reflected for a second before shooting up, I stopped her quickly.

"Woah hey, you stay there, I'll make coffee; there is plenty of time."

"I have so much to do, Ish, I…"

331

"I know, Essie, but you have not stopped for days. I am here to help you, whatever you need. Things will be perfect for them, I promise. Now let me make you breakfast, restore all that energy used; you are going to need it."

She took my chin then gave me one kiss before gazing into my eyes.

"You better believe it, Ish: after last night? I just can't get enough of you; you were amazing."

"Hmm, funny: I have the same problem, but I think, when we get another chance? We can do something about that."

"I would have to insist on it, Ish."

"No, you really wouldn't, Essie. Right: now I'm making breakfast."

I kissed her again, gave her a wink; then got up to make breakfast. The day was of great significance, I felt somewhat nervous. Essie had told the children about me, but they had not yet been introduced. I worried that they may not accept me, or would make things difficult. I had no idea what to expect, but, the younger ones showed interest, would ask Essie about me a lot, which I took to be a good sign. However, children were still unpredictable, Essie was confident things would be alright so that helped considerably; I wanted them all to be happy which was my priority, even if it came to the point where we had to split because the children weren't happy. I prayed that wouldn't be the case, I had a ready-made family I really wanted to be a part of. I also knew it wasn't mine, so I would have to do the right thing; no matter how hard.

We had breakfast then got ready; I took the dogs out, the children were due soon. Essie was busy doing what she needed which I helped with when I came back. She was so fidgety, which was understandable, I know she too had her worries. I walked into the lounge to see her staring out the window.

"Hey, beautiful, are you ready to have your kids back?"

"I still can't believe this is happening, Ish, I have so many mixed emotions, what if I can't do this?"

"Essie, I know; it is normal, I will be there for you all if they want that. I don't know what will happen, but you all come first, always. I know you can do this: you are, and will be an amazing mother, that I am certain of. I am there every step of the way for you, enjoy every moment"

"Oh Ish, I know you have your worries, that, too, is normal, but they will love you in time I'm sure, I hope you will love them too. I wish my father could be here: I would have loved him to meet them."

"He would have been a great grandfather to them; he will be so proud of you Essie, we speak of Avraham being around us, but I am sure Richie will be too, like Avraham, he will be smiling down on you."

That moment we heard a car door going, Essie looked out the window again.

"Ish, it is them; they are here."

"The first day of the rest of your life, I am so proud of you, Essie, I love you."

"The first day of our lives, Ish, I love you too."

She went to open the door, I stood a little way behind, Jonah came to stand by me. The children threw their arms around her as soon as they saw her, all except her eldest who only stood there; I was unsure why that was. I had a feeling in my stomach again, it was neither good or bad, it was strange: almost like I was waiting for something to be revealed. I was aware of it, but I could not see what the reason for it was, at least not yet. Essie said a few words to the lady then they unpacked the car. I was keen to help but I knew Essie had to do this her way. A few minutes later, I heard my name mentioned then Essie pulled the door back. The lady waved at me before saying her goodbyes; Essie then brought them inside.

"Okay children, this is Ishmael, that is Jonah, Issy is around somewhere too; why don't you go over, say hello?"

The three of them just looked at me curiously, especially her oldest. Looking back at him, the feeling I had eased; but again, I didn't know why, I only knew it had to be something to do with him. A minute later, her daughter came over to me holding a doll; she had little blonde pigtails held with blue ribbon and the biggest blue eyes I had ever seen; she was wearing blue shorts with a white t-shirt, and her pumps were white with blue laces. I kneeled to her level, while the others followed behind slowly.

"Hello, what's your name?"

"I am Maisy, I am eight."

"Wow, you're big aren't you, who is this?"

I pointed to her doll playfully.

"She is called Gabriel, Joseph picked it for me; she is my best friend."

"Oh, she is lovely isn't she, you are lucky having a doll like that aren't you?"

She stared deeply at me, then smiled before wandering off, looking back at me once; Essie called her over. Essie's youngest son had brown hair that was combed to the side, above his green eyes. He had a pair of brown pants on with a checked blue shirt; he stepped forward shyly.

"I... I am Elliott."

I put my hand out to shake his, he looked at me somewhat puzzled by this; he then took my had nervously, shaking it.

"It is a pleasure to meet you, Elliott, how old are you?"

"I am thirteen, nearly fourteen; you seem nice Ishmael."

Before I could speak he walked away, hiding behind Essie. I looked at her; she was smiling at me with a look to say I was doing fine. I smiled back then turned to Joseph.

"You must be Joseph, you seem to be older than the others?"

He stared at me too, just how Maisy had done, although he had a solemn look on his face, I smiled at him before he spoke in a confident tone.

"Much."

That was it, that was all he said. This comment threw me a little: something told me there was more meaning behind it, but I couldn't be sure because I had only just met him. I looked at him until he blinked then walked away. He had me very curious: he seemed to know something, but he was a child. I couldn't make sense of it, I just hoped Rabbi would be back soon, his advice was very much needed now. Jonah watched him too, his eyes followed him wherever he went. Issy came running out a moment later, then started jumping around Joseph, he turned then put his hand out, Issy immediately sat giving a whine, he then stroked her; I was just left stunned. He walked away so I left Essie to settle them in while I went back to my study. She popped her head in a while later.

"Ish, I'm going to make lunch with the children, they're in there now mixing. You were great today; they seem to really like you."

I looked up at her, I didn't want to bring Joseph up to her, not yet: I thought it to be unfair. I would speak to Rabbi then Essie when the time was right. I thought they were lovely children regardless so didn't hesitate to say so.

"They are great, Essie, it is obvious they're your children."

"You are sweet, Ish, I see Rabbi has not got back yet?"

I started laughing; leaving her baffled as to why.

"Ish, what are you laughing at?"

"Remember the line 'let him be'? Well that's what made me laugh; he will return when he is ready."

"I think I'm just anxious for him to meet them, it will be good for him."

"He will: when you're ready to do so."

"They know about him, Ish, although only that he is staying, I think any questions should be answered by you or Rabbi himself. Why don't you come to help; the children would like that?"

"Yes, I would too, I'll be in shortly; but before I do, I haven't showed you this"

I picked up my book, her face lit up as she rushed over.

"You published it? You kept that quiet. Oh, Ish, I knew you would do it. You know, you never cease to amaze me; come here."

Just before she went to kiss me we heard a smashing sound coming from the kitchen. We both dashed there. Maisy was standing over a bowl she had knocked off, now she became very upset by it.

"It was an accident, I'm sorry."

I went over to her bending down again.

"Maisy don't cry, it's alright; we all make mistakes, we have to so we can make things better. I bet your next lot of mixing will be even more lovely."

She had her hand to her eyes rubbing them while sniffling, trying to compose herself, she took one look at me.

"Will you help me?"

"I would love to help; but only if you put that smile back, we need that smile, do we have a deal?"

Her face brightened up again; bringing a smile back, jumping up once she shouted "deal" happily.

While Essie cleaned up I assisted the children, Joseph sat looking at a stone in his hand, I wasn't sure why or what he was doing, if anything. Soon I heard a knock on the door, I went to open it; Rabbi was back.

"Afternoon, Ishmael, are they here?"

"Yes, Rabbi, they are here; we are making lunch in the kitchen, come."

"Ishmael, I am not sure it to be right, I mustn't intrude."

"Rabbi it is right, you are family remember? Essie is keen for you to meet them, please, it's fine."

"Very well, Ishmael, I would love to meet them."

"How was your evening, good I hope?"

"Yes, it was interesting, how was yours?"

"Better than I imagined it to be, Rabbi."

I smirked at him: I couldn't stop myself. I seemed to throw him with that a little: he seemed unsure of what I meant, he looked at me while thinking. I'm convinced my smirk gave it away, he only grinned before patting me on the back; he never said another word. We walked into the kitchen, all was calm again, the children were busy while Essie was making coffee. Rabbi stood staring at them until Essie spoke.

"Rabbi, welcome back, how was your evening?"

"Not as interesting as yours seemed to be?"

She looked at me with a look as if to say: "you wait". Rabbi chuckled which made me laugh, it was clear he was winding her up. Moments like that were priceless, even if they were embarrassing, Essie would appreciate them too, regardless.

"Yes, I suppose I can't deny that, Rabbi."

She laughed now before turning around to pour coffee. Rabbi walked to the table then sat down. Joseph stared at him the whole time, I found the behavior odd but fascinating, too; it was unusual that much was certain. Essie, who noticed it, quickly introduced Rabbi properly.

"Rabbi, please meet Joseph; he is fifteen, this is Elliott who is thirteen and this is…"

She was abruptly stopped by Maisy.

"I am Maisy, I am eight."

We all laughed and then Rabbi spoke to her.

"That is a very pretty name, Maisy. Who is your friend?"

"She is called Gabriel, Joseph picked the name for me when I got her."

"Is that so? Well that, too, is a lovely name."

"He said her name is special, I talk to her; she looks after me."

"Yes, that is a special name, I am sure she will look after you always."

We all stood around the table preparing lunch, I looked round, I don't think I've ever felt so contented as I did in those few minutes, it was the simple things that meant the most, being round people that mattered in life. I had it all but hadn't fully appreciated it till now. After lunch Essie took the children out to show them around, Rabbi came to me as I cleaned the kitchen.

"Ishmael, I don't think I have enjoyed a day for so long, I don't think I've ever seen you so happy since Essie agreed to marry you; you're so different now, I am so happy for you all."

"I feel it Rabbi, I am very happy, but I…"

"Ishmael? But what?"

"That intuition you told me about?"

"Yes, what about it?"

"Rabbi, before the children came I had a peculiar feeling, neither good or bad, but when I saw Joseph it eased. I commented about his age saying he seemed older than the others, good-humouredly. He stared at me then just said 'Much?' Then there was the way he was with you, am I overthinking this? I can't make sense of it, he then did something with Issy, she was jumping around him, he turned putting his hand out, then she sat immediately. I was stunned by it: I've not seen anything like that before, what does it mean?"

"Ishmael, my knowledge of this type of thing isn't my greatest, however, I did sense this child is different. I, too, don't know how yet, but it will be revealed; perhaps you are to help him some way? Maybe that is what was being shown by those feelings. Let things be for now; enjoy each moment, you will know what to do in time."

"Rabbi, I have less knowledge than you, what if that is the case that I am to help him, but I can't? Like you said: I still have much to learn, especially about this."

"Ishmael, whether we know it or not we are not given things in life we cannot handle. You do have much to learn, yes, but Ishmael, I believe Joseph will be as much your teacher as you will be his. Trust him, trust yourself; things always work out, you know that better than anyone."

"I believe he is my next path, I have not told Essie yet, somehow it feels wrong: he is her son. But your advice has been helpful as always, all these years I wasted pushing you away. I was so reluctant getting you back in my life; but I'm so glad I did. I feel so bad about that Rabbi, I know all that has been said but…"

"Son, I know; but you are here now when I need you the most, just like you were for Avraham. When my time comes, I will leave this earth a happy man. Ishmael, Essie will support you as you know, talk to her, I see your concern; but you have nothing to worry about, she will help you too."

"I know, it's just so new, so odd; I know she is there. Rabbi, can I ask where you will be going after here, you didn't say?"

"Aah, I was waiting for that, but Ishmael, rest assured I won't be alone. I didn't say because I don't want you worrying or fussing. We are family, but you have your own life now with a young family to take care of; they will need you more. This is how I want it to be, this is the way it must be, Ishmael."

"I know I must let you go, but I find that difficult regardless. Rabbi, should you change your mind when you have left anytime, day or night: I will come for you."

"Yes, I know that, Son, I will do so if necessary; I give you my word. Ishmael, just remember the good times when I go; don't linger in hope I may call, it is more than likely I won't. That will be a sign that all is as I want it to be, find peace in that. I will miss you very much, Ishmael."

"Not as much as I will miss you, Rabbi, thank you for everything, I can't say it enough."

"Yes, I've noticed, Ishmael."

He smirked so I started laughing, shaking my head. I literally couldn't say it enough, he had done so much over the years, even when I pushed him away he still asked about me; he still cared. Every time I said it, it just never seemed to be sufficient. I found myself giving him a hug sincerely: I knew that would be something I wished I had done when he was gone. I prepared dinner while Rabbi went to rest, Essie arrived back with the children a couple of hours later; they came in looking happy but tired. Essie, too, was gleaming. I felt so blessed, more than I ever had, my worries melted away regarding the children. It was only Joseph I was unsure of how to approach: he was quiet, curious or as Rabbi put it, just different. In time I was sure we would become friends, I at least hoped it to be the case. Essie came over, then gave me a kiss; the children got themselves a drink.

"You look happy, Ish, it's the best look I've seen on you; you deserve this."

"I wouldn't be here without you, Avraham or Rabbi, I never thought I'd be this happy either, it's almost like all the bad was worth it; what's more bizarre is that I'm not dreaming it."

"Dreams do come true, Ish, you're proof of that, your fighter nature has got you here; helped you achieve all you have done. What we give out we get back, you have done so much good in your life, that's why it is how it is now. Like I just said; you deserve it all."

"Do you ever think about what life would have been like if we hadn't met?"

"No, Ish: that would take away what is happening in the moment, that is pointless."

"Meeting you has been the best thing to happen for me, I am glad it wasn't any other way. However, I think you have been hanging round Rabbi too much: all that wisdom is contagious."

She suddenly burst out laughing, even the children stopped what they were doing to look. I only grinned but I was serious too; but she knew that, it was another great moment. After she managed to stop laughing she turned to me.

"Ish, never lose that humour: it's priceless, I am not the only one to think it either"

We turned to see Maisy laughing with Elliott. Joseph only looked at me again before walking boldly over. I was a little uneasy: unsure of what would happen next, he just walked straight to me, staring deeply at me for a moment before he spoke.

"I can learn much from you, Ishmael."

Even Essie looked confused by this: it was so matter of fact. His ways were so mysterious; he was confident yet graceful, from his walk to his tone of voice. Some may think it was intimidating, however, I wasn't afraid of him, I just didn't understand his ways. I only knew there was reason as to why he was like that; it was also frustrating that he seemed to know things but would only hint, leaving me more puzzled every time he spoke. I quickly replied to him realising my mind was wandering.

"Joseph, I am sure you can teach me many things too?"

He glanced over, then to my surprise he smiled. With a very calm tone he spoke.

"Yes, Ishmael, much."

Staring at him, my attention was drawn to Rabbi who came in from his rest, popping his head around the door.

"Evening, Essie, children? Ishmael, a moment please?"

"Of course, Rabbi, what is it?"

He gestured his hand towards him, Essie grabbed me, still with puzzlement on her face.

"Ish, what was all that about?"

"I'm not sure, Essie; a few odd things have happened today. I will explain properly tonight; when the children are in bed, I love you."

"I love you too, Ish, you better go, Rabbi is waiting."

I walked out of the kitchen to where he was patiently standing, I knew I was in for some news I didn't want to hear. I led him to my study then sat down.

"Rabbi, I think I know why you have called me; I sense you're leaving, if so; then why so soon?"

"You have strong intuition, Ishmael, it is right too: I will be leaving shortly. I can't get too involved, as much as I would like to, it won't be fair on the children especially"

"Yes, I understand your decision as much as it saddens me. Just promise me you will be alright, Rabbi, remember what I said too?"

'Yes, I will Ishmael, I leave tomorrow. Let's enjoy the time we have left, it will be gone before we know it."

"Your visit was short; but it is one I won't forget. Thank you for giving me that, Rabbi: for coming back."

"I will take fond memories away with me also, however, we still have more to make yet, now is a perfect time as any?"

"Rabbi, before we go: something happened in the kitchen with Joseph. I made Essie laugh, then Joseph came over out the blue; saying: he could 'learn much from me' I replied: 'maybe he could teach me many things?' he looked at me then smiled before saying "yes, Ishmael, much'? Even Essie noticed something unusual, I must speak to her later: explain todays happenings. I find I'm becoming more confused every time he speaks? I am not sure I can handle it alone."

He sat in thought for a minute before sitting back.

"Ishmael, as peculiar as it appears, it is clear you have some sort of connection; he senses it, but your mind is clouded by all you have been through. Your intuition is strong now which could be because of him, but even though you have always had it, it is still new to you.

"It will be just as confusing for him too because he doesn't know you, he may just feel he does. His comments suggest he recognises something; but I don't know what or why. It is apparent to me that this is something you need to develop, understanding it is very important. You have been brought together for a reason, just as we all were. However, you will not know why yet, because neither of you are ready for that now. I do believe that you cannot ignore it any longer, the happenings today are proof of it. Ishmael, you have been thrown into the unknown your whole life, you handled it all whether in a good way or not; why should this be any different? This needs no reply, Son, only thought. Come: we should get back to Essie and the children."

Just then there was a tap on the door, Joseph walked in then came straight over to us, but right up close to me. I became uncomfortable again, he then took one step back gazing into my eyes. Rabbi watched him without saying a word.

"Ishmael, do not fear me: to fear me is to fear yourself, you have come far but we have much further to go. I am to tell you that dinner is ready."

He walked back out confidently; I was left dumbfounded, Rabbi was also amazed by this. I was so glad Rabbi was there to witness it, Joseph hadn't been fazed by the fact he was. Placing his hand on my arm, Rabbi then smiled at me.

"Listen to him, Ishmael, he is telling you what you need to know; no matter how many words are used, he has messages in each, they will help you one way or another, the child is extraordinary."

"I will, Rabbi, I've just realised that to fear or doubt will hold him back as much as it will hold me; he knows it too. I must prevent that however I can; if I can? Rabbi, thank you, I feel I understand a bit more."

"Not at all, Son; that's the main thing. Come they are waiting for us."

We sat around the dining table eating; happily chatting when Rabbi suddenly stood up.

"Essie, as I have told Ishmael, I am leaving tomorrow. I want to thank you for allowing me to be a part of your family, for all you have done for Ishmael; I leave with very fond memories of you all."

"Rabbi: that's so soon, will you not stay longer?"

"I have explained to Ishmael why, he will repeat it to you. But it must be this way; I know you will understand, Essie."

"It has been an honour knowing you, Rabbi, I wouldn't have such an amazing man if not for you; Avraham too of course, you know we are always here for you?"

"Yes, I have been told, thank you, Essie."

Elliott whispered something in her ear causing her to smile, she looked up turning to Rabbi again.

"Rabbi, seeing as it is your last night, when we put the children to bed, would you like to read stories for them; it appears they want you to?"

"I would love to Essie, yes; if you're sure it is alright?"

"It's more than alright: it's perfect, Rabbi."

He smiled at her then carried on eating. I thought that was such a lovely gesture, one Rabbi would have been incredibly grateful for. I was so sad he was leaving; but we did make the time we had together count. I hoped wherever he went that he enjoyed his final days, that he was happy, because he was so deserving of that.

We finished dinner then spent the evening chatting and playing games with the children. While Rabbi sat with them I told Essie about Joseph, he looked over often but didn't move. I told her all Rabbi had said; she listened until I stopped speaking, then turned to me.

"Ish, if my son needs your guidance in his life then I am so glad it is you. I know you are uncertain of many things, but I am positive you will both thrive when you get answers; I have every faith in you, Ish, even Joseph himself does."

"I knew you would understand, Essie; I don't know where my path will lead, or why this has happened. But I do know it is important I tell you what I know or feel about him. Rabbi called him extraordinary; but I feel we haven't seen half of it yet. I want to be there if he needs that, you are all very important to me so it's my job to make sure you're all happy in every way, I will do my upmost best to do so."

"You don't have to tell me that, Ish, I know, but it's my job to make sure that you are, too, in every way; I will also ensure I do that. I may not fully understand your spiritual path, but I am always here to listen, try to give a different view, it is you who will help me to understand that side of my son. You know: just when I thought I had seen it all with you, you still prove how amazing you can get. Hmm, I'm not sure my heart can handle the constant shock, Ish."

I erupted into laughter, I did not expect that, she started

giggling too; I don't think she expected my reaction either. Rabbi turned around looking very amused, followed by the children who, although laughing, still had looks of wonder as to what exactly was so funny. Joseph however: he just observed with no emotion. Rabbi stood up, his body language displaying much surprise.

"Ishmael, I don't think I've ever heard you laugh like that, neither do I believe it will be a memory I will ever forget in a hurry either; it is wonderful to see."

"You can…"

"I can what, Ishmael?"

"You can thank…"

I don't know what it was: but I couldn't speak for laughing. Every time I took a breath or tried to compose myself I got worse. Essie who was standing there while just grinning, turned to Rabbi.

"I think he is blaming me for it Rabbi, I think that is unfair, Ish, don't you think; considering?"

This just made me laugh even more, I had tears in my eyes before the aching sides set in. It didn't take long before we were all laughing; it would certainly be a memory I wouldn't forget either. After composing ourselves, Rabbi went back to the table with the children; I turned to Essie.

"You call me amazing? I certainly have competition with you."

"We can wrestle about it later, Ish; if you insist?"

"Well I think with my curiosity I am going to have to. But, I think for now we should relieve Rabbi of the children, he is looking tired."

"You read my mind, Ish."

"Hmm, well, after a day like today, I'm thinking anything is possible; come on."

We went over to see what they had been up to; they were drawing contentedly, talking to Rabbi. I wandered around to see their artwork, Joseph snatched his out of my view. I put my hand on his shoulder, he nudged me off him sharply, I knew it was wrong instantly.

"Joseph, may I look?"

"No, Ishmael."

"That is okay, Joseph; I can understand that."

He grabbed my arm to my surprise; just as I went to walk away.

"Not even I understand yet, Ishmael; but we will."

I stared at him confused, as he put his head down to continue. It was only then I knew I needed to speak to him in a different way to Maisy or Elliott: because of his ability to know things. The fact he was wise beyond his years too; just like Avraham was, although he'd even outdone him. He was similar in some ways, but so different in most others. Speaking to him in the same way as the other two children didn't work: he retaliated in a way which made me feel inadequate because of his abilities, whether he meant it to or not. I had to try to come to his level, or at least keep trying till I found the right one. I turned back to him; completely unaware of what was about to unfold.

"I trust your judgement to be right, Joseph."

He sat up abruptly then, slamming the pencil down, disturbing everyone. Maisy stared at him before calling out pleadingly.

"Joseph, no: calm remember? We must stay calm."

He looked at her then inhaled deeply, closing his eyes then opening them; staring straight at me he replied to her calmly.

"Yes, Maisy, I remember."

She stared at him then continued with what she was doing. Rabbi swapped glances between the two but kept quiet. Essie wasn't sure whether to intervene or not regarding Joseph; just as she took a step, Rabbi stopped her from going any further. It was clearly the wrong thing to have said once more but I needed to know why.

"Joseph?"

"Ishmael, you can't do that: you can only trust your own judgement, your own inner knowing."

"Joseph, I don't understand?"

"Ishmael, because it is what is right for your path, yours alone; what is right for me will not be right for you."

"Joseph, I believe I am meant to help you somehow, yet I don't know what way; am I right in thinking that?"

"Yes, Ishmael: we will learn from each other, but our end paths are not the same. I will gain much strength from you; I in return will give you higher knowledge. With your guidance I will fulfil my purpose; with my knowledge you will grow, enabling you to fulfil yours. There is much healing to be done, Ishmael; all you have done up to now is nothing to what you will do in the future, you will do many more great things. Your abilities will strengthen greatly, as will mine; but if you cannot trust yourself then I can't help you. Ishmael?"

I looked up at him.

"That is why we have been brought here."

"Why we have been brought here? Joseph what do you mean?"

"Ishmael, do not ask if I do not say: I will tell you what you need to know, when you need it. There are reasons to why that is; but you will see this way to be the right one, the reasons will be revealed in time. Your constant need of knowing must be eliminated: we don't need to know everything, only what is right for now. It must be this way Ishmael, otherwise you will lose focus. We must stay on the paths laid before us, that is crucial for what is needed; now do you understand?"

"Yes, Joseph, I think I do."

The whole table was deadly silent: nobody knew what to say, not even Rabbi. I pulled a chair then sat down; I was in complete shock. Joseph leaning over towards me, his voice much calmer.

"Ishmael, do not be troubled by what you don't yet understand, for that will create unnecessary barriers which will prohibit your abilities. In time you will recognise all I have said; it just requires patience. I, too, can help you with that, for it is a powerful necessity to achieve what we are here to do. You can trust my advice for it is true, Ishmael, but trusting yourself is the most vital thing for you, myself, but most of all this world, goodnight."

With that he got up then left the room. Essie stood shell-shocked by Joseph; tears were rolling down her face. She hadn't moved since Rabbi stopped her. I got up then went over placing my arm around her.

"Essie, hey, it is alright?"

"That's my son, Ish, that's my son; what… how… I…?"

"Yes, we have all seen just how incredible he is tonight, he is very special, Essie, nobody was prepared for just how much. He is powerful; yet only fifteen. I promise I will protect him; whatever it takes. He will do amazing things, Essie. I must help him, guide him, but you must love him as you already are; we are all a part of this in our own way."

Rabbi stepped in then, he still looked dazed from what had just happened.

"Essie, Ishmael, tonight's events have been a shock for us all, however, Joseph will need you both, just as much as you will both need him. Essie, I know you must be feeling many things; but he will know, he will help you. His relationship, I feel, will be much different with you, at times it will be challenging; but, like Ishmael, you too must trust him, allow him to do what is needed. Don't worry about things that have not yet happened, both of you only need to be there for him. Your son is remarkable, Essie, be proud of him. I will read to the children; we can speak afterwards if you want to."

"I am proud of him, Rabbi, I will always be that, like Ish said, none of us were prepared for that tonight, it is just hard to take it all in."

"But you will, Essie; you both will, come now, I am sure they will all want a cuddle from their mother."

She chuckled, a smile coming back on her face.

"I can do that, Rabbi."

"Yes, Essie, that as well as so much more, never doubt it."

She gave Rabbi a hug then we made our way upstairs to say goodnight to the children. Joseph was in the room with Maisy, we could hear her talking to him.

"Joseph, Ishmael is nice, I like him."

"He will get better, Maisy, much."

"We can help him Joseph, we must."

"We will Maisy, we are the same, he will need us. For now I will say no more. Rabbi is outside the door waiting to read your story; go now."

"I know Joseph, goodnight, I love you."

"Goodnight, Maisy."

We stood outside looking at each other, part of me felt uncomfortable listening to them after his words. If he knew Rabbi was outside, then he would know I was too; it was obvious that I would find containing my curiosity much more difficult. The realisation that Maisy, too, appeared to be, as Joseph put it, 'the same as him' was more unexpected news. I felt maybe I was meant to be there after all: Joseph would not have revealed that otherwise, knowing we were outside. Nonetheless, it was still unsettling because I didn't know what was right; I could only trust that where I came to be, that was meant to be.

We put the children to bed then Rabbi read to Maisy, then to Elliott. I was hovering around not sure what to do with myself: I was so restless now. Just when I was about to go downstairs, Joseph called me in a very calm tone. I knocked before I walked in.

"Ishmael, you are restless, why?"

"Joseph, so much has happened today, I am struggling with it all, I…"

"Ishmael, yes; but like you have always done, you overthink, you worry. Did you not listen to my words? You must contain your emotions, acknowledge them; but you can't let them cloud your mind or your heart now, they must be open for you to progress, to allow what you need in. Barriers, Ishmael, they are so quick to come, but difficult to break down, listen to what I am telling you? I may be a child;

but that is only physical, it has no relevance for me. My spirit is very old, Ishmael; as is yours. You have lived in the physical ways of the world for too long, you have forgotten; but now you must accept it is time to come into the spiritual, that is your priority. That is what will make you reach your true potential; Ishmael, that is not an option to ignore any longer. Life will continue to draw you to it, you have had a difficult life but now you know why: it has led us to this point. You have had purpose since you were born, however, Ishmael, your hardships gave you the strength I will need in future; it has made you the physical being you are now, that was your purpose first. Once you accept all that has been said, once you start separating yourself from the physical, then you will remember who you truly are, then you will truly understand. You will find answers for what you seek, but not before time, that too is crucial; it is up to you. Now I am done."

"I will come to you if I need to; thank you, Joseph."

"No, Ishmael, I will know: you cannot hide anything from me, I know before you do, therefore, I will come to you. Take this then rest easy, Ishmael; it will help. I am ready for Rabbi now, goodnight."

He handed me a coloured stone, like the one he had in the kitchen earlier; he gazed into my eyes as he gave me it.

"Joseph, what do I do with it?"

"Focus, Ishmael, just focus."

He smiled warmly this time, then turned away. I looked at him on my way out; he just sat there now, staring into space. I couldn't help but be in awe of him, regardless of the difficulties which lay ahead; I was so honoured I got to meet him, be a part of his life. I wished Avraham and Richie could have met him. He had changed everything for us all already, but I knew he was far from done; I knew that things would constantly change now. Rabbi was just coming out of Elliott's room as I came out of Joseph's.

"Aah, Ishmael, they are fast asleep."

"Rabbi, thank you, Joseph is expecting you."

"Yes, I thought he might, I want to speak with him too. Ishmael, you must go to Essie: much has happened today, you need to relax now. Keeping your thoughts positive may help, be aware of the negatives. I must not keep him waiting, it has been a long day for us all."

"Essie has gone for a bath, I will see you down there when you're ready Rabbi."

"Indeed, you will, Ishmael."

Rabbi knocked and then went inside, but I couldn't leave: I sensed there were things I needed to hear. It felt wrong to pry, it made me see Joseph's point about my curiosity, however, I wasn't curious now, I just knew more solidly that I needed to be here. As I was sitting on the stairs they began talking.

"Rabbi, please sit down?"

"Thank you, Joseph, you wanted to see me?"

"Rabbi, yes, Ishmael was led to you; over the years you have taught him well. I know why you are leaving; also, where you are going to. I feel your hidden fear; I see you are very troubled. But Rabbi, do not be afraid: for fear isn't necessary for you. Believe me when I say, you are never alone. I know you will leave this earth not knowing, but you will be surrounded by people who love you. Many will be in your heart, as well as your thoughts. You have given your life to helping others, you have shared your wisdom which has helped others on the right path so many times. Rabbi; you should be at peace, and I know when you leave here, this will come. I won't forget you, Rabbi, I knew of you for almost ten years, as well as Avraham: for I saw you both also. Avraham left peacefully, you will too. Now that your time is coming to an end, my time has come to begin my journey, I too have much to learn from the physical which is why Ishmael has crossed my path. You will understand why your time is ending now. You have done all you can; but you can't give him what he needs for the next part of his journey, I must do that now. Rabbi, I know you have other worries weighing heavy on your mind, you can speak of them if you wish?"

"Joseph, I don't know if my words are right: your knowledge is much greater than mine. However, I don't know what you know about Ishmael: he has been through so much, it is clear as to why now, but he has always been very important to me. I ask that you look after him in my absence, for I have always done so. His abilities are new to him; you must know him, his ways. He has always been very sensitive with a good heart, so I fear things may become too much for him, his mind is not easily swayed, this I know he has battled with always. Joseph, he will need you more than you need him, you must find balance between you both. I noticed him trying to change his way of approaching you, but you too must do that for him. He is a man of intelligence, but there is so much he needs to understand about this, about you especially. Your way of learning is not the same; I believe you know all this Joseph, but I must speak of it. He needs to heal still, that is why I am concerned."

"Rabbi, my ways may be abrupt, even come across as harsh or cold, but they are this way for a reason. Ever since my fourth birthday, I always knew my path would cross with Ishmael. I'd see him in my hours of rest, I could feel his pain, but more than anything: I am very aware of his capabilities, even those he is not aware of yet. Rabbi, although you fear my ways will push him to his limits negatively, you can rest assured that this way is the best way, my ways will bring out the best in him. I know of this, for I would be different in my approach otherwise. I will be there for him, I will know what he is feeling or thinking; he cannot hide anything from me, just like I said to him. Ishmael has healed Rabbi, but he is still in the physical, once he separates from it he will have complete peace, he will see the irrelevance of it all because now it has no purpose. His mind will become clear, his heart will be able to listen, I am only a child but again, like I said to Ishmael, my knowledge is pure, it is true because it is given from pure love. Ishmael is very sensitive, but he doesn't know how to use his gifts in the right way, so in the past they have reacted negatively for him; but he will learn. All you fear Rabbi, will be laid to rest, just as Ishmael's fear of his abilities, of me, will also be; I am here now to ensure that happens."

Rabbi looked at him now before putting his head down for a moment before speaking.

"Joseph, Ishmael does fear you; I know him well, and it is clear how powerful you are, that is something that would take anyone time to adjust to, but especially Ishmael. I trust all you have said, I now have much more understanding of you, thank you for speaking with me, Joseph. I, too, will never forget you either."

"Rabbi, as I said to Ishmael, to fear me is to fear himself; he did not understand this, that was also clear to me. But I am what we should all be, we are all capable of it, but through greed, ego, the world has forgotten this. They are blind to the reality; they are quick to accept the bad, yet question the good? Rabbi, all that was once good in the world has been destroyed, they fear love because it has been abused, just like trust; they judge or take advantage of people who care, they have forgotten the meaning of those words, but they are what will bring back the peace this planet needs. The way the world is now should never have come to be, man must be taught of its destruction; they cannot keep taking from it for their own selfish means. The world needs time to heal, animals must be allowed to roam free to bring harmony, to help the world replace what has been taken. We both have purpose to make that happen in our own way, and we will. Rabbi, you should rest, as must I, your body is not as strong as it once was. Remember: we are always with you, be at peace; goodnight."

"Yes, Joseph, I am confident of that now, I will let you rest also, goodnight."

I got up as Rabbi came out, he bumped into me, not knowing I was still up here.

"Rabbi, I…"

"Ishmael, why are you not with Essie? I assume you heard all that was said?"

"Yes Rabbi, I didn't mean to pry but I was meant to hear it, that I am sure about."

"It's fine, Ishmael, I must not intervene. That boy will do wonders, you both will; however, the path will be hard. I am confident Joseph knows all that is needed for you both, he will be your teacher now; so, you must listen to him, Ishmael, seek his guidance as you did mine. He will also seek yours as he too has much to learn, do not fear him now because you are the same; you just don't know it yet."

"I will, Rabbi. How about a game of chess before bed; I have brandy if you would like?"

"Yes, for a while will be good. Ishmael, Son, are you sure that having a brandy is wise?"

"Yes, Rabbi, I have not touched any for so long, I want my first, or rather, my last, with you; just the one for another memory?"

"I know, Ishmael, but alright, yes, we can have the one."

We retired to the lounge. We spoke of Avraham then Richie; the good times as well as the bad ones. I believed Joseph's words regarding myself being healed, speaking of it all didn't bother me, I didn't feel uncomfortable by talking of the bad things now. I knew he knew me better than I ever thought, I didn't need to doubt him or his intentions because, like Avraham's, they were good too, just different. We talked more than played; but Rabbi still managed to beat me which he was very pleased about. He was also quick to tease me about it too.

"Dear me, Ishmael, you can win at life but not at chess? You know, I can't make sense of that?"

"Hmm, that's simple, Rabbi: some are good at chess, but life just seems to be my game for some reason, but I am still figuring that reason out."

We both started laughing, it was good to see him laughing too. Rabbi turned to me a minute later.

"Ishmael, I have seen more sides of you while I have

been here this short time, than I have your whole life. I won't see your true self, I've only had a glimpse now. But embrace all you are; accept all that you will become, because like Joseph said to Maisy; you will only get better. Now, I think after that a brandy is in order?"

"Yes, I don't think I can handle any more speeches without one today, Rabbi; I'll grab some glasses."

That really tickled him, he howled at that comment, Essie came walking in seeing him in fits, she looked at me calmly pouring brandy; with a smirk on my face. With amusement in her voice she spoke to me.

"Ish, what have you done?"

"What I should've done many times before."

I winked at her, then she chuckled before rolling her eyes jokingly, walking over to Rabbi.

"Rabbi, I think we need to do something about his humour: it is dangerous, what do you think?"

He only gave a thumbs-up: he was still laughing. I came over with the brandies placing one in front of him.

"Rabbi, when you compose yourself, I would like to make a toast?"

"Ish, I don't think it wise: last time you spoke that happened."

Now I started to laugh: the seriousness on her face as she said it was what got to me more. Rabbi, who decided enough was enough, sat up, putting real effort in to control himself now. He picked his glass up taking a sip of brandy, then he sat back, inhaling deeply.

"Ishmael, Essie is right: your humour is dangerous but in the best possible way. Besides your other abilities, you can make people laugh. The world needs that, Son: laughter heals the soul. Do it as often as you can, don't lose sight of it as you once did."

"I won't, Rabbi, I am glad I was able to make you laugh: when you leave, that memory will make you smile too, use it when you need to, it will give comfort."

"I will, Ishmael, I will. Well, it is late: I must retire, I have

355

thoroughly enjoyed tonight, thank you both."

Essie stepped forward then hugged him; giving him a kiss on the cheek.

"Rabbi, it has been an absolute pleasure, goodnight."

"See you in the morning, Rabbi."

He looked at me then nodded.

"You will, Ishmael."

I thoroughly enjoyed that evening with him too, we had never really done that, but I realised there was so much we didn't do. However, I could not regret it now: as he said it is the now which mattered. We watched as he walked slowly towards the door. I felt emotional now, a tear was forming in my eye: every moment that passed was my last with him, it was hard to say goodnight, but he knew it. I realised that goodnight would not be as hard as the last goodbye, I knew I would regret not saying it because the little things are what were important. I rushed over to open the door for him.

"Goodnight, Rabbi, sleep well."

He smiled now resting his hand on my arm.

"You too, Son, you too."

I closed the door over after him, then put my hand to my head. Essie came to me.

"He has only been here a day, but it feels much longer; you made every second count. Ish. I know tomorrow will be incredibly difficult for you; but remember today, this evening. I am sure Joseph will be there for you more tomorrow, as much as any other day; as will I, we are all here for you."

"It is why I love you so much; it will be hard, but I will deal with what comes better than I have done before, I am ready to challenge whatever happens."

"What about our wrestling match, are you ready to challenge me on that?"

I grinned at her now, staring in her eyes.

"Anytime, Essie, anytime."

"Prove it, Ish?"

"You know, I have no problem with doing that; none

whatsoever."

She grinned then put her head down; I lifted it back up, smiling at her.

"Hey, you're too beautiful for that."

"You're right: after all, there are better places to look, you are proof of it."

"I don't know about me: but you certainly are."

She put her finger on my lips then stepped as close as she could.

"Okay, Ish? I'm done chatting, I suggest you make your move; otherwise I will."

Moving my head forward slightly, my lips locked with hers gently. I then, to her delight, carried her to bed.

Next morning, I woke up bewildered: I'd had an unsettled night. The dream I'd had was very vivid, but I could make no sense of it. My first thought was that the things I had seen were actual events that hadn't happened yet; I could not tell whether it was a vision or just a dream, I had not had anything like it before. Trying to put it out of my mind I got up then made my way downstairs. My thoughts changed when I saw Rabbi's belongings sitting there ready in the hallway, it was a sad sight knowing we only had a short time left with him. I felt panicked too, I could not brush it off. I had to try to remain optimistic: I could make the last bit of time happy for everyone by doing so. I walked into the kitchen where the children were having breakfast. Rabbi was chatting to them while Essie was pottering around.

"Good morning, everyone, how are we all?"

"We are great, Ish, coffee is ready, hope you're hungry?"

"I most certainly am. Rabbi, did you sleep well?"

"Yes, Ishmael, very well; come, sit with us."

I sat next to Maisy. They all spoke to me except Joseph, who only stared at me again. I noticed Maisy had suddenly stopped eating, she was just looking at her plate. I nudged her gently, but she didn't react at all.

"Maisy, what is wrong? Why have you stopped eating?"

Next thing she burst into tears. Rabbi looked at me then Essie came over. Joseph got up instantly then also came over to her, putting his hand on her shoulder before turning to me.

"She is highly sensitive to you, but you do not notice. Your heart is heavy, Ishmael: you fear today. Maisy knows this; we both do. She is still young so cannot yet fully understand this side; she only feels then reacts, Ishmael. Therefore, she is emotional. Now you will understand."

He was right, I was unaware how sensitive she was until now, Joseph had said they were the same, however, he was able to control his emotions. He was so calm, so balanced, gave nothing away but I realised Maisy couldn't do that yet. It was so important now for me to control my feelings; just as he had said. He hadn't mentioned Maisy to me, but there was reason: I now knew it was something I had to be shown. Now this had happened, it gave me real understanding.

"Joseph, I completely understand now. I, too, will be aware."

Again, he smiled, before turning to Maisy.

"Maisy, do not worry: they are not your feelings. Be calm now, dry your eyes; you will learn to control that part of you some day. I will always look after you until you do, eat now."

She looked up at him then smiled, wiping her eyes before she started eating again. The understanding they both had of each other was remarkable; breathtaking to witness, too. Elliott was very quiet, he kept looking at them both. I sensed he felt left out in a way: he would not understand them a lot of ways, but he was close with Maisy, too. Joseph, in the time since they had arrived, had barely spoken to him, I wondered why, was it because he knew Elliott's thoughts, or because he knew he wasn't like him? It concerned me, something told me that it was only a matter of time before Elliott came to blows, I had to find ways to stop it from happening; that is, of course, if I was meant to.

We ate while Rabbi chatted to Elliott at the other end of

the table. I wondered if he thought the same about him as I did: that he, too, had concerns, I knew Rabbi would say if he did, so, I left them to it. I was grateful he was who he was: not many would take the time to sit chatting to a child, but Rabbi knew it was important. If he had any inkling that Elliott felt left out, then he would be first to make him feel anything but that. Essie came to sit with us, we watched on, it wasn't long before Elliott was laughing. Maisy soon went over too, also starting to laugh. I smiled, I knew Rabbi had eased Elliott's mind, just like he had done mine so many times. I sat thinking: he was the finest Rabbi I had ever known. It was obvious they would miss him now, as well.

We soon finished breakfast; it was quite a morning already, another unforgettable one. Essie went to get the children ready while Rabbi went to finish gathering the rest of his things. Joseph sat with me in the kitchen, he hadn't said another word since Maisy got upset. I went to get up when he suddenly spoke.

"Ishmael, your night was unsettled, your dreams vivid; what is it you don't understand, why do you still doubt after all I have said?"

"My first thought was it maybe a vision, but that has not happened before, Joseph, I could not be sure?"

"Ishmael, there is no maybe about it: it is what it is. What you saw is an ability you possess, dreams are easy to forget, yet visions not so easy for they come with a knowing inside. What you felt is confirmation of it. You have had it many times, but you were blind. You doubt because you fear; you fear anything which has no answer that you want straight away. Ishmael, your first thought was truth; you can trust it to be true, you must. By shadowing it with what you want to believe, by ignoring what is, that will also create the blockages I have spoken about. There is reason for everything, accept what you see, believe all you feel; by doing so you allow more in. The visions will guide you, show you what you need to know. You know this for I am proof of it. By allowing yourself to see, you will get stronger, you will grow, that, too, you must allow."

"Joseph, I…?"

"I know, Ishmael, but not all needs questioning, not everything can be answered, time must be allowed to give you the answers. Ishmael, by questioning this, you question yourself, that is why your thoughts become muddled: your spirit knows. Now you will see why all I have said is so important. It is unnecessary to doubt what you don't understand, as I have said: time will reveal all. Patience, Ishmael, that will allow for acceptance. With patience you don't need to question what you know inside to be truth: you are truth, Ishmael."

"So many things have happened lately, none I was prepared for, you especially, Joseph."

"Ishmael, much change is going to come, that itself cannot be changed, you say you weren't prepared, yet you knew I was coming, but you did not listen, you panicked, questioned. You must calm your mind; listen to yourself, that will enable you to know, that will give no doubt. You sensed the feeling when I arrived was to do with me, I sensed the same from you; but you allow for ignorance rather than truth, this must stop, all I have told you will be clear as to why. It is almost time, Ishmael, Rabbi will be leaving shortly so I will not keep you any longer, I know he wants to see you alone."

He got up, then looked as though he was going to walk straight past me; he didn't, he turned to me again.

"Ishmael, the day will be an emotional one for many reasons, you will soon know this; remember what I have said, always remember that I am here."

I looked up at him then smiled.

"I know Joseph, yes, I know."

To my surprise he then touched me on my arm gently before walking out, he would not usually touch anyone who was fearful or heavy hearted, except Maisy; yet he wasn't afraid to bring that tranquility to them if needed. The morning events proved just how difficult my next path would be, but I knew Joseph would guide me in the right direction. With him by my side I would become my true self. It wouldn't be easy, but I was excited to find out what that was, what I would do in future, where life would take me next.

21 THE LAST GOODBYE

Rabbi soon came back into the kitchen to see me sitting there.

"Ishmael, Son: it is nearly time. I know this is hard for you but my time with you must end, I am contented to know that when I am gone, there won't be any bad reaction, any screaming or shouting like before; do not feel bad for this for you know much better than that now. Like Joseph said, you have come far but have much further to go, I know you will be fine, Ishmael; my heart is at peace knowing that."

"Yes, I know that too, you are a great man, Rabbi; one of the finest. I, too, know you will be at peace. I see why you do have to go now: to make way for Joseph. Nevertheless, you will always be very important to me, Rabbi. I'm here now because you gave us that chance, as I have said, that will never be forgotten."

"Ishmael, I have had this since just after I met you. I wanted to leave you something, you will know the importance it's had for me."

He handed me a diary, it was old but had been taken great care of over the years. It blew me away; I handed it back.

"Rabbi, I couldn't possibly take that."

"Please, Ishmael, I know it will be in safe hands with you. Open it when I am gone; you will see why it should go to you."

I looked at him curiously, he pushed it into my hands; holding it for a couple of seconds I smiled at him.

"Okay, Rabbi, I will look after it you have my word. In my dream, you gave me the same thing, yet it was new, it's so bizarre but I am not confused: I feel there is meaning from it, thank you, Rabbi."

"Ishmael, that is what Joseph is talking about: you accepted without question because you knew, always do that. Right, it's almost time for me to go, it's been some life for both of us, Ishmael, I don't regret one minute of it."

"It is impossible for me to regret any of it, Rabbi. I'll gather everyone."

I smiled as I had begun my new life with him, but now he was ending his with us; he had been there when it mattered, taught me, given guidance just as Avraham did. He was the father I needed, and he never hesitated to take on the role, I was so blessed for that. I was really going to miss him, but I knew that was acceptable. Soon we all gathered in the hallway. Rabbi picked up his case before he walked over to the children. He stood in front of Maisy.

"Maisy, you be good, one day you will be as wonderful as your mother is."

Maisy smiled before looking at him.

"I couldn't be anything else, Rabbi. I don't want you to go, but I know you must."

"Aah, Maisy, yes, I can believe that. You are all wonderful, children, I won't forget you little one, here, take these."

He handed her the beads he had had ever since I had known him; I looked at Essie who put her hand to her chest, she had a tear in her eye, too. Maisy's face lit up as she took them from him, she then looked at them for a minute before putting them round her neck. She looked back at Rabbi.

"Thank you, Rabbi, I will look after them, always."

"Aah, Maisy, I shall remember that, goodbye."

He then walked to Elliott.

"Elliott, remember what I said to you: that you are much loved by everyone here. Nevertheless, they will show it in different ways. You will grow strong, become great in your own way, don't ever compare yourself to others; you are just as unique as anybody, you will be a great man one day."

Elliott just hugged him tightly, pulling away he had tears, I knew for sure my instinct was right but felt confident he had been reassured by Rabbi.

"Thank you, Rabbi, I won't forget what you have said."

Rabbi gave him a friendly nudge while smiling.

"Make sure you don't, Elliott, goodbye."

"Goodbye, Rabbi."

He then moved on to Joseph.

"Joseph, I am not sure what else to say to you, I…"

Joseph stared at him solemnly.

"That is because there is no more to be said to me, Rabbi, other than goodbye."

Rabbi looked at him, then went to turn away with an unsettled look. Joseph touched him on the arm affectionately. He stared at Rabbi again before smiling. Rabbi returned it.

"I won't forget you, Joseph, goodbye."

"Goodbye, Rabbi."

Rabbi came to Essie who was emotional now. Rabbi was quick to bring comfort.

"Essie, your children are incredibly special, I want to thank you for allowing me to be part of their lives even for a while. The road will be hard for you all, but you are strong; I also want to thank you for all you have done for Ishmael, I know he will be in good hands with you. Love has conquered everything, you are the strongest couple I've ever seen. Take care of him for me. I will miss you all very much but do not cry for me, Essie, you have given me just as much happiness as you have given Ishmael. I will never forget that. Like Ishmael said to me, you're a beautiful person, that has been proven time and again, be proud of yourself because you have no reason not to be."

"Oh, Rabbi, I am blessed to have been a part of your life, I will really miss you too; we all will. I want to thank you for everything you have done for us all, especially Ishmael too; I will look after him just as you have done for so long, it has been a true honour, Rabbi."

She hugged him firmly, kissing him on the cheek, she had tears rolling which Rabbi soon sorted out.

"Now I see the reason for the tears: you wanted to leave me a souvenir, Essie?"

She started to laugh at this while fighting back her emotions. She then smiled.

"Of course, Rabbi, it is only right I leave a mark which you have left on us?"

Now he laughed nodding his head, he then came to me. I put my head down, but he put his hand on my shoulder.

"Ishmael, my son, I have said goodbye to many over the years, but this is the hardest goodbye I have ever done: we have been through so much, you have battled to get where you are. To watch you become the man you are has been extraordinary, all I've taught you, you have embraced. I thank God, every day, that he sent you to me. You've been challenging at times, difficult to watch, yet you've taught me so much. Ishmael, whatever path you follow now, I know you will make the most of it, I know you will embrace that, too. I don't see you as a friend: I see you as a son, that makes it harder. I have been able to smile when I think about you, you have done that by your actions, you changed your life, now here you are. I love you, Ishmael, my son, I always will."

"Rabbi, after my father passed you have stepped right up to the role; you've been there even when I distanced myself, you are one of the greatest men I will ever come across. All your teachings are what will help me in the future, all your wisdom I will share. You taught me the most important things in life with Avraham; thank you for all of it, for being who you are. I love you too, Rabbi, that will never fade."

I threw my arms around him now, I smiled but it was difficult, particularly seeing Essie emotional, I felt just the same as she expressed with her tears but I could contain myself now; I had to. We stood for a good minute, neither of us wanting to release. However, with Rabbi being Rabbi he soon pulled away, gripping both of my arms.

"Goodbye, Ishmael, don't forget the fighter you are or the strength you have, I will never forget you, especially."

"Like Avraham, I will continue to make you proud; goodbye, Rabbi."

"Like Avraham, I don't doubt it either, Ishmael."

Rabbi opened the door then stepped outside, he turned, smiling when he saw we all gathered around the doorway. It was raining again but I knew the offer of a lift would be something he would refuse; I had to let him be. He started to walk off, we all had our eyes fixed on him, watching him move slowly, further into the distance. I felt saddened but sure he would be alright now, wherever he ended up. He turned around giving one last wave; all of us waved back except Joseph. I turned to Essie.

"That is the finest Rabbi I have ever known; he will be at peace, so I am, too."

"Yes, Ish, he really was. You, too, are one of the finest; whatever happens you have us."

"I know, Essie, you all have me too."

She kissed me on the cheek then went into the lounge, I stood there a minute more. Rabbi turned a corner for the last time; he was really gone. I took a moment then rested my head against the door; I smiled now.

"Thank you, Rabbi, thank you my friend, you will be missed greatly, may your last days be blessed ones."

I closed the door then turned around, Joseph stood there just watching me. Issy and Jonah were sitting side by side.

"Ishmael, Rabbi left you something, you should open it."

"He did Joseph; come?"

Joseph followed me into the lounge, I closed the door behind us then sat down. Picking up the diary from Rabbi I opened it; inside there was a note. Essie grabbed my hand.

"Read it, Ish?"

Slowly I opened it.

"Ishmael, Son.

Over the years I have kept a record of your progress since you came to me: it allowed me to be reassured when I couldn't be around. You will see now why I could only give it to you: it's yours. I have marked specific dates as well as times, and through your coma I also marked your progress. Avraham always kept me informed but I knew one day you would be able to read it, to see just how much you have achieved. Now I believe you are ready. I'm very proud of you, Ishmael, I hope this, in times that maybe hard, will help to keep you moving forward. I know you won't stop doing that, you have a beautiful family; the world is yours. Be happy now, for I am because of you all. During my travels I visited your homeland; I met Benyamin too.

What you both did was inspiring, Ishmael, truly amazing. I saw the power you have inside yourself while I was there, I saw your potential. I did not say because I know you too well, but timing is everything, Ishmael; it's why I give you it now, that is just how it was meant to be, but now you will understand this? As you know, times ahead are going to be hard; but whatever happens in the future you will deal with it. Ishmael, whatever your purpose may be, I know you will fulfil it with everything you have; I won't be there, but I will be with you. Remember to enjoy your life no matter what it throws your way, because you can overcome anything.

I love you, Ishmael, just as Avraham did. My last bit of advice for you is: don't forget those close, they, too, will be there if you need them. Follow your heart, stay true to all you know; also, never be afraid to ask for help no matter how difficult it may be.

Well that is it, Ishmael. As a friend I would say it has been a real honour, but as a son I would say I wouldn't have wished for anyone else to take that role either.

This is my last goodbye, but we both know it's never that, not really, thank you for everything, Ishmael.

All my love

Rabbi

PS Look at the back of the diary.''

I turned a few pages, the detail he had written inside, dates, times was amazing; I was so moved by it. I put it to my chest but found myself welling up, too, which I tried to fight back. Joseph stood by me now with Maisy, they both stared at me. Essie put her arm around me while Elliott moved in closer.

"He really loved you, Ish, more than we ever knew, you have lost two very special people; but you have become all they were, it is okay to be emotional because they are feelings which come from love."

She whispered in my ear then.

"Look behind you."

I did, I saw that Joseph along with Maisy were smiling at me. I tried to suppress my feelings because I didn't want to upset Maisy, but I now knew the difference. I realised what Joseph meant, too, that is why he was so warm towards me, that's why now they were both smiling. Elliott turned to me.

"Ishmael, you haven't looked in the back yet?"

I chuckled at him then took a breath.

"So I haven't, Elliott, shall we see why Rabbi wants us too?"

Maisy stepped in now.

"It is a…"

Joseph stopped her from saying anymore, she looked at him then giggled.

I smirked at her, then opened the back of the diary. I was stunned to see that there were photographs sitting there neatly; along with another much shorter note.

"Ishmael,

You spoke of photographs in your dream of your family, but I have never seen you with any. I picked these up in your village with Benyamin's help. They are past, but they were family, we both know how precious that is; it will help you to remember, cherish them. I am sure now you can look at them with a smile on your face; once you get past the emotion that is. But now you know what I mean about timing for this. I can hear you saying thank you; but you know my answer to that, too.

Goodbye, Son
Rabbi ''

"Yes, Rabbi, it's not necessary."

I laughed at that; Essie joined in, too. Taking them out carefully, I looked through them. I was more touched he did that than I had been about the diary. I did have mixed emotions, but they were good ones I was no longer afraid to show. There was a photo of my parents wedding, one of when they were younger, also one I remember was taken a year before they died. There was also one of Avraham, as well as one of Rabbi, which was recently taken. I had never thought about getting a camera, but I could see the value of it; now it would be on my list of priorities.

We sat a good few hours, I told them about Rakira, about Avraham, too. They showed interest, Elliott more so, wanting to visit sometime which I promised we would do. Joseph did not stay around long: I knew he didn't need to hear about my life because he already knew, he was only there for the purpose of showing me the difference between my emotions, which had been fulfilled. Essie got up as it was almost dinner time.

"Who's hungry?"

I stood now putting my hands on her waist.

"I think we all are, how about we go out for some?"

"Can we, can we?"

We both grinned as we saw Maisy jumping excitedly. I bent down to her.

"Yes, Maisy, but you must get ready first, it is raining outside."

Her face lit up, she grabbed Elliott pulling on him; he certainly was not best pleased about it.

"Come on, we must go, Elliott, now."

"Maisy, alright, alright, I am coming."

They ran off, I stood back up next to Essie.

"I love you, Ish, more every day, I'd best help them; we won't be long."

"I love you too, Essie, more every minute, I'll be ready when you are."

I winked at her, making her chuckle as she followed the children upstairs; I began to straighten things out. Once done, I sat down again fixing the diary, placing the photos inside to keep safe until I got frames. I then walked to the window looking out. Joseph came back in a few minutes later; he came over to me but didn't say anything yet, only stood staring out. I heard the others coming down the stairs a few minutes later, I then went to turn away.

"Ishmael, pay attention to your dreams, take note for you will have many now. I have seen something; prepare for anything that will come, that is important for you."

"Joseph, what are you saying, is my end near?"

"No, Ishmael, for you it is just beginning."

"For me? What about you? Joseph, what about you?"

His eyes glistened and he smiled, touching my arm again. Elliott was hanging around the doorway, Joseph stared at him before turning to me with a serious expression.

"Be calm, Ishmael, have no fear: all will be revealed in time."

ABOUT THE AUTHOR

Born in Liverpool, England, Glenda Browne has recently been diagnosed with Asperger's syndrome and fibromyalgia. She has written throughout her life which has helped her through some very difficult times. As Glenda struggled to express herself, she found that writing poetry gave voice to her feelings and helped her to grow as a person. With the help of certain people who have encouraged her to challenge, as well as to believe in herself and her writing, Glenda now proudly brings you her first fictional novel.

"If you have a love or passion for something, no label or disability will stop you from achieving all you want to; a little help and support can make a real difference, it will bring the best out in people, with it we will all thrive."

"Always believe in you; let nobody tell you any different. We are only human, but we can do anything. We all have so much potential within us which can help make this world better. Follow your dreams, if you believe you can succeed – you will!"

"When we are given only the path of darkness – we can fight till we find the light!"